D1047808

A SAMPLING OF CITY LIFE AND LITERATURE . . .

"THE CABALIST OF EAST BROADWAY"
by ISAAC BASHEVIS SINGER

Two different women and two different cities are juxtaposed in this powerful story by the Nobel Prize–winning author to show the mystical allure of New York City. . . .

"THE ENORMOUS RADIO" by JOHN CHEEVER

In few stories is apartment life so wonderfully depicted as in this funny, wry tale of a radio that broadcasts the secrets and intimate lives of tenants in an urban high-rise. . . .

"LOOKING FOR MR. GREEN" by SAUL BELLOW

Nobel Prize–winner Bellow sends a newly hired white bureaucrat into an unfamiliar Chicago black neighborhood to deliver a relief check, and the results are as emotional as they are unexpected. . . .

"FAITH IN A TREE" by GRACE PALEY

A Brooklyn park, mothers and young children, and a writer in a tree paint a portrait of the lives, exterior and interior, of a city's women. . . .

BOOKS BY ILAN STAVANS IN ENGLISH

Fiction

The One-Handed Pianist and Other Stories

Nonfiction

Art & Anger

Bandido

The Hispanic Condition

Imagining Columbus

Editor

The Oxford Book of Latin American Essays

New World

Tropical Synagogues

Growing Up Latino
(co-edited with Harold Augenbraum)

Translator

Sentimental Songs by Felipe Alfau

THE URBAN MUSE

Stories on the American City

EDITED WITH AN INTRODUCTION BY

Ilan Stavans

Delta
Trade Paperbacks

A Delta Book
Published by
Dell Publishing
a division of
Bantam Doubleday Dell Publishing Group, Inc.
1540 Broadway
New York, New York 10036

Permissions follow on pages v–vi.
Copyright © 1998 by Ilan Stavans

All rights reserved. No part of this book may be reproduced or transmitted in any form or by any means, electronic or mechanical, including photocopying, recording, or by any information storage and retrieval system, without the written permission of the Publisher, except where permitted by law.

The trademark Delta® is registered in the U.S. Patent and Trademark Office and in other countries.

Library of Congress Cataloging in Publication Data
The urban muse : stories on the American city / edited with an introduction by Ilan Stavans.
p. cm.
"A Delta book"—T.p. verso.
ISBN 0-385-31368-3
1. City and town life—United States—Fiction. 2. United States—Social life and customs—Fiction. 3. Cities and towns—United States—Fiction. 4. Short stories, American. I. Stavans, Ilan.
PS648.C5U73 1998
813.008'0321732—dc21 97-24135
CIP

Manufactured in the United States of America
Published simultaneously in Canada

January 1998

10 9 8 7 6 5 4 3 2

BVG

The editor gratefully acknowledges permission to reprint the following material:

Nathaniel Hawthorne: "My Kinsman, Major Molineux." From *The Snow-Image and Other Twice-Told Tales*, 1852.

Herman Melville: "Bartleby the Scrivener." First published in *Putnam's Monthly Magazine*, November-December, 1853. Collected in *The Piazza Tales*, 1856.

Henry James: "The Jolly Corner." Published in Vol. 17, *The New York Edition* ["The Beast in the Jungle," "The Birthplace," and Other Tales], Charles Scribner's Sons, 1909. Collected in *The Short Stories of Henry James*. Random House, 1945.

Anzia Yezierska: "My Own People." From *Hungry Hearts and Other Stories*, by Anzia Yezierska, copyright © 1985 by Louise Levitas Henriksen. Reprinted by permission of Persea Books, Inc.

Dorothy Parker: "From the Diary of a New York Lady." From *The Collected Stories of Dorothy Parker*. Copyright © 1939 by Dorothy Parker. Published by Viking Press.

Dashiell Hammett: "The House in Turk Street." From *The Continental Op* by Dashiell Hammett. Copyright © 1974 by Lillian Hellman, executrix for the Estate of Dashiell Hammett. Reprinted by permission of Random House, Inc.

F. Scott Fitzgerald: "May Day." From *The Short Stories of F. Scott Fitzgerald*, edited with a preface by Matthew J. Bruccoli. Charles Scribner's Sons, 1989. Reprinted by permission of Scribner, a division of Simon and Schuster.

Zora Neale Hurston: "Spunk." First published in *Opportunity Magazine*, June 1925, and reprinted in the anthology *The New Negro*, edited by Alain Locke (New York: Albert and Charles Boni, 1925). Collected in *The Complete Stories* by Zora Neale Hurston. Introduction copyright © 1995 by Henry Louis Gates, Jr., and Sieglinde Lemke. Compilation copyright © 1995 by Vivian Bowden, Lois J. Hurston Gaston, Clifford Hurston, Lucy Ann Hurston, Winifred Hurston Clark, Zora Mack Goins, Edgar Hurston, Sr., and Barbara Hurston Lewis. Afterword and Bibliography copyright © Henry Louis Gates, Jr. Reprinted by permission of HarperCollins Publishers, Inc.

Langston Hughes: "Little Dog." Originally published in *The Ways of White Folks*, reprinted in *Something in Common and Other Stories*. Copyright © 1963 by the Langston Hughes Estate. Reprinted by permission.

Isaac Bashevis Singer: "The Cabalist of East Broadway." From *The Collected Stories of Isaac Bashevis Singer* by Isaac Bashevis Singer. Copyright © 1982 by Isaac Bashevis Singer. Reprinted by permission of Farrar, Straus and Giroux.

John Cheever: "The Enormous Radio." From *The Stories of John Cheever* by John Cheever. Copyright © 1947 by John Cheever. Reprinted by permission of Alfred A. Knopf, Inc.

Delmore Schwartz: "In Dreams Begin Responsibilities." From *In Dreams Begin Responsibilities*. Copyright © 1961 by Delmore Schwartz. Reprinted by permission of New Directions Publishing Corp.

Saul Bellow: "Looking for Mr. Green." First published in 1951, renewed © 1979 by Saul Bellow. Collected in *Mosby's Memoirs and Other Stories* by Saul Bellow. Reprinted by permission of Viking Penguin, a division of Penguin Books USA, Inc.

James Baldwin: "Sonny's Blues." Originally published in *Partisan Review*. Collected in *Going to Meet the Man*, copyright © 1965 by James Baldwin, copyright renewed. Published by Vintage Books. Reprinted by agreement with the James Baldwin Estate.

Cynthia Ozick: "The Pagan Rabbi." From *The Pagan Rabbi and Other Stories* by Cynthia Ozick. Copyright © 1971 by Cynthia Ozick. Reprinted by permission of Alfred A. Knopf, Inc.

Grace Paley: "Faith in a Tree." First published in *Enormous Changes at the Last Minute* by Grace Paley. Collected in *The Collected Stories of Grace Paley*. Copyright © 1994 by Grace Paley. Reprinted by permission of Farrar, Straus and Giroux.

Paul Auster: "Auggie Wren's Christmas Story." First published in *The New York Times*, December 25, 1990. Copyright © 1990 by Paul Auster. Reprinted by permission.

Contents

For what is the city if not our prison,
Not a triumph over Nature but a betrayal?
. . . Or am I wrong? Did God design it?
Why then is it so jumbled, so obtuse? Is it that He loves chaos?

—Mordechai Calman,
Tales of a Drunken World

Introduction

Ilan Stavans

I am packing my library. One by one, the books lose their configuration, what Walter Benjamin called "the mild boredom of order." I reach for them on the heights of a shelf, browse calmly through their pages, dust off the jackets, and proceed to store them in an empty carton. I will number these boxes from one to sixty. When the books come out again, they will follow an altogether different order. Their overall setting will be different, too. I wonder if they will resent the change? Can books feel? Do they experience emotion? There is a certain sweetness to the whole enterprise in which I am involved, for, as I advance, I realize how much my library and I have changed together this past decade. We began modestly and now we hardly recognize each other. Are all these volumes really mine? When did they grow to be so many? What do they say about me? And what can I, their collector, say about them?

This has been a decade of enlightenment. I had come to New York with only a handful of them. It was here I thought I would either become a genuine writer or vanish altogether into anonymity. I was in my mid-twenties. Even before landing, I had given myself until age thirty-three to come to terms with my fate: literature is a passion that ought not to be wasted, I repeated in my heart. The journey, I foresaw, would be difficult, for somewhere along the line I had made the conscious decision to find my voice in a language and habitat not my own. How rewarding a pursuit it has been is made clear by how much I am endeared to the books I am packing. Ours is a marriage of love.

Moving out of the city doesn't mean defeat. On the contrary, it is a sign of success. The books are already too many. They need room to breathe. The floor might not be strong enough to sustain their weight. I first arrived with one suitcase in hand and a dozen books, mostly in Spanish. Selecting them had made me feel like a doomed sailor forced to rescue only a handful of items from a shipwreck. These were the books I couldn't do without, the ones I would unequivocally return to time and again in sleepless nights. They were a talisman, a code of survival. They included a pair of collections by Borges, *The Aleph* and *Other Inquisitions.* Having them at my side was an assurance. Not only had they convinced me of the relevance of literature, but, most important, they had a mystical quality to them. Years ago I had memorized numerous segments from these collections and each time I recited them, I realized the world made more sense: it seemed brighter, more intelligible. I also took along novels by writers I idolized: Kafka, Conrad, Gabriel García Márquez, Joyce, Nabokov, and Mario Vargas Llosa. Their literature was for me a religion.

I had come to New York to be a newspaper correspondent and also to study at The Jewish Theological Seminary, located on Broadway and 122nd Street. This institution would become a door to medieval philosophy and mysticism as well as to nineteenth-century Yiddish. The fact that it was in New York made it the perfect site: I would be able to send my dispatches and also to explore the links between fantasy and the intellect. My experience growing up in Mexico had instigated a sense of marginality in me: I had been born in the margins of culture, I thought, and a move to what in the words of George Steiner was "the capital of the twentieth century," was a way to overcome the handicap. When I got a letter from the Seminary granting me tuition, room, and board, I was spellbound. True, I knew next to nothing about the Seminary and about New York. I had the tools of a first-time tourist: a guide, my rudimentary English, and a lot of excitement. I could not wait to experience New York's roughness, its acerbic rhythms. That, I told myself, was in and of itself the best education I could ever aspire to.

The room I first lived in, a block away from the Seminary, was no larger than 7′ × 7′. It had a kitchen nearby and a shared bathroom only a few steps away. Fortunately, it wasn't dark; I did not have a spectacular view, but its mid-size windows allowed me to experience the change of seasons with some accuracy, although traffic jams would form beneath my windows and the noise would be offensive. Never did I complain about how small my room was; most New Yorkers, after all, lived in similarly inhuman conditions, restricted in space and overwhelmed by a cacophony of a street life not known for its tonality. What else was the city about but intensity and speed—attributes I actually found quite stimulating. Among the first things I did shortly after my arrival was to buy myself a book shelf. I needed to have my books out in the open, right in front of me. I unpacked them and stared at the haphazard order I had found for them. Were they really as invaluable as I thought? Would I reread them with the regularity I had envisioned in Mexico? The answer came faster than I realized.

The only thing I wanted to do every day was to be out and about. The room might not have looked small to me, but I always wanted to be elsewhere, walking the city, *reading* it, navigating through its heterogeneous neighborhoods, deciphering its countless mysteries. For ever since I stepped into it, it appeared to me like a huge book, a novel-in-progress perhaps, filled with anecdotes, with a kind of poetry impossible to repress. What an astonishing place it was! My encounter with it had actually come tangentially, after seeing other American cities and feeling disappointed with them. My parents took me on a trip through the Southwest when I was in my mid-teens. We entered the United States through Laredo and from there reached San Antonio, Houston, and Dallas. Eventually, our vacation took us farther west into California, where we visited *Disneylandia.* (The word still rings louder in Spanish.) I entered these cities with the deep desire to find out how different they were from the monstrous metropolis, *Distrito Federal,* where I had grown up. And indeed they were. No previous experience could have prepared me for their ugliness: they were vibrating places, no doubt, but banal and pretentious and without a single hint of mystery. Mexico's capital might well have been less livable, but it had a charm, an ethos none of these urban centers knew anything about. They had absolutely no weight, no sense of history, as if a disoriented God had created them while drunk. The few historic sites I found in San Antonio, most notably the Alamo, seemed to be tourist attractions: they appeared to have been built with an eye on commerce, not by artistic architects but by plastic surgeons.

In fact from no matter what viewpoint I approached them, these places presented themselves as amusement parks. People moved around with a sense of satisfaction, of professed happiness. Everything was for sale but nothing had enough value to be irreplaceable. The mercantile frenzy would come to you through the syncopated rhythm of advertisement: I would turn the TV on and immediately a station would begin begging for public money to subsist; I would wander through a downtown square and a gospel preacher would promote a fashionable chamber of heaven, which for a few dollars I could acquire right away; or I would take a bus and a captivating photo of a nearby zoo would invite me to experience fear and a sense of adventure. This bombardment of stimulation made these cities move at an incredible speeeeeeed. . . . People seemed to be robots: they marched forward while walking or driving their car, obsessed with reaching a destination that would make them more fulfilled. In Mexico, by comparison, the population allowed itself an afternoon siesta to catch its breath, to reconnect with itself, to become human again. But in these cities the absence of movement was equated with death, so nobody stopped to reconsider. Prophetically, Tom Wolfe's image of "the bonfire of vanities," which became available a decade later, already seemed suitable: in the American city, I came to believe, everyone and everything was on the run and made out of plastic; it was illusory in the way T. S. Eliot announced it in *The Waste Land:* "Unreal City . . . , I had not thought death had undone so many." In retrospect, Disneyland struck me as the most archetypal of them all: artificial but without false pretensions.

It took me four or five years more to make it to New York, but once it happened it was clear I had made it to *the real thing.* This, surely, is the source of sources, a city of fraternal strangers, of cultural sophistication and high civilization, the city of Walt Whitman and Federico García Lorca and Henry Roth, where tongues intermingle to such a degree that a new language seems to be born every other second, where everybody pretends to be a bit more than what he really is, where all nationalities and backgrounds coexist by seeing each other without an alibi. Mixture, impurity, promiscuity, heat . . . In New York every fake item becomes original. The mercantile frenzy in other American cities is, by contrast, but an innuendo: fortunes are done and undone here at the speed of light, and so are reputations; life is elusive, transitory; people are always exhausted, but they keep themselves going by sheer magic. Most important, nothing is sacred. Among the first memories I have of the city is of an irreverent sign promoting the different religions of the world:

Taoism: Shit happens.
Hinduism: This shit happened before.
Confucianism: Confucius says, "Shit happens."
Buddhism: If shit happens, it really isn't shit.
Zen: What is the sound of shit happening?
Islam: If shit happens, it is the Will of Allah.
Jehovah's Witnesses: Knock, Knock: "Shit Happens."
Atheism: There is no shit.
Agnosticism: I don't know whether shit happens.
Protestantism: Shit won't happen if I work harder.
Catholicism: If shit happens, I deserve it.
Judaism: Why does shit always happen to us?

In the ten years I lived in the city I must have walked it a thousand times during the day. Each block had its own style, its own atmosphere. So much variety, so much electricity. Would I ever come across the same face twice? It took me no time to realize the degree to which New Yorkers are concerned with their own identity. Their body is their most cherished asset: they live to show it around, to trim it, to polish its edges; their clothes, their gestures are a message: "Look at me," they shriek, "I've managed to become myself, to be distinct, unique, unlike you." But this obsession is but a mirage, for New Yorkers are all alike: they talk alike, they dress alike, they eat and dream alike. And each of them has a double. You walk the city and suddenly a face you saw days ago appears to you again, only somewhat redesigned. It is a double you've come across, an alter ego. In "The Jolly Corner," Henry James makes his protagonist, Spencer Brydon, return to his New York home after an absence of thirty-three years. The house might be empty, but Brydon is convinced it is inhabited by his alter ego, the man he himself would have been had he stayed in America rather than lived in Europe. New York is filled with Brydons in constant dialogue with their own reflected selves. They look themselves in the mirror and wonder: who am I?

What has attracted me most since the beginning are the complex ways in which the city communicates. This is a milieu where chaos and order are in constant conflict and their battle emerges most clearly in the way people talk, always invading each other's space, overlapping words, or failing to finish a sentence, as if life is short and one needs to move quickly to the next stage. I would wander from one section of the city to another realizing the extent to which its citizens live in parallel, disconnected universes. Polyglotism is a common characteristic: New Yorkers know three, four different tongues, each useful to transmit a different meaning and to communicate with a different type of person. These tongues strive for space. They interact by polluting each other, to the point where a mixture of tongues becomes the only alternative for clarity. Someone might not understand a certain term, but it doesn't matter; the context will solve the enigma.

Linguistic chaos goes beyond this verbal *mish-mash,* though. New York is always immersed in an eternal war against graffiti. No sooner is one battle over, another one breaks out. It is like cancer: you extirpate an organ, you apply a forceful treatment, but the sickness resists, for graffiti is as much a part of the landscape as advertising is. But this anarchic, nonverbal language forces itself in one's eyes in a more subtle, less digestible way. Graffiti exists to prove that order and civilization cannot exist without a cancer growing within and threatening to collapse the whole urban structure. Graffiti is often portrayed as obnoxious and rebellious by government figures but it has an enchanting harmony to it. It manages to say the unpronounceable: that the city is inhabited by a type of citizen who refuses to go by its laws; that beauty and class are deceiving attributes; that for as much as we strive to eradicate barbarism from our lives, it will always palpitate in our unconscious. Its message is clear: we, civilized creatures, carry along our own manure.

Verbal or otherwise, the printed word is at the heart of New York: newsstands are veritable fairs of letters and images; the amount of books on sale and recycled, trashy and sophisticated, is astonishing. Everyone reads: bums, secretaries, subway conductors, nannies. This is a city that is omnipresent in literature, so much so that if a catastrophe ever occurred, one would be able to re-create its sidewalks, dance clubs, and subway stations, its love affairs and robberies, even the shadow projected by a restless fly on a rained-soaked umbrella, through what its inhabitants write about it. This literature slowly made its way into my library. I allowed myself to be hypnotized by this literary outpour: Paul Auster's over-intellectualized mysteries, Nicholson Baker's minimalist rendezvous, Abraham Cahan's odyssey of a *shtetl* Jew into an urban dweller, Edith Wharton's invocations of a *belle époque*. One day I would read a story by Isaac Bashevis Singer about a cafeteria, and a few days later I would wander around the neighborhood looking to contrast the real site with its imaginary wobble. Literature was my compass: I visited bars near Columbia at the suggestion of Allen Ginsberg and Jack Kerouac; I wandered around the Lower East Side tracing David Schearl's path in *Call It Sleep;* I looked for the Harlem *rumberos* Oscar Hijuelos sang to in *The Mambo Kings Play Song of Love;* I visited Wall Street and saw a Bartleby in the faces of bums sheltered under a stairway or behind a revolving door.

My library began to grow, and so did I. Since I didn't have much money, I would first read a book from the public library and only if I became infatuated by it would I buy it. Purchase meant possession: I needed to make these volumes my own, to shape my personal library as a mirror of who I was turning into. Walter Benjamin was right when he claimed that a real library is always somewhat impenetrable and at the same time uniquely itself. Mine, clearly, is the product of an urban spirit set free. Its sensibility is more suited to the experience of alien immigrants arriving from far and wide without enough tools to handle the environment at first. Jewish and black writers in particular fascinated me: in James Baldwin I found a haunting essayist turning a somber Harlem into a field of lyrical possibilities; in Cynthia Ozick, a religious dilettante making sense of the pagan rituals that surrounded her. Literature became a map to New York and the world at large in a way I had never expected. *Orbis et urbis:* I would not only read about the city but about other American urban centers—Saul Bellow's Chicago, Dashiell Hammett's and Raymond Chandler's Los Angeles, Henry James's Boston. . . . And yet, New York, increasingly, was the whole universe for me. *Topos* became the issue: place and text went hand in hand. This made perspective all the more attractive: I would carefully study the fashion in which a certain writer had experienced a place, and then I would visit it; the result would be nothing short of thrilling. Countless writers obviously locate their fictions in places only half real, but so what? I would spend long afternoons discovering what was real and what wasn't. Or better, to realize that no place is ever *real* until a writer touches it. This topography also manifested itself by making me invoke the site in which I first penetrated a book. When I think of a certain location, I immediately picture myself having a particular novel under my arm. My memory of 116th Street and Broadway is attached to Felipe Alfau's *Locos,* for it was there where I waited for a friend while reading it; 82nd Street and Broadway, where I would walk on Sunday afternoons, belongs to

Truman Capote's *In Cold Blood;* and Varick Street near the offices of *El Diario/La Prensa,* a stop I frequented while writing my newspaper column, corresponds to Don DeLillo's *The Names*. Most of what I read were novels, instinctually trusting that this literary genre was by nature so multifaceted that the excesses of New York and other American cities would fit only in it. But human life is in itself multifaceted. One doesn't need to be immoderate to penetrate its richness. Reading a novel, while it takes longer, is really a lazy act; it allows for attention lapses and lack of consistency. The short story, on the other hand, is a challenge in every sense; it is subtle, astute, and discriminating. Its power is without mistake: it insinuates rather than overwhelms; it takes the reader by surprise rather than massages his attention.

Can an entire city, with all its complexities, be captured in a dozen pages? Yes, albeit rarely. A good short story is but an accident. Writers make what they can of their condition by means of the written word, but success has little to do with money and public attention. Instead, it is the result of casual circumstances. How many perfect ones is a single writer allowed in his lifetime? It is, I think, impossible to predict when and why a good story will appear; it simply does, as if by sheer magic. The world is without it for so long, but once the story is among us, it seems inevitable and irreplaceable. For a country that has not a minute to waste, the short story loses no time in taking our breath away; too, it is redeeming in that it redefines life in a single stroke, and what is America about if not reinventing itself *ad nauseam*. America in the eighteenth century was a patriotic song (Paine: "In a chariot of light from the regions of day, the Goddess of Liberty came"); afterward it became an epic poem (Emerson: "Spirit, that made those heroes dare / To die, and leave their children free"), only to be turned into a total novel during the Depression and after World War II. But in its magisterial egomania, in its fractured texture and everlasting impatience, the story, I think, is the genre closest to its heart.

I am almost finished packing my library and I realize that the handful of books I originally brought with me from Mexico have been pushed to a corner. In Joyce I have completely lost interest. My Spanish translations of Nabokov and Conrad were replaced by their originals, thus acquiring a pale and derivative status. The work of Mario Vargas Llosa I have ceased to read: he belongs to a period of the early eighties when I thought art and politics were siblings; but I no longer think that way. Gabriel García Márquez remains a favorite. Through his Spanish I reconnect with my native roots, and each of his books has a special place in my library. But Borges is the real survivor of the initial bunch: he is both a compass and a totem. (He said: "I only exist when I write.") Not long ago I began reading the pages I had memorized in English, which, magically, turned them into an exercise in transcendentalism. This, to me, makes him seem a cousin of Emerson and Hawthorne. The fact that none of the original books have disappeared is comforting. Who would I be without them today? Knowledge is not achieved but accumulated. We never get to know things completely, we only get a grasp of what they are at a certain moment. A library, much like life itself, is a work in eternal mutation. The coming decade will surely push the titles I now hold dearest to another corner.

For the time being, though, I feel at peace. Speed will soon give way to quietude. The cartons include a harvest of books written by myself. And I am taking New York—and all the cities it encompasses—along with me.

Editorial Note

In selecting seventeen among my most endeared stories on the modern American city, I followed only my instinct and predisposition and paid no attention to pity as a form of art. I am of course not at odds with the fact that most of these stories (actually, all but one) are set in New England and New York City. About a third of my contributors are what James Russell Lowell once called "stalwart old iconoclasts," although, as their tales attest, they can be ignoble and impure. The remaining two thirds are real and metaphorical Jews, e.g., blacks, Eastern Europeans, women. . . . But their background carries no consequence. Their stories are not a boutique of types and idiosyncrasies, but a rendezvous to the order and chaos of modern urban existence. Through them I have learned to understand the bargainings of America. They thrive by exploring the heaviness of its doubt. Together they constitute the city I carry within.

A note of gratitude: I wish to thank Trish Todd for inviting me to gather a handful of my favorite urban stories regardless of ideological value; Alison Stavchansky, the "perfect" reader; Jill Kneerim for her embrace; Kathleen Jayes for her perseverance; José Matosantos and Laura Santiago for their help; Jules Chametzky for his friendship; and Harold Augenbraum, whose idea it was to turn an itinerant dweller's eye into a viewpoint.

Author's Note

[illegible]

Auggie Wren's Christmas Story

Paul Auster (1947–)

Often labeled a "postmodern" poet and prose writer, New Jersey native **Paul Auster** depicts a complex, dark humanity where reality itself is incomprehensible. This dark existence is expressed especially in his *New York Trilogy,* mystery novels that include *City of Glass* (1985), *Ghosts* (1986), and *The Locked Room* (1987). Other novels include *In the Country of Last Things* (1988), *Moon Palace* (1989), *The Music of Chance* (1990), and *Mr. Vertigo* (1994). *Disappearances: Selected Poems* (1989) and *The Art of Hunger* (1991), an essay compilation, are other works. "Auggie Wren's Christmas Story" appeared as an Op-Ed piece in *The New York Times,* 25 December 1990. It was subsequently adapted by Auster himself into the screenplay of the film *Smoke.*

I heard this story from Auggie Wren. Since Auggie doesn't come off too well in it, at least not as well as he'd like to, he's asked me not to use his real name. Other than that, the whole business about the lost wallet and the blind woman and the Christmas dinner is just as he told it to me.

Auggie and I have known each other for close to eleven years now. He works behind the counter of a cigar store on Court Street in downtown Brooklyn, and since it's the only store that carries the little Dutch cigars I like to smoke, I go in there fairly often. For a long time, I didn't give much thought to Auggie Wren. He was the strange little man who wore a hooded blue sweatshirt and sold me cigars and magazines, the impish, wisecracking character who always had something funny to say about the weather or the Mets or the politicians in Washington, and that was the extent of it.

correlates w/ look @ end

But then one day several years ago he happened to be looking through a magazine in the store, and he stumbled across a review of one of my books. He knew it was me because a photograph accompanied the review, and after that things changed between us. I was no longer just another customer to Auggie, I had become a distinguished person. Most people couldn't care less about books and writers, but it turned out that Auggie considered himself an artist. Now that he had cracked the secret of who I was, he embraced me as an ally, a confidant, a brother-in-arms. To tell the truth, I found it rather embarrassing. Then, almost inevitably, a moment came when he asked if I would be willing to look at his photographs. Given his enthusiasm and good will, there didn't seem to be any way I could turn him down.

God knows what I was expecting. At the very least, it wasn't what Auggie showed me the next day. In a small, windowless room at the back of the store, he opened a cardboard box and pulled out twelve identical black photo albums. This was his life's work, he said, and it didn't take him more than five minutes a day to do it. Every morning for the past twelve years, he had stood at the corner of Atlantic Avenue and Clinton Street at precisely seven o'clock and had taken a single color photograph of precisely the same view. The project now ran to more than four thousand photographs. Each album represented a different year, and all the pictures were laid out in sequence, from January 1 to December 31, with the dates carefully recorded under each one.

As I flipped through the albums and began to study Auggie's work, I didn't know what to think. My first impression was that it was the oddest, most bewildering thing I had ever seen. All the pictures were the same. The whole project was a numbing onslaught of repetition, the same street and the same buildings over and over again, an unrelenting delirium of redundant images. I couldn't think of anything to say to Auggie, so I continued turning pages, nodding my head in feigned appreciation. Auggie himself seemed unperturbed, watching me with a broad smile on his face, but after I'd been at it for several minutes, he suddenly interrupted me and said, "You're going too fast. You'll never get it if you don't slow down."

He was right, of course. If you don't take the time to look, you'll never manage to see anything. I picked up another album and forced myself to go more deliberately. I paid closer attention to details, took note of shifts in the weather, watched for the changing angles of light as the seasons advanced. Eventually, I was able to detect subtle differences in the traffic flow, to anticipate the rhythm of the different days (the commotion of workday mornings, the relative stillness of weekends, the contrast between Saturdays and Sundays). And then, little by little, I began to recognize the faces of the people in the background, the passersby on their way to work, the same people in the same spot every morning, living an instant of their lives in the field of Auggie's camera.

Once I got to know them, I began to study their postures, the way they carried themselves from one morning to the next, trying to discover their moods from these surface indications, as if I could imagine stories for them, as if I could penetrate the invisible dramas locked inside their bodies. I picked up another album. I was no longer bored, no longer puzzled as I had been at first. Auggie was photographing time, I realized, both natural time and human time, and he was doing it by planting himself in one tiny corner of the world and willing it to be his own, by standing guard in the space he had chosen for himself. As he watched me pore over his work, Auggie continued to smile with pleasure. Then, almost as if he had been reading my thoughts, he began to recite a line from Shakespeare. "Tomorrow and tomorrow and tomorrow," he muttered under his breath, "time creeps on its petty pace." I understood then that he knew exactly what he was doing.

That was more than two thousand pictures ago. Since that day, Auggie and I have discussed his work many times, but it was only last week that I learned how he acquired his camera and started taking pictures in the first place. That was the subject of the story he told me, and I'm still struggling to make sense of it.

Earlier that same week, a man from the *New York Times* called me and asked if I would be willing to write a short story that would appear in the paper on Christmas morning. My first impulse was to say no, but the man was very charming and persistent, and by the end of the conversation I told him I would give it a try. The moment I hung up the phone, however, I fell into a deep panic. What did I know about Christmas? I asked myself. What did I know about writing short stories on commission?

I spent the next several days in despair, warring with the ghosts of Dickens, O. Henry and other masters of the Yuletide spirit. The very phrase "Christmas story" had unpleasant associations for me, evoking dreadful outpourings of hypocritical mush and treacle. Even at their best, Christmas stories were no more than wish-fulfillment dreams, fairy tales for adults, and I'd be damned if I'd ever allowed myself to write something like that. And yet, how could anyone propose to write an unsentimental Christmas story? It was a contradiction in terms, an impossibility, an out-and-out conundrum. One might just as well try to imagine a racehorse without legs, or a sparrow without wings.

I got nowhere. On Thursday I went out for a long walk, hoping the air would clear my head. Just past noon, I stopped in at the cigar store to replenish my supply, and there was Auggie, standing behind the counter as always. He asked me how I was. Without really meaning to, I found myself unburdening my troubles to him. "A Christmas story?" he said after I had finished. "Is that all? If you buy me lunch, my friend, I'll tell you the best Christmas story you ever heard. And I guarantee that every word of it is true."

We walked down the block to Jack's, a cramped and boisterous delicatessen with good pastrami sandwiches and photographs of old Dodger teams hanging on the walls. We found a table at the back, ordered our food, and then Auggie launched into his story.

"It was the summer of '72," he said. "A kid came in one morning and started stealing things from the store. He must have been about nineteen or twenty, and I don't think I've ever seen a more pathetic shoplifter in my life. He's standing by the rack of paperbacks along the far wall and stuffing books into the pockets of his raincoat. It was crowded around the counter just then, so I didn't see him at first. But once I noticed what he was up to, I started to shout. He took off like a jackrabbit, and by the time I managed to get out from behind the counter, he was already tearing down Atlantic Avenue. I chased after him for about half a block, and then I gave up. He'd dropped something along the way, and since I didn't feel like running anymore, I bent down to see what it was.

"It turned out to be his wallet. There wasn't any money inside, but his driver's license was there along with three or four snapshots. I suppose I could have called the cops and had him arrested. I had his name and address from the license, but I felt kind of sorry for him. He was just a measly little punk, and once I looked at those pictures in his wallet, I couldn't bring myself to feel very angry at him. Robert Goodwin. That was his name. In one of the pictures, I remember, he was standing with his arm around his mother or grandmother. In another one, he was sitting there at age nine or ten dressed in a baseball uniform with a big smile on his face. I just didn't have the heart. He was probably on dope now, I figured. A poor kid from Brooklyn without much going for him, and who cared about a couple of trashy paperbacks anyway?

"So I held onto the wallet. Every once in a while I'd get a little urge to send it back to him, but I kept delaying and never did anything about it. Then Christmas rolls around and I'm stuck with nothing to do. The boss usually invites me over to his house to spend the day, but that year he and his family were down in Florida visiting relatives. So I'm sitting in my apartment that morning feeling a little sorry for myself, and then I see Robert Goodwin's wallet lying on a shelf in the kitchen. I figure what the hell, why not do something nice for once, and I put on my coat and go out to return the wallet in person.

"The address was over in Boerum Hill, somewhere in the projects. It was freezing out that day, and I remember getting lost a few times trying to find the right building. Everything looks the same in that place, and you keep going over the same ground thinking you're somewhere else. Anyway, I finally get to the apartment I'm looking for and ring the bell. Nothing happens. I assume no one's there, but I try again just to make sure. I wait a little longer, and just when I'm about to give up, I hear someone shuffling to the door. An old woman's voice asks who's there, and I say I'm looking for Robert Goodwin. 'Is that you, Robert?' the old woman says, and then she undoes about fifteen locks and opens the door.

"She has to be at least eighty, maybe ninety years old, and the first thing I notice about her is that she's blind. 'I knew you'd come, Robert,' she says. 'I knew you wouldn't forget your Granny Ethel on Christmas.' And then she opens her arms as if she's about to hug me.

"I didn't have much time to think, you understand. I had to say something real fast, and before I knew what was happening, I could hear the words coming out of my mouth. 'That's right, Granny Ethel,' I said. 'I came back to see you on Christmas.' Don't ask me why I did it. I don't have any idea. Maybe I didn't want to disappoint her or something, I don't know. It just came out that way, and then this old woman was suddenly hugging me there in front of the door, and I was hugging her back.

"I didn't exactly say that I was her grandson. Not in so many words, at least, but that was the implication. I wasn't trying to trick her, though. It was like a game we'd both decided to play—without having to discuss the rules. I mean, that woman *knew* I wasn't her grandson Robert. She was old and dotty, but she wasn't so far gone that she couldn't tell the difference between a stranger and her own flesh and blood. But it made her happy to pretend, and since I had nothing better to do anyway, I was happy to go along with her.

"So we went into the apartment and spent the day together. The place was a real dump, I might add, but what else can you expect from a blind woman who does her own housekeeping? Every time she asked me a question about how I was, I would lie to her. I told her I'd found a good job working in a cigar store, I told her I was about to get married, I told her a hundred pretty stories, and she made like she believed every one of them. 'That's fine, Robert,' she would say, nodding her head and smiling. 'I always knew things would work out for you.'

"After a while, I started getting pretty hungry. There didn't seem to be much food in the house, so I went out to a store in the neighborhood and brought back a mess of stuff. A precooked chicken, vegetable soup, a bucket of potato salad, a chocolate cake, all kinds of things. Ethel had a couple of bottles of wine stashed in her bedroom, and so between us we managed to put together a fairly decent Christmas dinner. We both got a little tipsy from the wine, I remember, and after the meal was over we went out to sit in the living room, where the chairs were more comfortable. I had to take a pee, so I excused myself and went to the bathroom down the hall. That's where things took yet another turn. It was ditsy enough doing my little jig as Ethel's grandson, but what I did next was positively crazy, and I've never forgiven myself for it.

"I go into the bathroom, and stacked up against the wall next to the shower, I see a pile of six or seven cameras. Brand-new thirty-five-millimeter cameras, still in their boxes, top-quality merchandise. I figure this is the work of the real Robert, a storage place for one of his recent hauls. I've never taken a picture in my life, and I've certainly never stolen anything, but the moment I see those cameras sitting in the bathroom, I decide I want one of them for myself. Just like that. And without even stopping to think about it, I tuck one of the boxes under my arm and go back to the living room.

"I couldn't have been gone for more than three minutes, but in that time Granny Ethel had fallen asleep in her chair. Too much Chianti, I suppose. I went into the kitchen to wash the dishes, and she slept on through the whole racket, snoring like a baby. There didn't seem to be any point in disturbing her, so I decided to leave. I couldn't even write a note to say good-bye, seeing that she was blind and all, and so I just left. I put her grandson's wallet on the table, picked up the camera again, and walked out of the apartment. And that's the end of the story."

"Did you ever go back to see her?" I asked.

"Once," he said. "About three or four months later. I felt so bad about stealing the camera, I hadn't even used it yet. I finally made up my mind to return it, but Ethel wasn't there anymore. I don't know what happened to her, but someone else had moved into the apartment, and he couldn't tell me where she was."

"She probably died."

"Yeah, probably."

"Which means that she spent her last Christmas with you."

"I guess so. I never thought of it that way."

"It was a good deed, Auggie. It was a nice thing you did for her."

"I lied to her, and then I stole from her. I don't see how you can call that a good deed."

"You made her happy. And the camera was stolen anyway. It's not as if the person you took it from really owned it."

"Anything for art, eh Paul?"

"I wouldn't say that. But at least you've put the camera to good use."

"And now you've got your Christmas story, don't you?"

"Yes," I said. "I suppose I do."

I paused for a moment, studying Auggie as a wicked grin spread across his face. I couldn't be sure, but the look in his eyes at that moment was so mysterious, so fraught with the glow of some inner delight, that it suddenly occurred to me that he had made the whole thing up. I was about to ask him if he'd been putting me on, but then I realized he would never tell. I had been tricked into believing him, and that was the only thing that mattered. As long as there's one person to believe it, there's no story that can't be true.

"You're an ace, Auggie," I said. "Thanks for being so helpful."

"Any time," he answered, still looking at me with that maniacal light in his eyes. "After all, if you can't share your secrets with your friends, what kind of a friend are you?"

"I guess I owe you one."

"No you don't. Just put it down the way I told it to you, and you don't owe me a thing."

"Except the lunch."

"That's right. Except the lunch."

I returned Auggie's smile with a smile of my own, and then I called out to the waiter and asked for the check.

Spunk

Zora Neale Hurston (1901?–1960)

Born in Eatonville, Florida, **Zora Neale Hurston** grew up in the South and eventually moved to New York City, where she studied at Barnard College, wrote, and was central to the Harlem Renaissance. A novelist, folklorist, and anthropologist who made a tremendous impact on African-American cultural studies and literature, Hurston collected tales, studied voodoo, and researched southern and Caribbean black culture, invoking the surroundings, dialects, and customs of these areas and cultures. This work eventually resulted in books of fluid, beautiful prose. Her last years were painful: she worked as a maid and died anonymously and in poverty back in Florida, but was brought back to mainstream culture by writer Alice Walker. Her novels include *Jonah's Gourd Vine* (1934), *Their Eyes Were Watching God* (1937), *Moses, Man of the Mountain* (1939), and *Seraph on the Swanee* (1948). Her folklore and anthropology books include *Mules and Men* (1935) and *Tell My Horse* (1938). She also wrote an autobiography entitled *Dust Tracks on a Road* (1942).

A giant of a brown-skinned man sauntered up the one street of the Village and out into the palmetto thickets with a small pretty woman clinging lovingly to his arm.

"Looka theah, folkses!" cried Elijah Mosley, slapping his leg gleefully. "Theah they go, big as life an' brassy as tacks."

All the loungers in the store tried to walk to the door with an air of nonchalance but with small success.

"Now pee-eople!" Walter Thomas gasped. "Will you look at 'em!"

"But that's one thing Ah likes about Spunk Banks—he ain't skeered of nothin' on God's green footstool—*nothin'!* He rides that log down at saw-mill jus' like he struts 'round wid another man's wife—jus' don't give a kitty. When Tes' Miller got cut to giblets on that circle-saw, Spunk steps right up and starts ridin'. The rest of us was skeered to go near it."

A round-shouldered figure in overalls much too large, came nervously in the door and the talking ceased. The men looked at each other and winked.

"Gimme some soda-water. Sass'prilla Ah reckon," the new-comer ordered, and stood far down the counter near the open pickled pig-feet tub to drink it.

Elijah nudged Walter and turned with mock gravity to the new-comer.

"Say, Joe, how's everything up yo' way? How's yo' wife?"

Joe started and all but dropped the bottle he held in his hands. He swallowed several times painfully and his lips trembled.

"Aw 'Lige, you oughtn't to do nothin' like that," Walter grumbled. Elijah ignored him.

"She jus' passed heah a few minutes ago goin' thata way," with a wave of his hand in the direction of the woods.

Now Joe knew his wife had passed that way. He knew that the men lounging in the general store had seen her, moreover, he knew that the men knew *he* knew. He stood there silent for a long moment staring blankly, with his Adam's apple twitching nervously up and down his throat. One could actually *see* the pain he was suffering, his eyes, his face, his hands and even the dejected slump of his shoulders. He set the bottle down upon the counter. He didn't bang it, just eased it out of his hand silently and fiddled with his suspender buckle.

"Well, Ah'm goin' after her to-day. Ah'm goin' an' fetch her back. Spunk's done gone too fur."

He reached deep down into his trouser pocket and drew out a hollow ground razor, large and shiny, and passed his moistened thumb back and forth over the edge.

"Talkin' like a man, Joe. Course that's *yo'* fambly affairs, but Ah like to see grit in anybody."

Joe Kanty laid down a nickel and stumbled out into the street.

Dusk crept in from the woods. Ike Clarke lit the swinging oil lamp that was almost immediately surrounded by candle-flies. The men laughed boisterously behind Joe's back as they watched him shamble woodward.

"You oughtn't to said whut you did to him, Lige—look how it worked him up," Walter chided.

"And Ah hope it did work him up. 'Tain't even decent for a man to take and take like he do."

"Spunk will sho' kill him."

"Aw, Ah doan't know. You never kin tell. He might turn him up an' spank him fur gettin' in the way, but Spunk wouldn't shoot no unarmed man. Dat razor he carried outa heah ain't gonna run Spunk down an' cut him, an' Joe ain't got the nerve to go up to Spunk with it knowing he totes that Army .45. He makes that break outa heah to bluff us. He's gonna hide that razor behind the first likely palmetto root an' sneak back home to bed. Don't tell me nothin' 'bout that rabbit-foot colored man. Didn't he meet Spunk an' Lena face to face one day las' week an' mumble sumthin' to Spunk 'bout lettin' his wife alone?"

"What did Spunk say?" Walter broke in—"Ah like him fine but 'tain't right the way he carries on wid Lena Kanty, jus' cause Joe's timid 'bout fightin'."

"You wrong theah, Walter. 'Tain't cause Joe's timid at all, it's cause Spunk wants Lena. If Joe was a passle of wile cats Spunk would tackle the job just the same. He'd go after *anything* he wanted the same way. As Ah wuz sayin' a minute ago, he tole Joe right to his face that Lena was his. 'Call her,' he says to Joe. 'Call her and see if she'll come. A woman knows her boss an' she answers when he calls.' 'Lena, ain't I yo' husband?' Joe sorter whines out. Lena looked at him real disgusted but she don't answer and she don't move outa her tracks. Then Spunk reaches out an' takes hold of her arm an' says: 'Lena, youse mine. From now on Ah works for you an' fights for you an' Ah never wants you to look to nobody for a crumb of bread, a stitch of close or a shingle to go over yo' head, but *me* long as Ah live. Ah'll git the lumber foh owah house to-morrow. Go home an' git yo' things together!'

" 'Thass mah house,' Lena speaks up. 'Papa gimme that.'

" 'Well,' says Spunk, 'doan give up whut's yours, but when youse inside don't forgit youse mine, an' let no other man git outa his place wid you!'

"Lena looked up at him with her eyes so full of love that they wuz runnin' over, an' Spunk seen it an' Joe seen it too, and his lip started to tremblin' and his Adam's apple was galloping up and down his neck like a race horse. Ah bet he's wore out half a dozen Adam's apples since Spunk's been on the job with Lena. That's all he'll do. He'll be back heah after while swallowin' an' workin' his lips like he wants to say somethin' an' can't."

"But didn't he do *nothin'* to stop 'em?"

"Nope, not a frazzlin' thing—jus' stood there. Spunk took Lena's arm and walked off jus' like nothin' ain't happened and he stood there gazin' after them till they was outa sight. Now you know a woman don't want no man like that. I'm jus' waitin' to see whut he's goin' to say when he gits back."

II

But Joe Kanty never came back, never. The men in the store heard the sharp report of a pistol somewhere distant in the palmetto thicket and soon Spunk came walking leisurely, with his big black Stetson set at the same rakish angle and Lena clinging to his arm, came walking right into the general store. Lena wept in a frightened manner.

"Well," Spunk announced calmly, "Joe come out there wid a meatax an' made me kill him."

He sent Lena home and led the men back to Joe—Joe crumpled and limp with his right hand still clutching his razor.

"See mah back? Mah cloes cut clear through. He sneaked up an' tried to kill me from the back, but Ah got him, an' got him good, first shot," Spunk said.

The men glared at Elijah, accusingly.

"Take him up an' plant him in 'Stoney lonesome,' " Spunk said in a careless voice. "Ah didn't wanna shoot him but he made me do it. He's a dirty coward, jumpin' on a man from behind."

Spunk turned on his heel and sauntered away to where he

knew his love wept in fear for him and no man stopped him. At the general store later on, they all talked of locking him up until the sheriff should come from Orlando, but no one did anything but talk.

A clear case of self-defense, the trial was a short one, and Spunk walked out of the court house to freedom again. He could work again, ride the dangerous log-carriage that fed the singing, snarling, biting, circle-saw; he could stroll the soft dark lanes with his guitar. He was free to roam the woods again; he was free to return to Lena. He did all of these things.

III

"Whut you reckon, Walt?" Elijah asked one night later. "Spunk's gittin' ready to marry Lena!"

"Naw! Why, Joe ain't had time to git cold yit. Nohow Ah didn't figger Spunk was the marryin' kind."

"Well, he is," rejoined Elijah. "He done moved most of Lena's things—and her along wid 'em—over to the Bradley house. He's buying it. Jus' like Ah told yo' all right in heah the night Joe wuz kilt. Spunk's crazy 'bout Lena. He don't want folks to keep on talkin' 'bout her—thass reason he's rushin' so. Funny thing 'bout that bob-cat, wan't it?"

"Whut bob-cat, 'Lige? Ah ain't heered 'bout none."

"Ain't cher? Well, night befo' las' was the fust night Spunk an' Lena moved together an' jus' as they was goin' to bed, a big black bob-cat, black all over, you hear me, *black,* walked round and round that house and howled like forty, an' when Spunk got his gun an' went to the winder to shoot it, he says it stood right still an' looked him in the eye, an' howled right at him. The thing got Spunk so nervoused up he couldn't shoot. But Spunk says twan't no bob-cat nohow. He says it was Joe done sneaked back from Hell!"

"Humph!" sniffed Walter, "he oughter be nervous after what he done. Ah reckon Joe come back to dare him to marry Lena, or to come out an' fight. Ah bet he'll be back time and agin, too. Know what Ah think? Joe wuz a braver man than Spunk."

There was a general shout of derision from the group.

"Thass a fact," went on Walter. "Lookit whut he done; took a razor an' went out to fight a man he knowed toted a gun an' wuz a crack shot, too; 'nother thing Joe wuz skeered of Spunk, skeered plumb stiff! But he went jes' the same. It took him a long time to get his nerve up. 'Tain't nothin' for Spunk to fight when he ain't skeered of nothin'. Now, Joe's done come back to have it out wid the man that's got all he ever had. Y'll know Joe ain't never had nothin' nor wanted nothin' besides Lena. It musta been a h'ant cause ain' nobody never seen no black bob-cat."

" 'Nother thing," cut in one of the men, "Spunk wuz cussin' a blue streak to-day 'cause he 'lowed dat saw wuz wobblin'—almos' got 'im once. The machinist come, looked it over an' said it wuz alright. Spunk musta been leanin' t'wards it some. Den he claimed somebody pushed 'im but 'twant nobody close to 'im. Ah wuz glad when knockin' off time come. I'm skeered of dat man when he gits hot. He'd beat you full of button holes as quick as he's look atcher."

IV

The men gathered the next evening in a different mood, no laughter. No badinage this time.

"Look, 'Lige, you goin' to set up wid Spunk?"

"Naw, Ah reckon not, Walter. Tell yuh the truth, Ah'm a lil bit skittish. Spunk died too wicket—died cussin' he did. You know he thought he wuz done outa life."

"Good Lawd, who'd he think done it?"

"Joe."

"Joe Kanty? How come?"

"Walter, Ah b'leeve Ah will walk up thata way an' set. Lena would like it Ah reckon."

"But whut did he say, 'Lige?"

Elijah did not answer until they had left the lighted store and were strolling down the dark street.

"Ah wuz loadin' a wagon wid scantlin' right near the saw when Spunk fell on the carriage but 'fore Ah could git to him the saw got him in the body—awful sight. Me an' Skint Miller got him off but it was too late. Anybody could see that. The fust thing he said wuz: 'He pushed me, 'Lige—the dirty hound pushed me in the back!'—He was spittin' blood at ev'ry breath. We laid him on the sawdust pile with his face to the East so's he could die easy. He helt mah han' till the last, Walter, and said: 'It was Joe, 'Lige—the dirty sneak shoved me . . . he didn't dare come to mah face . . . but Ah'll git the son-of-a-wood louse soon's Ah get there an' make hell too hot for him. . . . Ah felt him shove me . . . !' Thass how he died."

"If spirits kin fight, there's a powerful tussle goin' on somewhere ovah Jordan 'cause Ah b'leeve Joe's ready for Spunk an' ain't skeered any more—yas, Ah b'leeve Joe pushed 'im mahself."

They had arrived at the house. Lena's lamentations were deep and loud. She had filled the room with magnolia blossoms that gave off a heavy sweet odor. The keepers of the wake tipped about whispering in frightened tones. Everyone in the village was there, even old Jeff Kanty, Joe's father, who a few hours before would have been afraid to come within ten feet of him, stood leering triumphantly down upon the fallen giant as if his fingers had been the teeth of steel that laid him low.

The cooling board consisted of three sixteen-inch boards on saw horses, a dingy sheet was his shroud.

The women ate heartily of the funeral baked meats and wondered who would be Lena's next. The men whispered coarse conjectures between guzzles of whiskey.

The Cabalist of East Broadway

Isaac Bashevis Singer (1904–1991)

Isaac Bashevis Singer is regarded by many to be the greatest American Yiddish writer. The son of a rabbi, he was born in Radzymin, Poland, and emigrated to New York City in 1935. He became a journalist for the *Jewish Daily Forward* and eventually began publishing short stories and novels. Isaac Bashevis Singer offers psychological insight and visual force as he describes the lives and experiences of Jews in Poland, America, and Germany. His descriptions are lyrically invoked, his characters original and imaginative, and his gift as storyteller first and foremost is unquestionable. Among Isaac Bashevis Singer's novels are *The Family Moskat* (1950), *Satan in Goray* (1955), *The Magician of Lublin* (1960), *The Manor* (1967), *The Estate* (1970), and *Enemies: A Love Story* (1972). His short story collections include *Gimpel the Fool and Other Stories* (1957), *The Spinoza of Market Street* (1961), *The Seance* (1968), *A Friend of Kafka* (1970), and *A Crown of Feathers* (1973). He also wrote several children's stories, a 1966 autobiography entitled *In My Father's Court*, and in 1978 he won the Nobel Prize. "The Cabalist of East Broadway" appears in *The Collected Stories of Isaac Bashevis Singer* (1982).

As happens so often in New York, the neighborhood changed. The synagogues became churches, the yeshivas restaurants or garages. Here and there one could still see a Jewish old people's home, a shop selling Hebrew books, a meeting place for *landsleit* from some village in Rumania or Hungary. I had to come downtown a few times a week, because the Yiddish newspaper to which I contributed was still there. In the cafeteria on the corner, in former times one could meet Yiddish writers, journalists, teach-

Translated by Alma Singer and Herbert Lottman

ers, fund raisers for Israel, and the like. Blintzes, borscht, kreplech, chopped liver, rice pudding, and egg cookies were the standard dishes. Now the place catered mainly to Negroes and Puerto Ricans. The voices were different, the smells were different. Still, I used to go there occasionally to eat a quick lunch or to drink a cup of coffee. Each time I entered the cafeteria, I would immediately see a man I'll call Joel Yabloner, an old Yiddish writer who specialized in the Cabala. He had published books about Holy Isaac Luria, Rabbi Moshe of Cordova, the Baal Shem, Rabbi Nachman of Bratslav. Yabloner had translated part of the Zohar into Yiddish. He also wrote in Hebrew. According to my calculations, he must have been in his early seventies.

Joel Yabloner, tall, lean, his face sallow and wrinkled, had a shiny skull without a single hair, a sharp nose, sunken cheeks, a throat with a prominent Adam's apple. His eyes bulged and were the color of amber. He wore a shabby suit and an unbuttoned shirt that revealed the white hair on his chest. Yabloner had never married. In his youth he suffered from consumption, and the doctors had sent him to a sanatorium in Colorado. Someone told me that there he was forced to eat pork, and as a result he fell into melancholy. I seldom heard him utter a word. When I greeted him, he barely nodded and often averted his eyes. He lived on the few dollars a week the Yiddish Writers' Union could spare him. His apartment on Broome Street had no bath, telephone, central heating. He ate neither fish nor meat, not even eggs or milk—only bread, vegetables, and fruit. In the cafeteria he always ordered a cup of black coffee and a dish of prunes. He would sit for hours staring at the revolving door, at the cashier's desk, or the wall where, years ago, a commercial artist had painted the market on Orchard Street, with its pushcarts and peddlers. The paint was peeling now.

The president of the Writers' Union told me that although all of Joel Yabloner's friends and admirers had died out here in New York, he still had relatives and disciples in the land of Israel. They had often invited him to come there to live. They would publish his works, they promised (he had trunks filled with manuscripts), find an apartment for him, and see that he was taken care of in every way. Yabloner had a nephew in Jerusalem who was a professor at the university. There were still some Zionist leaders who considered Joel Yabloner their spiritual father. So why should he sit here on East Broadway, a silent and forgotten man? The Writers' Union would have sent his pension to him in Israel, and he could also have received Social Security, which he had never bothered to claim. Here in New York he had already been burglarized a few times. A mugger had knocked out his last three teeth. Eiserman, the dentist who had translated Shakespeare's sonnets into Yiddish, told me that he had offered to make Yabloner a set of false teeth, but Yabloner had said to him, "There is only one step from false teeth to a false brain."

"A great man, but a queer one," Eiserman said to me while he drilled and filled my own teeth. "Or perhaps he wants to atone for his sins this way. I've heard that he had love affairs in his youth."

"Yabloner—love affairs?"

"Yes, love affairs. I myself knew a Hebrew teacher, Deborah Soltis, who was madly in love with him. She was my patient. She died about ten years ago."

In connection with this, Eiserman told me of a curious episode. Joel Yabloner and Deborah Soltis saw each other over a period of twenty years, indulging in long conversations, often discussing Hebrew literature, the fine points of grammar, Maimonides, and Rabbi Judah ha-Levi, but the pair never went so far as to kiss. The closest they came was once when both of them were looking up the meaning of a word or an idiom in Ben-Yahudah's great dictionary and their heads met accidentally. Yabloner fell into a playful mood and said, "Deborah, let's trade eyeglasses."

"What for?" Deborah Soltis asked.

"Oh, just like that. Only for a little while."

The two lovers exchanged reading glasses, but he couldn't read with hers and she couldn't read with his. So they replaced their own glasses on their own noses—and that was the most intimate contact the two ever achieved.

* * *

Eventually, I stopped going down to East Broadway. I sent my articles to the newspaper by mail. I forgot Joel Yabloner. I didn't even know that he was still alive. Then one day when I walked into a hotel lobby in Tel Aviv I heard applause in an adjoining hall. The door to the hall was half open and I looked in. There was Joel Yabloner behind a lectern, making a speech. He wore an alpaca suit, a white shirt, a silk skullcap, and his face appeared fresh, rosy, young. He had a full set of new teeth and had sprouted a white goatee. I happened not to be especially busy, so I found an empty chair and sat down.

Yabloner did not speak modern Hebrew but the old holy tongue with the Ashkenazi pronunciation. When he gesticulated, I noticed the sparkling links in his immaculate shirt cuffs. I heard him say in a Talmudic singsong, "Since the Infinite One filled all space and, as the Zohar expresses it, 'No space is empty of Him,' how did He create the universe? Rabbi Chaim Vital gave the answer: 'Before creation, the attributes of the Almighty were all potential, not actual. How can one be a king without subjects, and how can there be mercy without anyone to receive it?' "

Yabloner clutched his beard, glanced at his notes. Once in a while, he took a sip from a glass of tea. I observed quite a number of women and even young girls in the audience. A few students took notes. How strange—there was also a nun. She must have understood Hebrew. "The Jewish state has resuscitated Joel Yabloner," I said to myself. One seldom has a chance to enjoy someone else's good fortune, and for me Yabloner's triumph was a symbol of the Eternal Jew. He had spent decades as a lonely, neglected man. Now he seemed to have come into his own. I listened to the rest of the lecture, which was followed by a question period. Unbelievable, but that sad man had a sense of humor. I learned that the lecture had been organized by a committee which had undertaken to publish Yabloner's work. One of the members of the committee knew me, and asked if I wished to attend a banquet in Yabloner's honor. "Since you are a vegetarian," he added, "here is your chance. They will serve only vegetables, fruits, nuts. When do they ever have a vegetarian banquet? Once in a lifetime."

Between the lecture and the banquet, Joel Yabloner went out on the terrace for a rest. The day had been hot, and now in the late afternoon a breeze was blowing from the sea. I approached him, saying, "You don't remember me, but I know you."

"I know you very well. I read everything you write," he replied. "Even here I try not to miss your stories."

"Really, it is a great honor for me to hear you say so."

"Please sit down," he said, indicating a chair.

God in Heaven, that silent man had become talkative. He asked me all kinds of questions about America, East Broadway, Yiddish literature. A woman came over to us. She wore a turban over her white hair, a satin cape, and men's shoes with low, wide heels. She had a large head, high cheekbones, the complexion of a gypsy, black eyes that blazed with anger. The beginnings of a beard could be seen on her chin. In a strong, mannish voice she said to me, "*Adoni* [Sir], my husband just finished an important lecture. He must speak at the banquet, and I want him to rest for a while. Be so good as to leave him alone. He is not a young man any more and he should not exert himself."

"Oh, excuse me."

Yabloner frowned. "Abigail, this man is a Yiddish writer and my friend."

"He may be a writer and a friend, but your throat is overstrained. If you argue with him, you will be hoarse later."

"Abigail, we aren't arguing."

"*Adoni,* please listen to me. He doesn't know how to take care of himself."

"Well, we shall talk later," I said. "You have a devoted wife."

"So they tell me."

I took part in the banquet—ate the nuts, almonds, avocados, cheese, bananas that were served. Yabloner again made a speech, this time about the author of the cabalistic book *The Treatise of the Hasidim*. His wife sat near him on the stage. Each time his voice became scratchy she handed him a glass of white fluid—some variety of yogurt. After the speech, in the course of which Yabloner demonstrated much erudition, the chairman announced that an assistant professor at the Hebrew University was writing Yabloner's biography and that funds were being raised to publish it. The author was called out on the stage. He was a young man with a round face, shining eyes, and the tiniest of skullcaps, which blended into his pomaded hair. In his closing words, Yabloner thanked his old friends, his students, all those who came to honor him. He paid tribute to his wife, Abigail, saying that without her help he would never have been able to put his manuscripts in order. He mentioned her first husband, whom he referred to as a genius, a saint, a pillar of wisdom. From a huge handbag that resembled a valise more than a lady's purse, Mrs. Yabloner took out a red kerchief like the ones used by old-fashioned rabbis and blew her nose with a blast that reverberated throughout the hall. "Let him intercede for us at the Throne of Glory!" she called out.

After the banquet I went over to Yabloner and said, "Often when I saw you sitting all alone in the cafeteria I was tempted to ask you why you didn't go to Israel. What was your reason for waiting so long?"

He paused, closing his eyes as if the question required pondering, and finally shrugged his shoulders. "Man does not live according to reason."

Again a few years passed. The typesetter on the newspaper for which I worked had lost a page of my most recent article, and since the article had to appear the next day—Saturday—there wasn't time to send the copy by mail. I had to take a cab to deliver it to the composing room myself. I gave the missing page to the foreman and went down to the editorial department to see the editor and some of my old colleagues. The winter day was short, and when I came back onto the street I felt the long-forgotten hustle and bustle of the oncoming Sabbath. Even though the neighborhood was no longer predominantly Jewish, some synagogues, yeshivas, and Hasidic study houses had refused to leave. Here and there I saw in a window a woman lighting her Sabbath candles. Men in wide-brimmed velvet or fur hats were going to prayers, accompanied by boys with long sidelocks. My father's words came to my mind: "The Almighty will always have His quorum." I remembered the chants of the Sabbath-eve liturgy: "Let us exalt," "Come my bridegroom," "The temple of the King."

I was not in a hurry any more, and I decided to have a cup of coffee in the cafeteria before I took the subway home. I pushed the revolving door. For a moment I imagined that nothing had changed, and I thought I could hear those voices of my first years in America—the cafeteria filled with Old World intellectuals shouting their opinions of Zionism, Jewish Socialism, the life and culture in America. But the faces were not familiar. Spanish was the language I heard. The walls had been painted over, and the scenes of Orchard Street with its pushcarts and peddlers had disappeared. Suddenly I saw something I could not believe. At a table in the middle of the room sat Joel Yabloner—without a beard, in a shabby suit and an unbuttoned shirt. He was emaciated, wrinkled, and disheveled, and his mouth again appeared sunken and empty. His bulging eyes stared at the empty wall opposite. Was I mistaken? No, it was Yabloner, all right. In his expression there was the desperation of a man caught in a dilemma from which there is no escape. With the cup of coffee in my hand, I stopped. Should I approach him to greet him, should I ask permission to sit down at his table?

Someone pushed me, and half of my coffee spilled over. The spoon fell on the floor with a clang. Yabloner turned around and our eyes met for a second. I nodded to him, but he did not respond. Then he turned his face away. Yes, he recognized me, but he was not in a mood for conversation. I even imagined that he had shaken his head in refusal. I found a table against the wall and sat down. I drank what was left of my coffee, all the while looking at him sideways. Why had he left Israel? Did he miss something here? Was he running away from someone? I had a strong desire to go over and ask him, but I knew that I would not get anything out of him.

A power stronger than man and his calculations has driven him out of Paradise, back to Hell, I decided. He did not even go to the Friday-night services. He was hostile not only to people but to the Sabbath itself. I finished the coffee and left.

A few weeks later, I read among the obituaries that Joel Yabloner had died. He was buried somewhere in Brooklyn. That night I lay awake until three o'clock, thinking about him. Why did he return? Had he not atoned enough for the sins of his youth? Had his return to East Broadway some explanation in the lore of the Cabala? Had some holy sparks strayed from the World of Emanation into the Evil Host? And could they have been found and brought back to their sacred origin only in this cafeteria? Another idea came into my head—perhaps he wanted to lie near that teacher with whom he exchanged eyeglasses? I remembered the last words I heard from him: "Man does not live according to reason."

Bartleby the Scrivener
A Story of Wall Street

Herman Melville (1819–1891)

Herman Melville was born and grew up in New York City, but most of his rhythmical and realistic narrative and prose works describe adventures on the sea, a sea he loved. Melville's experiences on ships and in the South Seas shine through in novels such as *Typee* (1846), *Omoo* (1847), *Mardi* (1849), *Redburn* (1849), *White Jacket* (1850) and his most famous novel, *Moby Dick* (1851). In addition to these novels, Melville wrote *The Piazza Tales* (1856), a book of short fiction that includes "Bartleby the Scrivener"; *Billy Budd,* an 1890 novella; and some verse: *Battle Pieces and Aspects of War* (1866) and *Clarel* (1876).

I am a rather elderly man. The nature of my avocations, for the last thirty years, has brought me into more than ordinary contact with what would seem an interesting and somewhat singular set of men, of whom, as yet, nothing, that I know of, has ever been written—I mean, the law-copyists, or scriveners. I have known very many of them, professionally and privately, and, if I pleased, could relate divers histories, at which good-natured gentlemen might smile, and sentimental souls might weep. But I waive the biographies of all other scriveners, for a few passages in the life of Bartleby, who was a scrivener, the strangest I ever saw, or heard of. While, of other law-copyists, I might write the complete life, of Bartleby nothing of that sort can be done. I believe that no materials exist, for a full and satisfactory biography of this man. It is an irreparable loss to literature. Bartleby was one of those beings of whom nothing is ascertainable, except from the original sources, and, in his case, those are very small. What my own astonished eyes saw of Bartleby, *that* is all I know of him, except, indeed, one vague report, which will appear in the sequel.

Ere introducing the scrivener, as he first appeared to me, it is fit I make some mention of myself, my *employés,* my business, my chambers, and general surroundings; because some such description is indispensable to an adequate understanding of the chief character about to be presented. Imprimis: I am a man who, from his youth upwards, has been filled with a profound conviction that the easiest way of life is the best. Hence, though I belong to a profession proverbially energetic and nervous, even to turbulence, at times, yet nothing of that sort have I ever suffered to invade my peace. I am one of those unambitious lawyers who never addresses a jury, or in any way draws down public applause; but, in the cool tranquillity of a snug retreat, do a snug business among rich men's bonds, and mortgages, and title-deeds. All who know me, consider me an eminently *safe* man. The late John Jacob Astor, a personage little given to poetic enthusiasm, had no hesitation in pronouncing my first grand point to be prudence; my next, method. I do not speak it in vanity, but simply record the fact, that I was not unemployed in my profession by the late John Jacob Astor; a name which, I admit, I love to repeat; for it hath a rounded and orbicular sound to it, and rings like unto bullion. I will freely add, that I was not insensible to the late John Jacob Astor's good opinion.

Some time prior to the period at which this little history begins, my avocations had been largely increased. The good old office now extinct in the State of New York, of a Master in Chancery, had been conferred upon me. It was not a very arduous office, but very pleasantly remunerative. I seldom lose my temper; much more seldom indulge in dangerous indignation at wrongs and outrages; but I must be permitted to be rash here and declare, that I consider the sudden and violent abrogation of the office of Master in Chancery, by the new Constitution, as a ——— premature act; inasmuch as I had counted upon a life-lease of the profits, whereas I only received those of a few short years. But this is by the way.

My chambers were up stairs, at No. — Wall Street. At one end, they looked upon the white wall of the interior of a spacious skylight shaft, penetrating the building from top to bottom.

This view might have been considered rather tame than otherwise, deficient in what landscape painters call "life." But, if so, the view from the other end of my chambers offered, at least, a contrast, if nothing more. In that direction, my windows commanded an unobstructed view of a lofty brick wall, black by age and everlasting shade; which wall required no spy-glass to bring out its lurking beauties, but, for the benefit of all near-sighted spectators, was pushed up to within ten feet of my window panes. Owing to the great height of the surrounding buildings, and my chambers being on the second floor, the interval between this wall and mine not a little resembled a huge square cistern.

At the period just preceding the advent of Bartleby, I had two persons as copyists in my employment, and a promising lad as an office-boy. First, Turkey; second, Nippers; third, Ginger Nut. These may seem names, the like of which are not usually found in the Directory. In truth, they were nicknames, mutually conferred upon each other by my three clerks, and were deemed expressive of their respective persons or characters. Turkey was a short, pursy Englishman, of about my age—that is, somewhere not far from sixty. In the morning, one might say, his face was of a fine florid hue, but after twelve o'clock, meridian—his dinner hour—it blazed like a grate full of Christmas coals; and continued blazing—but, as it were, with a gradual wane—till six o'clock, P.M., or thereabouts; after which, I saw no more of the proprietor of the face, which, gaining its meridian with the sun, seemed to set with it, to rise, culminate, and decline the following day, with the like regularity and undiminished glory. There are many singular coincidences I have known in the course of my life, not the least among which was the fact, that, exactly when Turkey displayed his fullest beams from his red and radiant countenance, just then, too, at that critical moment, began the daily period when I considered his business capacities as seriously disturbed for the remainder of the twenty-four hours. Not that he was absolutely idle, or averse to business, then; far from it. The difficulty was, he was apt to be altogether too energetic. There was a strange, inflamed, flurried, flighty recklessness of activity about him. He would be incautious in dipping his pen into his ink-stand. All his blots upon my documents were dropped there after twelve o'clock, meridian. Indeed, not only would he be reckless, and sadly given to making blots in the afternoon, but, some days, he went further, and was rather noisy. At such times, too, his face flamed with augmented blazonry, as if cannel coal had been heaped on anthracite. He made an unpleasant racket with his chair; spilled his sand-box; in mending his pens, impatiently split them all to pieces, and threw them on the floor in a sudden passion; stood up, and leaned over his table, boxing his papers about in a most indecorous manner, very sad to behold in an elderly man like him. Nevertheless, as he was in many ways a most valuable person to me, and all the time before twelve o'clock meridian, was the quickest, steadiest creature, too, accomplishing a great deal of work in a style not easily to be matched—for these reasons, I was willing to overlook his eccentricities, though, indeed, occasionally, I remonstrated with him. I did this very gently, however, because, though the civilest, nay, the blandest and most reverential of men in the morning, yet, in the afternoon, he was disposed, upon provocation, to be slightly rash with his tongue—in fact, insolent. Now, valuing his morning services as I did, and resolved not to lose them—yet, at the same time, made uncomfortable by his inflamed ways after twelve o'clock—and being a man of peace, unwilling by my admonitions to call forth unseemly retorts from him, I took upon me, one Saturday noon (he was always worse on Saturdays) to hint to him, very kindly, that, perhaps, now that he was growing old, it might be well to abridge his labors; in short, he need not come to my chambers after twelve o'clock, but, dinner over, had best go home to his lodgings, and rest himself till tea-time. But no; he insisted upon his afternoon devotions. His countenance became intolerably fervid, as he oratorically assured me—gesticulating with a long ruler at the other end of the room—that if his services in the morning were useful, how indispensable, then, in the afternoon?

"With submission, sir," said Turkey, on this occasion, "I consider myself your right-hand man. In the morning I but marshal and deploy my columns; but in the afternoon I put myself at their head, and gallantly charge the foe, thus"—and he made a violent thrust with the ruler.

"But the blots, Turkey," intimated I.

"True; but, with submission, sir, behold these hairs! I am getting old. Surely, sir, a blot or two of a warm afternoon is not to be severely urged against gray hairs. Old age—even if it blot the page—is honorable. With submission, sir, we *both* are getting old."

This appeal to my fellow-feeling was hardly to be resisted. At all events, I saw that go he would not. So, I made up my mind to let him stay, resolving, nevertheless, to see to it that, during the afternoon, he had to do with my less important papers.

Nippers, the second on my list, was a whiskered, sallow, and, upon the whole, rather piratical-looking young man, of about five-and-twenty. I always deemed him the victim of two evil powers—ambition and indigestion. The ambition was evinced by a certain impatience of the duties of a mere copyist, and unwarrantable usurpation of strictly professional affairs, such as the original drawing up of legal documents. The indigestion seemed betokened in an occasional nervous testiness and grinning irritability, causing the teeth to audibly grind together over mistakes committed in copying; unnecessary maledictions, hissed, rather than spoken, in the heat of business; and especially by a continual discontent with the height of the table where he worked. Though of a very ingenious mechanical turn, Nippers could never get this table to suit him. He put chips under it, blocks of various sorts, bits of pasteboard, and at last went so far as to attempt an exquisite adjustment, by final pieces of folded blotting-paper. But no invention would answer. If, for the sake of easing his back, he brought the table-lid at a sharp angle well up towards his chin, and wrote there like a man using the steep roof of a Dutch house for his desk, then he declared that it stopped the circulation in his arms. If now he lowered the table to his waistbands, and stooped over it in writing, then there was a sore aching in his back. In short, the truth of the matter was, Nippers knew not what he wanted. Or, if he wanted anything, it was to be rid of a scrivener's table altogether. Among the manifestations of his diseased ambition was a fondness he had for receiving visits from certain ambiguous-looking fellows in seedy coats, whom he called his clients. Indeed, I was aware that not only was he, at times, considerable of a ward-politician, but he occasionally did a little business at the Justices' courts, and was not unknown on the steps of the Tombs. I have good reason to believe, however, that one individual who called upon him at my chambers, and who, with a grand air, he insisted was his client, was no other than a dun, and the alleged title-deed, a bill. But, with all his failings, and the annoyances he caused me, Nippers, like his compatriot Turkey, was a very useful man to me; wrote a neat, swift hand; and, when he chose, was not deficient in a gentlemanly sort of deportment. Added to this, he always dressed in a gentlemanly sort of way; and so, incidentally, reflected credit upon my chambers. Whereas, with respect to Turkey, I had much ado to keep him from being a reproach to me. His clothes were apt to look oily, and smell of eatinghouses. He wore his pantaloons very loose and baggy in summer. His coats were execrable; his hat not to be handled. But while the hat was a thing of indifference to me, inasmuch as his natural civility and deference, as a dependent Englishman, always led him to doff it the moment he entered the room, yet his coat was another matter. Concerning his coats, I reasoned with him; but with no effect. The truth was, I suppose, that a man with so small an income could not afford to sport such a lustrous face and a lustrous coat at one and the same time. As Nippers once observed, Turkey's money went chiefly for red ink. One winter day, I presented Turkey with a highly respectable-looking coat of my own—a padded gray coat, of a most comfortable warmth, and which buttoned straight up from the knee to the neck. I thought Turkey would appreciate the favor, and abate his rashness and obstreperousness of afternoons. But no; I verily believe that buttoning himself up in so downy and blanket-like a coat had a pernicious effect upon him—upon the same principle that too much oats are bad for horses. In fact, precisely as a rash, restive horse is said to feel his oats, so Turkey felt his coat. It made him insolent. He was a man whom prosperity harmed.

Though, concerning the self-indulgent habits of Turkey, I had my own private surmises, yet, touching Nippers, I was well persuaded that, whatever might be his faults in other respects, he was, at least, a temperate young man. But, indeed, nature herself seemed to have been his vintner, and, at his birth, charged him so thoroughly with an irritable, brandy-like disposition, that all subsequent potations were needless. When I consider how, amid the stillness of my chambers, Nippers would sometimes impatiently rise from his seat, and stooping over his table, spread his arms wide apart, seize the whole desk, and move it, and jerk it, with a grim, grinding motion on the floor, as if the table were a perverse voluntary agent, intent on thwarting and vexing him, I plainly perceive that, for Nippers, brandy-and-water were altogether superfluous.

It was fortunate for me that, owing to its peculiar cause—indigestion—the irritability and consequent nervousness of Nippers were mainly observable in the morning, while in the afternoon he was comparatively mild. So that, Turkey's paroxysms only coming on about twelve o'clock, I never had to do with their eccentricities at one time. Their fits relieved each other, like guards. When Nippers's was on, Turkey's was off; and *vice versa.* This was a good natural arrangement, under the circumstances.

Ginger Nut, the third on my list, was a lad, some twelve years old. His father was a carman, ambitious of seeing his son on the bench instead of a cart, before he died. So he sent him to my office, as student at law, errand-boy, cleaner and sweeper, at the rate of one dollar a week. He had a little desk to himself, but he did not use it much. Upon inspection, the drawer exhibited a great array of the shells of various sorts of nuts. Indeed, to this quick-witted youth, the whole noble science of the law was contained in a nut-shell. Not the least among the employments of Ginger Nut, as well as one which he discharged with the most alacrity, was his duty as cake and apple purveyor for Turkey and Nippers. Copying law-papers being proverbially a dry, husky sort of business, my two scriveners were fain to moisten their mouths very often with Spitzenbergs, to be had at the numerous stalls nigh the Custom House and Post Office. Also, they sent Ginger Nut very frequently for that peculiar cake—small, flat, round, and very spicy—after which he had been named by them. Of a cold morning, when business was but dull, Turkey would gobble up scores of these cakes, as if they were mere wafers—indeed, they sell them at the rate of six or eight for a penny—the scrape of his pen blending with the crunching of the crisp particles in his mouth. Rashest of all the fiery afternoon blunders and flurried rashnesses of Turkey, was his once moistening a ginger-cake between his lips, and clapping it on to a mortgage, for a seal. I came within an ace of dismissing him then. But he mollified me by making an oriental bow, and saying—

"With submission, sir, it was generous of me to find you in stationery on my own account."

Now my original business—that of a conveyancer and title hunter, and drawer-up of recondite documents of all sorts—was considerably increased by receiving the master's office. There was now great work for scriveners. Not only must I push the clerks already with me, but I must have additional help.

In answer to my advertisement, a motionless young man one morning stood upon my office threshold, the door being open, for it was summer. I can see that figure now—pallidly neat, pitiably respectable, incurably forlorn! It was Bartleby.

After a few words touching his qualifications, I engaged him, glad to have among my corps of copyists a man of so singularly sedate an aspect, which I thought might operate beneficially upon the flighty temper of Turkey, and the fiery one of Nippers.

I should have stated before that ground-glass folding-doors divided my premises into two parts, one of which was occupied by my scriveners, the other by myself. According to my humor, I threw open these doors, or closed them. I resolved to assign Bartleby a corner by the folding-doors, but on my side of them, so as to have this quiet man within easy call, in case any trifling thing was to be done. I placed his desk close up to a small side-window in that part of the room, a window which originally had afforded a lateral view of certain grimy back-yards and bricks, but which, owing to subsequent erections, commanded at present no view at all, though it gave some light. Within three feet of the panes was a wall, and the light came down from far above, between two lofty buildings, as from a very small opening in a dome. Still further to a satisfactory arrangement, I procured a high green folding screen, which might entirely isolate Bartleby from my sight, though not remove him from my voice. And thus, in a manner, privacy and society were conjoined.

At first, Bartleby did an extraordinary quantity of writing. As if long famishing for something to copy, he seemed to gorge himself on my documents. There was no pause for digestion. He ran a day and night line, copying by sun-light and by candle-light. I should have been quite delighted with his application, had he been cheerfully industrious. But he wrote on silently, palely, mechanically.

It is, of course, an indispensable part of a scrivener's business to verify the accuracy of his copy, word by word. Where there are two or more scriveners in an office, they assist each other in this examination, one reading from the copy, the other holding the original. It is a very dull, wearisome, and lethargic affair. I can readily imagine that, to some sanguine temperaments, it would be altogether intolerable. For example, I cannot credit that the mettlesome poet, Byron, would have contentedly sat down with Bartleby to examine a law document of, say five hundred pages, closely written in a crimpy hand.

Now and then, in the haste of business, it had been my habit to assist in comparing some brief document myself, calling Turkey or Nippers for this purpose. One object I had, in placing Bartleby so handy to me behind the screen, was, to avail myself of his services on such trivial occasions. It was on the third day, I think, of his being with me, and before any necessity had arisen for having his own writing examined, that, being much hurried to complete a small affair I had in hand, I abruptly called to Bartleby. In my haste and natural expectancy of instant compliance, I sat with my head bent over the original on my desk, and my right hand sideways, and somewhat nervously extended with the copy, so that, immediately upon emerging from his retreat, Bartleby might snatch it and proceed to business without the least delay.

In this very attitude did I sit when I called to him, rapidly stating what it was I wanted him to do—namely, to examine a small paper with me. Imagine my surprise, nay, my consternation, when, without moving from his privacy, Bartleby, in a singularly mild, firm voice, replied, "I would prefer not to."

I sat awhile in perfect silence, rallying my stunned faculties. Immediately it occurred to me that my ears had deceived me, or Bartleby had entirely misunderstood my meaning. I repeated my request in the clearest tone I could assume; but in quite as clear a one came the previous reply, "I would prefer not to."

"Prefer not to," echoed I, rising in high excitement, and crossing the room with a stride. "What do you mean? Are you moonstruck? I want you to help me compare this sheet here—take it," and I thrust it towards him.

"I would prefer not to," said he.

I looked at him steadfastly. His face was leanly composed; his gray eye dimly calm. Not a wrinkle of agitation rippled him. Had there been the least uneasiness, anger, impatience or impertinence in his manner; in other words, had there been anything ordinarily human about him, doubtless I should have violently dismissed him from the premises. But as it was, I should have as soon thought of turning my pale plaster-of-paris bust of Cicero out of doors. I stood gazing at him awhile, as he went on with his own writing, and then reseated myself at my desk. This is very strange, thought I. What had one best do? But my business hurried me. I concluded to forget the matter for the present, reserving it for my future leisure. So, calling Nippers from the other room, the paper was speedily examined.

A few days after this, Bartleby concluded four lengthy documents, being quadruplicates of a week's testimony taken before me in my High Court of Chancery. It became necessary to examine them. It was an important suit, and great accuracy was imperative. Having all things arranged, I called Turkey, Nippers and Ginger Nut, from the next room, meaning to place the four copies in the hands of my four clerks, while I should read from the original. Accordingly, Turkey, Nippers, and Ginger Nut had taken their seats in a row, each with his document in his hand, when I called to Bartleby to join this interesting group.

"Bartleby! quick, I am waiting."

I heard a slow scrape of his chair legs on the uncarpeted floor, and soon he appeared standing at the entrance of his hermitage.

"What is wanted?" said he, mildly.

"The copies, the copies," said I, hurriedly. "We are going to examine them. There"—and I held towards him the fourth quadruplicate.

"I would prefer not to," he said, and gently disappeared behind the screen.

For a few moments I was turned into a pillar of salt, standing at the head of my seated column of clerks. Recovering myself, I advanced towards the screen, and demanded the reason for such extraordinary conduct.

"*Why* do you refuse?"

"I would prefer not to."

With any other man I should have flown outright into a dreadful passion, scorned all further words, and thrust him ignominiously from my presence. But there was something about Bartleby that not only strangely disarmed me, but, in a wonderful manner, touched and disconcerted me. I began to reason with him.

"These are your own copies we are about to examine. It is labor saving to you, because one examination will answer for your four papers. It is common usage. Every copyist is bound to help examine his copy. Is it not so? Will you not speak? Answer!"

"I prefer not to," he replied in a flute-like tone. It seemed to me that, while I had been addressing him, he carefully revolved every statement that I made; fully comprehended the meaning; could not gainsay the irresistible conclusion; but, at the same time, some paramount consideration prevailed with him to reply as he did.

"You are decided, then, not to comply with my request—a request made according to common usage and common sense?"

He briefly gave me to understand, that on that point my judgment was sound. Yes: his decision was irreversible.

It is not seldom the case that, when a man is browbeaten in some unprecedented and violently unreasonable way, he begins to stagger in his own plainest faith. He begins, as it were, vaguely to surmise that, wonderful as it may be, all the justice and all the reason is on the other side. Accordingly, if any disinterested persons are present, he turns to them for some reinforcement for his own faltering mind.

"Turkey," said I, "what do you think of this? Am I not right?"

"With submission, sir," and Turkey, in his blandest tone, "I think that you are."

"Nippers," said I, "what do *you* think of it?"

"I think I should kick him out of the office."

(The reader of nice perceptions will here perceive that, it being morning, Turkey's answer is couched in polite and tranquil terms, but Nippers replies in ill-tempered ones. Or, to repeat a previous sentence, Nippers's ugly mood was on duty, and Turkey's off.)

"Ginger Nut," said I, willing to enlist the smallest suffrage in my behalf, "what do *you* think of it?"

"I think, sir, he's a little *luny,*" replied Ginger Nut, with a grin.

"You hear what they say," said I, turning towards the screen, "come forth and do your duty."

But he vouchsafed no reply. I pondered a moment in sore perplexity. But once more business hurried me. I determined again to postpone the consideration of this dilemma to my future leisure. With a little trouble we made out to examine the papers without Bartleby, though at every page or two Turkey deferentially dropped his opinion, that this proceeding was quite out of the common; while Nippers, twitching in his chair with a dyspeptic nervousness, ground out, between his set teeth, occasional hissing maledictions against the stubborn oaf behind the screen. And for his (Nippers's) part, this was the first and the last time he would do another man's business without pay.

Meanwhile Bartleby sat in his hermitage, oblivious to everything but his own peculiar business there.

Some days passed, the scrivener being employed upon another lengthy work. His late remarkable conduct led me to regard his ways narrowly. I observed that he never went to dinner; indeed, that he never went anywhere. As yet I had never, of my personal knowledge, known him to be outside of my office. He was a perpetual sentry in the corner. At about eleven o'clock though, in the morning, I noticed that Ginger Nut would advance toward the opening in Bartleby's screen, as if silently beckoned thither by a gesture invisible to me where I sat. The boy would then leave the office, jingling a few pence, and reappear with a handful of ginger-nuts, which he delivered in the hermitage, receiving two of the cakes for his trouble.

He lives, then, on ginger-nuts, thought I; never eats a dinner, properly speaking; he must be a vegetarian, then, but no; he never eats even vegetables, he eats nothing but ginger-nuts. My mind then ran on in reveries concerning the probable effects upon the human constitution of living entirely on ginger-nuts. Ginger-nuts are so called, because they contain ginger as one of their peculiar constituents, and the final flavoring one. Now, what was ginger? A hot, spicy thing. Was Bartleby hot and spicy? Not at all. Ginger, then, had no effect upon Bartleby. Probably he preferred it should have none.

Nothing so aggravates an earnest person as a passive resistance. If the individual so resisted be of a not inhumane temper, and the resisting one perfectly harmless in his passivity, then, in the better moods of the former, he will endeavor charitably to construe to his imagination what proves impossible to be solved by his judgment. Even so, for the most part, I regarded Bartleby and his ways. Poor fellow! thought I, he means no mischief; it is plain he intends no insolence; his aspect sufficiently evinces that his eccentricities are involuntary. He is useful to me. I can get along with him. If I turn him away, the chances are he will fall in with some less-indulgent employer, and then he will be rudely treated, and perhaps driven forth miserably to starve. Yes. Here I can cheaply purchase a delicious self-approval. To befriend Bartleby; to humor him in his strange willfulness, will cost me little or nothing, while I lay up in my soul what will eventually prove a sweet morsel for my conscience. But this mood was not invariable with me. The passiveness of Bartleby sometimes irritated me. I felt strangely goaded on to encounter him in new opposition—to elicit some angry spark from him answerable to my own. But, indeed, I might as well have essayed to strike fire with my knuckles against a bit of Windsor soap. But one afternoon the evil impulse in me mastered me, and the following little scene ensued:

"Bartleby," said I, "when those papers are all copied, I will compare them with you."

"I would prefer not to."

"How? Surely you do not mean to persist in that mulish vagary?"

No answer.

I threw open the folding-doors near by, and, turning upon Turkey and Nippers, exclaimed:

"Bartleby a second time says, he won't examine his papers. What do you think of it, Turkey?"

It was afternoon, be it remembered. Turkey sat glowing like a brass boiler; his bald head steaming; his hands reeling among his blotted papers.

"Think of it?" roared Turkey. "I think I'll just step behind his screen, and black his eyes for him!"

So saying, Turkey rose to his feet and threw his arms into a pugilistic position. He was hurrying away to make good his promise, when I detained him, alarmed at the effect of incautiously rousing Turkey's combativeness after dinner.

"Sit down, Turkey," said I, "and hear what Nippers has to say. What do you think of it, Nippers? Would I not be justified in immediately dismissing Bartleby?"

"Excuse me, that is for you to decide, sir. I think his conduct quite unusual, and, indeed, unjust, as regards Turkey and myself. But it may only be a passing whim."

"Ah," exclaimed I, "you have strangely changed your mind, then—you speak very gently of him now."

"All beer," cried Turkey; "gentleness is effects of beer—Nippers and I dined together to-day. You see how gentle *I* am, sir. Shall I go and black his eyes?"

"You refer to Bartleby, I suppose. No, not to-day, Turkey," I replied; "pray, put up your fists."

I closed the doors, and again advanced towards Bartleby. I felt additional incentives tempting me to my fate. I burned to be rebelled against again. I remembered that Bartleby never left the office.

"Bartleby," said I, "Ginger Nut is away; just step around to the Post Office, won't you?" (it was but a three minutes' walk) "and see if there is anything for me."

"I would prefer not to."

"You *will* not?"

"I *prefer* not."

I staggered to my desk, and sat there in a deep study. My blind inveteracy returned. Was there any other thing in which I could procure myself to be ignominiously repulsed by this lean, penniless wight?—my hired clerk? What added thing is there, perfectly reasonable, that he will be sure to refuse to do?

"Bartleby!"

No answer.

"Bartleby," in a louder tone.

No answer.

"Bartleby," I roared.

Like a very ghost, agreeably to the laws of magical invocation, at the third summons, he appeared at the entrance of his hermitage.

"Go to the next room, and tell Nippers to come to me."

"I prefer not to," he respectfully and slowly said, and mildly disappeared.

"Very good, Bartleby," said I, in a quiet sort of serenely-severe self-possessed tone, intimating the unalterable purpose of some terrible retribution very close at hand. At the moment I half intended something of the kind. But upon the whole, as it was drawing towards my dinner-hour, I thought it best to put on my hat and walk home for the day, suffering much from perplexity and distress of mind.

Shall I acknowledge it? The conclusion of this whole business was, that it soon became a fixed fact of my chambers, that a pale young scrivener, by the name of Bartleby, had a desk there; that he copied for me at the usual rate of four cents a folio (one hundred words); but he was permanently exempt from examining the work done by him, that duty being transferred to Turkey and Nippers, out of compliment, doubtless, to their superior acuteness; moreover, said Bartleby was never, on any account, to be dispatched on the most trivial errand of any sort; and that even if entreated to take upon him such a matter, it was generally understood that he would "prefer not to"—in other words, that he would refuse point-blank.

As days passed on, I became considerably reconciled to Bartleby. His steadiness, his freedom from all dissipation, his incessant industry (except when he chose to throw himself into a standing revery behind his screen), his great stillness, his unalterableness of demeanor under all circumstances, made him a valuable acquisition. One prime thing was this—*he was always there*—first in the morning, continually through the day, and the last at night. I had a singular confidence in his honesty. I felt my most precious papers perfectly safe in his hands. Sometimes, to be sure, I could not, for the very soul of me, avoid falling into sudden spasmodic passions with him. For it was exceeding difficult to bear in mind all the time those strange peculiarities, privileges, and unheard-of exemptions, forming the tacit stipulations on Bartleby's part under which he remained in my office. Now and then, in the eagerness of dispatching pressing business, I would inadvertently summon Bartleby, in a short, rapid tone, to put his finger, say, on the incipient tie of a bit of red tape with which I was about compressing some papers. Of course, from behind the screen the usual answer, "I prefer not to," was sure to come; and then, how could a human creature, with the common infirmities of our nature, refrain from bitterly exclaiming upon such perverseness—such unreasonableness? However, every added repulse of this sort which I received only tended to lessen the probability of my repeating the inadvertence.

Here it must be said, that, according to the custom of most legal gentlemen occupying chambers in densely-populated law buildings, there were several keys to my door. One was kept by a woman residing in the attic, which person weekly scrubbed and daily swept and dusted my apartments. Another was kept by Turkey for convenience sake. The third I sometimes carried in my own pocket. The fourth I knew not who had.

Now, one Sunday morning I happened to go to Trinity Church, to hear a celebrated preacher, and finding myself rather early on the ground I thought I would walk round to my chambers for a while. Luckily I had my key with me; but upon applying it to the lock, I found it resisted by something inserted from the inside. Quite surprised, I called out; when to my consternation a key was turned from within; and thrusting his lean visage at me, and holding the door ajar, the apparition of Bartleby appeared, in his shirtsleeves, and otherwise in a strangely tattered *déshabillé,* saying quietly that he was sorry, but he was deeply engaged just then, and—preferred not admitting me at present. In a brief word or two, he moreover added, that perhaps I had better walk round the block two or three times, and by that time he would probably have concluded his affairs.

Now, the utterly unsurmised appearance of Bartleby, tenanting my law-chambers of a Sunday morning, with his cadaverously gentlemanly *nonchalance,* yet withal firm and self-possessed, had such a strange effect upon me, that incontinently I slunk away from my own door, and did as desired. But not without sundry twinges of impotent rebellion against the mild effrontery of this unaccountable scrivener. Indeed, it was his wonderful mildness chiefly, which not only disarmed me, but unmanned me as it were. For I consider that one, for the time, is sort of unmanned when he tranquilly permits his hired clerk to dictate to him, and order him away from his own premises. Furthermore, I was full of uneasiness as to what Bartleby could possibly be doing in my office in his shirt sleeves, and in an otherwise dismantled condition of a Sunday morning. Was anything amiss going on? Nay, that was out of the question. It was not to be thought of for a moment that Bartleby was an immoral person. But what could he be doing there?—copying? Nay again, whatever might be his eccentricities, Bartleby was an eminently decorous person. He would be the last man to sit down to his desk in any state approaching to nudity. Besides, it was Sunday; and there was something about Bartleby that forbade the supposition that he would by any secular occupation violate the proprieties of the day.

Nevertheless, my mind was not pacified; and full of a restless curiosity, at last I returned to the door. Without hindrance I inserted my key, opened it, and entered. Bartleby was not to be seen. I looked round anxiously, peeped behind his screen; but it was very plain that he was gone. Upon more closely examining the place, I surmised that for an indefinite period Bartleby must have eaten, dressed, and slept in my office, and that too without plate, mirror, or bed. The cushioned seat of a ricketty old sofa in one corner bore the faint impress of a lean, reclining form. Rolled away under his desk, I found a blanket; under the empty grate, a blacking box and brush; on a chair, a tin basin, with soap and a ragged towel; in a newspaper a few crumbs of ginger-nuts and a morsel of cheese. Yes, thought I, it is evident enough that Bartleby has been making his home here, keeping bachelor's hall all by himself. Immediately then the thought came sweeping across me, what miserable friendlessness and loneliness are here revealed! His poverty is great; but his solitude, how horrible! Think of it. Of a Sunday, Wall Street is deserted as Petra; and every night of every day it is an emptiness. This building, too, which of week-days hums with industry and life, at nightfall echoes with sheer vacancy, and all through Sunday is forlorn. And here Bartleby makes his home; sole spectator of a solitude which he has seen all populous—a sort of innocent and transformed Marius brooding among the ruins of Carthage!

For the first time in my life a feeling of overpowering stinging melancholy seized me. Before, I had never experienced aught but a not unpleasing sadness. The bond of a common humanity now drew me irresistibly to gloom. A fraternal melancholy! For both I and Bartleby were sons of Adam. I remembered the bright silks and sparkling faces I had seen that day, in gala trim, swan-like sailing down the Mississippi of Broadway; and I contrasted them with the pallid copyist, and thought to myself, Ah, happiness courts the light, so we deem the world is gay; but misery hides aloof, so we deem that misery there is none. These sad fancyings—chimeras, doubtless, of a sick and silly brain—led on to other and more special thoughts, concerning the eccentricities of Bartleby. Presentiments of strange discoveries hovered round me. The scrivener's pale form appeared to me laid out, among uncaring strangers, in its shivering winding-sheet.

Suddenly I was attracted by Bartleby's closed desk, the key in open sight left in the lock.

I mean no mischief, seek the gratification of no heartless curiosity, thought I; besides, the desk is mine, and its contents, too, so I will make bold to look within. Everything was methodically arranged, the papers smoothly placed. The pigeon holes were deep, and removing the files of documents, I groped into their recesses. Presently I felt something there, and dragged it out. It was an old bandana handkerchief, heavy and knotted. I opened it, and saw it was a savings' bank.

I now recalled all the quiet mysteries which I had noted in the man. I remembered that he never spoke but to answer; that, though at intervals he had considerable time to himself, yet I had never seen him reading—no, not even a newspaper; that for long periods he would stand looking out, at his pale window behind the screen, upon the dead brick wall; I was quite sure he never visited any refectory or eating house; while his pale face clearly indicated that he never drank beer like Turkey, or tea and coffee even, like other men; that he never went anywhere in particular that I could learn; never went out for a walk, unless, indeed, that was the case at present; that he had declined telling who he was, or whence he came, or whether he had any relatives in the world;

that though so thin and pale, he never complained of ill health. And more than all, I remembered a certain unconscious air of pallid—how shall I call it?—of pallid haughtiness, say, or rather an austere reserve about him, which had positively awed me into my tame compliance with his eccentricities, when I had feared to ask him to do the slightest incidental thing for me, even though I might know, from his long-continued motionlessness, that behind his screen he must be standing in one of those dead-wall reveries of his.

Revolving all these things, and coupling them with the recently discovered fact, that he made my office his constant abiding place and home, and not forgetful of his morbid moodiness; revolving all these things, a prudential feeling began to steal over me. My first emotions had been those of pure melancholy and sincerest pity; but just in proportion as the forlornness of Bartleby grew and grew to my imagination, did that same melancholy merge into fear, that pity into repulsion. So true it is, and so terrible, too, that up to a certain point the thought or sight of misery enlists our best affections; but, in certain special cases, beyond that point it does not. They err who would assert that invariably this is owing to the inherent selfishness of the human heart. It rather proceeds from a certain hopelessness of remedying excessive and organic ill. To a sensitive being, pity is not seldom pain. And when at last it is perceived that such pity cannot lead to effectual succor, common sense bids the soul be rid of it. What I saw that morning persuaded me that the scrivener was the victim of innate and incurable disorder. I might give alms to his body; but his body did not pain him; it was his soul that suffered, and his soul I could not reach.

I did not accomplish the purpose of going to Trinity Church that morning. Somehow, the things I had seen disqualified me for the time from church-going. I walked homeward, thinking what I would do with Bartleby. Finally, I resolved upon this—I would put certain calm questions to him the next morning, touching his history, etc., and if he declined to answer them openly and unreservedly (and I supposed he would prefer not), then to give him a twenty dollar bill over and above whatever I might owe him, and tell him his services were no longer required; but that if in any other way I could assist him, I would be happy to do so, especially if he desired to return to his native place, wherever that might be, I would willingly help to defray the expenses. Moreover, if, after reaching home, he found himself at any time in want of aid, a letter from him would be sure of a reply.

The next morning came.

"Bartleby," said I, gently calling to him behind his screen.

No reply.

"Bartleby," said I, in a still gentler tone, "come here; I am not going to ask you to do anything you would prefer not to do—I simply wish to speak to you."

Upon this he noiselessly slid into view.

"Will you tell me, Bartleby, where you were born?"

"I would prefer not to."

"Will you tell me *anything* about yourself?"

"I would prefer not to."

"But what reasonable objection can you have to speak to me? I feel friendly towards you."

He did not look at me while I spoke, but kept his glance fixed upon my bust of Cicero, which, as I then sat, was directly behind me, some six inches above my head.

"What is your answer, Bartleby?" said I, after waiting a considerable time for a reply, during which his countenance remained immovable, only there was the faintest conceivable tremor of the white attenuated mouth.

"At present I prefer to give no answer," he said, and retired into his hermitage.

It was rather weak in me I confess, but his manner, on this occasion, nettled me. Not only did there seem to lurk in it a certain calm disdain, but his perverseness seemed ungrateful, considering the undeniable good usage and indulgence he had received from me.

Again I sat ruminating what I should do. Mortified as I was at his behavior, and resolved as I had been to dismiss him when I entered my office, nevertheless I strangely felt something superstitious knocking at my heart, and forbidding me to carry out my purpose, and denouncing me for a villain if I dared to breathe one bitter word against this forlornest of mankind. At last, familiarly drawing my chair behind his screen, I sat down and said: "Bartleby, never mind, then, about revealing your history; but let me entreat you, as a friend, to comply as far as may be with the usages of this office. Say now, you will help to examine papers tomorrow or next day: in short, say now, that in a day or two you will begin to be a little reasonable:—say so, Bartleby."

"At present I would prefer not to be a little reasonable," was his mildly cadaverous reply.

Just then the folding-doors opened, and Nippers approached. He seemed suffering from an unusually bad night's rest, induced by severer indigestion than common. He overheard those final words of Bartleby.

"*Prefer not,* eh?" gritted Nippers—"I'd *prefer* him, if I were you, sir," addressing me—"I'd *prefer* him; I'd give him preferences, the stubborn mule! What is it, sir, pray, that he *prefers* not to do now?"

Bartleby moved not a limb.

"Mr. Nippers," said I, "I'd prefer that you would withdraw for the present."

Somehow, of late, I had got into the way of involuntarily using this word "prefer" upon all sorts of not exactly suitable occasions. And I trembled to think that my contact with the scrivener had already and seriously affected me in a mental way. And what further and deeper aberration might it not yet produce? This apprehension had not been without efficacy in determining me to summary measures.

As Nippers, looking very sour and sulky, was departing, Turkey blandly and deferentially approached.

"With submission, sir," said he, "yesterday I was thinking about Bartleby here, and I think that if he would but prefer to take a quart of good ale every day, it would do much towards mending him, and enabling him to assist in examining his papers."

"So you have got the word, too," said I, slightly excited.

"With submission, what word, sir?" asked Turkey, respectfully crowding himself into the contracted space behind the screen, and by so doing, making me jostle the scrivener. "What word, sir?"

"I would prefer to be left alone here," said Bartleby, as if offended at being mobbed in his privacy.

"*That*'s the word, Turkey," said I—"*that*'s it."

"Oh, *prefer?* oh yes—queer word. I never use it myself. But, sir, as I was saying, if he would but prefer—"

"Turkey," interrupted I, "you will please withdraw."

"Oh certainly, sir, if you prefer that I should."

As he opened the folding-door to retire, Nippers at his desk caught a glimpse of me, and asked whether I would prefer to have a certain paper copied on blue paper or white. He did not in the least roguishly accent the word "prefer." It was plain that it involuntarily rolled from his tongue. I thought to myself, surely I must get rid of a demented man, who already has in some degree turned the tongues, if not the heads, of myself and clerks. But I thought it prudent not to break the dismission at once.

The next day I noticed that Bartleby did nothing but stand at his window in his dead-wall revery. Upon asking him why he did not write, he said that he had decided upon doing no more writing.

"Why, how now? what next?" exclaimed I, "do no more writing?"

"No more."

"And what is the reason?"

"Do you not see the reason for yourself?" he indifferently replied.

I looked steadfastly at him, and perceived that his eyes looked dull and glazed. Instantly it occurred to me, that his unexampled diligence in copying by his dim window for the first few weeks of his stay with me might have temporarily impaired his vision.

I was touched. I said something in condolence with him. I hinted that of course he did wisely in abstaining from writing for a while; and urged him to embrace that opportunity of taking wholesome exercise in the open air. This, however, he did not do.

A few days after this, my other clerks being absent, and being in a great hurry to dispatch certain letters by the mail, I thought that, having nothing else earthly to do, Bartleby would surely be less inflexible than usual, and carry these letters to the post-office. But he blankly declined. So, much to my inconvenience, I went myself.

Still added days went by. Whether Bartleby's eyes improved or not, I could not say. To all appearance, I thought they did. But when I asked him if they did, he vouchsafed no answer. At all events, he would do no copying. At last, in reply to my urgings, he informed me that he had permanently given up copying.

"What!" exclaimed I; "suppose your eyes should get entirely well—better than ever before—would you not copy then?"

"I have given up copying," he answered, and slid aside.

He remained as ever, a fixture in my chamber. Nay—if that were possible—he became still more of a fixture than before. What was to be done? He would do nothing in the office; why should he stay there? In plain fact, he had now become a millstone to me, not only useless as a necklace, but afflictive to bear. Yet I was sorry for him. I speak less than truth when I say that, on his own account, he occasioned me uneasiness. If he would but have named a single relative or friend, I would instantly have written, and urged their taking the poor fellow away to some convenient retreat. But he seemed alone, absolutely alone in the universe. A bit of wreck in the mid Atlantic. At length, necessities connected with my business tyrannized over all other considerations. Decently as I could, I told Bartleby that in six days' time he must unconditionally leave the office. I warned him to take measures, in the interval, for procuring some other abode. I offered to assist him in this endeavor, if he himself would but take the first step towards a removal. "And when you finally quit me, Bartleby," added I, "I shall see that you go not away entirely unprovided. Six days from this hour, remember."

At the expiration of that period, I peeped behind the screen, and lo! Bartleby was there.

I buttoned up my coat, balanced myself; advanced slowly towards him, touched his shoulder, and said, "The time has come; you must quit this place; I am sorry for you; here is money; but you must go."

"I would prefer not," he replied, with his back still towards me.

"You *must.*"

He remained silent.

Now I had an unbounded confidence in this man's common honesty. He had frequently restored to me sixpences and shillings carelessly dropped upon the floor, for I am apt to be very reckless in such shirt-button affairs. The proceeding, then, which followed will not be deemed extraordinary.

"Bartleby," said I, "I owe you twelve dollars on account; here are thirty-two; the odd twenty are yours— Will you take it?" and I handed the bills towards him.

But he made no motion.

"I will leave them here, then," putting them under a weight on the table. Then taking my hat and cane and going to the door, I tranquilly turned and added—"After you have removed your things from these offices, Bartleby, you will of course lock the door—since every one is now gone for the day but you—and if you please, slip your key underneath the mat, so that I may have it in the morning. I shall not see you again; so good-by to you. If, hereafter, in your new place of abode, I can be of any service to you, do not fail to advise me by letter. Good-by, Bartleby, and fare you well."

But he answered not a word; like the last column of some ruined temple, he remained standing mute and solitary in the middle of the otherwise deserted room.

As I walked home in a pensive mood, my vanity got the better of my pity. I could not but highly plume myself on my masterly management in getting rid of Bartleby. Masterly I call it, and such it must appear to any dispassionate thinker. The beauty of my procedure seemed to consist in its perfect quietness. There was no vulgar bullying, no bravado of any sort, no choleric hectoring, and striding to and fro across the apartment, jerking out vehement commands for Bartleby to bundle himself off with his beggarly traps. Nothing of the kind. Without loudly bidding Bartleby depart—as an inferior genius might have done—I *assumed* the ground that depart he must; and upon that assumption built all I had to say. The more I thought over my procedure, the more I was charmed with it. Nevertheless, next morning, upon awakening, I had my doubts—I had somehow slept off the fumes of vanity. One of the coolest and wisest hours a man has, is just after he awakes in the morning. My procedure seemed as sagacious as ever—but only in theory. How it would prove in practice—there was the rub. It was truly a beautiful thought to have assumed Bartleby's departure; but, after all, that assumption was simply my own, and none of Bartleby's. The great point was, not whether I had assumed that he would quit me, but whether he would prefer so to do. He was more a man of preferences than assumptions.

After breakfast, I walked down town, arguing the probabilities *pro* and *con*. One moment I thought it would prove a miserable failure, and Bartleby would be found all alive at my office as usual; the next moment it seemed certain that I should find his chair empty. And so I kept veering about. At the corner of Broadway and Canal Street, I saw quite an excited group of people standing in earnest conversation.

"I'll take odds he doesn't," said a voice as I passed.

"Doesn't go?—done!" said I, "put up your money."

I was instinctively putting my hand in my pocket to produce my own, when I remembered that this was an election day. The words I had overheard bore no reference to Bartleby, but to the success or non-success of some candidate for the mayoralty. In my intent frame of mind, I had, as it were, imagined that all Broadway shared in my excitement, and were debating the same question with me. I passed on, very thankful that the uproar of the street screened my momentary absent-mindedness.

As I had intended, I was earlier than usual at my office door. I stood listening for a moment. All was still. He must be gone. I tried the knob. The door was locked. Yes, my procedure had worked to a charm; he indeed must be vanished. Yet a certain melancholy mixed with this: I was almost sorry for my brilliant success. I was fumbling under the door mat for the key, which Bartleby was to have left there for me, when accidentally my knee knocked against a panel, producing a summoning sound, and in response a voice came to me from within—"Not yet; I am occupied."

It was Bartleby.

I was thunderstruck. For an instant I stood like the man who, pipe in mouth, was killed one cloudless afternoon long ago in Virginia, by summer lightning; at his own warm open window he was killed, and remained leaning out there upon the dreamy afternoon, till some one touched him, when he fell.

"Not gone!" I murmured at last. But again obeying that wondrous ascendancy which the inscrutable scrivener had over me, and from which ascendancy, for all my chafing, I could not completely escape, I slowly went down stairs and out into the street, and while walking round the block, considered what I should next do in this unheard-of perplexity. Turn the man out by an actual thrusting I could not; to drive him away by calling him hard names would not do; calling in the police was an unpleasant idea; and yet, permit him to enjoy his cadaverous triumph over me—this, too, I could not think of. What was to be done? or, if nothing could be done, was there anything further that I could *assume* in the matter? Yes, as before I had prospectively assumed that Bartleby would depart, so now I might retrospectively assume that departed he was. In the legitimate carrying out of this assumption, I might enter my office in a great hurry, and pretending not to see Bartleby at all, walk straight against him as if he were air. Such a proceeding would in a singular degree have the appearance of a home-thrust. It was hardly possible that Bartleby could withstand such an application of the doctrine of assumptions. But upon second thoughts the success of the plan seemed rather dubious. I resolved to argue the matter over with him again.

"Bartleby," said I, entering the office, with a quietly severe expression, "I am seriously displeased. I am pained, Bartleby. I had thought better of you. I had imagined you of such a gentlemanly organization, that in any delicate dilemma a slight hint would suffice—in short, an assumption. But it appears I am deceived. Why," I added, unaffectedly starting, "you have not even touched that money yet," pointing to it, just where I had left it the evening previous.

He answered nothing.

"Will you, or will you not, quit me?" I now demanded in a sudden passion, advancing close to him.

"I would prefer *not* to quit you," he replied, gently emphasizing the *not*.

"What earthly right have you to stay here? Do you pay any rent? Do you pay my taxes? Or is this property yours?"

He answered nothing.

"Are you ready to go on and write now? Are your eyes recovered? Could you copy a small paper for me this morning? or help examine a few lines? or step round to the post-office? In a word, will you do anything at all, to give a coloring to your refusal to depart the premises?"

He silently retired into his hermitage.

I was now in such a state of nervous resentment that I thought it but prudent to check myself at present from further demonstrations. Bartleby and I were alone. I remembered the tragedy of the unfortunate Adams and the still more unfortunate Colt in the solitary office of the latter; and how poor Colt, being dreadfully incensed by Adams, and imprudently permitting himself to get wildly excited, was at unawares hurried into his fatal act—an act which certainly no man could possibly deplore more than the actor himself. Often it had occurred to me in my ponderings upon the subject that had that altercation taken place in the public street, or at a private residence, it would not have terminated as it did. It was the circumstance of being alone in a solitary office, up stairs, of a building entirely unhallowed by humanizing domestic associations—an uncarpeted office, doubtless, of a dusty, haggard sort of appearance—this it must have been, which greatly helped to enhance the irritable desperation of the hapless Colt.

But when this old Adam of resentment rose in me and tempted me concerning Bartleby, I grappled him and threw him. How?

Why, simply by recalling the divine injunction: "A new commandment give I unto you, that ye love one another." Yes, this it was that saved me. Aside from higher considerations, charity often operates as a vastly wise and prudent principle—a great safeguard to its possessor. Men have committed murder for jealousy's sake, and anger's sake, and hatred's sake, and selfishness' sake, and spiritual pride's sake; but no man, that ever I heard of, ever committed a diabolical murder for sweet charity's sake. Mere self-interest, then, if no better motive can be enlisted, should, especially with high-tempered men, prompt all beings to charity and philanthropy. At any rate, upon the occasion in question, I strove to drown my exasperated feelings towards the scrivener by benevolently construing his conduct. Poor fellow, poor fellow! thought I, he don't mean anything; and besides, he has seen hard times, and ought to be indulged.

I endeavored, also, immediately to occupy myself, and at the same time to comfort my despondency. I tried to fancy, that in the course of the morning, at such time as might prove agreeable to him, Bartleby, of his own free accord, would emerge from his hermitage and take up some decided line of march in the direction of the door. But no. Half-past twelve o'clock came; Turkey began to glow in the face, overturn his inkstand, and become generally obstreperous; Nippers abated down into quietude and courtesy; Ginger Nut munched his noon apple; and Bartleby remained standing at his window in one of his profoundest dead-wall reveries. Will it be credited? Ought I to acknowledge it? That afternoon I left the office without saying one further word to him.

Some days now passed, during which, at leisure intervals I looked a little into "Edwards on the Will," and "Priestley on Necessity." Under the circumstances, those books induced a salutary feeling. Gradually I slid into the persuasion that these troubles of mine, touching the scrivener, had been all predestinated from eternity, and Bartleby was billeted upon me for some mysterious purpose of an allwise Providence, which it was not for a mere mortal like me to fathom. Yes, Bartleby, stay there behind your screen, thought I; I shall persecute you no more; you are harmless and noiseless as any of these old chairs; in short, I never feel so private as when I know you are here. At last I see it, I feel it; I penetrate to the predestinated purpose of my life. I am content. Others may have loftier parts to enact; but my mission in this world, Bartleby, is to furnish you with office-room for such period as you may see fit to remain.

I believe that this wise and blessed frame of mind would have continued with me, had it not been for the unsolicited and uncharitable remarks obtruded upon me by my professional friends who visited the rooms. But thus it often is, that the constant friction of illiberal minds wears out at last the best resolves of the more generous. Though to be sure, when I reflected upon it, it was not strange that people entering my office should be struck by the peculiar aspect of the unaccountable Bartleby, and so be tempted to throw out some sinister observations concerning him. Sometimes an attorney, having business with me, and calling at my office, and finding no one but the scrivener there, would undertake to obtain some sort of precise information from him touching my whereabouts; but without heeding his idle talk, Bartleby would remain standing immovable in the middle of the room. So after contemplating him in that position for a time, the attorney would depart, no wiser than he came.

Also, when a Reference was going on, and the room full of lawyers and witnesses, and business driving fast, some deeply-occupied legal gentleman present, seeing Bartleby wholly unemployed, would request him to run round to his (the legal gentleman's) office and fetch some papers for him. Thereupon, Bartleby would tranquilly decline, and yet remain idle as before. Then the lawyer would give a great stare, and turn to me. And what could I say? At last I was made aware that all through the circle of my professional acquaintance, a whisper of wonder was running round, having reference to the strange creature I kept at my office. This worried me very much. And as the idea came upon me of his possibly turning out a long-lived man, and keep occupying my chambers, and denying my authority; and perplexing my visitors; and scandalizing my professional reputation; and casting a general gloom over the premises; keeping soul and body together to the last upon his savings (for doubtless he spent but half a dime a day), and in the end perhaps outlive me, and claim possession of my office by right of his perpetual occupancy: as all these dark anticipations crowded upon me more and more, and my friends continually intruded their relentless remarks upon the apparition in my room; a great change was wrought in me. I resolved to gather all my faculties together, and forever rid me of this intolerable incubus.

Ere revolving any complicated project, however, adapted to this end, I first simply suggested to Bartleby the propriety of his permanent departure. In a calm and serious tone, I commended the idea to his careful and mature consideration. But, having taken three days to meditate upon it, he apprised me, that his original determination remained the same; in short, that he still preferred to abide with me.

What shall I do? I now said to myself, buttoning up my coat to the last button. What shall I do? what ought I to do? what does conscience say I *should* do with this man, or, rather, ghost. Rid myself of him, I must; go, he shall. But how? You will not thrust him, the poor, pale, passive mortal—you will not thrust such a helpless creature out of your door? you will not dishonor yourself by such cruelty? No, I will not, I cannot do that. Rather would I let him live and die here, and then mason up his remains in the wall. What, then, will you do? For all your coaxing, he will not budge. Bribes he leaves under your own paperweight on your table; in short, it is quite plain that he prefers to cling to you.

Then something severe, something unusual must be done. What! surely you will not have him collared by a constable, and commit his innocent pallor to the common jail? And upon what ground could you procure such a thing to be done?—a vagrant, is he? What! he a vagrant, a wanderer, who refuses to budge? It is because he will *not* be a vagrant, then, that you seek to count him *as* a vagrant. That is too absurd. No visible means of support: there I have him. Wrong again: for indubitably he *does* support himself, and that is the only unanswerable proof that any man can show of his possessing the means so to do. No more, then. Since he will not quit me, I must quit him. I will change my offices; I will move elsewhere, and give him fair notice, that if I find him on my new premises I will then proceed against him as a common trespasser.

Acting accordingly, next day I thus addressed him: "I find these chambers too far from the City Hall; the air is unwholesome. In a word, I propose to remove my offices next week, and shall no longer require your services. I tell you this now, in order that you may seek another place."

He made no reply, and nothing more was said.

On the appointed day I engaged carts and men, proceeded to my chambers, and, having but little furniture, everything was removed in a few hours. Throughout, the scrivener remained standing behind the screen, which I directed to be removed the last thing. It was withdrawn; and, being folded up like a huge folio, left him the motionless occupant of a naked room. I stood in the entry watching him a moment, while something from within me upbraided me.

I re-entered, with my hand in my pocket—and—and my heart in my mouth.

"Good-by, Bartleby; I am going—good-by, and God some way bless you; and take that," slipping something in his hand. But it dropped upon the floor, and then—strange to say—I tore myself from him whom I had so longed to be rid of.

Established in my new quarters, for a day or two I kept the door locked, and started at every footfall in the passages. When I returned to my rooms, after any little absence, I would pause at the threshold for an instant, and attentively listen, ere applying my key. But these fears were needless. Bartleby never came nigh me.

I thought all was going well, when a perturbed-looking stranger visited me, inquiring whether I was the person who had recently occupied rooms at No. — Wall Street.

Full of forebodings, I replied that I was.

"Then, sir," said the stranger, who proved a lawyer, "you are responsible for the man you left there. He refuses to do any copying; he refuses to do anything; he says he prefers not to; and he refuses to quit the premises."

"I am very sorry, sir," said I, with assumed tranquillity, but an inward tremor, "but, really, the man you allude to is nothing to me—he is no relation or apprentice of mine, that you should hold me responsible for him."

"In mercy's name, who is he?"

"I certainly cannot inform you. I know nothing about him. Formerly I employed him as a copyist; but he has done nothing for me now for some time past."

"I shall settle him, then—good morning, sir."

Several days passed, and I heard nothing more; and, though I often felt a charitable prompting to call at the place and see poor Bartleby, yet a certain squeamishness, of I know not what, withheld me.

All is over with him, by this time, thought I, at last, when, through another week, no further intelligence reached me. But, coming to my room the day after, I found several persons waiting at my door in a high state of nervous excitement.

"That's the man—here he comes," cried the foremost one, whom I recognized as the lawyer who had previously called upon me alone.

"You must take him away, sir, at once," cried a portly person among them, advancing upon me, and whom I knew to be the landlord of No. — Wall Street. "These gentlemen, my tenants, cannot stand it any longer; Mr. B——," pointing to the lawyer, "has turned him out of his room, and he now persists in haunting the building generally, sitting upon the banisters of the stairs by day, and sleeping in the entry by night. Everybody is concerned; clients are leaving the offices; some fears are entertained of a mob; something you must do, and that without delay."

Aghast at this torrent, I fell back before it, and would fain have locked myself in my new quarters. In vain I persisted that Bartleby was nothing to me—no more than to any one else. In vain—I was the last person known to have anything to do with him, and they held me to the terrible account. Fearful, then, of being exposed in the papers (as one person present obscurely threatened), I considered the matter, and, at length, said, that if the lawyer would give me a confidential interview with the scrivener, in his (the lawyer's) own room, I would, that afternoon, strive my best to rid them of the nuisance they complained of.

Going up stairs to my old haunt, there was Bartleby silently sitting upon the banister at the landing.

"What are you doing here, Bartleby?" said I.

"Sitting upon the banister," he mildly replied.

I motioned him into the lawyer's room, who then left us.

"Bartleby," said I, "are you aware that you are the cause of great tribulation to me, by persisting in occupying the entry after being dismissed from the office?"

No answer.

"Now one of two things must take place. Either you must do something, or something must be done to you. Now what sort of business would you like to engage in? Would you like to re-engage in copying for some one?"

"No; I would prefer not to make any change."

"Would you like a clerkship in a dry-goods store?"

"There is too much confinement about that. No, I would not like a clerkship; but I am not particular."

"Too much confinement," I cried, "why, you keep yourself confined all the time!"

"I would prefer not to take a clerkship," he rejoined, as if to settle that little item at once.

"How would a bar-tender's business suit you? There is no trying of the eye-sight in that."

"I would not like it at all; though, as I said before, I am not particular."

His unwonted wordiness inspirited me. I returned to the charge.

"Well, then, would you like to travel through the country collecting bills for the merchants? That would improve your health."

"No, I would prefer to be doing something else."

"How, then, would going as a companion to Europe, to enter-tain some young gentleman with your conversation—how would that suit you?"

"Not at all. It does not strike me that there is anything definite about that. I like to be stationary. But I am not particular."

"Stationary you shall be, then," I cried, now losing all patience, and, for the first time in all my exasperating connection with him, fairly flying into a passion. "If you do not go away from these premises before night, I shall feel bound—indeed, I *am* bound—to—to—to quit the premises myself!" I rather absurdly concluded, knowing not with what possible threat to try to frighten his immobility into compliance. Despairing of all further efforts, I was precipitately leaving him, when a final thought occurred to me—one which had not been wholly unindulged before.

"Bartleby," said I, in the kindest tone I could assume under such exciting circumstances, "will you go home with me now—not to my office, but my dwelling—and remain there till we can conclude upon some convenient arrangement for you at our leisure? Come, let us start now, right away."

"No: at present I would prefer not to make any change at all."

I answered nothing; but, effectually dodging every one by the suddenness and rapidity of my flight, rushed from the building, ran up Wall Street towards Broadway, and, jumping into the first omnibus, was soon removed from pursuit. As soon as tranquillity returned, I distinctly perceived that I had now done all that I possibly could, both in respect to the demands of the landlord and his tenants, and with regard to my own desire and sense of duty, to benefit Bartleby, and shield him from rude persecution. I now strove to be entirely care-free and quiescent; and my conscience justified me in the attempt; though, indeed, it was not so successful as I could have wished. So fearful was I of being again hunted out by the incensed landlord and his exasperated tenants, that, surrendering my business to Nippers, for a few days, I drove about the upper part of the town and through the suburbs, in my rockaway; crossed over to Jersey City and Hoboken, and paid fugitive visits to Manhattanville and Astoria. In fact, I almost lived in my rockaway for the time.

When again I entered my office, lo, a note from the landlord lay upon the desk. I opened it with trembling hands. It informed me that the writer had sent to the police, and had Bartleby removed to the Tombs as a vagrant. Moreover, since I knew more about him than any one else, he wished me to appear at that place, and make a suitable statement of the facts. These tidings had a conflicting effect upon me. At first I was indignant; but, at last, almost approved. The landlord's energetic, summary disposition, had led him to adopt a procedure which I do not think I would have decided upon myself; and yet, as a last resort, under such peculiar circumstances, it seemed the only plan.

As I afterwards learned, the poor scrivener, when told that he must be conducted to the Tombs, offered not the slightest obstacle, but, in his pale, unmoving way, silently acquiesced.

Some of the compassionate and curious bystanders joined the party; and headed by one of the constables arm-in-arm with Bartleby, the silent procession filed its way through all the noise, and heat, and joy of the roaring thoroughfares at noon.

The same day I received the note, I went to the Tombs, or, to speak more properly, the Halls of Justice. Seeking the right officer, I stated the purpose of my call, and was informed that the individual I described was, indeed, within. I then assured the functionary that Bartleby was a perfectly honest man, and greatly to be compassionated, however unaccountably eccentric. I narrated all I knew, and closed by suggesting the idea of letting him remain in as indulgent confinement as possible, till something less harsh might be done—though, indeed, I hardly knew what. At all events, if nothing else could be decided upon, the alms-house must receive him. I then begged to have an interview.

Being under no disgraceful charge, and quite serene and harmless in all his ways, they had permitted him freely to wander about the prison, and, especially, in the inclosed grass-platted yards thereof. And so I found him there, standing all alone in the quietest of the yards, his face towards a high wall, while all around, from the narrow slits of the jail windows, I thought I saw peering out upon him the eyes of murderers and thieves.

"Bartleby!"

"I know you," he said, without looking round—"and I want nothing to say to you."

"It was not I that brought you here, Bartleby," said I, keenly pained at his implied suspicion. "And to you, this should not be so vile a place. Nothing reproachful attaches to you by being here. And see, it is not so sad a place as one might think. Look, there is the sky, and here is the grass."

"I know where I am," he replied, but would say nothing more, and so I left him.

As I entered the corridor again, a broad meat-like man, in an apron, accosted me, and, jerking his thumb over his shoulder, said—"Is that your friend?"

"Yes."

"Does he want to starve? If he does, let him live on the prison fare, that's all."

"Who are you?" asked I, not knowing what to make of such an unofficially speaking person in such a place.

"I am the grub-man. Such gentlemen as have friends here, hire me to provide them with something good to eat."

"Is this so?" said I, turning to the turnkey.

He said it was.

"Well, then," said I, slipping some silver into the grub-man's hands (for so they called him), "I want you to give particular attention to my friend there; let him have the best dinner you can get. And you must be as polite to him as possible."

"Introduce me, will you?" said the grub-man, looking at me with an expression which seemed to say he was all impatience for an opportunity to give a specimen of his breeding.

Thinking it would prove of benefit to the scrivener, I acquiesced; and, asking the grub-man his name, went up with him to Bartleby.

"Bartleby, this is a friend; you will find him very useful to you."

"Your sarvant, sir, your sarvant," said the grub-man, making a low salutation behind his apron. "Hope you find it pleasant here, sir; nice grounds—cool apartments—hope you'll stay with us some time—try to make it agreeable. What will you have for dinner to-day?"

"I prefer not to dine to-day," said Bartleby, turning away. "It would disagree with me; I am unused to dinners." So saying, he slowly moved to the other side of the inclosure, and took up a position fronting the dead-wall.

"How's this?" said the grub-man, addressing me with a stare of astonishment. "He's odd, ain't he?"

"I think he is a little deranged," said I, sadly.

"Deranged? deranged is it? Well, now, upon my word, I thought that friend of yourn was a gentleman forger; they are always pale and genteel-like, them forgers. I can't help pity 'em—can't help it, sir. Did you know Monroe Edwards?" he added, touchingly, and paused. Then, laying his hand piteously on my shoulder, sighed, "he died of consumption at Sing-Sing. So you weren't acquainted with Monroe?"

"No, I was never socially acquainted with any forgers. But I cannot stop longer. Look to my friend yonder. You will not lose by it. I will see you again."

Some few days after this, I again obtained admission to the Tombs, and went through the corridors in quest of Bartleby; but without finding him.

"I saw him coming from his cell not long ago," said a turnkey, "may be he's gone to loiter in the yards."

So I went in that direction.

"Are you looking for the silent man?" said another turnkey, passing me. "Yonder he lies—sleeping in the yard there. 'Tis not twenty minutes since I saw him lie down."

The yard was entirely quiet. It was not accessible to the common prisoners. The surrounding walls, of amazing thickness, kept off all sounds behind them. The Egyptian character of the masonry weighed upon me with its gloom. But a soft imprisoned turf grew under foot. The heart of the eternal pyramids, it seemed, wherein, by some strange magic, through the clefts, grass-seed, dropped by birds, had sprung.

Strangely huddled at the base of the wall, his knees drawn up, and lying on his side, his head touching the cold stones, I saw the wasted Bartleby. But nothing stirred. I paused; then went close up to him; stooped over, and saw that his dim eyes were open; otherwise he seemed profoundly sleeping. Something prompted me to touch him. I felt his hand, when a tingling shiver ran up my arm and down my spine to my feet.

The round face of the grub-man peered upon me now. "His dinner is ready. Won't he dine to-day, either? Or does he live without dining?"

"Lives without dining," said I, and closed the eyes.

"Eh!—He's asleep, ain't he?"

"With kings and counselors," murmured I.

There would seem little need for proceeding further in this history. Imagination will readily supply the meagre recital of poor Bartleby's interment. But, ere parting with the reader, let me say, that if this little narrative has sufficiently interested him, to awaken curiosity as to who Bartleby was, and what manner of life he led prior to the present narrator's making his acquaintance, I can only reply, that in such curiosity I fully share, but am wholly unable to gratify it. Yet here I hardly know whether I should divulge one little item of rumor, which came to my ear a few months after the scrivener's decease. Upon what basis it rested, I could never ascertain; and hence, how true it is I cannot now tell. But, inasmuch as this vague report has not been without a certain suggestive interest to me, however sad, it may prove the same with some others; and so I will briefly mention it. The report was this: that Bartleby had been a subordinate clerk in the Dead Letter Office at Washington, from which he had been suddenly removed by a change in the administration. When I think over this rumor, hardly can I express the emotions which seize me. Dead letters! does it not sound like dead men? Conceive a man by nature and misfortune prone to a pallid hopelessness, can any business seem more fitted to heighten it than that of continually handling these dead letters, and assorting them for the flames? For by the cartload they are annually burned. Sometimes from out the folded paper the pale clerk takes a ring—

the finger it was meant for, perhaps, moulders in the grave; a bank-note sent in swiftest charity—he whom it would relieve, nor eats nor hungers any more; pardon for those who died despairing; hope for those who died unhoping; good tidings for those who died stifled by unrelieved calamities. On errands of life, these letters speed to death.

Ah, Bartleby! Ah, humanity!

Sonny's Blues

James Baldwin (1924–1987)

A novelist and essayist born in Harlem, **James Baldwin** is known for his brilliant writing style and powerful prose. Baldwin's style was influenced by Henry James and his prose was influenced by sermon rhetoric from his evangelical upbringing and, later on, by his involvement in the Civil Rights struggles. His first novel, the widely acclaimed *Go Tell It on the Mountain* (1953), describes black life in the United States. His next novel, *Giovanni's Room* (1956), takes place in Paris, where Baldwin lived for many years. Other novels include *Another Country* (1962), *Tell Me How Long the Train's Been Gone* (1968), *If Beale Street Could Talk* (1974), and *Just Above My Head* (1979). Some nonfiction works are *Notes of a Native Son* (1955), *The Fire Next Time* (1963), *No Name in the Street* (1972), and *The Devil Finds Work* (1976). "Sonny's Blues" is part of *Going to Meet the Man* (1965), a story collection.

I read about it in the paper, in the subway, on my way to work. I read it, and I couldn't believe it, and I read it again. Then perhaps I just stared at it, at the newsprint spelling out his name, spelling out the story. I stared at it in the swinging lights of the subway car, and in the faces and bodies of the people, and in my own face, trapped in the darkness which roared outside.

It was not to be believed and I kept telling myself that, as I walked from the subway station to the high school. And at the same time I couldn't doubt it. I was scared, scared for Sonny. He became real to me again. A great block of ice got settled in my belly and kept melting there slowly all day long, while I taught my classes algebra. It was a special kind of ice. It kept melting, sending trickles of ice water all up and down my veins, but it never got less. Sometimes it hardened and seemed to expand until I felt my guts were going to come spilling out or that I was going to choke or scream. This would always be at a moment when I was remembering some specific thing Sonny had once said or done.

When he was about as old as the boys in my classes his face had been bright and open, there was a lot of copper in it; and he'd had wonderfully direct brown eyes, and great gentleness and privacy. I wondered what he looked like now. He had been picked up, the evening before, in a raid on an apartment downtown, for peddling and using heroin.

I couldn't believe it: but what I mean by that is that I couldn't find any room for it anywhere inside me. I had kept it outside me for a long time. I hadn't wanted to know. I had had suspicions, but I didn't name them, I kept putting them away. I told myself that Sonny was wild, but he wasn't crazy. And he'd always been a good boy, he hadn't ever turned hard or evil or disrespectful, the way kids can, so quick, so quick, especially in Harlem. I didn't want to believe that I'd ever see my brother going down, coming to nothing, all that light in his face gone out, in the condition I'd already seen so many others. Yet it had happened and here I was, talking about algebra to a lot of boys who might, every one of them for all I knew, be popping off needles every time they went to the head. Maybe it did more for them than algebra could.

I was sure that the first time Sonny had ever had horse, he couldn't have been much older than these boys were now. These boys, now, were living as we'd been living then, they were growing up with a rush and their heads bumped abruptly against the low ceiling of their actual possibilities. They were filled with rage. All they really knew were two darknesses, the darkness of their lives, which was now closing in on them, and the darkness of the movies, which had blinded them to that other darkness, and in which they now, vindictively, dreamed, at once more together than they were at any other time, and more alone.

When the last bell rang, the last class ended, I let out my breath. It seemed I'd been holding it for all that time. My clothes were wet—I may have looked as though I'd been sitting in a steam bath, all dressed up, all afternoon. I sat alone in the classroom a long time. I listened to the boys outside, downstairs, shouting and cursing and laughing. Their laughter struck me for perhaps the first time. It was not the joyous laughter which—God knows why—one associates with children. It was mocking and insular, its intent to denigrate. It was disenchanted, and in this, also, lay the authority of their curses. Perhaps I was listening to them because I was thinking about my brother and in them I heard my brother. And myself.

One boy was whistling a tune, at once very complicated and very simple, it seemed to be pouring out of him as though he were a bird, and it sounded very cool and moving through all that harsh, bright air, only just holding its own through all those other sounds.

I stood up and walked over to the window and looked down into the courtyard. It was the beginning of the spring and the sap was rising in the boys. A teacher passed through them every now and again, quickly, as though he or she couldn't wait to get out of that courtyard, to get those boys out of their sight and off their minds. I started collecting my stuff. I thought I'd better get home and talk to Isabel.

The courtyard was almost deserted by the time I got downstairs. I saw this boy standing in the shadow of a doorway, looking just like Sonny. I almost called his name. Then I saw that it wasn't Sonny, but somebody we used to know, a boy from around our block. He'd been Sonny's friend. He'd never been mine, having been too young for me, and, anyway, I'd never liked him. And now, even though he was a grown-up man, he still hung around that block, still spent hours on the street corners, was always high and raggy. I used to run into him from time to time and he'd often work around to asking me for a quarter or fifty cents. He always had some real good excuse, too, and I always gave it to him, I don't know why.

But now, abruptly, I hated him. I couldn't stand the way he looked at me, partly like a dog, partly like a cunning child. I wanted to ask him what the hell he was doing in the school courtyard.

He sort of shuffled over to me, and he said, "I see you got the papers. So you already know about it."

"You mean about Sonny? Yes, I already know about it. How come they didn't get you?"

He grinned. It made him repulsive and it also brought to mind what he'd looked like as a kid. "I wasn't there. I stay away from them people."

"Good for you." I offered him a cigarette and I watched him through the smoke. "You come all the way down here just to tell me about Sonny?"

"That's right." He was sort of shaking his head and his eyes looked strange, as though they were about to cross. The bright sun deadened his damp dark brown skin and it made his eyes look yellow and showed up the dirt in his kinked hair. He smelled funky. I moved a little way from him and I said, "Well, thanks. But I already know about it and I got to get home."

"I'll walk you a little ways," he said. We started walking. There were a couple of kids still loitering in the courtyard and one of them said goodnight to me and looked strangely at the boy beside me.

"What're you going to do?" he asked me. "I mean, about Sonny?"

"Look. I haven't seen Sonny for over a year, I'm not sure I'm going to do anything. Anyway, what the hell *can* I do?"

"That's right," he said quickly, "ain't nothing you can do. Can't much help old Sonny no more, I guess."

It was what I was thinking and so it seemed to me he had no right to say it.

"I'm surprised at Sonny, though," he went on—he had a funny way of talking, he looked straight ahead as though he were talking to himself—"I thought Sonny was a smart boy, I thought he was too smart to get hung."

"I guess he thought so too," I said sharply, "and that's how he got hung. And how about you? You're pretty goddamn smart, I bet."

Then he looked directly at me, just for a minute. "I ain't

smart," he said. "If I was smart, I'd have reached for a pistol a long time ago."

"Look. Don't tell *me* your sad story, if it was up to me, I'd give you one." Then I felt guilty—guilty, probably, for never having supposed that the poor bastard *had* a story of his own, much less a sad one, and I asked, quickly, "What's going to happen to him now?"

He didn't answer this. He was off by himself some place. "Funny thing," he said, and from his tone we might have been discussing the quickest way to get to Brooklyn, "when I saw the papers this morning, the first thing I asked myself was if I had anything to do with it. I felt sort of responsible."

I began to listen more carefully. The subway station was on the corner, just before us, and I stopped. He stopped, too. We were in front of a bar and he ducked slightly, peering in, but whoever he was looking for didn't seem to be there. The juke box was blasting away with something black and bouncy and I half watched the barmaid as she danced her way from the juke box to her place behind the bar. And I watched her face as she laughingly responded to something someone said to her, still keeping time to the music. When she smiled one saw the little girl, one sensed the doomed, still-struggling woman beneath the battered face of the semi-whore.

"I never *give* Sonny nothing," the boy said finally, "but a long time ago I come to school high and Sonny asked me how it felt." He paused, I couldn't bear to watch him, I watched the barmaid, and I listened to the music which seemed to be causing the pavement to shake. "I told him it felt great." The music stopped, the barmaid paused and watched the juke box until the music began again. "It did."

All this was carrying me some place I didn't want to go. I certainly didn't want to know how it felt. It filled everything, the people, the houses, the music, the dark, quicksilver barmaid, with menace; and this menace was their reality.

"What's going to happen to him now?" I asked again.

"They'll send him away some place and they'll try to cure

him." He shook his head. "Maybe he'll even think he's kicked the habit. Then they'll let him loose"—he gestured, throwing his cigarette into the gutter. "That's all."

"What do you mean, that's *all?*"

But I knew what he meant.

"I *mean,* that's *all.*" He turned his head and looked at me, pulling down the corners of his mouth. "Don't you know what I mean?" he asked, softly.

"How the hell *would* I know what you mean?" I almost whispered it, I don't know why.

"That's right," he said to the air, "how would *he* know what I mean?" He turned toward me again, patient and calm, and yet I somehow felt him shaking, shaking as though he were going to fall apart. I felt that ice in my guts again, the dread I'd felt all afternoon; and again I watched the barmaid, moving about the bar, washing glasses, and singing. "Listen. They'll let him out and then it'll just start all over again. That's what I mean."

"You mean—they'll let him out. And then he'll just start working his way back in again. You mean he'll never kick the habit. Is that what you mean?"

"That's right," he said, cheerfully. "*You* see what I mean."

"Tell me," I said at last, "why does he want to die? He must want to die, he's killing himself, why does he want to die?"

He looked at me in surprise. He licked his lips. "He don't want to die. He wants to live. Don't nobody want to die, ever."

Then I wanted to ask him—too many things. He could not have answered, or if he had, I could not have borne the answers. I started walking. "Well, I guess it's none of my business."

"It's going to be rough on old Sonny," he said. We reached the subway station. "This is your station?" he asked. I nodded. I took one step down. "Damn!" he said, suddenly. I looked up at him. He grinned again. "Damn it if I didn't leave all my money home. You ain't got a dollar on you, have you? Just for a couple of days, is all."

All at once something inside gave and threatened to come

pouring out of me. I didn't hate him any more. I felt that in another moment I'd start crying like a child.

"Sure," I said. "Don't sweat." I looked in my wallet and didn't have a dollar, I only had a five. "Here," I said. "That hold you?"

He didn't look at it—he didn't want to look at it. A terrible closed look came over his face, as though he were keeping the number on the bill a secret from him and me. "Thanks," he said, and now he was dying to see me go. "Don't worry about Sonny. Maybe I'll write him or something."

"Sure," I said. "You do that. So long."

"Be seeing you," he said. I went on down the steps.

And I didn't write Sonny or send him anything for a long time. When I finally did, it was just after my little girl died, he wrote me back a letter which made me feel like a bastard.

Here's what he said:

Dear brother,

You don't know how much I needed to hear from you. I wanted to write you many a time but I dug how much I must have hurt you and so I didn't write. But now I feel like a man who's been trying to climb up out of some deep, real deep and funky hole and just saw the sun up there, outside. I got to get outside.

I can't tell you much about how I got here. I mean I don't know how to tell you. I guess I was afraid of something or I was trying to escape from something and you know I have never been very strong in the head (smile). I'm glad Mama and Daddy are dead and can't see what's happened to their son and I swear if I'd known what I was doing I would never have hurt you so, you and a lot of other fine people who were nice to me and who believed in me.

I don't want you to think it had anything to do with me being a musician. It's more than that. Or maybe less than that. I can't get anything straight in my head down here and I try not to think about what's going to happen to me when I get outside again. Sometime I think I'm going to flip and *never* get outside and sometime I think I'll come straight back. I tell you one thing, though, I'd rather blow my brains out than go through this again. But that's what they all say, so they tell me. If I tell you when I'm coming to New York and if you could meet me, I sure would appreciate it. Give my love to Isabel and the kids and I was sure sorry to hear about little Gracie. I wish I could be like Mama and say the Lord's will be done, but I don't know it seems to me that trouble is the one thing that never does get stopped and I don't know what good it does to blame it on the Lord. But maybe it does some good if you believe it.

Your brother,
Sonny

Then I kept in constant touch with him and I sent him whatever I could and I went to meet him when he came back to New York. When I saw him many things I thought I had forgotten came flooding back to me. This was because I had begun, finally, to wonder about Sonny, about the life that Sonny lived inside. This life, whatever it was, had made him older and thinner and it had deepened the distant stillness in which he had always moved. He looked very unlike my baby brother. Yet, when he smiled, when we shook hands, the baby brother I'd never known looked out from the depths of his private life, like an animal waiting to be coaxed into the light.

"How you been keeping?" he asked me.

"All right. And you?"

"Just fine." He was smiling all over his face. "It's good to see you again."

"It's good to see you."

The seven years' difference in our ages lay between us like a chasm: I wondered if these years would ever operate between us as a bridge. I was remembering, and it made it hard to catch my breath, that I had been there when he was born; and I had heard the first word he had ever spoken. When he started to walk, he walked from our mother straight to me. I caught him just before he fell when he took the first steps he ever took in this world.

"How's Isabel?"

"Just fine. She's dying to see you."

"And the boys?"

"They're fine, too. They're anxious to see their uncle."

"Oh, come on. You know they don't remember me."

"Are you kidding? Of course they remember you."

He grinned again. We got into a taxi. We had a lot to say to each other, far too much to know how to begin.

As the taxi began to move, I asked, "You still want to go to India?"

He laughed. "You still remember that. Hell, no. This place is Indian enough for me."

"It used to belong to them," I said.

And he laughed again. "They damn sure knew what they were doing when they got rid of it."

Years ago, when he was around fourteen, he'd been all hipped on the idea of going to India. He read books about people sitting on rocks, naked, in all kinds of weather, but mostly bad, naturally, and walking barefoot through hot coals and arriving at wisdom. I used to say that it sounded to me as though they were getting away from wisdom as fast as they could. I think he sort of looked down on me for that.

"Do you mind," he asked, "if we have the driver drive alongside the park? On the west side—I haven't seen the city in so long."

"Of course not," I said. I was afraid that I might sound as though I were humoring him, but I hoped he wouldn't take it that way.

So we drove along, between the green of the park and the stony, lifeless elegance of hotels and apartment buildings, toward the vivid, killing streets of our childhood. These streets hadn't changed, though housing projects jutted up out of them now like rocks in the middle of a boiling sea. Most of the houses in which we had grown up had vanished, as had the stores from which we had stolen, the basements in which we had first tried sex, the rooftops from which we had hurled tin cans and bricks. But houses exactly like the houses of our past yet dominated the landscape, boys exactly like the boys we once had been found themselves smothering in these houses, came down into the streets for light and air and found themselves encircled by disaster. Some escaped the trap, most didn't. Those who got out always left something of themselves behind, as some animals amputate a leg and leave it in the trap. It might be said, perhaps, that I had escaped, after all, I was a school teacher; or that Sonny had, he hadn't lived in Harlem for years. Yet, as the cab moved uptown through streets which seemed, with a rush, to darken with dark people, and as I covertly studied Sonny's face, it came to me that what we both were seeking through our separate cab windows was that part of ourselves which had been left behind. It's always at the hour of trouble and confrontation that the missing member aches.

We hit 110th Street and started rolling up Lenox Avenue. And I'd known this avenue all my life, but it seemed to me again, as it had seemed on the day I'd first heard about Sonny's trouble, filled with a hidden menace which was its very breath of life.

"We almost there," said Sonny.

"Almost." We were both too nervous to say anything more.

We live in a housing project. It hasn't been up long. A few days after it was up it seemed uninhabitably new, now, of course, it's already rundown. It looks like a parody of the good, clean, faceless life—God knows the people who live in it do their best to make it a parody. The beat-looking grass lying around isn't enough to make their lives green, the hedges will never hold out the streets, and they know it. The big windows fool no one, they aren't big enough to make space out of no space. They don't bother with the windows, they watch the TV screen instead. The playground is most popular with the children who don't play at jacks, or skip rope, or roller skate, or swing, and they can be found in it after dark. We moved in partly because it's not too far from where I teach, and partly for the kids; but it's really just like the houses in which Sonny and I grew up. The same things happen, they'll have the same things to remember. The moment Sonny and I started into the house I had the feeling that I was simply bringing him back into the danger he had almost died trying to escape.

Sonny has never been talkative. So I don't know why I was sure he'd be dying to talk to me when supper was over the first night. Everything went fine, the oldest boy remembered him, and the youngest boy liked him, and Sonny had remembered to bring something for each of them; and Isabel, who is really much nicer than I am, more open and giving, had gone to a lot of trouble about dinner and was genuinely glad to see him. And she's always been able to tease Sonny in a way that I haven't. It was nice to see her face so vivid again and to hear her laugh and watch her make Sonny laugh. She wasn't, or, anyway, she didn't seem to be, at all uneasy or embarrassed. She chatted as though there were no subject which had to be avoided and she got Sonny past his first, faint stiffness. And thank God she was there, for I was filled with that icy dread again. Everything I did seemed awkward to me, and everything I said sounded freighted with hidden meaning. I was trying to remember everything I'd heard about dope addiction and I couldn't help watching Sonny for signs. I wasn't doing it out of malice. I was trying to find out something about my brother. I was dying to hear him tell me he was safe.

"Safe?" my father grunted, whenever Mama suggested trying to move to a neighborhood which might be safer for children. "Safe, hell! Ain't no place safe for kids, nor nobody."

He always went on like this, but he wasn't, ever, really as bad as he sounded, not even on weekends, when he got drunk. As a matter of fact, he was always on the lookout for "something a little better," but he died before he found it. He died suddenly, during a drunken weekend in the middle of the war, when Sonny was fifteen. He and Sonny hadn't ever got on too well. And this was partly because Sonny was the apple of his father's eye. It was because he loved Sonny so much and was frightened for him, that he was always fighting with him. It doesn't do any good to fight with Sonny. Sonny just moves back, inside himself, where he can't be reached. But the principal reason that they never hit it off is that they were so much alike. Daddy was big and rough and loud-talking, just the opposite of Sonny, but they both had—that same privacy.

Mama tried to tell me something about this, just after Daddy died. I was home on leave from the army.

This was the last time I ever saw my mother alive. Just the same, this picture gets all mixed up in my mind with pictures I had of her when she was younger. The way I always see her is the way she used to be on a Sunday afternoon, say, when the old folks were talking after the big Sunday dinner. I always see her wearing pale blue. She'd be sitting on the sofa. And my father would be sitting in the easy chair, not far from her. And the living room would be full of church folks and relatives. There they sit, in chairs all around the living room, and the night is creeping up outside, but nobody knows it yet. You can see the darkness growing against the window-panes and you hear the street noises every now and again, or maybe the jangling beat of a tambourine from one of the churches close by, but it's real quiet in the room. For a moment nobody's talking, but every face looks darkening, like the sky outside. And my mother rocks a little from the waist, and my father's eyes are closed. Everyone is looking at something a child can't see. For a minute they've forgotten the children. Maybe a kid is lying on the rug, half asleep. Maybe somebody's got a kid in his lap and is absent-mindedly stroking the kid's head. Maybe there's a kid, quiet and big-eyed, curled up in a big chair in the corner. The silence, the darkness coming, and the darkness in the faces frightens the child obscurely. He hopes that the hand which strokes his forehead will never stop—will never die. He hopes that there will never come a time when the old folks won't be sitting around the living room, talking about where they've come from, and what they've seen, and what's happened to them and their kinfolk.

But something deep and watchful in the child knows that this is bound to end, is already ending. In a moment someone will get up and turn on the light. Then the old folks will remember the children and they won't talk any more that day. And when light fills the room, the child is filled with darkness. He knows that everytime this happens he's moved just a little closer to that darkness outside. The darkness outside is what the old folks have been talking about. It's what they've come from. It's what they endure. The child knows that they won't talk any more because if he knows too much about what's happened to *them,* he'll know too much too soon, about what's going to happen to *him.*

The last time I talked to my mother, I remember I was restless. I wanted to get out and see Isabel. We weren't married then and we had a lot to straighten out between us.

There Mama sat, in black, by the window. She was humming an old church song, *Lord, you brought me from a long ways off.* Sonny was out somewhere. Mama kept watching the streets.

"I don't know," she said, "if I'll ever see you again, after you go off from here. But I hope you'll remember the things I tried to teach you."

"Don't talk like that," I said, and smiled. "You'll be here a long time yet."

She smiled, too, but she said nothing. She was quiet for a long time. And I said, "Mama, don't you worry about nothing. I'll be writing all the time, and you be getting the checks. . . ."

"I want to talk to you about your brother," she said, suddenly. "If anything happens to me he ain't going to have nobody to look out for him."

"Mama," I said, "ain't nothing going to happen to you or Sonny. Sonny's all right. He's a good boy and he's got good sense."

"It ain't a question of his being a good boy," Mama said, "nor of his having good sense. It ain't only the bad ones, nor yet the dumb ones that gets sucked under." She stopped, looking at me. "Your Daddy once had a brother," she said, and she smiled in a way that made me feel she was in pain. "You didn't never know that, did you?"

"No," I said, "I never knew that," and I watched her face.

"Oh, yes," she said, "your Daddy had a brother." She looked

out the window again. "I know you never saw your Daddy cry. But *I* did—many a time, through all these years."

I asked her, "What happened to his brother? How come nobody's ever talked about him?"

This was the first time I ever saw my mother look old.

"His brother got killed," she said, "when he was just a little younger than you are now. I knew him. He was a fine boy. He was maybe a little full of the devil, but he didn't mean nobody no harm."

Then she stopped and the room was silent, exactly as it had sometimes been on those Sunday afternoons. Mama kept looking out into the streets.

"He used to have a job in the mill," she said, "and, like all young folks, he just liked to perform on Saturday nights. Saturday nights him and your father would drift around to different places, go to dances and things like that, or just sit around with people they knew, and your father's brother would sing, he had a fine voice, and play along with himself on his guitar. Well, this particular Saturday night, him and your father was coming home from some place, and they were both a little drunk and there was a moon that night, it was bright like day. Your father's brother was feeling kind of good, and he was whistling to himself, and he had his guitar slung over his shoulder. They was coming down a hill and beneath them was a road that turned off from the highway. Well, your father's brother, being always kind of frisky, decided to run down this hill, and he did, with that guitar banging and clanging behind him, and he ran across the road, and he was making water behind a tree. And your father was sort of amused at him and he was still coming down the hill, kind of slow. Then he heard a motor and that same minute his brother stepped from behind the tree, into the road, in the moonlight. And he started to cross the road. And your father started to run down the hill, he says he don't know why. This car was full of white men. They was all drunk, and when they seen your father's brother they let out a great whoop and holler and they aimed the car straight at him. They was having fun, they just wanted to scare him, the way they do sometimes, you know. But they was drunk. And I guess the boy, being drunk, too, and scared, kind of lost his head. By the time he jumped it was too late. Your father says he heard his brother scream when the car rolled over him, and he heard the wood of that guitar when it give, and heard them strings go flying, and he heard them white men shouting, and the car kept on a-going and it ain't stopped till this day. And, time your father got down the hill, his brother weren't nothing but blood and pulp."

Tears were gleaming on my mother's face. There wasn't anything I could say.

"He never mentioned it," she said, "because I never let him mention it before you children. Your Daddy was like a crazy man that night and for many a night thereafter. He says he never in his life seen anything as dark as that road after the lights of that car had gone away. Weren't nothing, weren't nobody on that road, just your Daddy and his brother and that busted guitar. Oh, yes. Your Daddy never did really get right again. Till the day he died he weren't sure but that every white man he saw was the man that killed his brother."

She stopped and took out her handkerchief and dried her eyes and looked at me.

"I ain't telling you all this," she said, "to make you scared or bitter or to make you hate nobody. I'm telling you this because you got a brother. And the world ain't changed."

I guess I didn't want to believe this. I guess she saw this in my face. She turned away from me, toward the window again, searching those streets.

"But I praise my Redeemer," she said at last, "that He called your Daddy home before me. I ain't saying it to throw no flowers at myself, but, I declare, it keeps me from feeling too cast down to know I helped your father get safely through this world. Your father always acted like he was the roughest, strongest man on earth. And everybody took him to be like that. But if he hadn't had *me* there—to see his tears!"

She was crying again. Still, I couldn't move. I said, "Lord, Lord, Mama, I didn't know it was like that."

"Oh, honey," she said, "there's a lot that you don't know. But you are going to find it out." She stood up from the window and came over to me. "You got to hold on to your brother," she said, "and don't let him fall, no matter what it looks like is happening to him and no matter how evil you gets with him. You going to be evil with him many a time. But don't you forget what I told you, you hear?"

"I won't forget," I said. "Don't you worry, I won't forget. I won't let nothing happen to Sonny."

My mother smiled as though she were amused at something she saw in my face. Then, "You may not be able to stop nothing from happening. But you got to let him know you's *there*."

Two days later I was married, and then I was gone. And I had a lot of things on my mind and I pretty well forgot my promise to Mama until I got shipped home on a special furlough for her funeral.

And, after the funeral, with just Sonny and me alone in the empty kitchen, I tried to find out something about him.

"What do you want to do?" I asked him.

"I'm going to be a musician," he said.

For he had graduated, in the time I had been away, from dancing to the juke box to finding out who was playing what, and what they were doing with it, and he had bought himself a set of drums.

"You mean, you want to be a drummer?" I somehow had the feeling that being a drummer might be all right for other people but not for my brother Sonny.

"I don't think," he said, looking at me very gravely, "that I'll ever be a good drummer. But I think I can play a piano."

I frowned. I'd never played the role of the older brother quite so seriously before, had scarcely ever, in fact, *asked* Sonny a damn thing. I sensed myself in the presence of something I didn't really know how to handle, didn't understand. So I made my frown a little deeper as I asked: "What kind of musician do you want to be?"

He grinned. "How many kinds do you think there are?"

"Be *serious,*" I said.

He laughed, throwing his head back, and then looked at me. "I am serious."

"Well, then, for Christ's sake, stop kidding around and answer a serious question. I mean, do you want to be a concert pianist, you want to play classical music and all that, or—or what?" Long before I finished he was laughing again. "For Christ's *sake,* Sonny!"

He sobered, but with difficulty. "I'm sorry. But you sound so—*scared!*" and he was off again.

"Well, you think it's funny now, baby, but it's not going to be so funny when you have to make your living at it, let me tell you *that.*" I was furious because I knew he was laughing at me and I didn't know why.

"No," he said, very sober now, and afraid, perhaps, that he'd hurt me, "I don't want to be a classical pianist. That isn't what interests me. I mean—" he paused, looking hard at me, as though his eyes would help me to understand, and then gestured helplessly, as though perhaps his hand would help—"I mean, I'll have a lot of studying to do, and I'll have to study *everything,* but, I mean, I want to play *with*—jazz musicians." He stopped. "I want to play jazz," he said.

Well, the word had never before sounded as heavy, as real, as it sounded that afternoon in Sonny's mouth. I just looked at him and I was probably frowning a real frown by this time. I simply couldn't see why on earth he'd want to spend his time hanging around nightclubs, clowning around on bandstands, while people pushed each other around a dance floor. It seemed—beneath him, somehow. I had never thought about it before, had never been forced to, but I suppose I had always put jazz musicians in a class with what Daddy called "good-time people."

"Are you *serious?*"

"Hell, *yes,* I'm serious."

He looked more helpless than ever, and annoyed, and deeply hurt.

I suggested, helpfully: "You mean—like Louis Armstrong?"

His face closed as though I'd struck him. "No. I'm not talking about none of that old-time, down home crap."

"Well, look, Sonny, I'm sorry, don't get mad. I just don't altogether get it, that's all. Name somebody—you know, a jazz musician you admire."

"Bird."

"Who?"

"Bird! Charlie Parker! Don't they teach you nothing in the goddamn army?"

I lit a cigarette. I was surprised and then a little amused to discover that I was trembling. "I've been out of touch," I said. "You'll have to be patient with me. Now. Who's this Parker character?"

"He's just one of the greatest jazz musicians alive," said Sonny, sullenly, his hands in his pockets, his back to me. "Maybe *the* greatest," he added, bitterly, "that's probably why *you* never heard of him."

"All right," I said, "I'm ignorant. I'm sorry. I'll go out and buy all the cat's records right away, all right?"

"It don't," said Sonny, with dignity, "make any difference to me. I don't care what you listen to. Don't do me no favors."

I was beginning to realize that I'd never seen him so upset before. With another part of my mind I was thinking that this would probably turn out to be one of those things kids go through and that I shouldn't make it seem important by pushing it too hard. Still, I didn't think it would do any harm to ask: "Doesn't all this take a lot of time? Can you make a living at it?"

He turned back to me and half leaned, half sat, on the kitchen table. "Everything takes time," he said, "and—well, yes, sure, I can make a living at it. But what I don't seem to be able to make you understand is that it's the only thing I want to do."

"Well, Sonny," I said, gently, "you know people can't always do exactly what they *want* to do—"

"*No,* I don't know that," said Sonny, surprising me. "I think people *ought* to do what they want to do, what else are they alive for?"

"You getting to be a big boy," I said desperately, "it's time you started thinking about your future."

"I'm thinking about my future," said Sonny, grimly. "I think about it all the time."

I gave up. I decided, if he didn't change his mind, that we could always talk about it later. "In the meantime," I said, "you got to finish school." We had already decided that he'd have to move in with Isabel and her folks. I knew this wasn't the ideal arrangement because Isabel's folks are inclined to be dicty and they hadn't especially wanted Isabel to marry me. But I didn't know what else to do. "And we have to get you fixed up at Isabel's."

There was a long silence. He moved from the kitchen table to the window. "That's a terrible idea. You know it yourself."

"Do you have a *better* idea?"

He just walked up and down the kitchen for a minute. He was as tall as I was. He had started to shave. I suddenly had the feeling that I didn't know him at all.

He stopped at the kitchen table and picked up my cigarettes. Looking at me with a kind of mocking, amused defiance, he put one between his lips. "You mind?"

"You smoking already?"

He lit the cigarette and nodded, watching me through the smoke. "I just wanted to see if I'd have the courage to smoke in front of you." He grinned and blew a great cloud of smoke to the ceiling. "It was easy." He looked at my face. "Come on, now. I bet you was smoking at my age, tell the truth."

I didn't say anything but the truth was on my face, and he laughed. But now there was something very strained in his laugh. "Sure. And I bet that ain't all you was doing."

He was frightening me a little. "Cut the crap," I said. "We already decided that you was going to go and live at Isabel's. Now what's got into you all of a sudden?"

"*You* decided it," he pointed out. "I didn't decide nothing." He stopped in front of me, leaning against the stove, arms loosely folded. "Look, brother. I don't want to stay in Harlem no more, I really don't." He was very earnest. He looked at me, then over toward the kitchen window. There was something in his eyes I'd never seen before, some thoughtfulness, some worry all his own. He rubbed the muscle of one arm. "It's time I was getting out of here."

"Where do you want to *go,* Sonny?"

"I want to join the army. Or the navy, I don't care. If I say I'm old enough, they'll believe me."

Then I got mad. It was because I was so scared. "You must be crazy. You goddamn fool, what the hell do you want to go and join the *army* for?"

"I just told you. To get out of Harlem."

"Sonny, you haven't even finished *school.* And if you really want to be a musician, how do you expect to study if you're in the *army?*"

He looked at me, trapped, and in anguish. "There's ways. I might be able to work out some kind of deal. Anyway, I'll have the G.I. bill when I come out."

"If you come out." We stared at each other. "Sonny, please. Be reasonable. I know the setup is far from perfect. But we got to do the best we can."

"I ain't learning nothing in school," he said. "Even when I go." He turned away from me and opened the window and threw his cigarette out into the narrow alley. I watched his back. "At least, I ain't learning nothing you'd want me to learn." He slammed the window so hard I thought the glass would fly out, and turned back to me. "And I'm sick of the stink of these garbage cans!"

"Sonny," I said, "I know how you feel. But if you don't finish school now, you're going to be sorry later that you didn't." I grabbed him by the shoulders. "And you only got another year. It ain't so bad. And I'll come back and I swear I'll help you do *whatever* you want to do. Just try to put up with it till I come back. Will you please do that? For me?"

He didn't answer and he wouldn't look at me.

"Sonny. You hear me?"

He pulled away. "I hear you. But you never hear anything I say."

I didn't know what to say to that. He looked out of the window and then back at me. "OK," he said, and sighed. "I'll try."

Then I said, trying to cheer him up a little, "They got a piano at Isabel's. You can practice on it."

And as a matter of fact, it did cheer him up for a minute. "That's right," he said to himself. "I forgot that." His face relaxed a little. But the worry, the thoughtfulness, played on it still, the way shadows play on a face which is staring into the fire.

But I thought I'd never hear the end of that piano. At first, Isabel would write me, saying how nice it was that Sonny was so serious about his music and how, as soon as he came in from school, or wherever he had been when he was supposed to be at school, he went straight to that piano and stayed there until suppertime. And, after supper, he went back to that piano and stayed there until everybody went to bed. He was at the piano all day Saturday and all day Sunday. Then he bought a record player and started playing records. He'd play one record over and over again, all day long sometimes, and he'd improvise along with it on the piano. Or he'd play one section of the record, one chord, one change, one progression, then he'd do it on the piano. Then back to the record. Then back to the piano.

Well, I really don't know how they stood it. Isabel finally confessed that it wasn't like living with a person at all, it was like living with sound. And the sound didn't make any sense to her, didn't make any sense to any of them—naturally. They began, in a way, to be afflicted by this presence that was living in their home. It was as though Sonny were some sort of god, or monster. He moved in an atmosphere which wasn't like theirs at all. They fed him and he ate, he washed himself, he walked in and out of their door; he certainly wasn't nasty or unpleasant or rude. Sonny isn't any of those things; but it was as though he were all wrapped up in some cloud, some fire, some vision all his own; and there wasn't any way to reach him.

At the same time, he wasn't really a man yet, he was still a child, and they had to watch out for him in all kinds of ways. They certainly couldn't throw him out. Neither did they dare to make a great scene about that piano because even they dimly sensed, as I sensed, from so many thousands of miles away, that Sonny was at that piano playing for his life.

But he hadn't been going to school. One day a letter came from the school board and Isabel's mother got it—there had, apparently, been other letters but Sonny had torn them up. This day, when Sonny came in, Isabel's mother showed him the letter and asked where he'd been spending his time. And she finally got it out of him that he'd been down in Greenwich Village, with musicians and other characters, in a white girl's apartment. And this scared her and she started to scream at him and what came up, once she began—though she denies it to this day—was what sacrifices they were making to give Sonny a decent home and how little he appreciated it.

Sonny didn't play the piano that day. By evening, Isabel's mother had calmed down but then there was the old man to deal with, and Isabel herself. Isabel says she did her best to be calm but she broke down and started crying. She says she just watched Sonny's face. She could tell, by watching him, what was happening with him. And what was happening was that they penetrated his cloud, they had reached him. Even if their fingers had been a thousand times more gentle than human fingers ever are, he could hardly help feeling that they had stripped him naked and were spitting on that nakedness. For he also had to see that his presence, that music, which was life or death to him, had been torture for them and that they had endured it, not at all for his sake, but only for mine. And Sonny couldn't take that. He can take it a little better today than he could then but he's still not very good at it and, frankly, I don't know anybody who is.

The silence of the next few days must have been louder than the sound of all the music ever played since time began. One morning, before she went to work, Isabel was in his room for something and she suddenly realized that all of his records were gone. And she knew for certain that he was gone. And he was. He went as far as the navy would carry him. He finally sent me a postcard from some place in Greece and that was the first I knew that Sonny was still alive. I didn't see him any more until we were both back in New York and the war had long been over.

He was a man by then, of course, but I wasn't willing to see it. He came by the house from time to time, but we fought almost every time we met. I didn't like the way he carried himself, loose and dreamlike all the time, and I didn't like his friends, and his music seemed to be merely an excuse for the life he led. It sounded just that weird and disordered.

Then we had a fight, a pretty awful fight, and I didn't see him for months. By and by I looked him up, where he was living, in a furnished room in the Village, and I tried to make it up. But there were lots of people in the room and Sonny just lay on his bed, and he wouldn't come downstairs with me, and he treated these other people as though they were his family and I weren't. So I got mad and then he got mad, and then I told him that he might just as well be dead as live the way he was living. Then he stood up and he told me not to worry about him any more in life, that he *was* dead as far as I was concerned. Then he pushed me to the door and the other people looked on as though nothing were happening, and he slammed the door behind me. I stood in the hallway, staring at the door. I heard somebody laugh in the room and then the tears came to my eyes. I started down the steps, whistling to keep from crying. I kept whistling to myself, *You going to need me, baby, one of these cold, rainy days.*

I read about Sonny's trouble in the spring. Little Grace died in the fall. She was a beautiful little girl. But she only lived a little over two years. She died of polio and she suffered. She had a slight fever for a couple of days, but it didn't seem like anything and we just kept her in bed. And we would certainly have called the doctor, but the fever dropped, she seemed to be all right. So we thought it had just been a cold. Then, one day, she was up, playing, Isabel was in the kitchen fixing lunch for the two boys when they'd come in from school, and she heard Grace fall down in the living room. When you have a lot of children you don't always start running when one of them falls, unless they start screaming or something. And, this time, Grace was quiet. Yet, Isabel says that when she heard that thump and then that silence, something happened in her to make her afraid. And she ran to the living room and there was little Grace on the floor, all twisted up, and the reason she hadn't screamed was that she couldn't get her breath. And when she did scream, it was the worst sound, Isabel says, that she'd ever heard in all her life, and she still hears it sometimes in her dreams. Isabel will sometimes wake me up with a low, moaning, strangled sound and I have to be quick to awaken her and hold her to me and where Isabel is weeping against me seems a mortal wound.

I think I may have written Sonny the very day that little Grace was buried. I was sitting in the living room in the dark, by myself, and I suddenly thought of Sonny. My trouble made his real.

One Saturday afternoon, when Sonny had been living with us, or, anyway, been in our house, for nearly two weeks, I found myself wandering aimlessly about the living room, drinking from a can of beer, and trying to work up the courage to search Sonny's room. He was out, he was usually out whenever I was home, and Isabel had taken the children to see their grandparents. Suddenly I was standing still in front of the living room window, watching Seventh Avenue. The idea of searching Sonny's room made me still. I scarcely dared to admit to myself what I'd be searching for. I didn't know what I'd do if I found it. Or if I didn't.

On the sidewalk across from me, near the entrance to a barbecue joint, some people were holding an old-fashioned revival meeting. The barbecue cook, wearing a dirty white apron, his conked hair reddish and metallic in the pale sun, and a cigarette between his lips, stood in the doorway, watching them. Kids and older people paused in their errands and stood there, along with some older men and a couple of very tough-looking women who watched everything that happened on the avenue, as though they owned it, or were maybe owned by it. Well, they were watching this, too. The revival was being carried on by three sisters in black, and a brother. All they had were their voices and their Bibles and a tambourine. The brother was testifying and while he testified two of the sisters stood together, seeming to say, amen, and the third sister walked around with the tambourine outstretched and a couple of people dropped coins into it. Then the brother's testimony ended and the sister who had been taking up the collection dumped the coins into her palm and transferred them to the pocket of her long black robe. Then she raised both hands, striking the tambourine against the air, and then against one hand, and she started to sing. And the two other sisters and the brother joined in.

It was strange, suddenly, to watch, though I had been seeing these street meetings all my life. So, of course, had everybody else down there. Yet, they paused and watched and listened and I stood still at the window. *" 'Tis the old ship of Zion,"* they sang, and the sister with the tambourine kept a steady, jangling beat, *"it has rescued many a thousand!"* Not a soul under the sound of their voices was hearing this song for the first time, not one of them had been rescued. Nor had they seen much in the way of rescue work being done around them. Neither did they especially believe in the holiness of the three sisters and the brother, they knew too much about them, knew where they lived, and how. The woman with the tambourine, whose voice dominated the air, whose face was bright with joy, was divided by very little from the woman who stood watching her, a cigarette between her heavy, chapped lips, her hair a cuckoo's nest, her face scarred and swollen from many beatings, and her black eyes glittering like coal. Perhaps they both knew this, which was why, when, as rarely, they addressed each other, they addressed each other as Sister. As the singing filled the air the watching, listening faces underwent a change, the eyes focusing on something within; the music seemed to soothe a poison out of them; and time seemed, nearly, to fall away from the sullen, belligerent, battered faces, as though they were fleeing back to their first condition, while dreaming of their last. The barbecue cook half shook his head and smiled, and dropped his cigarette and disappeared into his joint. A man fumbled in his pockets for change and stood holding it in his hand impatiently, as though he had just remembered a pressing appointment further up the avenue. He looked furious. Then I saw Sonny, standing on the edge of the crowd. He was carrying a wide, flat notebook with a green cover, and it made him look, from where I was standing, almost like a schoolboy. The coppery sun brought out the copper in his skin, he was very faintly smiling, standing very still. Then the singing stopped, the tambourine turned into a collection plate again. The furious man dropped in his coins and vanished, so did a couple of the women, and Sonny dropped some change in the plate, looking directly at the woman with a little smile. He started across the avenue, toward the house. He has a slow, loping walk, something like the way Harlem hipsters walk, only he's imposed on this his own half-beat. I had never really noticed it before.

I stayed at the window, both relieved and apprehensive. As Sonny disappeared from my sight, they began singing again. And they were still singing when his key turned in the lock.

"Hey," he said.

"Hey yourself. You want some beer?"

"No. Well, maybe." But he came up to the window and stood beside me, looking out. "What a warm voice," he said.

They were singing *If I could only hear my mother pray again!*

"Yes," I said, "and she can sure beat that tambourine."

"But what a terrible song," he said, and laughed. He dropped his notebook on the sofa and disappeared into the kitchen. "Where's Isabel and the kids?"

"I think they went to see their grandparents. You hungry?"

"No." He came back into the living room with his can of beer. "You want to come some place with me tonight?"

I sensed, I don't know how, that I couldn't possibly say no. "Sure. Where?"

He sat down on the sofa and picked up his notebook and

started leafing through it. "I'm going to sit in with some fellows in a joint in the Village."

"You mean, you're going to play, tonight?"

"That's right." He took a swallow of his beer and moved back to the window. He gave me a sidelong look. "If you can stand it."

"I'll try," I said.

He smiled to himself and we both watched as the meeting across the way broke up. The three sisters and the brother, heads bowed, were singing *God be with you till we meet again.* The faces around them were very quiet. Then the song ended. The small crowd dispersed. We watched the three women and the lone man walk slowly up the avenue.

"When she was singing before," said Sonny, abruptly, "her voice reminded me for a minute of what heroin feels like sometimes—when it's in your veins. It makes you feel sort of warm and cool at the same time. And distant. And—and sure." He sipped his beer, very deliberately not looking at me. I watched his face. "It makes you feel—in control. Sometimes you've got to have that feeling."

"Do you?" I sat down slowly in the easy chair.

"Sometimes." He went to the sofa and picked up his notebook again. "Some people do."

"In order," I asked, "to play?" And my voice was very ugly, full of contempt and anger.

"Well"—he looked at me with great, troubled eyes, as though, in fact, he hoped his eyes would tell me things he could never otherwise say—"they *think* so. And if they think so—!"

"And what do *you* think?" I asked.

He sat on the sofa and put his can of beer on the floor. "I don't know," he said, and I couldn't be sure if he were answering my question or pursuing his thoughts. His face didn't tell me. "It's not so much to *play*. It's to *stand* it, to be able to make it at all. On any level." He frowned and smiled: "In order to keep from shaking to pieces."

"But these friends of yours," I said, "they seem to shake themselves to pieces pretty goddamn fast."

"Maybe." He played with the notebook. And something told me that I should curb my tongue, that Sonny was doing his best to talk, that I should listen. "But of course you only know the ones that've gone to pieces. Some don't—or at least they haven't *yet* and that's just about all *any* of us can say." He paused. "And then there are some who just live, really, in hell, and they know it and they see what's happening and they go right on. I don't know." He sighed, dropped the notebook, folded his arms. "Some guys, you can tell from the way they play, they are something *all* the time. And you can see that, well, it makes something real for them. But of course," he picked up his beer from the floor and sipped it and put the can down again, "they *want* to, too, you've got to see that. Even some of them that say they don't—*some,* not all."

"And what about you?" I asked—I couldn't help it. "What about you? Do *you* want to?"

He stood up and walked to the window and remained silent for a long time. Then he sighed. "Me," he said. Then: "While I was downstairs before, on my way here, listening to that woman sing, it struck me all of a sudden how much suffering she must have had to go through—to sing like that. It's *repulsive* to think you have to suffer that much."

I said: "But there's no way not to suffer—is there, Sonny?"

"I believe not," he said and smiled, "but that's never stopped anyone from trying." He looked at me. "Has it?" I realized, with this mocking look, that there stood between us, forever, beyond the power of time or forgiveness, the fact that I had held silence—so long!—when he had needed human speech to help him. He turned back to the window. "No, there's no way not to suffer. But you try all kinds of ways to keep from drowning in it, to keep on top of it, and to make it seem—well, like *you.* Like you did something, all right, and now you're suffering for it. You know?" I said nothing. "Well you know," he said, impatiently, "why *do* people suffer? Maybe it's better to do something to give it a reason, *any* reason."

"But we just agreed," I said, "that there's no way not to suffer. Isn't it better, then, just to—take it?"

"But nobody just takes it," Sonny cried, "that's what I'm telling you! *Everybody* tries not to. You're just hung up on the *way* some people try—it's not *your* way!"

The hair on my face began to itch, my face felt wet. "That's not true," I said, "that's not true. I don't give a damn what other people do, I don't even care how they suffer. I just care how *you* suffer." And he looked at me. "Please believe me," I said, "I don't want to see you—die—trying not to suffer."

"I won't," he said, flatly, "die trying not to suffer. At least, not any faster than anybody else."

"But there's no need," I said, trying to laugh, "is there? in killing yourself."

I wanted to say more, but I couldn't. I wanted to talk about will power and how life could be—well, beautiful. I wanted to say that it was all within; but was it? or, rather, wasn't that exactly the trouble? And I wanted to promise that I would never fail him again. But it would all have sounded—empty words and lies.

So I made the promise to myself and prayed that I would keep it.

"It's terrible sometimes, inside," he said, "that's what's the trouble. You walk these streets, black and funky and cold, and there's not really a living ass to talk to, and there's nothing shaking, and there's no way of getting it out—that storm inside. You can't talk it and you can't make love with it, and when you finally try to get with it and play it, you realize *nobody*'s listening. So *you've* got to listen. You got to find a way to listen."

And then he walked away from the window and sat on the sofa again, as though all the wind had suddenly been knocked out of him. "Sometimes you'll do *anything* to play, even cut your mother's throat." He laughed and looked at me. "Or your brother's." Then he sobered. "Or your own." Then: "Don't worry. I'm all right now and I think I'll *be* all right. But I can't forget—where I've been. I don't mean just the physical place I've been, I mean where I've *been*. And *what* I've been."

"What have you been, Sonny?" I asked.

He smiled—but sat sideways on the sofa, his elbow resting on the back, his fingers playing with his mouth and chin, not looking at me. "I've been something I didn't recognize, didn't know I could be. Didn't know anybody could be." He stopped, looking inward, looking helplessly young, looking old. "I'm not talking about it now because I feel *guilty* or anything like that—maybe it would be better if I did, I don't know. Anyway, I can't really talk about it. Not to you, not to anybody," and now he turned and faced me. "Sometimes, you know, and it was actually when I was most *out* of the world, I felt that I was in it, that I was *with* it, really, and I could play or I didn't really have to *play,* it just came out of me, it was there. And I don't know how I played, thinking about it now, but I know I did awful things, those times, sometimes, to people. Or it wasn't that I *did* anything to them—it was that they weren't real." He picked up the beer can; it was empty; he rolled it between his palms: "And other times—well, I needed a fix, I needed to find a place to lean, I needed to clear a space to *listen*—and I couldn't find it, and I—went crazy, I did terrible things to *me,* I was terrible *for* me." He began pressing the beer can between his hands, I watched the metal begin to give. It glittered, as he played with it, like a knife, and I was afraid he would cut himself, but I said nothing. "Oh well. I can never tell you. I was all by myself at the bottom of something, stinking and sweating and crying and shaking, and I smelled it, you know? *my* stink, and I thought I'd die if I couldn't get away from it and yet, all the same, I knew that everything I was doing was just locking me in with it. And I didn't know, I still *don't* know, something kept telling me that maybe it was good to smell your own stink, but I didn't think that *that* was what I'd been trying to do—and—who can stand it?" and he abruptly dropped the ruined beer can, looking at me with a small, still smile, and then rose, walking to the window as though it were the lodestone rock. I watched his face, he watched the avenue. "I couldn't tell you when Mama died—but the reason I wanted to leave Harlem so bad was to get away from drugs. And then, when I ran away, that's what I was running from—really. When I came back, nothing had changed, *I* hadn't changed, I was just—older." And he stopped, drumming with his fingers on the windowpane. The sun had vanished, soon darkness would fall. I watched his face. "It can come again," he said, almost as though speaking to himself. Then he turned to me. "It can come again," he repeated. "I just want you to know that."

"All right," I said, at last. "So it can come again, All right."

He smiled, but the smile was sorrowful. "I had to try to tell you," he said.

"Yes," I said. "I understand that."

"You're my brother," he said, looking straight at me, and not smiling at all.

"Yes," I repeated, "yes. I understand that."

He turned back to the window, looking out. "All that hatred down there," he said, "all that hatred and misery and love. It's a wonder it doesn't blow the avenue apart."

We went to the only nightclub on a short, dark street, downtown. We squeezed through the narrow, chattering, jam-packed bar to the entrance of the big room, where the bandstand was. And we stood there for a moment, for the lights were very dim in this room and we couldn't see. Then, "Hello, boy," said a voice and an enormous black man, much older than Sonny or myself, erupted out of all that atmospheric lighting and put an arm around Sonny's shoulder. "I been sitting right here," he said, "waiting for you."

He had a big voice, too, and heads in the darkness turned toward us.

Sonny grinned and pulled a little away, and said, "Creole, this is my brother. I told you about him."

Creole shook my hand. "I'm glad to meet you, son," he said, and it was clear that he was glad to meet me *there,* for Sonny's sake. And he smiled, "You got a real musician in *your* family," and he took his arm from Sonny's shoulder and slapped him, lightly, affectionately, with the back of his hand.

"Well. Now I've heard it all," said a voice behind us. This was another musician, and a friend of Sonny's, a coal-black, cheerful-looking man, built close to the ground. He immediately began confiding to me, at the top of his lungs, the most terrible things about Sonny, his teeth gleaming like a lighthouse and his laugh coming up out of him like the beginning of an earthquake. And it turned out that everyone at the bar knew Sonny, or almost everyone; some were musicians, working there, or nearby, or not working, some were simply hangers-on, and some were there to hear Sonny play. I was introduced to all of them and they were all very polite to me. Yet, it was clear that, for them, I was only Sonny's brother. Here, I was in Sonny's world. Or, rather: his kingdom. Here, it was not even a question that his veins bore royal blood.

They were going to play soon and Creole installed me, by myself, at a table in a dark corner. Then I watched them, Creole, and the little black man, and Sonny, and the others, while they horsed around, standing just below the bandstand. The light from the bandstand spilled just a little short of them and, watching them laughing and gesturing and moving about, I had the feeling that they, nevertheless, were being most careful not to step into that circle of light too suddenly: that if they moved into the light too suddenly, without thinking, they would perish in flame. Then, while I watched, one of them, the small, black man, moved into the light and crossed the bandstand and started fooling around with his drums. Then—being funny and being, also, extremely ceremonious—Creole took Sonny by the arm and led him to the piano. A woman's voice called Sonny's name and a few hands started clapping. And Sonny, also being funny and being ceremonious, and so touched, I think, that he could have cried, but neither hiding it nor showing it, riding it like a man, grinned, and put both hands to his heart and bowed from the waist.

Creole then went to the bass fiddle and a lean, very bright-skinned brown man jumped up on the bandstand and picked up his horn. So there they were, and the atmosphere on the bandstand and in the room began to change and tighten. Someone stepped up to the microphone and announced them. Then there were all kinds of murmurs. Some people at the bar shushed others.

The waitress ran around, frantically getting in the last orders, guys and chicks got closer to each other, and the lights on the bandstand, on the quartet, turned to a kind of indigo. Then they all looked different there. Creole looked about him for the last time, as though he were making certain that all his chickens were in the coop, and then he—jumped and struck the fiddle. And there they were.

All I know about music is that not many people ever really hear it. And even then, on the rare occasions when something opens within, and the music enters, what we mainly hear, or hear corroborated, are personal, private, vanishing evocations. But the man who creates the music is hearing something else, is dealing with the roar rising from the void and imposing order on it as it hits the air. What is evoked in him, then, is of another order, more terrible because it has no words, and triumphant, too, for that same reason. And his triumph, when he triumphs, is ours. I just watched Sonny's face. His face was troubled, he was working hard, but he wasn't with it. And I had the feeling that, in a way, everyone on the bandstand was waiting for him, both waiting for him and pushing him along. But as I began to watch Creole, I realized that it was Creole who held them all back. He had them on a short rein. Up there, keeping the beat with his whole body, wailing on the fiddle, with his eyes closed, he was listening to everything, but he was listening to Sonny. He was having a dialogue with Sonny. He wanted Sonny to leave the shoreline and strike out for the deep water. He was Sonny's witness that deep water and drowning were not the same thing—he had been there, and he knew. And he wanted Sonny to know. He was waiting for Sonny to do the things on the keys which would let Creole know that Sonny was in the water.

And, while Creole listened, Sonny moved, deep within, exactly like someone in torment. I had never before thought of how awful the relationship must be between the musician and his instrument. He has to fill it, this instrument, with the breath of life, his own. He has to make it do what he wants it to do. And a piano is just a piano. It's made out of so much wood and wires and little hammers and big ones, and ivory. While there's only so much you can do with it, the only way to find this out is to try; to try and make it do everything.

And Sonny hadn't been near a piano for over a year. And he wasn't on much better terms with his life, not the life that stretched before him now. He and the piano stammered, started one way, got scared, stopped; started another way, panicked, marked time, started again; then seemed to have found a direction, panicked again, got stuck. And the face I saw on Sonny I'd never seen before. Everything had been burned out of it, and, at the same time, things usually hidden were being burned in, by the fire and fury of the battle which was occurring in him up there.

Yet, watching Creole's face as they neared the end of the first set, I had the feeling that something had happened, something I hadn't heard. Then they finished, there was scattered applause, and then, without an instant's warning, Creole started into something else, it was almost sardonic, it was *Am I Blue*. And, as though he commanded, Sonny began to play. Something began to happen. And Creole let out the reins. The dry, low, black man said something awful on the drums, Creole answered, and the drums talked back. Then the horn insisted, sweet and high, slightly detached perhaps, and Creole listened, commenting now and then, dry, and driving, beautiful and calm and old. Then they all came together again, and Sonny was part of the family again. I could tell this from his face. He seemed to have found, right there beneath his fingers, a damn brand-new piano. It seemed that he couldn't get over it. Then, for a while, just being happy with Sonny, they seemed to be agreeing with him that brand-new pianos certainly were a gas.

Then Creole stepped forward to remind them that what they were playing was the blues. He hit something in all of them, he hit something in me, myself, and the music tightened and deepened, apprehension began to beat the air. Creole began to tell us what the blues were all about. They were not about anything very new. He and his boys up there were keeping it new, at the risk of ruin, destruction, madness, and death, in order to find new ways to make us listen. For, while the tale of how we suffer, and how we are delighted, and how we may triumph is never new, it always must be heard. There isn't any other tale to tell, it's the only light we've got in all this darkness.

And this tale, according to that face, that body, those strong hands on those strings, has another aspect in every country, and a new depth in every generation. Listen, Creole seemed to be saying, listen. Now these are Sonny's blues. He made the little black man on the drums know it, and the bright, brown man on the horn. Creole wasn't trying any longer to get Sonny in the water. He was wishing him Godspeed. Then he stepped back, very slowly, filling the air with the immense suggestion that Sonny speak for himself.

Then they all gathered around Sonny and Sonny played. Every now and again one of them seemed to say, amen. Sonny's fingers filled the air with life, his life. But that life contained so many others. And Sonny went all the way back, he really began with the spare, flat statement of the opening phrase of the song. Then he began to make it his. It was very beautiful because it wasn't hurried and it was no longer a lament. I seemed to hear with what burning he had made it his, with what burning we had yet to make it ours, how we could cease lamenting. Freedom lurked around us and I understood, at last, that he could help us to be free if we would listen, that he would never be free until we did. Yet, there was no battle in his face now. I heard what he had gone through, and would continue to go through until he came to rest in earth. He had made it his: that long line, of which we knew only Mama and Daddy. And he was giving it back, as everything must be given back, so that, passing through death, it can live forever. I saw my mother's face again, and felt, for the first time, how the stones of the road she had walked on must have bruised her feet. I saw the moonlit road where my father's brother died. And it brought something else back to me, and carried me past it. I saw my little girl again and felt Isabel's tears again, and I felt my own tears begin to rise. And I was yet aware that this was only a

Turned the lament of his life into something positive (he liberates himself)

moment, that the world waited outside, as hungry as a tiger, and that trouble stretched above us, longer than the sky.

Then it was over. Creole and Sonny let out their breath, both soaking wet, and grinning. There was a lot of applause and some of it was real. In the dark, the girl came by and I asked her to take drinks to the bandstand. There was a long pause, while they talked up there in the indigo light and after awhile I saw the girl put a Scotch and milk on top of the piano for Sonny. He didn't seem to notice it, but just before they started playing again, he sipped from it and looked toward me, and nodded. Then he put it back on top of the piano. For me, then, as they began to play again, it glowed and shook above my brother's head like the very cup of trembling.

No longer a prisoner. He has been freed!

the Bible

Faith in a Tree

Grace Paley (1922–)

Grace Paley was born in Brooklyn, the daughter of Jewish immigrants from Eastern Europe. She attended Hunter College and New York University. Her first stories appeared in *Accent* and other literary magazines. Her titles include *The Little Disturbances of Man* (1959), *Enormous Changes at the Last Minute* (1974), where "Faith in a Tree" comes from, and *Later the Same Day* (1985), all of which were collected in 1994 in *The Collected Stories of Grace Paley*. She is also responsible for *Leaning Forward* (1985), *Long Walks and Intimate Talk* (1991), and *New and Collected Poems* (1992).

Just when I most needed important conversation, a sniff of the man-wide world, that is, at least one brainy companion who could translate my friendly language into his tongue of undying carnal love, I was forced to lounge in our neighborhood park, surrounded by children.

All the children were there. Among the trees, in the arms of statues, toes in the grass, they hopped in and out of dog shit and dug tunnels into mole holes. Wherever the children ran, their mothers stopped to talk.

What a place in democratic time! One God, who was King of the Jews, who unravels the stars to this day with little hydrogen explosions. He can look down from His Holy Headquarters and see us all: heads of girl, ponytails riding the springtime luck, short black bobs, and an occasional eminence of golden wedding rings. He sees south into Brooklyn how Prospect Park lies in its sand-rooted trees among Japanese gardens and police, and beyond us north to dangerous Central Park. Far north, the deer-eyed eland and kudu survive, grazing the open pits of the Bronx Zoo.

Same view that Faith has w/ a larger perspective

But me, the creation of His soft second thought, I am sitting on the twelve-foot-high, strong, long arm of a sycamore, my feet swinging, and I can only see Kitty, a co-worker in the mother trade—a topnotch craftsman. She is below, leaning on my tree, rumpled in a black cotton skirt made of shroud remnants at about fourteen cents a yard. Another colleague, Anne Kraat, is close by on a hard park bench, gloomy, beautiful, waiting for her luck to change.

Although I can't see them, I know that on the other side of the dry pool, the thick snout of the fountain spout, hurrying along the circumference of the parched sun-struck circle (in which, when Henry James could see, he saw lilies floating), Mrs. Hyme Caraway pokes her terrible seedlings, Gowan, Michael, and Christopher, astride an English bike, a French tricycle, and a Danish tractor. Beside her, talking all the time in fear of no response, Mrs. Steamy Lewis, mother of Matthew, Mark, and Lucy, tells of happy happy life in a thatched hotel on a Greek island where total historical recall is indigenous. Lucy limps along at her skirt in muddy cashmere. Mrs. Steamy Lewis really swings within the seconds of her latitude and swears she will have six, but Mr. Steamy Lewis is not expected to live.

I can easily see Mrs. Junius Finn, my up-the-block neighbor and evening stoop companion, a broad barge, like a lady, moving slow—a couple of redheaded cabooses dragged by clothesline at her stern; on her fat upper deck, Wiltwyck,* a pale three-year-old roaring captain with smoky eyes, shoves his wet thumb into the wind. "Hurry! Hurry!" he howls. Mrs. Finn goes puff puffing toward the opinionated playground, that sandy harbor.

Along the same channel, but near enough now to spatter with spite, tilting delicately like a boy's sailboat, Lynn Ballard floats past my unconcern to drop light anchor, a large mauve handbag, over the green bench slats. She sighs and looks up to see what (if anything) the heavens are telling. In this way, once a week, toes in,

* Wiltwyck is named for the school of his brother Junior, where Junior, who was bad and getting worse, is still bad, but is getting better (as man is perfectible).

head high and in three-quarter turn, arms at her side, graceful as a seal's flippers, she rests, quiet and expensive. She never grabs another mother's kid when he falls and cries. Her particular Michael on his little red bike rides round and round the sandbox, while she dreams of private midnight.

"Like a model," hollers Mrs. Junius Finn over Lynn Ballard's head.

I'm too close to the subject to remark. I sniff, however, and accidentally take sweetness into my lungs. Because it's the month of May.

Kitty and I are nothing like Lynn Ballard. You will see Kitty's darling face, as I tell her, slowly, but me—quick—what am I? Not bad if you're a basement shopper. On my face are a dozen messages, easy to read, strictly for friends, Bargains Galore! I admit it now.

However, the most ordinary life is illuminated by a great event like fame. Once I was famous. From the meaning of that glow, the modest hardhearted me is descended.

Once, all the New York papers that had the machinery to do so carried a rotogravure picture of me in a stewardess's arms. I was, it is now thought, the third commercial air-flight baby passenger in the entire world. This picture is at the Home now, mounted on laundry cardboard. My mother fixed it with glass to assail eternity. The caption says: One of Our Youngest. Little Faith Decided to Visit Gramma. Here She Is, Gently Cuddled in the Arms of Stewardess Jeannie Carter.

Why would anyone send a little baby anywhere alone? What was my mother trying to prove? That I was independent? That she wasn't the sort to hang on? That in the sensible, socialist, Zionist world of the future, she wouldn't cry at my wedding? "You're an American child. Free. Independent." Now what does that mean? I have always required a man to be dependent on, even when it appeared that I had one already. I own two small boys whose dependence on me takes up my lumpen time and my bourgeois feelings. I'm not the least bit ashamed to say that I tie their shoes and I have wiped their backsides well beyond the recommendations of my friends, Ellen and George Hellesbraun, who are psychiatric social workers and appalled. I kiss those kids forty times a day. I punch them just like a father should. When I have a date and come home late at night, I wake them with a couple of good hard shakes to complain about the miserable entertainment. When I'm not furiously exhausted from my low-level job and that bedraggled soot-slimy house, I praise God for them. One Sunday morning, my neighbor, Mrs. Raftery, called the cops because it was 3 a.m. and I was vengefully singing a praising song.

Since I have already mentioned singing, I have to tell you: it is not Sunday. For that reason, all the blue-eyed, boy-faced policemen in the park are worried. They can see that lots of our vitamin-enlarged high-school kids are planning to lug their guitar cases around all day long. They're scared that one of them may strum and sing a mountain melody or that several, a gang, will gather to raise their voices in medieval counterpoint.

Question: Does the world know, does the average freedman realize that, except for a few hours on Sunday afternoon, the playing of fretted instruments is banned by municipal decree? Absolutely forbidden is the song of the flute and oboe.

Answer (explanation): This *is* a great ballswinger of a city on the constant cement-mixing remake, battering and shattering, and a high note out of a wild clarinet could be the decibel to break a citizen's eardrum. But what if you were a city-loving planner leaning on your drawing board? Tears would drop to the delicate drafting sheets.

Well, you won't be pulled in for whistling and here come the whistlers—the young Saturday fathers, open-shirted and ambitious. By and large they are trying to get somewhere and have to go to a lot of parties. They are sleepy but pretend to great energy for the sake of their two-year-old sons (little boys need a recollection of Energy as a male resource). They carry miniature footballs though the season's changing. Then the older fathers trot in, just a few minutes slower, their faces scraped to a clean smile, every one of them wearing a fine gray head and eager eyes, his breath caught, his hand held by the baby daughter of a third intelligent marriage.

One of them, passing my tree, stubs his toe on Kitty's sandal. He shades his eyes to look up at me against my sun. That is Alex O. Steele, who was a man organizing tenant strikes on Ocean Parkway when I was a Coney Island Girl Scout against my mother's socialist will. He says, "Hey, Faith, how's the world? Heard anything from Ricardo?"

I answer him in lecture form:

> Alex Steele. Sasha. Yes. I have heard from Ricardo. Ricardo even at the present moment when I am trying to talk with you in a civilized way, Ricardo has rolled his dove-gray brain into a glob of spit in order to fly secretly into my ear right off the poop deck of Foamline's World Tour Cruiseship *Eastern Sunset.* He is stretched out in my head, exhausted before dawn from falling in love with an *Eastern Sunset* lady passenger on the first leg of her many-masted journey round the nighttimes of the world. He is *this minute* saying to me,
>
> "Arcturus Rise, Orion Fall . . ."
>
> "Cock-proud son of a bitch," I mutter.
>
> "Ugh," he says, blinking.
>
> "How are the boys?" I make him say.
>
> "Well, he really wants to know how the boys are," I reply.
>
> "No, I don't," he says. "Please don't answer. Just make sure they don't get killed crossing the street. That's your job."

"What?" says Alex Steele. "Speak clearly, Faith, you're garbling like you used to."

"I'm joking. Forget it. But I did hear from him the other day." Out of the pocket of my stretch denims I drag a mashed letter with the exotic stamp of a new underdeveloped nation. It is a large stamp with two smiling lions on a field of barbed wire. The letter says: "I am not well. I hope I never see another rain forest. I am sick. Are you working? Have you seen Ed Snead? He owes me $180. Don't badger him about it if he looks broke. Otherwise send me some to Guerra Verde c/o Dotty Wasserman. Am living here with her. She's on a Children's Mission. Wonderful girl. Reminds me of you ten years ago. She acts on her principles. I *need* the money."

"That is Ricardo. Isn't it, Alex? I mean, there's no signature."

"Dotty Wasserman!" Alex says. "So that's where she is . . . a funny plain girl. Faith, let's have lunch some time. I work up in the East Fifties. How're your folks? I hear they put themselves into a Home. They're young for that. Listen, I'm the executive director of Incurables, Inc., a fund-raising organization. We do wonderful things, Faith. The speed of life-extending developments . . . By the way, what do you think of this little curly Sharon of mine?"

"Oh, Alex, how old is she? She's darling, she's a little golden baby, I love her. She's a peach."

"Of course! *She's* a peach, you like anyone better'n you like us," says my son Richard, who is jealous—because he came first and was deprived at two and one-half by his baby brother of my singlehearted love, my friend Ellie Hellesbraun says. Of course, that's a convenient professional lie, a cheap hindsight, as Richard, my older son, is brilliant, and I knew it from the beginning. When he was a baby all alone with me, and Ricardo, his daddy, was off exploring some deep creepy jungle, we often took the ferry to Staten Island. Then we sometimes took the ferry to Hoboken. We walked bridges, just he and I, I said to him, Richie, see the choo-choos on the barges, Richie, see the strong fast tugboat, see the merchant ships with their tall cranes, see the *United States* sail away for a week and a day, see the Hudson River with its white current. Oh, it isn't really the Hudson River, I told him, it's the North River; it isn't really a river, it's an estuary, part of the sea, I told him, though he was only two. I could tell him scientific things like that, because I considered him absolutely brilliant. See how beautiful the ice is on the river, see the stony palisades, I said, I hugged him, my pussycat, I said, see the interesting world.

So he really has no kicks coming, he's just peevish.

"We're really a problem to you, Faith, we keep you not free,"

Richard says. "Anyway, it's true you're crazy about anyone but us."

It's true I do like the other kids. I am not too cool to say Alex's Sharon really is a peach. But you, you stupid kid, Richard! Who could match me for pride or you for brilliance? Which one of the smart third-grade kids in a class of learned Jews, Presbyterians, and bohemians? You are one of the two smartest and the other one is Chinese—Arnold Lee, who does make Richard look a little simple, I admit it. But did you ever hear of a child who, when asked to write a sentence for the word "who" (they were up to the hard *wh*'s), wrote and then magnificently, with Oriental lisp, read the following: "Friend, tell me who among the Shanghai merchants does the largest trade?"*

"That's a typical yak yak out of you, Faith," says Richard.

"Now Richard, listen to me, Arnold's an interesting boy; you wouldn't meet a kid like him anywhere but here or Hong Kong. So use some of these advantages I've given you. I could be living in the country, which I love, but I know how hard that is on children—I stay here in this creepy slum. I dwell in soot and slime just so you can meet kids like Arnold Lee and live on this wonderful block with all the Irish and Puerto Ricans, although God knows why there aren't any Negro children for you to play with . . ."

"Who needs it?" he says, just to tease me. "All those guys got knives anyway. But you don't care if I get killed much, do you?"

How can you answer that boy?

"You don't," says Mrs. Junius Finn, glad to say a few words. "You don't have to answer them. God didn't give out tongues for that. You answer too much, Faith Asbury, and it shows. Nobody fresher than Richard."

"Mrs. Finn," I scream in order to be heard, for she's some distance away and doesn't pay attention the way I do, "what's so

* The teacher, Marilyn Gewirtz, the only real person in this story, a child admirer, told me this.

terrible about fresh. EVIL is bad. WICKED is bad. ROBBING, MURDER, and PUTTING HEROIN IN YOUR BLOOD is bad."

"Blah blah," she says, deaf to passion. "Blah to you."

Despite no education, Mrs. Finn always is more in charge of word meanings than I am. She is especially in charge of Good and Bad. My language limitations here are real. My vocabulary is adequate for writing notes and keeping journals but absolutely useless for an active moral life. If I really knew this language, there would surely be in my head, as there is in Webster's or the *Dictionary of American Slang,* that unreducible verb designed to tell a person like me what to do next.

Mrs. Finn knows my problems because I do not keep them to myself. And I am reminded of them particularly at this moment, for I see her roughly the size of life, held up at the playground by Wyllie, who has rolled off the high ruddy deck of her chest to admire all the English bikes filed in the park bike stand. Of course that is what Junior is upstate for: love that forced possession. At first his father laced him on his behind, cutting the exquisite design known to generations of daddies who labored at home before the rise of industrialism and group therapy. Then Mr. Finn remembered his childhood, that it was Adam's Fall not Junior that was responsible. Now the Finns never see a ten-speed Italian racer without family sighs for Junior, who is still not home as there were about 176 bikes he loved.

Something is wrong with the following tenants: Mrs. Finn, Mrs. Raftery, Ginnie, and me. Everyone else in our building is on the way up through the affluent society, putting five to ten years into low rent before moving to Jersey or Bridgeport. But our four family units, as people are now called, are doomed to stand culturally still as this society moves on its caterpillar treads from ordinary affluent to absolute empire. All this in mind, I name names and dates. "Mrs. Finn, darling, look at my Richard, the time Junior took his Schwinn and how Richard hid in the coal in the basement thinking of a way to commit suicide," but she coolly answers, "Faith, you're not a bit fair, for Junior give it right back when he found out it was Richard's."

O.K.

Kitty says, "Faith, you'll fall out of the tree, calm yourself." She looks up, rolling her eyes to show direction, and I see a handsome man in narrow pants whom we remember from other Saturdays. He has gone to sit beside Lynn Ballard. He speaks softly to her left ear while she maintains her profile. He has never spoken to her Michael. He is a famous actor trying to persuade her to play opposite him in a new production of *She*. That's what Kitty, my kind friend, says.

I am above that kindness. I often see through the appearance of things right to the apparition itself. It's obvious that he's a weekend queer, talking her into the possibilities of a neighborhood threesome. When her nose quivers and she agrees, he will easily get his really true love, the magnificent manager of the supermarket, who has been longing for her at the check-out counter. What they will do then, I haven't the vaguest idea. I am the child of puritans and I'm only halfway here.

"Don't even think like that," says Kitty. No. She can see a contract in his pocket.

There is no one like Kitty Skazka. Unlike other people who have similar flaws that doom, she is tolerant and loving. I wish Kitty could live forever, bearing daughters and sons to open the heart of man. Meanwhile, mortal, pregnant, she has three green-eyed daughters and they aren't that great. Of course, Kitty thinks they are. And they are no worse than the average gifted, sensitive child of a wholehearted mother and half a dozen transient fathers. Her youngest girl is Antonia, who has no respect for grownups. Kitty has always liked her to have no respect; so in this, she is quite satisfactory to Kitty.

At some right moment on this Saturday afternoon, Antonia decided to talk to Tonto, my second son. He lay on his belly in the grass, his bare heels exposed to the eye of flitting angels, and he worked at a game that included certain ants and other bugs as players.

"Tonto," she asked, "what are you playing, can I?"

"No, it's my game, no girls," Tonto said.

"Are you the boss of the world?" Antonia asked politely.

"Yes," said Tonto.

He thinks, he really believes, he is. To which I must say, Righto! you are the boss of the world, Anthony, you are prince of the day-care center for the deprived children of working mothers, you are the Lord of the West Side loading zone whenever it rains on Sundays. I have seen you, creepy chief of the dark forest of four ginkgo trees. The Boss! If you would only look up, Anthony, and boss me what to do, I would immediately slide down this scabby bark, ripping my new stretch slacks, and do it.

"Give me a nickel, Faith," he ordered at once.

"Give him a nickel, Kitty," I said.

"Nickels, nickels, nickels, whatever happened to pennies?" Anna Kraat asked.

"Anna, you're rich. You're against us," I whispered, but loud enough to be heard by Mrs. Junius Finn, still stopped at the mouth of the playground.

"Don't blame the rich for everything," she warned. She herself, despite the personal facts of her economic position, is disgusted with the neurotic rise of the working class.

Lynn Ballard bent her proud and shameless head.

Kitty sighed, shifted her yardage, and began to shorten the hem of the enormous skirt which she was wearing. "Here's a nickel, love," she said.

"Oh boy! Love!" said Anna Kraat.

Antonia walked in a wide circle around the sycamore tree and put her arm on Kitty, who sewed, the sun just barely over her left shoulder—a perfect light. At that very moment, a representational artist passed. I think it was Edward Roster. He stopped and kneeled, peering at the scene. He squared them off with a filmmaker's viewfinder and said, "Ah, what a picture!" then left.

"Number one!" I announced to Kitty, which he was, the very first of the squint-eyed speculators who come by to size up the stock. Pretty soon, depending on age and intention, they would move in groups along the paths or separately take notes in the shadows of the statues.

"The trick," said Anna, downgrading the world, "is to know the speculators from the investors . . ."

"I will never live like that. Not I," Kitty said softly.

"Balls!" I shouted, as two men strolled past us, leaning toward one another. They weren't lovers, they were Jack Resnick and Tom Weed, music lovers inclining toward their transistor, which was playing the "Chromatic Fantasy." They paid no attention to us because of their relation to this great music. However, Anna heard them say, "Jack, do you hear what I hear?" "Damnit yes, the overromanticizing and the under-Baching, I can't believe it."

Well, I must say when darkness covers the earth and great darkness the people, I will think of you: two men with smart ears. I don't believe civilization can do a lot more than educate a person's senses. If it's truth and honor you want to refine, I think the Jews have some insight. Make no images, imitate no God. After all, in His field, the graphic arts, He is pre-eminent. Then let that One who made the tan deserts and the blue Van Allen belt and the green mountains of New England be in charge of Beauty, which He obviously understands, and let man, who was full of forgiveness at Jerusalem, and full of survival at Troy, let man be in charge of Good.

"Faith, will you quit with your all-the-time philosophies," says Richard, my first- and disapproving-born. Into our midst, he'd galloped, riding an all-day rage. Brand-new ball bearings, roller skates, heavy enough for his big feet, hung round his neck.

I decided not to give in to Richard by responding. I digressed and was free: A cross-eyed man with a red beard became president of the Parent-Teachers Association. He appointed a committee of fun-loving ladies who met in the lunchroom and touched up the coffee with little gurgles of brandy.

He had many clever notions about how to deal with the money shortage in the public schools. One of his great plots was to promote the idea of the integrated school in such a way that private-school people would think their kids were missing the real thing. And at 5 a.m., the envious hour, the very pit of the morning of middle age, they would think of all the public-school children deeply involved in the urban tragedy, something their children might never know. He suggested that one month of public-school attendance might become part of the private-school curriculum, as natural and progressive an experience as a visit to the boiler room in first grade. Funds could be split 50-50 or 30-70 or 40-60 with the Board of Education. If the plan failed, still the projected effort would certainly enhance the prestige of the public school.

Actually something did stir. Delegations of private progressive-school parents attacked the Board of Ed. for what became known as the Shut-out, and finally even the parents-and-teachers associations of the classical schools (whose peculiar concern always had been educating the child's head) began to consider the value of exposing children who had read about the horror at Ilium to ordinary street fights, so they could understand the Iliad better. Public School (in Manhattan) would become a minor like typing, required but secondary.

Mr. Terry Koln, full of initiative, energy, and lightheartedness, was re-elected by unanimous vote and sent on to the United Parents and Federated Teachers Organization as special council member, where in a tiny office all his own he grew marijuana on the windowsills, swearing it was deflowered marigolds.

He was the joy of our P.T.A. But it was soon discovered that he had no children, and Kitty and I have to meet him now surreptitiously in bars.

"Oh," said Richard, his meanness undeflected by this jolly digression:

"The ladies of the P.T.A.
wear baggies in their blouses
they talk on telephones all day
and never clean their houses."

He really wrote that, my Richard. I thought it was awfully good, rhyme and meter and all, and I brought it to his teacher. I took the afternoon off to bring it to her. "Are you joking, Mrs. Asbury?" she asked.

Looking into her kind teaching eyes, I remembered schools and what it might be like certain afternoons and I replied, "May I have my Richard, please, he has a dental appointment. His teeth are just like his father's. Rotten."

"Do take care of them, Mrs. Asbury."

"God, yes, it's the least," I said, taking his hand.

"Faith," said Richard, who had not gone away. "Why did you take me to the dentist that afternoon?"

"I thought you wanted to get out of there."

"Why? Why? Why?" asked Richard, stamping his feet and shouting. I didn't answer. I closed my eyes to make him disappear.

"Why not?" asked Philip Mazzano, who was standing there looking up at me when I opened my eyes.

"Where's Richard?" I asked.

"This is Philip," Kitty called up to me. "You know Philip, that I told you about?"

"Yes?"

"Philip," she said.

"Oh," I said and left the arm of the sycamore with as delicate a jump as can be made by a person afraid of falling, twisting an ankle, and being out of work for a week.

"I don't mind school," said Richard, shouting from behind the tree. "It's better than listening to her whine."

He really talks like that.

Philip looked puzzled. "How old are you, sonny?"

"Nine."

"Do nine-year-olds talk like that? I think I have a boy who's nine."

"Yes," said Kitty. "Your Johnny's nine, David's eleven, and Mike's fourteen."

"Ah," said Philip, sighing; he looked up into the tree I'd flopped from—and there was Judy, Anna's kid, using my nice warm branch. "God," said Philip, "more!"

Silence followed and embarrassment, because we outnumbered him, though clearly, we tenderly liked him.

"How is everything, Kitty?" he said, kneeling to tousle her

hair. "How's everything, my old honey girl? Another one?" He tapped Kitty's tummy lightly with an index finger. "God!" he said, standing up. "Say, Kitty, I saw Jerry in Newark day before yesterday. Just like that. He was standing in a square scratching his head."

"Jerry?" Kitty asked in a high loving squeak. "Oh, I know. Newark all week . . . Why were you there?"

"Me? I had to see someone, a guy named Vincent Hall, a man in my field."

"What's your field?" I asked.

"Daisies," he said. "I happen to be in the field of daisies."

What an answer! How often does one meet, in this black place, a man, woman, or child who can think up a pastoral reply like that?

For that reason I looked at him. He had dark offended eyes deep in shadow, with a narrow rim of whiteness under the eyes, the result, I invented, of lots of late carousing nights, followed by eye-wrinkling examinations of mortalness. All this had marked him lightly with sobriety, the first enhancing manifest of ravage.

Even Richard is stunned by this uncynical openhearted notation of feeling. Forty bare seconds then, while Jack Resnick puts his transistor into the hollow of an English elm, takes a tattered score of *The Messiah* out of his rucksack, and writes a short Elizabethan melody in among the long chorus holds to go with the last singing sentence of my ode to Philip.

"Nice day," said Anna.

"Please, Faith," said Richard. "Please. You see that guy over there?" He pointed to a fat boy seated among adults on a park bench not far from listening Lynn Ballard. "He has a skate key and he won't lend it to me. He stinks. It's your fault you lost the skate key, Faith. You know you did. You never put anything away."

"Ask him again, Richard."

"You ask him, Faith. You're a grownup."

"I will not. You want the skate key, you ask him. You have to go after your own things in this life. I'm not going to be around forever."

Richard gave me a gloomy, lip-curling look. No. It was worse than that. It was a baleful, foreboding look; a look which as far as our far-in-the-future relations were concerned could be named ill-auguring.

"You never do me a favor, do you?" he said.

"*I'll* go with you, Richard." Philip grabbed his hand. "We'll talk to that kid. He probably hasn't got a friend in the world. I'm not kidding you, boy, it's hard to be a fat kid." He rapped his belly, where, I imagine, certain memories were stored.

Then he took Richard's hand and they went off, man and boy, to tangle.

"Kitty! Richard just hands him his skate, his hand, and just goes off with him . . . That's not like my Richard."

"Children sense how good he is," said Kitty.

"He's good?"

"He's really not so good. Oh, he's good. He's considerate. You know what kind he is, Faith. But if you don't really want him to be good, he will be. And he's very strong. Physically. Someday I'll tell you about him. Not now. He has a special meaning to me."

Actually everyone has a special meaning to Kitty, even me, a dictionary of particular generalities, even Anna and all our children.

Kitty sewed as she spoke. She looked like a delegate to a Conference of Youth from the People's Republic of Ubmonsk from Lower Tartaria. A single dark braid hung down her back. She wore a round-necked white blouse with capped sleeves made of softened muslin, woven for aged bridesbeds. I have always listened carefully to my friend Kitty's recommendations, for she has made one mistake after another. Her experience is invaluable.

Kitty's kids have kept an eye on her from their dear tiniest times. They listened to her reasons, but the two eldest, without meaning any disrespect, had made different plans for their lives. Children are all for John Dewey. Lisa and Nina have never believed that Kitty's life really worked. They slapped Antonia for scratching the enameled kitchen table. When Kitty caught them, she said, "Antonia's a baby. Come on now girls, what's a table?"

"What's a *table*?" said Lisa. "What a nut! She wants to know what a table is."

"Well, Faith," said Richard, "*he* got the key for me."

Richard and Philip were holding hands, which made Richard look like a little boy with a daddy. I could cry when I think that I always treat Richard as though he's about forty-seven.

Philip felt remarkable to have extracted that key. "He's quite a kid, Faith, your boy. I wish that my Johnny in Chicago was as great as Richard here. Is Johnny really nine, Kitty?"

"You bet," she said.

He kept his puzzled face for some anticipated eventuality and folded down to cross-legged comfort, leaning familiarly on Nina's and Lisa's backs. "How are you two fairy queens?" he asked and tugged at their long hair gently. He peeked over their shoulders. They were reading Classic Comics, *Ivanhoe* and *Robin Hood.*

"I hate to read," said Antonia.

"Me too," hollered Tonto.

"Antonia, I wish *you'd* read more," said Philip. "Antonia, little beauty. These two little ones. Forest babies. Little sunny brown creatures. I think you would say, Kitty, that they understand their bodies?"

"Oh, yes, I would," said Kitty, who believed all that.

Although I'm very shy, I tend to persevere, so I said, "You're pretty sunny and brown yourself. How do you make out? What are you? An actor or a French teacher, or something?"

"French . . ." Kitty smiled. "He could teach Sanskrit if he wanted to. Or Filipino or Cambodian."

"Cambodge . . ." Philip said. He said this softly as though the wars in Indochina might be the next subject for discussion.

"French teacher?" asked Anna Kraat, who had been silent, grieved by spring, for one hour and forty minutes. "Judy," she yelled into the crossed branches of the sycamore. "Judy . . . French . . ."

"So?" said Judy. "What's so great? Je m'appelle Judy Solomon. Ma père s'appelle Pierre Solomon. How's that, folks?"

"Mon père," said Anna. "I told you that before."

"Who cares?" said Judy, who didn't care.

"She's lost two fathers," said Anna, "within three years."

Tonto stood up to scratch his belly and back, which were itchy with wet grass. "Mostly nobody has fathers, Anna," he said.

"Is that true, little boy?" asked Philip.

"Oh yes," Tonto said. "My father is in the Equator. They never even had fathers," pointing to Kitty's daughters. "Judy has two fathers, Peter and Dr. Kraat. Dr. Kraat takes care of you if you're crazy."

"Maybe I'll be your father."

Tonto looked at me. I was too rosy. "Oh no," he said. "Not right now. My father's name is Ricardo. He's a famous explorer. Like an explorer, I mean. He went in the Equator to make contacts. I have two books by him."

"Do you like him?"

"He's all right."

"Do you miss him?"

"He's very fresh when he's home."

"That's enough of that!" I said. It's stupid to let a kid talk badly about his father in front of another man. Men really have too much on their minds without that.

"He's quite a boy," said Philip. "You and your brother are real boys." He turned to me. "What do I do? Well, I make a living. Here. Chicago. Wherever I am. I'm not in financial trouble. I figured it all out ten years ago. But what I really am, really . . ." he said, driven to lying confidence because he thought he ought to try that life anyway. "What I truly am is a comedian."

"That's a joke, that's the first joke you've said."

"But that's what I want to be . . . a comedian."

"But you're not funny."

"But I am. You don't know me yet. I want to be one. I've been a teacher and I've worked for the State Department. And now what I want to be's a comedian. People have changed professions before."

"You can't be a comedian," said Anna, "unless you're funny."

He took a good look at Anna. Anna's character is terrible, but she's beautiful. It took her husbands about two years apiece to see how bad she was, but it takes the average passer, answerer, or asker about thirty seconds to see how beautiful she is. You can't warn men. As for Kitty and me, well, we love her because she's beautiful.

"Anna's all right," said Richard.

"Be quiet," said Philip. "Say, Anna, are you interested in the French tongue, the French people, French history, or French civilization?"

"No," said Anna.

"Oh," he said, disappointed.

"I'm not interested in anything," said Anna.

"Say!" said Philip, getting absolutely red with excitement, blushing from his earlobes down into his shirt, making me think as I watched the blood descend from his brains that I would like to be the one who was holding his balls very gently, to be exactly present so to speak when all the thumping got there.

Since it was clearly Anna, not I, who would be in that affectionate position, I thought I'd better climb the tree again just for the oxygen or I'd surely suffer the same sudden descent of blood. That's the way nature does things, swishing those quarts and quarts to wherever they're needed for power and action.

Luckily, a banging of pots and pans came out of the playground and a short parade appeared—four or five grownups, a few years behind me in the mommy-and-daddy business, pushing little go-carts with babies in them, a couple of three-year-olds hanging on. They were the main bangers and clangers. The grownups carried three posters. The first showed a prime-living, prime-earning, well-dressed man about thirty-five years old next to a small girl. A question was asked: would you burn a child? In the next poster he placed a burning cigarette on the child's arm. The cool answer was given: WHEN NECESSARY. The third poster carried no words, only a napalmed Vietnamese baby, seared, scarred, with twisted hands.

We were very quiet. Kitty put her head down into the dark skirt of her lap. I trembled. I said, Oh! Anna said to Philip,

"They'll only turn people against them," and turned against them herself at once.

"You people will have to go," said Douglas, our neighborhood cop. He had actually arrived a few minutes earlier to tell Kitty to beg Jerry not to sell grass at this end of the park. But he was ready. "You just have to go," he said. "No parades in the park."

Kitty lifted her head and with sweet bossiness said, "Hey Doug, leave them alone. They're O.K."

Tonto said, "I know that girl, she goes to Greenwich House. You're in the fours," he told her.

Doug said, "Listen Tonto, there's a war on. You'll be a soldier too someday. I know you're no sissy like some kids around here. You'll fight for your country."

"Ha ha," said Mrs. Junius Finn, "that'll be the day. Oh, say, can you see?"

The paraders made a little meeting just outside our discussion. They had to decide what next. The four grownups held the tongues of the children's bells until that decision could be made. They were a group of that kind of person.

"What they're doing is treason," said Douglas. He had decided to explain and educate. "Signs on sticks aren't allowed. In case of riot. It's for their own protection too. They might turn against each other." He was afraid that no one would find the real perpetrator if that should happen.

"But Officer, I know these people. They're decent citizens of this community," said Philip, though he didn't live in the borough, city, or state, let alone vote in it.

Doug looked at him thoroughly. "Mister, I could take you in for interference." He pulled his cop voice out of his healthy diaphragm.

"Come on . . ." said Kitty.

"You too," he said fiercely. "Disperse," he said, "disperse, disperse."

Behind his back, the meeting had been neatly dispersed for about three minutes. He ran after them, but they continued on the park's circumference, their posters on the carriage handles, very solemn, making friends and enemies.

"They look pretty legal to me," I hollered after Doug's blue back.

Tonto fastened himself to my leg and stuck his thumb in his mouth.

Richard shouted, "Ha! Ha!" and punched me. He also began to grind his teeth, which would lead, I knew, to great expense.

"Oh, that's funny, Faith," he said. He cried, he stamped his feet dangerously, in skates. "I hate you. I hate your stupid friends. Why didn't they just stand up to that stupid cop and say fuck you. They should of just stood up and hit him." He ripped his skates off, twisting his bad ankle. "Gimme that chalk box, Lisa, just give it to me."

In a fury of tears and disgust, he wrote on the near blacktop in pink flamingo chalk—in letters fifteen feet high, so the entire Saturday walking world could see—WOULD YOU BURN A CHILD? and under it, a little taller, the red reply, WHEN NECESSARY.

And I think that is exactly when events turned me around, changing my hairdo, my job uptown, my style of living and telling. Then I met women and men in different lines of work, whose minds were made up and directed out of that sexy playground by my children's heartfelt brains, I thought more and more and every day about the world.

The Enormous Radio

John Cheever (1912–1982)

John Cheever's short stories and novels focus on the problems and isolation of contemporary American life, especially among affluent New Englanders in the midst of suburbia—a suburbia where marriages and families break apart. Born in Quincy, Massachusetts, Cheever grew up near those he wrote about. He received a Guggenheim Fellowship in 1951, which allowed him to focus on writing. He carefully balances humor and irony, sophistication and melancholy; this effective style is clearly visible within his first novel *The Wapshot Chronicle* (1957), for which he received the National Book Award, and within *The Stories of John Cheever* (1979), which won the Pulitzer Prize and the National Book Critics Award, and includes the story in this anthology. Other notable works include *The Enormous Radio and Other Stories* (1953), *The Wapshot Scandal* (1964; a sequel to *The Wapshot Chronicle*), *Bullet Park* (1969), *The World of Apples* (1973), and *Falconer* (1977).

Jim and Irene Westcott were the kind of people who seem to strike that satisfactory average of income, endeavor, and respectability that is reached by the statistical reports in college alumni bulletins. They were the parents of two young children, they had been married nine years, they lived on the twelfth floor of an apartment house near Sutton Place, they went to the theatre on an average of 10.3 times a year, and they hoped someday to live in Westchester. Irene Westcott was a pleasant, rather plain girl with soft brown hair and a wide, fine forehead upon which nothing at all had been written, and in the cold weather she wore a coat of fitch skins dyed to resemble mink. You could not say that Jim Westcott looked younger than he was, but you could at least say of him that he seemed to feel younger. He wore his graying hair cut very short, he dressed in the kind of clothes his class had worn at Andover, and his manner was earnest, vehement, and intentionally naïve. The Westcotts differed from their friends, their classmates, and their neighbors only in an interest they shared in serious music. They went to a great many concerts—although they seldom mentioned this to anyone—and they spent a good deal of time listening to music on the radio.

Their radio was an old instrument, sensitive, unpredictable, and beyond repair. Neither of them understood the mechanics of radio—or of any of the other appliances that surrounded them—and when the instrument faltered, Jim would strike the side of the cabinet with his hand. This sometimes helped. One Sunday afternoon, in the middle of a Schubert quartet, the music faded away altogether. Jim struck the cabinet repeatedly, but there was no response; the Schubert was lost to them forever. He promised to buy Irene a new radio, and on Monday when he came home from work he told her that he had got one. He refused to describe it, and said it would be a surprise for her when it came.

The radio was delivered at the kitchen door the following afternoon, and with the assistance of her maid and the handyman Irene uncrated it and brought it into the living room. She was struck at once with the physical ugliness of the large gumwood cabinet. Irene was proud of her living room, she had chosen its furnishings and colors as carefully as she chose her clothes, and now it seemed to her that the new radio stood among her intimate possessions like an aggressive intruder. She was confounded by the number of dials and switches on the instrument panel, and she studied them thoroughly before she put the plug into a wall socket and turned the radio on. The dials flooded with a malevolent green light, and in the distance she heard the music of a piano quintet. The quintet was in the distance for only an instant; it bore down upon her with a speed greater than light and filled the apartment with the noise of music amplified so mightily that it knocked a china ornament from a table to the floor. She rushed to the instrument and reduced the volume. The violent forces that were snared in the ugly gumwood cabinet made her uneasy. Her children came home from school then, and she took them to the Park. It was not until later in the afternoon that she was able to return to the radio.

The maid had given the children their suppers and was supervising their baths when Irene turned on the radio, reduced the volume, and sat down to listen to a Mozart quintet that she knew and enjoyed. The music came through clearly. The new instrument had a much purer tone, she thought, than the old one. She decided that tone was most important and that she could conceal the cabinet behind a sofa. But as soon as she had made her peace with the radio, the interference began. A crackling sound like the noise of a burning powder fuse began to accompany the singing of the strings. Beyond the music, there was a rustling that reminded Irene unpleasantly of the sea, and as the quintet progressed, these noises were joined by many others. She tried all the dials and switches but nothing dimmed the interference, and she sat down, disappointed and bewildered, and tried to trace the flight of the melody. The elevator shaft in her building ran beside the living-room wall, and it was the noise of the elevator that gave her a clue to the character of the static. The rattling of the elevator cables and the opening and closing of the elevator doors were reproduced in her loudspeaker, and, realizing that the radio was sensitive to electrical currents of all sorts, she began to discern through the Mozart the ringing of telephone bells, the dialing of phones, and the lamentation of a vacuum cleaner. By listening more carefully, she was able to distinguish doorbells, elevator bells, electric razors, and Waring mixers, whose sounds had been picked up from the apartments that surrounded hers and transmitted through her loudspeaker. The powerful and ugly instrument, with its mistaken sensitivity to discord, was more than she could hope to master, so she turned the thing off and went into the nursery to see her children.

When Jim Westcott came home that night, he went to the radio confidently and worked the controls. He had the same sort of experience Irene had had. A man was speaking on the station Jim had chosen, and his voice swung instantly from the distance into a force so powerful that it shook the apartment. Jim turned the volume control and reduced the voice. Then, a minute or two later, the interference began. The ringing of telephones and doorbells set in, joined by the rasp of the elevator doors and the whir of cooking appliances. The character of the noise had changed since Irene had tried the radio earlier; the last of the electric razors was being unplugged, the vacuum cleaners had all been returned to their closets, and the static reflected that change in pace that overtakes the city after the sun goes down. He fiddled with the knobs but couldn't get rid of the noises, so he turned the radio off and told Irene that in the morning he'd call the people who had sold it to him and give them hell.

The following afternoon, when Irene returned to the apartment from a luncheon date, the maid told her that a man had come and fixed the radio. Irene went into the living room before she took off her hat or her furs and tried the instrument. From the loudspeaker came a recording of the "Missouri Waltz." It reminded her of the thin, scratchy music from an old-fashioned phonograph that she sometimes heard across the lake where she spent her summers. She waited until the waltz had finished, expecting an explanation of the recording, but there was none. The music was followed by silence, and then the plaintive and scratchy record was repeated. She turned the dial and got a satisfactory burst of Caucasian music—the thump of bare feet in the dust and the rattle of coin jewelry—but in the background she could hear the ringing of bells and a confusion of voices. Her children came home from school then, and she turned off the radio and went to the nursery.

When Jim came home that night, he was tired, and he took a bath and changed his clothes. Then he joined Irene in the living room. He had just turned on the radio when the maid announced dinner, so he left it on, and he and Irene went to the table.

Jim was too tired to make even a pretense of sociability, and there was nothing about the dinner to hold Irene's interest, so her attention wandered from the food to the deposits of silver polish on the candlesticks and from there to the music in the other room. She listened for a few minutes to a Chopin prelude and then was surprised to hear a man's voice break in. "For Christ's sake, Kathy," he said, "do you always have to play the piano when I get home?" The music stopped abruptly. "It's the only chance I have," a woman said. "I'm at the office all day." "So am I," the man said. He added something obscene about an upright piano, and slammed a door. The passionate and melancholy music began again.

"Did you hear that?" Irene asked.

"What?" Jim was eating his dessert.

"The radio. A man said something while the music was still going on—something dirty."

"It's probably a play."

"I don't think it *is* a play," Irene said.

They left the table and took their coffee into the living room. Irene asked Jim to try another station. He turned the knob. "Have you seen my garters?" a man asked. "Button me up," a woman said. "Have you seen my garters?" the man said again. "Just button me up and I'll find your garters," the woman said. Jim shifted to another station. "I wish you wouldn't leave apple cores in the ashtrays," a man said. "I hate the smell."

"This is strange," Jim said.

"Isn't it?" Irene said.

Jim turned the knob again. " 'On the coast of Coromandel where the early pumpkins blow,' " a woman with a pronounced English accent said, " 'in the middle of the woods lived the Yonghy-Bonghy-Bò. Two old chairs, and half a candle, one old jug without a handle . . .' "

"My God!" Irene cried. "That's the Sweeneys' nurse."

" 'These were all his worldly goods,' " the British voice continued.

"Turn that thing off," Irene said. "Maybe they can hear *us*." Jim switched the radio off. "That was Miss Armstrong, the Sweeneys' nurse," Irene said. "She must be reading to the little girl. They live in 17-B. I've talked with Miss Armstrong in the Park. I know her voice very well. We must be getting other people's apartments."

"That's impossible," Jim said.

"Well, that was the Sweeneys' nurse," Irene said hotly. "I know her voice. I know it very well. I'm wondering if they can hear us."

Jim turned the switch. First from a distance and then nearer, nearer, as if borne on the wind, came the pure accents of the Sweeneys' nurse again: " '*Lady Jingly! Lady Jingly!*' " she said, " '*sitting where the pumpkins blow, will you come and be my wife?* said the Yonghy-Bonghy-Bò . . .' "

Jim went over to the radio and said "Hello" loudly into the speaker.

" '*I am tired of living singly,*' " the nurse went on, " '*on this coast so wild and shingly, I'm a-weary of my life; if you'll come and be my wife, quite serene would be my life . . . .*' "

"I guess she can't hear us," Irene said. "Try something else."

Jim turned to another station, and the living room was filled with the uproar of a cocktail party that had overshot its mark. Someone was playing the piano and singing the "Whiffenpoof Song," and the voices that surrounded the piano were vehement and happy. "Eat some more sandwiches," a woman shrieked. There were screams of laughter and a dish of some sort crashed to the floor.

"Those must be the Fullers, in 11-E," Irene said. "I knew they were giving a party this afternoon. I saw her in the liquor store. Isn't this too divine? Try something else. See if you can get those people in 18-C."

The Westcotts overheard that evening a monologue on salmon fishing in Canada, a bridge game, running comments on home movies of what had apparently been a fortnight at Sea Island, and a bitter family quarrel about an overdraft at the bank. They turned off their radio at midnight and went to bed, weak with laughter. Sometime in the night, their son began to call for a glass of water and Irene got one and took it to his room. It was very early. All the lights in the neighborhood were extinguished, and from the boy's window she could see the empty street. She went into the living room and tried the radio. There was some faint coughing, a moan, and then a man spoke. "Are you all right, darling?" he asked. "Yes," a woman said wearily. "Yes, I'm all right, I guess," and then she added with great feeling, "But, you know, Charlie, I don't feel like myself any more. Sometimes there are about fifteen or twenty minutes in the week when I feel like myself. I don't like to go to another doctor, because the doctor's bills are so awful already, but I just don't feel like myself, Charlie. I just never feel like myself." They were not young, Irene thought. She guessed from the timbre of their voices that they were middle-aged. The restrained melancholy of the dialogue and the draft from the bedroom window made her shiver, and she went back to bed.

The following morning, Irene cooked breakfast for the family—the maid didn't come up from her room in the basement until ten—braided her daughter's hair, and waited at the door until her children and her husband had been carried away in the elevator. Then she went into the living room and tried the radio. "I don't want to go to school," a child screamed. "I hate school. I won't go to school. I hate school." "You will go to school," an enraged woman said. "We paid eight hundred dollars to get you into that school and you'll go if it kills you." The next number on the dial produced the worn record of the "Missouri Waltz." Irene shifted the control and invaded the privacy of several breakfast tables. She overheard demonstrations of indigestion, carnal love, abysmal vanity, faith, and despair. Irene's life was nearly as simple and sheltered as it appeared to be, and the forthright and sometimes brutal language that came from the loudspeaker that morning astonished and troubled her. She continued to listen until her maid came in. Then she turned off the radio quickly, since this insight, she realized, was a furtive one.

Irene had a luncheon date with a friend that day, and she left her apartment at a little after twelve. There were a number of women in the elevator when it stopped at her floor. She stared at their handsome and impassive faces, their furs, and the cloth flowers in their hats. Which one of them had been to Sea Island? she wondered. Which one had overdrawn her bank account? The elevator stopped at the tenth floor and a woman with a pair of

Skye terriers joined them. Her hair was rigged high on her head and she wore a mink cape. She was humming the "Missouri Waltz."

Irene had two Martinis at lunch, and she looked searchingly at her friend and wondered what her secrets were. They had intended to go shopping after lunch, but Irene excused herself and went home. She told the maid that she was not to be disturbed; then she went into the living room, closed the doors, and switched on the radio. She heard, in the course of the afternoon, the halting conversation of a woman entertaining her aunt, the hysterical conclusion of a luncheon party, and a hostess briefing her maid about some cocktail guests. "Don't give the best Scotch to anyone who hasn't white hair," the hostess said. "See if you can get rid of that liver paste before you pass those hot things, and could you lend me five dollars? I want to tip the elevator man."

As the afternoon waned, the conversations increased in intensity. From where Irene sat, she could see the open sky above the East River. There were hundreds of clouds in the sky, as though the south wind had broken the winter into pieces and were blowing it north, and on her radio she could hear the arrival of cocktail guests and the return of children and businessmen from their schools and offices. "I found a good-sized diamond on the bathroom floor this morning," a woman said. "It must have fallen out of that bracelet Mrs. Dunston was wearing last night." "We'll sell it," a man said. "Take it down to the jeweler on Madison Avenue and sell it. Mrs. Dunston won't know the difference, and we could use a couple of hundred bucks . . ." " 'Oranges and lemons, say the bells of St. Clement's,' " the Sweeneys' nurse sang. " 'Halfpence and farthings, say the bells of St. Martin's. When will you pay me? say the bells at old Bailey . . .' " "It's not a hat," a woman cried, and at her back roared a cocktail party. "It's not a hat, it's a love affair. That's what Walter Florell said. He said it's not a hat, it's a love affair," and then, in a lower voice, the same woman added, "Talk to somebody, for Christ's sake, honey, talk to somebody. If she catches you standing here not talking to anybody, she'll take us off her invitation list, and I love these parties."

The Westcotts were going out for dinner that night, and when Jim came home, Irene was dressing. She seemed sad and vague, and he brought her a drink. They were dining with friends in the neighborhood, and they walked to where they were going. The sky was broad and filled with light. It was one of those splendid spring evenings that excite memory and desire, and the air that touched their hands and faces felt very soft. A Salvation Army band was on the corner playing "Jesus Is Sweeter." Irene drew on her husband's arm and held him there for a minute, to hear the music. "They're really such nice people, aren't they?" she said. "They have such nice faces. Actually, they're so much nicer than a lot of the people we know." She took a bill from her purse and walked over and dropped it into the tambourine. There was in her face, when she returned to her husband, a look of radiant melancholy that he was not familiar with. And her conduct at the dinner party that night seemed strange to him, too. She interrupted her hostess rudely and stared at the people across the table from her with an intensity for which she would have punished her children.

It was still mild when they walked home from the party, and Irene looked up at the spring stars. " 'How far that little candle throws its beams,' " she exclaimed. " 'So shines a good deed in a naughty world.' " She waited that night until Jim had fallen asleep, and then went into the living room and turned on the radio.

Jim came home at about six the next night. Emma, the maid, let him in, and he had taken off his hat and was taking off his coat when Irene ran into the hall. Her face was shining with tears and her hair was disordered. "Go up to 16-C, Jim!" she screamed. "Don't take off your coat. Go up to 16-C. Mr. Osborn's beating his wife. They've been quarreling since four o'clock, and now he's hitting her. Go up there and stop him."

From the radio in the living room, Jim heard screams, obscenities, and thuds. "You know you don't have to listen to this sort of thing," he said. He strode into the living room and turned the switch. "It's indecent," he said. "It's like looking in windows. You know you don't have to listen to this sort of thing. You can turn it off."

"Oh, it's so horrible, it's so dreadful," Irene was sobbing. "I've been listening all day, and it's so depressing."

"Well, if it's so depressing, why do you listen to it? I bought this damned radio to give you some pleasure," he said. "I paid a great deal of money for it. I thought it might make you happy. I wanted to make you happy."

"Don't, don't, don't, don't quarrel with me," she moaned, and laid her head on his shoulder. "All the others have been quarreling all day. Everybody's been quarreling. They're all worried about money. Mrs. Hutchinson's mother is dying of cancer in Florida and they don't have enough money to send her to the Mayo Clinic. At least, Mr. Hutchinson says they don't have enough money. And some woman in this building is having an affair with the handyman—with that hideous handyman. It's too disgusting. And Mrs. Melville has heart trouble and Mr. Hendricks is going to lose his job in April and Mrs. Hendricks is horrid about the whole thing and that girl who plays the 'Missouri Waltz' is a whore, a common whore, and the elevator man has tuberculosis and Mr. Osborn has been beating Mrs. Osborn." She wailed, she trembled with grief and checked the stream of tears down her face with the heel of her palm.

"Well, why do you have to listen?" Jim asked again. "Why do you have to listen to this stuff if it makes you so miserable?"

"Oh, don't, don't, don't," she cried. "Life is too terrible, too sordid and awful. But we've never been like that, have we, darling? Have we? I mean, we've always been good and decent and loving to one another, haven't we? And we have two children, two beautiful children. Our lives aren't sordid, are they, darling? Are they?" She flung her arms around his neck and drew his face down to hers. "We're happy, aren't we, darling? We are happy, aren't we?"

"Of course we're happy," he said tiredly. He began to surrender his resentment. "Of course we're happy. I'll have that damned radio fixed or taken away tomorrow." He stroked her soft hair. "My poor girl," he said.

"You love me, don't you?" she asked. "And we're not hypercritical or worried about money or dishonest, are we?"

"No, darling," he said.

A man came in the morning and fixed the radio. Irene turned it on cautiously and was happy to hear a California-wine commercial and a recording of Beethoven's Ninth Symphony, including Schiller's "Ode to Joy." She kept the radio on all day and nothing untoward came from the speaker.

A Spanish suite was being played when Jim came home. "Is everything all right?" he asked. His face was pale, she thought. They had some cocktails and went in to dinner to the "Anvil Chorus" from *Il Trovatore.* This was followed by Debussy's "La Mer."

"I paid the bill for the radio today," Jim said. "It cost four hundred dollars. I hope you'll get some enjoyment out of it."

"Oh, I'm sure I will," Irene said.

"Four hundred dollars is a good deal more than I can afford," he went on. "I wanted to get something that you'd enjoy. It's the last extravagance we'll be able to indulge in this year. I see that you haven't paid your clothing bills yet. I saw them on your dressing table." He looked directly at her. "Why did you tell me you'd paid them? Why did you lie to me?"

"I just didn't want you to worry, Jim," she said. She drank some water. "I'll be able to pay my bills out of this month's allowance. There were the slipcovers last month, and that party."

"You've got to learn to handle the money I give you a little more intelligently, Irene," he said. "You've got to understand that we won't have as much money this year as we had last. I had a very sobering talk with Mitchell today. No one is buying anything. We're spending all our time promoting new issues, and you know how long that takes. I'm not getting any younger, you know. I'm thirty-seven. My hair will be gray next year. I haven't done as well as I'd hoped to do. And I don't suppose things will get any better."

"Yes, dear," she said.

"We've got to start cutting down," Jim said. "We've got to think of the children. To be perfectly frank with you, I worry about money a great deal. I'm not at all sure of the future. No one is. If anything should happen to me, there's the insurance, but that wouldn't go very far today. I've worked awfully hard to give you and the children a comfortable life," he said bitterly. "I don't like to see all of my energies, all of my youth, wasted in fur coats and radios and slipcovers and—"

"Please, Jim," she said. "Please. They'll hear us."

"*Who'll hear us?* Emma can't hear us."

"The radio."

"Oh, I'm sick!" he shouted. "I'm sick to death of your apprehensiveness. The radio can't hear us. Nobody can hear us. And what if they can hear us? Who cares?"

Irene got up from the table and went into the living room. Jim went to the door and shouted at her from there. "Why are you so Christly all of a sudden? What's turned you overnight into a convent girl? You stole your mother's jewelry before they probated her will. You never gave your sister a cent of that money that was intended for her—not even when she needed it. You made Grace Howland's life miserable, and where was all your piety and your virtue when you went to that abortionist? I'll never forget how cool you were. You packed your bag and went off to have that child murdered as if you were going to Nassau. If you'd had any reasons, if you'd had any good reasons—"

Irene stood for a minute before the hideous cabinet, disgraced and sickened, but she held her hand on the switch before she extinguished the music and the voices, hoping that the instrument might speak to her kindly, that she might hear the Sweeneys' nurse. Jim continued to shout at her from the door. The voice on the radio was suave and noncommittal. "An early-morning railroad disaster in Tokyo," the loudspeaker said, "killed twenty-nine people. A fire in a Catholic hospital near Buffalo for the care of blind children was extinguished early this morning by nuns. The temperature is forty-seven. The humidity is eighty-nine."

May Day

F. Scott Fitzgerald (1896–1940)

F. Scott Fitzgerald was born in St. Paul, Minnesota. He attended Princeton University, and later, in both his writing and lifestyle, went on to epitomize the glitter and fast living of the 1920s "Jazz Age." He is renowned for his brilliant invocations of 1920s mood and spirit and for the way in which he objectively portrayed this age while simultaneously immersing himself in it. The notion of aspiration in spite of inherent societal cynicism and the illusory nature of the American Dream is key to his works. His novels include *This Side of Paradise* (1920), which is partly autobiographical; *The Beautiful and Damned* (1922); *The Great Gatsby* (1925), his most famous novel; *Tender Is the Night* (1934); and the uncompleted *The Last Tycoon* (1941). Two of his short story collections are *Flappers and Philosophers* (1920) and *Tales of the Jazz Age* (1922).

There had been a war fought and won and the great city of the conquering people was crossed with triumphal arches and vivid with thrown flowers of white, red, and rose. All through the long spring days the returning soldiers marched up the chief highway behind the strump of drums and the joyous, resonant wind of the brasses, while merchants and clerks left their bickerings and figurings and, crowding to the windows, turned their white-bunched faces gravely upon the passing battalions.

Never had there been such splendor in the great city, for the victorious war had brought plenty in its train, and the merchants had flocked thither from the South and West with their households to taste of all the luscious feasts and witness the lavish entertainments prepared—and to buy for their women furs against the next winter and bags of golden mesh and varicolored slippers of silk and silver and rose satin and cloth of gold.

So gaily and noisily were the peace and prosperity impending hymned by the scribes and poets of the conquering people that more and more spenders had gathered from the provinces to drink the wine of excitement, and faster and faster did the merchants dispose of their trinkets and slippers until they sent up a mighty cry for more trinkets and more slippers in order that they might give in barter what was demanded of them. Some of them even flung up their hands helplessly, shouting:

"Alas! I have no more slippers! and alas! I have no more trinkets! May Heaven help me, for I know not what I shall do!"

But no one listened to their great outcry, for the throngs were far too busy—day by day, the foot-soldiers trod jauntily the highway and all exulted because the young men returning were pure and brave, sound of tooth and pink of cheek, and the young women of the land were virgins and comely both of face and of figure.

So during all this time there were many adventures that happened in the great city, and, of these, several—or perhaps one—are here set down.

I

At nine o'clock on the morning of the first of May, 1919, a young man spoke to the room clerk at the Biltmore Hotel, asking if Mr. Philip Dean were registered there, and if so, could he be connected with Mr. Dean's rooms. The inquirer was dressed in a well-cut, shabby suit. He was small, slender, and darkly handsome; his eyes were framed above with unusually long eyelashes and below with the blue semicircle of ill health, this latter effect heightened by an unnatural glow which colored his face like a low, incessant fever.

Mr. Dean was staying there. The young man was directed to a telephone at the side.

After a second his connection was made; a sleepy voice hello'd from somewhere above.

"Mr. Dean?"—this very eagerly—"it's Gordon, Phil. It's Gordon Sterrett. I'm down-stairs. I heard you were in New York and I had a hunch you'd be here."

The sleepy voice became gradually enthusiastic. Well, how was Gordy, old boy! Well, he certainly was surprised and tickled! Would Gordy come right up, for Pete's sake!

A few minutes later Philip Dean, dressed in blue silk pajamas, opened his door and the two young men greeted each other with a half-embarrassed exuberance. They were both about twenty-four, Yale graduates of the year before the war; but there the resemblance stopped abruptly. Dean was blond, ruddy, and rugged under his thin pajamas. Everything about him radiated fitness and bodily comfort. He smiled frequently, showing large and prominent teeth.

"I was going to look you up," he cried enthusiastically. "I'm taking a couple of weeks off. If you'll sit down a sec I'll be right with you. Going to take a shower."

As he vanished into the bathroom his visitor's dark eyes roved nervously around the room, resting for a moment on a great English travelling bag in the corner and on a family of thick silk shirts littered on the chairs amid impressive neckties and soft woollen socks.

Gordon rose and, picking up one of the shirts, gave it a minute examination. It was of very heavy silk, yellow, with a pale blue stripe—and there were nearly a dozen of them. He stared involuntarily at his own shirt-cuffs—they were ragged and linty at the edges and soiled to a faint gray. Dropping the silk shirt, he held his coat-sleeves down and worked the frayed shirt-cuffs up till they were out of sight. Then he went to the mirror and looked at himself with listless, unhappy interest. His tie, of former glory, was faded and thumb-creased—it served no longer to hide the jagged button-holes of his collar. He thought, quite without amusement, that only three years before he had received a scattering vote in the senior elections at college for being the best-dressed man in his class.

Dean emerged from the bathroom polishing his body.

"Saw an old friend of yours last night," he remarked. "Passed her in the lobby and couldn't think of her name to save my neck. That girl you brought up to New Haven senior year."

Gordon started.

"Edith Bradin? That whom you mean?"

" 'At's the one. Damn good looking. She's still sort of a pretty doll—you know what I mean: as if you touched her she'd smear."

He surveyed his shining self complacently in the mirror, smiled faintly, exposing a section of teeth.

"She must be twenty-three anyway," he continued.

"Twenty-two last month," said Gordon absently.

"What? Oh, last month. Well, I imagine she's down for the Gamma Psi dance. Did you know we're having a Yale Gamma Psi dance to-night at Delmonico's? You better come up, Gordy. Half of New Haven'll probably be there. I can get you an invitation."

Draping himself reluctantly in fresh underwear, Dean lit a cigarette and sat down by the open window, inspecting his calves and knees under the morning sunshine which poured into the room.

"Sit down, Gordy," he suggested, "and tell me all about what you've been doing and what you're doing now and everything."

Gordon collapsed unexpectedly upon the bed; lay there inert and spiritless. His mouth, which habitually dropped a little open when his face was in repose, became suddenly helpless and pathetic.

"What's the matter?" asked Dean quickly.

"Oh, God!"

"What's the matter?"

"Every God damn thing in the world," he said miserably. "I've absolutely gone to pieces, Phil. I'm all in."

"Huh?"

"I'm all in." His voice was shaking.

Dean scrutinized him more closely with appraising blue eyes.

"You certainly look all shot."

"I am. I've made a hell of a mess of everything." He paused. "I'd better start at the beginning—or will it bore you?"

"Not at all; go on." There was, however, a hesitant note in

Dean's voice. This trip East had been planned for a holiday—to find Gordon Sterrett in trouble exasperated him a little.

"Go on," he repeated, and then added half under his breath, "Get it over with."

"Well," began Gordon unsteadily, "I got back from France in February, went home to Harrisburg for a month, and then came down to New York to get a job. I got one—with an export company. They fired me yesterday."

"Fired you?"

"I'm coming to that, Phil. I want to tell you frankly. You're about the only man I can turn to in a matter like this. You won't mind if I just tell you frankly, will you, Phil?"

Dean stiffened a bit more. The pats he was bestowing on his knees grew perfunctory. He felt vaguely that he was being unfairly saddled with responsibility; he was not even sure he wanted to be told. Though never surprised at finding Gordon Sterrett in mild difficulty, there was something in this present misery that repelled him and hardened him, even though it excited his curiosity.

"Go on."

"It's a girl."

"Hm." Dean resolved that nothing was going to spoil his trip. If Gordon was going to be depressing, then he'd have to see less of Gordon.

"Her name is Jewel Hudson," went on the distressed voice from the bed. "She used to be 'pure,' I guess, up to about a year ago. Lived here in New York—poor family. Her people are dead now and she lives with an old aunt. You see it was just about the time I met her that everybody began to come back from France in droves—and all I did was to welcome the newly arrived and go on parties with 'em. That's the way it started, Phil, just from being glad to see everybody and having them glad to see me."

"You ought to've had more sense."

"I know," Gordon paused, and then continued listlessly. "I'm on my own now, you know, and Phil, I can't stand being poor. Then came this darn girl. She sort of fell in love with me for a while and, though I never intended to get so involved, I'd always seem to run into her somewhere. You can imagine the sort of work I was doing for those exporting people—of course, I always intended to draw; do illustrating for magazines; there's a pile of money in it."

"Why didn't you? You've got to buckle down if you want to make good," suggested Dean with cold formalism.

"I tried, a little, but my stuff's crude. I've got talent, Phil; I can draw—but I just don't know how. I ought to go to art school and I can't afford it. Well, things came to a crisis about a week ago. Just as I was down to about my last dollar this girl began bothering me. She wants some money; claims she can make trouble for me if she doesn't get it."

"Can she?"

"I'm afraid she can. That's one reason I lost my job—she kept calling up the office all the time, and that was sort of the last straw down there. She's got a letter all written to send to my family. Oh, she's got me, all right. I've got to have some money for her."

There was an awkward pause. Gordon lay very still, his hands clenched by his side.

"I'm all in," he continued, his voice trembling. "I'm half crazy, Phil. If I hadn't known you were coming East, I think I'd have killed myself. I want you to lend me three hundred dollars."

Dean's hands, which had been patting his bare ankles, were suddenly quiet—and the curious uncertainty playing between the two became taut and strained.

After a second Gordon continued:

"I've bled the family until I'm ashamed to ask for another nickel."

Still Dean made no answer.

"Jewel says she's got to have two hundred dollars."

"Tell her where she can go."

"Yes, that sounds easy, but she's got a couple of drunken letters I wrote her. Unfortunately she's not at all the flabby sort of person you'd expect."

Dean made an expression of distaste.

"I can't stand that sort of woman. You ought to have kept away."

"I know," admitted Gordon wearily.

"You've got to look at things as they are. If you haven't got money you've got to work and stay away from women."

"That's easy for you to say," began Gordon, his eyes narrowing. "You've got all the money in the world."

"I most certainly have not. My family keep darn close tab on what I spend. Just because I have a little leeway I have to be extra careful not to abuse it."

He raised the blind and let in a further flood of sunshine.

"I'm no prig, Lord knows," he went on deliberately. "I like pleasure—and I like a lot of it on a vacation like this, but you're—you're in awful shape. I never heard you talk just this way before. You seem to be sort of bankrupt—morally as well as financially."

"Don't they usually go together?"

Dean shook his head impatiently.

"There's a regular aura about you that I don't understand. It's a sort of evil."

"It's an air of worry and poverty and sleepless nights," said Gordon, rather defiantly.

"I don't know."

"Oh, I admit I'm depressing. I depress myself. But, my God, Phil, a week's rest and a new suit and some ready money and I'd be like—like I was. Phil, I can draw like a streak, and you know it. But half the time I haven't had the money to buy decent drawing materials—and I can't draw when I'm tired and discouraged and all in. With a little ready money I can take a few weeks off and get started."

"How do I know you wouldn't use it on some other woman?"

"Why rub it in?" said Gordon quietly.

"I'm not rubbing it in. I hate to see you this way."

"Will you lend me the money, Phil?"

"I can't decide right off. That's a lot of money and it'll be darn inconvenient for me."

"It'll be hell for me if you can't—I know I'm whining, and it's all my own fault but—that doesn't change it."

"When could you pay it back?"

This was encouraging. Gordon considered. It was probably wisest to be frank.

"Of course, I could promise to send it back next month, but—I'd better say three months. Just as soon as I start to sell drawings."

"How do I know you'll sell any drawings?"

A new hardness in Dean's voice sent a faint chill of doubt over Gordon. Was it possible that he wouldn't get the money?

"I supposed you had a little confidence in me."

"I did have—but when I see you like this I begin to wonder."

"Do you suppose if I wasn't at the end of my rope I'd come to you like this? Do you think I'm enjoying it?" He broke off and bit his lip, feeling that he had better subdue the rising anger in his voice. After all, he was the suppliant.

"You seem to manage it pretty easily," said Dean angrily. "You put me in the position where, if I don't lend it to you, I'm a sucker—oh, yes, you do. And let me tell you it's no easy thing for me to get hold of three hundred dollars. My income isn't so big but that a slice like that won't play the deuce with it."

He left his chair and began to dress, choosing his clothes carefully. Gordon stretched out his arms and clenched the edges of the bed, fighting back a desire to cry out. His head was splitting and whirring, his mouth was dry and bitter and he could feel the fever in his blood resolving itself into innumerable regular counts like a slow dripping from a roof.

Dean tied his tie precisely, brushed his eyebrows, and removed a piece of tobacco from his teeth with solemnity. Next he filled his cigarette case, tossed the empty box thoughtfully into the waste basket, and settled the case in his vest pocket.

"Had breakfast?" he demanded.

"No; I don't eat it any more."

"Well, we'll go out and have some. We'll decide about that money later. I'm sick of the subject. I came East to have a good time.

"Let's go over to the Yale Club," he continued moodily, and then added with an implied reproof: "You've given up your job. You've got nothing else to do."

"I'd have a lot to do if I had a little money," said Gordon pointedly.

"Oh, for Heaven's sake drop the subject for a while! No point in glooming on my whole trip. Here, here's some money."

He took a five-dollar bill from his wallet and tossed it over to Gordon, who folded it carefully and put it in his pocket. There was an added spot of color in his cheeks, an added glow that was not fever. For an instant before they turned to go out their eyes met and in that instant each found something that made him lower his own glance quickly. For in that instant they quite suddenly and definitely hated each other.

II

Fifth Avenue and Forty-fourth Street swarmed with the noon crowd. The wealthy, happy sun glittered in transient gold through the thick windows of the smart shops, lighting upon mesh bags and purses and strings of pearls in gray velvet cases; upon gaudy feather fans of many colors; upon the laces and silks of expensive dresses; upon the bad paintings and the fine period furniture in the elaborate show rooms of interior decorators.

Working-girls, in pairs and groups and swarms, loitered by these windows, choosing their future boudoirs from some resplendent display which included even a man's silk pajamas laid domestically across the bed. They stood in front of the jewelry stores and picked out their engagement rings, and their wedding rings and their platinum wrist watches, and then drifted on to inspect the feather fans and opera cloaks; meanwhile digesting the sandwiches and sundaes they had eaten for lunch.

All through the crowd were men in uniform, sailors from the great fleet anchored in the Hudson, soldiers with divisional insignia from Massachusetts to California, wanting fearfully to be noticed, and finding the great city thoroughly fed up with soldiers unless they were nicely massed into pretty formations and uncomfortable under the weight of a pack and rifle.

Through this medley Dean and Gordon wandered; the former interested, made alert by the display of humanity at its frothiest and gaudiest; the latter reminded of how often he had been one of the crowd, tired, casually fed, overworked, and dissipated. To Dean the struggle was significant, young, cheerful; to Gordon it was dismal, meaningless, endless.

In the Yale Club they met a group of their former classmates who greeted the visiting Dean vociferously. Sitting in a semicircle of lounges and great chairs, they had a highball all around.

Gordon found the conversation tiresome and interminable. They lunched together *en masse,* warmed with liquor as the afternoon began. They were all going to the Gamma Psi dance that night—it promised to be the best party since the war.

"Edith Bradin's coming," said some one to Gordon. "Didn't she used to be an old flame of yours? Aren't you both from Harrisburg?"

"Yes." He tried to change the subject. "I see her brother occasionally. He's sort of a socialistic nut. Runs a paper or something here in New York."

"Not like his gay sister, eh?" continued his eager informant. "Well, she's coming to-night with a junior named Peter Himmel."

Gordon was to meet Jewel Hudson at eight o'clock—he had promised to have some money for her. Several times he glanced nervously at his wrist watch. At four, to his relief, Dean rose and announced that he was going over to Rivers Brothers to buy some collars and ties. But as they left the Club another of the party joined them, to Gordon's great dismay. Dean was in a jovial mood now, happy, expectant of the evening's party, faintly hilarious. Over in Rivers' he chose a dozen neckties, selecting each one after long consultations with the other man. Did he think narrow ties were coming back? And wasn't it a shame that Rivers couldn't get any more Welsh Margotson collars? There never was a collar like the "Covington."

Gordon was in something of a panic. He wanted the money immediately. And he was now inspired also with a vague idea of attending the Gamma Psi dance. He wanted to see Edith—Edith whom he hadn't met since one romantic night at the Harrisburg Country Club just before he went to France. The affair had died, drowned in the turmoil of the war and quite forgotten in the arabesque of these three months, but a picture of her, poignant, debonair, immersed in her own inconsequential chatter, recurred to him unexpectedly and brought a hundred memories with it. It was Edith's face that he had cherished through college with a sort of detached yet affectionate admiration. He had loved to draw her—around his room had been a dozen sketches of her—playing golf, swimming—he could draw her pert, arresting profile with his eyes shut.

They left Rivers' at five-thirty and paused for a moment on the sidewalk.

"Well," said Dean genially, "I'm all set now. Think I'll go back to the hotel and get a shave, haircut, and massage."

"Good enough," said the other man, "I think I'll join you."

Gordon wondered if he was to be beaten after all. With difficulty he restrained himself from turning to the man and snarling out, "Go on away, damn you!" In despair he suspected that perhaps Dean had spoken to him, was keeping him along in order to avoid a dispute about the money.

They went into the Biltmore—a Biltmore alive with girls—mostly from the West and South, the stellar débutantes of many cities gathered for the dance of a famous fraternity of a famous university. But to Gordon they were faces in a dream. He gathered together his forces for a last appeal, was about to come out with he knew not what, when Dean suddenly excused himself to the other man and taking Gordon's arm led him aside.

"Gordy," he said quickly, "I've thought the whole thing over carefully and I've decided that I can't lend you that money. I'd like to oblige you, but I don't feel I ought to—it'd put a crimp in me for a month."

Gordon, watching him dully, wondered why he had never before noticed how much those upper teeth projected.

"—I'm mighty sorry, Gordon," continued Dean, "but that's the way it is."

He took out his wallet and deliberately counted out seventy-five dollars in bills.

"Here," he said, holding them out, "here's seventy-five; that makes eighty all together. That's all the actual cash I have with me, besides what I'll actually spend on the trip."

Gordon raised his clenched hand automatically, opened it as though it were a tongs he was holding, and clenched it again on the money.

"I'll see you at the dance," continued Dean. "I've got to get along to the barber shop."

"So-long," said Gordon in a strained and husky voice.

"So-long."

Dean began to smile, but seemed to change his mind. He nodded briskly and disappeared.

But Gordon stood there, his handsome face awry with distress, the roll of bills clenched tightly in his hand. Then, blinded by sudden tears, he stumbled clumsily down the Biltmore steps.

III

About nine o'clock of the same night two human beings came out of a cheap restaurant in Sixth Avenue. They were ugly, ill-nourished, devoid of all except the very lowest form of intelligence, and without even that animal exuberance that in itself brings color into life; they were lately vermin-ridden, cold, and hungry in a dirty town of a strange land; they were poor, friendless; tossed as driftwood from their births, they would be tossed as driftwood to their deaths. They were dressed in the uniform of the United States Army, and on the shoulder of each was the insignia of a drafted division from New Jersey, landed three days before.

The taller of the two was named Carrol Key, a name hinting that in his veins, however thinly diluted by generations of degeneration, ran blood of some potentiality. But one could stare endlessly at the long, chinless face, the dull, watery eyes, and high cheek-bones, without finding a suggestion of either ancestral worth or native resourcefulness.

His companion was swart and bandy-legged, with rat-eyes and a much-broken hooked nose. His defiant air was obviously a pretense, a weapon of protection borrowed from that world of snarl and snap, of physical bluff and physical menace, in which he had always lived. His name was Gus Rose.

Leaving the café they sauntered down Sixth Avenue, wielding toothpicks with great gusto and complete detachment.

"Where to?" asked Rose, in a tone which implied that he would not be surprised if Key suggested the South Sea Islands.

"What you say we see if we can getta holda some liquor?" Prohibition was not yet. The ginger in the suggestion was caused by the law forbidding the selling of liquor to soldiers.

Rose agreed enthusiastically.

"I got an idea," continued Key, after a moment's thought, "I got a brother somewhere."

"In New York?"

"Yeah. He's an old fella." He meant that he was an elder brother. "He's a waiter in a hash joint."

"Maybe he can get us some."

"I'll say he can!"

"B'lieve me, I'm goin' to get this darn uniform off me tomorra. Never get me in it again, neither. I'm goin' to get me some regular clothes."

"Say, maybe I'm not."

As their combined finances were something less than five dollars, this intention can be taken largely as a pleasant game of words, harmless and consoling. It seemed to please both of them, however, for they reinforced it with chuckling and mention of personages high in biblical circles, adding such further emphasis as "Oh, boy!" "You know!" and "I'll say so!" repeated many times over.

The entire mental pabulum of these two men consisted of an offended nasal comment extended through the years upon the institution—army, business, or poorhouse—which kept them alive, and toward their immediate superior in that institution. Until that very morning the institution had been the "government" and the immediate superior had been the "Cap'n"—from these two they had glided out and were now in the vaguely uncomfortable state before they should adopt their next bondage. They were uncertain, resentful, and somewhat ill at ease. This they hid by pretending an elaborate relief at being out of the army, and by assuring each other that military discipline should never again rule their stubborn, liberty-loving wills. Yet, as a matter of fact, they would have felt more at home in a prison than in this new-found and unquestionable freedom.

Suddenly Key increased his gait. Rose, looking up and following his glance, discovered a crowd that was collecting fifty yards down the street. Key chuckled and began to run in the direction of the crowd; Rose thereupon also chuckled and his short bandy legs twinkled beside the long, awkward strides of his companion.

Reaching the outskirts of the crowd they immediately became an indistinguishable part of it. It was composed of ragged civilians somewhat the worse for liquor, and of soldiers representing many divisions and many stages of sobriety, all clustered around a gesticulating little Jew with long black whiskers, who was waving his arms and delivering an excited but succinct harangue. Key and Rose, having wedged themselves into the approximate parquet, scrutinized him with acute suspicion, as his words penetrated their common consciousness.

"—What have you got outa the war?" he was crying fiercely. "Look arounja, look arounja! Are you rich? Have you got a lot of money offered you?—no; you're lucky if you're alive and got both your legs; you're lucky if you came back an' find your wife ain't gone off with some other fella that had the money to buy himself out of the war! That's when you're lucky! Who got anything out of it except J. P. Morgan an' John D. Rockerfeller?"

At this point the little Jew's oration was interrupted by the hostile impact of a fist upon the point of his bearded chin and he toppled backward to a sprawl on the pavement.

"God damn Bolsheviki!" cried the big soldier-blacksmith who had delivered the blow. There was a rumble of approval, the crowd closed in nearer.

The Jew staggered to his feet, and immediately went down again before a half-dozen reaching-in fists. This time he stayed down, breathing heavily, blood oozing from his lip where it was cut within and without.

There was a riot of voices, and in a minute Rose and Key found themselves flowing with the jumbled crowd down Sixth Avenue under the leadership of a thin civilian in a slouch hat and the brawny soldier who had summarily ended the oration. The crowd had marvellously swollen to formidable proportions and a stream of more non-committal citizens followed it along the sidewalks lending their moral support by intermittent huzzas.

"Where we goin'?" yelled Key to the man nearest him.

His neighbor pointed up to the leader in the slouch hat.

"That guy knows where there's a lot of 'em! We're goin' to show 'em!"

"We're goin' to show 'em!" whispered Key delightedly to Rose, who repeated the phrase rapturously to a man on the other side.

Down Sixth Avenue swept the procession, joined here and there by soldiers and marines, and now and then by civilians, who came up with the inevitable cry that they were just out of the army themselves, as if presenting it as a card of admission to a newly formed Sporting and Amusement Club.

Then the procession swerved down a cross street and headed for Fifth Avenue and the word filtered here and there that they were bound for a Red meeting at Tolliver Hall.

"Where is it?"

The question went up the line and a moment later the answer floated back. Tolliver Hall was down on Tenth Street. There was a bunch of other sojers who was goin' to break it up and was down there now!

But Tenth Street had a faraway sound and at the word a general groan went up and a score of the procession dropped out. Among these were Rose and Key, who slowed down to a saunter and let the more enthusiastic sweep on by.

"I'd rather get some liquor," said Key as they halted and made their way to the sidewalk amid cries of "Shell hole!" and "Quitters!"

"Does your brother work around here?" asked Rose, assuming the air of one passing from the superficial to the eternal.

"He oughta," replied Key. "I ain't seen him for a coupla years. I been out to Pennsylvania since. Maybe he don't work at night anyhow. It's right along here. He can get us some o'right if he ain't gone."

They found the place after a few minutes' patrol of the street—a shoddy tablecloth restaurant between Fifth Avenue and Broadway. Here Key went inside to inquire for his brother George, while Rose waited on the sidewalk.

"He ain't here no more," said Key emerging. "He's a waiter up to Delmonico's."

Rose nodded wisely, as if he'd expected as much. One should not be surprised at a capable man changing jobs occasionally. He knew a waiter once—there ensued a long conversation as they walked as to whether waiters made more in actual wages than in tips—it was decided that it depended on the social tone of the joint wherein the waiter labored. After having given each other vivid pictures of millionaires dining at Delmonico's and throwing away fifty-dollar bills after their first quart of champagne, both men thought privately of becoming waiters. In fact, Key's narrow brow was secreting a resolution to ask his brother to get him a job.

"A waiter can drink up all the champagne those fellas leave in bottles," suggested Rose with some relish, and then added as an afterthought, "Oh, boy!"

By the time they reached Delmonico's it was half past ten, and they were surprised to see a stream of taxis driving up to the door one after the other and emitting marvelous, hatless young ladies, each one attended by a stiff young gentleman in evening clothes.

"It's a party," said Rose with some awe. "Maybe we better not go in. He'll be busy."

"No, he won't. He'll be o'right."

After some hesitation they entered what appeared to them to be the least elaborate door and, indecision falling upon them immediately, stationed themselves nervously in an inconspicuous corner of the small dining-room in which they found themselves. They took off their caps and held them in their hands. A cloud of gloom fell upon them and both started when a door at one end of the room crashed open, emitting a comet-like waiter who streaked across the floor and vanished through another door on the other side.

There had been three of these lightning passages before the seekers mustered the acumen to hail a waiter. He turned, looked at them suspiciously, and then approached with soft, catlike steps, as if prepared at any moment to turn and flee.

"Say," began Key, "say, do you know my brother? He's a waiter here."

"His name is Key," annotated Rose.

Yes, the waiter knew Key. He was up-stairs, he thought. There was a big dance going on in the main ballroom. He'd tell him.

Ten minutes later George Key appeared and greeted his brother with the utmost suspicion; his first and most natural thought being that he was going to be asked for money.

George was tall and weak chinned, but there his resemblance to his brother ceased. The waiter's eyes were not dull, they were alert and twinkling, and his manner was suave, in-door, and faintly superior. They exchanged formalities. George was married and had three children. He seemed fairly interested, but not impressed by the news that Carrol had been abroad in the army. This disappointed Carrol.

"George," said the younger brother, these amenities having been disposed of, "we want to get some booze, and they won't sell us none. Can you get us some?"

George considered.

"Sure. Maybe I can. It may be half an hour, though."

"All right," agreed Carrol, "we'll wait."

At this Rose started to sit down in a convenient chair, but was hailed to his feet by the indignant George.

"Hey! Watch out, you! Can't sit down here! This room's all set for a twelve o'clock banquet."

"I ain't goin' to hurt it," said Rose resentfully. "I been through the delouser."

"Never mind," said George sternly, "if the head waiter seen me here talkin' he'd romp all over me."

"Oh."

The mention of the head waiter was full explanation to the other two; they fingered their overseas caps nervously and waited for a suggestion.

"I tell you," said George, after a pause, "I got a place you can wait; you just come here with me."

They followed him out the far door, through a deserted pantry and up a pair of dark winding stairs, emerging finally into a small room chiefly furnished by piles of pails and stacks of scrubbing brushes, and illuminated by a single dim electric light. There he left them, after soliciting two dollars and agreeing to return in half an hour with a quart of whiskey.

"George is makin' money, I bet," said Key gloomily as he seated himself on an inverted pail. "I bet he's making fifty dollars a week."

Rose nodded his head and spat.

"I bet he is, too."

"What'd he say the dance was of?"

"A lot of college fellas. Yale College."

They both nodded solemnly at each other.

"Wonder where that crowda sojers is now?"

"I don't know. I know that's too damn long to walk for me."

"Me too. You don't catch me walkin' that far."

Ten minutes later restlessness seized them.

"I'm goin' to see what's out here," said Rose, stepping cautiously toward the other door.

It was a swinging door of green baize and he pushed it open a cautious inch.

"See anything?"

For answer Rose drew in his breath sharply.

"Doggone! Here's some liquor I'll say!"

"Liquor?"

Key joined Rose at the door, and looked eagerly.

"I'll tell the world that's liquor," he said, after a moment of concentrated gazing.

It was a room about twice as large as the one they were in—and in it was prepared a radiant feast of spirits. There were long walls of alternating bottles set along two white covered tables; whiskey, gin, brandy, French and Italian vermouths, and orange juice, not to mention an array of syphons and two great empty punch bowls. The room was as yet uninhabited.

"It's for this dance they're just starting," whispered Key; "hear the violins playin'? Say, boy, I wouldn't mind havin' a dance."

They closed the door softly and exchanged a glance of mutual comprehension. There was no need of feeling each other out.

"I'd like to get my hands on a coupla those bottles," said Rose emphatically.

"Me too."

"Do you suppose we'd get seen?"

Key considered.

"Maybe we better wait till they start drinkin' 'em. They got 'em all laid out now, and they know how many of them there are."

They debated this point for several minutes. Rose was all for getting his hands on a bottle now and tucking it under his coat before any one came into the room. Key, however, advocated caution. He was afraid he might get his brother in trouble. If they waited till some of the bottles were opened it'd be all right to take one, and everybody'd think it was one of the college fellas.

While they were still engaged in argument George Key hurried through the room and, barely grunting at them, disappeared by way of the green baize door. A minute later they heard several corks pop, and then the sound of cracking ice and splashing liquid. George was mixing the punch.

The soldiers exchanged delighted grins.

"Oh, boy!" whispered Rose.

George reappeared.

"Just keep low, boys," he said quickly. "I'll have your stuff for you in five minutes."

He disappeared through the door by which he had come.

As soon as his footsteps receded down the stairs, Rose, after a cautious look, darted into the room of delights and reappeared with a bottle in his hand.

"Here's what I say," he said, as they sat radiantly digesting their first drink. "We'll wait till he comes up, and we'll ask him if we can't just stay here and drink what he brings us—see. We'll tell him we haven't got any place to drink it—see. Then we can sneak in there whenever there ain't nobody in that there room and tuck a bottle under our coats. We'll have enough to last us a coupla days—see?"

"Sure," agreed Key enthusiastically. "Oh, boy! And if we want to we can sell it to sojers any time we want to."

They were silent for a moment thinking rosily of this idea. Then Key reached up and unhooked the collar of his O. D. coat.

"It's hot in here, ain't it?"

Rose agreed earnestly.

"Hot as hell."

IV

She was still quite angry when she came out of the dressing-room and crossed the intervening parlor of politeness that opened onto the hall—angry not so much at the actual happening which was, after all, the merest commonplace of her social existence, but because it had occurred on this particular night. She had no quarrel with herself. She had acted with that correct mixture of dignity and reticent pity which she always employed. She had succinctly and deftly snubbed him.

It had happened when their taxi was leaving the Biltmore—hadn't gone half a block. He had lifted his right arm awkwardly—she was on his right side—and attempted to settle it snugly around the crimson fur-trimmed opera cloak she wore. This in itself had been a mistake. It was inevitably more graceful for a young man attempting to embrace a young lady of whose acquiescence he was not certain, to first put his far arm around her. It avoided that awkward movement of raising the near arm.

His second *faux pas* was unconscious. She had spent the afternoon at the hairdresser's; the idea of any calamity overtaking her hair was extremely repugnant—yet as Peter made his unfortunate attempt the point of his elbow had just faintly brushed it. That was his second *faux pas*. Two were quite enough.

He had begun to murmur. At the first murmur she had decided that he was nothing but a college boy—Edith was twenty-two, and anyhow, this dance, first of its kind since the war, was reminding her, with the accelerating rhythm of its associations, of something else—of another dance and another man, a man for whom her feelings had been little more than a sad-eyed, adolescent mooniness. Edith Bradin was falling in love with her recollection of Gordon Sterrett.

So she came out of the dressing-room at Delmonico's and stood for a second in the doorway looking over the shoulders of a black dress in front of her at the groups of Yale men who flitted like dignified black moths around the head of the stairs. From the room she had left drifted out the heavy fragrance left by the passage to and fro of many scented young beauties—rich perfumes and the fragile memory-laden dust of fragrant powders. This odor drifting out acquired the tang of cigarette smoke in the hall, and then settled sensuously down the stairs and permeated the ballroom where the Gamma Psi dance was to be held. It was an odor she knew well, exciting, stimulating, restlessly sweet—the odor of a fashionable dance.

She thought of her own appearance. Her bare arms and shoulders were powdered to a creamy white. She knew they looked very soft and would gleam like milk against the black backs that were to silhouette them tonight. The hairdressing had been a success; her reddish mass of hair was piled and crushed and creased to an arrogant marvel of mobile curves. Her lips were finely made of deep carmine; the irises of her eyes were delicate, breakable blue, like china eyes. She was a complete, infinitely delicate, quite perfect thing of beauty, flowing in an even line from a complex coiffure to two small slim feet.

She thought of what she would say to-night at this revel, faintly prestiged already by the sounds of high and low laughter and slippered footsteps, and movements of couples up and down the stairs. She would talk the language she had talked for many years—her line—made up of the current expressions, bits of journalese and college slang strung together into an intrinsic whole, careless, faintly provocative, delicately sentimental. She smiled faintly as she heard a girl sitting on the stairs near her say: "You don't know the half of it, dearie!"

And as she smiled her anger melted for a moment, and closing her eyes she drew in a deep breath of pleasure. She dropped her arms to her side until they were faintly touching the sleek sheath that covered and suggested her figure. She had never felt her own softness so much nor so enjoyed the whiteness of her own arms.

"I smell sweet," she said to herself simply, and then came another thought—"I'm made for love."

She liked the sound of this and thought it again; then in inevitable succession came her new-born riot of dreams about Gordon. The twist of her imagination which, two months before, had disclosed to her her unguessed desire to see him again, seemed now to have been leading up to this dance, this hour.

For all her sleek beauty, Edith was a grave, slow-thinking girl. There was a streak in her of that same desire to ponder, of that adolescent idealism that had turned her brother socialist and pacifist. Henry Bradin had left Cornell, where he had been an instructor in economics, and had come to New York to pour the latest cures for incurable evils into the columns of a radical weekly newspaper.

Edith, less fatuously, would have been content to cure Gordon Sterrett. There was a quality of weakness in Gordon that she wanted to take care of; there was a helplessness in him that she wanted to protect. And she wanted someone she had known a long while, someone who had loved her a long while. She was a little tired; she wanted to get married. Out of a pile of letters, half a dozen pictures and as many memories, and this weariness, she had decided that next time she saw Gordon their relations were going to be changed. She would say something that would change them. There was this evening. This was her evening. All evenings were her evenings.

Then her thoughts were interrupted by a solemn undergraduate with a hurt look and an air of strained formality who presented himself before her and bowed unusually low. It was the man she had come with, Peter Himmel. He was tall and humorous, with horned-rimmed glasses and an air of attractive whimsicality. She suddenly rather disliked him—probably because he had not succeeded in kissing her.

"Well," she began, "are you still furious at me?"

"Not at all."

She stepped forward and took his arm.

"I'm sorry," she said softly. "I don't know why I snapped out that way. I'm in a bum humor to-night for some strange reason. I'm sorry."

"S'all right," he mumbled, "don't mention it."

He felt disagreeably embarrassed. Was she rubbing in the fact of his late failure?

"It was a mistake," she continued, on the same consciously gentle key. "We'll both forget it." For this he hated her.

A few minutes later they drifted out on the floor while the dozen swaying, sighing members of the specially hired jazz orchestra informed the crowded ballroom that "if a saxophone and me are left alone why then two is compan-ee!"

A man with a mustache cut in.

"Hello," he began reprovingly. "You don't remember me."

"I can't just think of your name," she said lightly—"and I know you so well."

"I met you up at—" His voice trailed disconsolately off as a man with very fair hair cut in. Edith murmured a conventional "Thanks, loads—cut in later," to the *inconnu*.

The very fair man insisted on shaking hands enthusiastically. She placed him as one of the numerous Jims of her acquaintance—last name a mystery. She remembered even that he had a peculiar rhythm in dancing and found as they started that she was right.

"Going to be here long?" he breathed confidentially.

She leaned back and looked up at him.

"Couple of weeks."

"Where are you?"

"Biltmore. Call me up some day."

"I mean it," he assured her. "I will. We'll go to tea."

"So do I—Do."

A dark man cut in with intense formality.

"You don't remember me, do you?" he said gravely.

"I should say I do. Your name's Harlan."

"No-ope. Barlow."

"Well, I knew there were two syllables anyway. You're the boy that played the ukulele so well up at Howard Marshall's house party."

"I played—but not——"

A man with prominent teeth cut in. Edith inhaled a slight cloud of whiskey. She liked men to have had something to drink; they were so much more cheerful, and appreciative and complimentary—much easier to talk to.

"My name's Dean, Philip Dean," he said cheerfully. "You don't remember me, I know, but you used to come up to New Haven with a fellow I roomed with senior year, Gordon Sterrett."

Edith looked up quickly.

"Yes, I went up with him twice—to the Pump and Slipper and the Junior prom."

"You've seen him, of course," said Dean carelessly. "He's here to-night. I saw him just a minute ago."

Edith started. Yet she had felt quite sure he would be here.

"Why, no, I haven't——"

A fat man with red hair cut in.

"Hello, Edith," he began.

"Why—hello there——"

She slipped, stumbled lightly.

"I'm sorry, dear," she murmured mechanically.

She had seen Gordon—Gordon very white and listless, leaning against the side of a doorway, smoking and looking into the ballroom. Edith could see that his face was thin and wan—that the hand he raised to his lips with a cigarette was trembling. They were dancing quite close to him now.

"—They invite so darn many extra fellas that you—" the short man was saying.

"Hello, Gordon," called Edith over her partner's shoulder. Her heart was pounding wildly.

His large dark eyes were fixed on her. He took a step in her direction. Her partner turned her away—she heard his voice bleating——

"—but half the stags get lit and leave before long, so——"

Then a low tone at her side.

"May I, please?"

She was dancing suddenly with Gordon; one of his arms was around her; she felt it tighten spasmodically; felt his hand on her back with the fingers spread. Her hand holding the little lace handkerchief was crushed in his.

"Why Gordon," she began breathlessly.

"Hello, Edith."

She slipped again—was tossed forward by her recovery until her face touched the black cloth of his dinner coat. She loved him—she knew she loved him—then for a minute there was silence while a strange feeling of uneasiness crept over her. Something was wrong.

Of a sudden her heart wrenched, and turned over as she realized what it was. He was pitiful and wretched, a little drunk, and miserably tired.

"Oh——" she cried involuntarily.

His eyes looked down at her. She saw suddenly that they were blood-streaked and rolling uncontrollably.

"Gordon," she murmured, "we'll sit down; I want to sit down."

They were nearly in mid-floor, but she had seen two men start toward her from opposite sides of the room, so she halted, seized Gordon's limp hand and led him bumping through the crowd, her mouth tight shut, her face a little pale under her rouge, her eyes trembling with tears.

She found a place high up on the soft-carpeted stairs, and he sat down heavily beside her.

"Well," he began, staring at her unsteadily, "I certainly am glad to see you, Edith."

She looked at him without answering. The effect of this on her was immeasurable. For years she had seen men in various stages of intoxication, from uncles all the way down to chauffeurs, and her feelings had varied from amusement to disgust, but here for the first time she was seized with a new feeling—an unutterable horror.

"Gordon," she said accusingly and almost crying, "you look like the devil."

He nodded. "I've had trouble, Edith."

"Trouble?"

"All sorts of trouble. Don't you say anything to the family, but I'm all gone to pieces. I'm a mess, Edith."

His lower lip was sagging. He seemed scarcely to see her.

"Can't you—can't you," she hesitated, "can't you tell me about it, Gordon? You know I'm always interested in you."

She bit her lip—she had intended to say something stronger, but found at the end that she couldn't bring it out.

Gordon shook his head dully. "I can't tell you. You're a good woman. I can't tell a good woman the story."

"Rot," she said, defiantly. "I think it's a perfect insult to call any one a good woman in that way. It's a slam. You've been drinking, Gordon."

"Thanks." He inclined his head gravely. "Thanks for the information."

"Why do you drink?"

"Because I'm so damn miserable."

"Do you think drinking's going to make it any better?"

"What you doing—trying to reform me?"

"No; I'm trying to help you, Gordon. Can't you tell me about it?"

"I'm in an awful mess. Best thing you can do is to pretend not to know me."

"Why, Gordon?"

"I'm sorry I cut in on you—it's unfair to you. You're pure woman—and all that sort of thing. Here, I'll get some one else to dance with you."

He rose clumsily to his feet, but she reached up and pulled him down beside her on the stairs.

"Here, Gordon. You're ridiculous. You're hurting me. You're acting like a—like a crazy man——"

"I admit it. I'm a little crazy. Something's wrong with me, Edith. There's something left me. It doesn't matter."

"It does, tell me."

"Just that. I was always queer—little bit different from other boys. All right in college, but now it's all wrong. Things have been snapping inside me for four months like little hooks on a dress, and it's about to come off when a few more hooks go. I'm very gradually going loony."

He turned his eyes full on her and began to laugh, and she shrank away from him.

"What *is* the matter?"

"Just me," he repeated. "I'm going loony. This whole place is like a dream to me—this Delmonico's—"

As he talked she saw he had changed utterly. He wasn't at all light and gay and careless—a great lethargy and discouragement had come over him. Revulsion seized her, followed by a faint, surprising boredom. His voice seemed to come out of a great void.

"Edith," he said, "I used to think I was clever, talented, an artist. Now I know I'm nothing. Can't draw, Edith. Don't know why I'm telling you this."

She nodded absently.

"I can't draw, I can't do anything. I'm poor as a church mouse." He laughed, bitterly and rather too loud. "I've become a damn beggar, a leech on my friends. I'm a failure. I'm poor as hell."

Her distaste was growing. She barely nodded this time, waiting for her first possible cue to rise.

Suddenly Gordon's eyes filled with tears.

"Edith," he said, turning to her with what was evidently a strong effort at self-control, "I can't tell you what it means to me to know there's one person left who's interested in me."

He reached out and patted her hand, and involuntarily she drew it away.

"It's mighty fine of you," he repeated.

"Well," she said slowly, looking him in the eye, "any one's always glad to see an old friend—but I'm sorry to see you like this, Gordon."

There was a pause while they looked at each other, and the momentary eagerness in his eyes wavered. She rose and stood looking at him, her face quite expressionless.

"Shall we dance?" she suggested, coolly.

—Love is fragile—she was thinking—but perhaps the pieces are saved, the things that hovered on lips, that might have been said. The new love words, the tendernesses learned, are treasured up for the next lover.

V

Peter Himmel, escort to the lovely Edith, was unaccustomed to being snubbed; having been snubbed, he was hurt and embarrassed, and ashamed of himself. For a matter of two months he had been on special delivery terms with Edith Bradin, and knowing that the one excuse and explanation of the special delivery letter is its value in sentimental correspondence, he had believed himself quite sure of his ground. He searched in vain for any reason why she should have taken this attitude in the matter of a simple kiss.

Therefore when he was cut in on by the man with the mustache he went out into the hall and, making up a sentence, said it over to himself several times. Considerably deleted, this was it:

"Well, if any girl ever led a man on and then jolted him, she did—and she has no kick coming if I go out and get beautifully boiled."

So he walked through the supper room into a small room adjoining it, which he had located earlier in the evening. It was a room in which there were several large bowls of punch flanked by many bottles. He took a seat beside the table which held the bottles.

At the second highball, boredom, disgust, the monotony of time, the turbidity of events, sank into a vague background before which glittering cobwebs formed. Things became reconciled to themselves, things lay quietly on their shelves; the troubles of the day arranged themselves in trim formation and at his curt wish of dismissal, marched off and disappeared. And with the departure of worry came brilliant, permeating symbolism. Edith became a flighty, negligible girl, not to be worried over; rather to be laughed at. She fitted like a figure of his own dream into the surface world forming about him. He himself became in a measure symbolic, a type of the continent bacchanal, the brilliant dreamer at play.

Then the symbolic mood faded and as he sipped his third highball his imagination yielded to the warm glow and he lapsed into a state similar to floating on his back in pleasant water. It was at this point that he noticed that a green baize door near him was open about two inches, and that through the aperture a pair of eyes were watching him intently.

"Hm," murmured Peter calmly.

The green door closed—and then opened again—a bare half inch this time.

"Peek-a-boo," murmured Peter.

The door remained stationary and then he became aware of a series of tense intermittent whispers.

"One guy."

"What's he doin'?"

"He's sittin' lookin'."

"He better beat it off. We gotta get another li'l' bottle."

Peter listened while the words filtered into his consciousness.

"Now this," he thought, "is most remarkable."

He was excited. He was jubilant. He felt that he had stumbled upon a mystery. Affecting an elaborate carelessness he arose and walked around the table—then, turning quickly, pulled open the green door, precipitating Private Rose into the room.

Peter bowed.

"How do you do?" he said.

Private Rose set one foot slightly in front of the other, poised for fight, flight, or compromise.

"How do you do?" repeated Peter politely.

"I'm o'right."

"Can I offer you a drink?"

Private Rose looked at him searchingly, suspecting possible sarcasm.

"O'right," he said finally.

Peter indicated a chair.

"Sit down."

"I got a friend," said Rose, "I got a friend in there." He pointed to the green door.

"By all means let's have him in."

Peter crossed over, opened the door and welcomed in Private Key, very suspicious and uncertain and guilty. Chairs were found and the three took their seats around the punch bowl. Peter gave them each a highball and offered them a cigarette from his case. They accepted both with some diffidence.

"Now," continued Peter easily, "may I ask why you gentlemen prefer to lounge away your leisure hours in a room which is chiefly furnished, as far as I can see, with scrubbing brushes. And when the human race has progressed to the stage where seventeen thousand chairs are manufactured on every day except Sunday—" he paused. Rose and Key regarded him vacantly. "Will you tell me," went on Peter, "why you choose to rest yourselves on articles intended for the transportation of water from one place to another?"

At this point Rose contributed a grunt to the conversation.

"And lastly," finished Peter, "will you tell me why, when you are in a building beautifully hung with enormous candelabra, you prefer to spend these evening hours under one anemic electric light?"

Rose looked at Key; Key looked at Rose. They laughed; they laughed uproariously; they found it was impossible to look at each other without laughing. But they were not laughing with this man—they were laughing at him. To them a man who talked after this fashion was either raving drunk or raving crazy.

"You are Yale men, I presume," said Peter, finishing his highball and preparing another.

They laughed again.

"Na-ah."

"So? I thought perhaps you might be members of that lowly section of the university known as the Sheffield Scientific School."

"Na-ah."

"Hm. Well, that's too bad. No doubt you are Harvard men, anxious to preserve your incognito in this—this paradise of violet blue, as the newspapers say."

"Na-ah," said Key scornfully, "we was just waitin' for somebody."

"Ah," exclaimed Peter, rising and filling their glasses, "very interestin'. Had a date with a scrublady, eh?"

They both denied this indignantly.

"It's all right," Peter reassured them, "don't apologize. A scrublady's as good as any lady in the world. Kipling says 'Any lady and Judy O'Grady under the skin.' "

"Sure," said Key, winking broadly at Rose.

"My case, for instance," continued Peter, finishing his glass. "I got a girl up here that's spoiled. Spoildest darn girl I ever saw. Refused to kiss me; no reason whatsoever. Led me on deliberately to think sure I want to kiss you and then plunk! Threw me over! What's the younger generation comin' to?"

"Say tha's hard luck," said Key—"that's awful hard luck."

"Oh, boy!" said Rose.

"Have another?" said Peter.

"We got in a sort of fight for a while," said Key after a pause, "but it was too far away."

"A fight?—tha's stuff!" said Peter, seating himself unsteadily. "Fight 'em all! I was in the army."

"This was with a Bolshevik fella."

"Tha's stuff!" exclaimed Peter, enthusiastic. "That's what I say! Kill the Bolshevik! Exterminate 'em!"

"We're Americuns," said Rose, implying a sturdy, defiant patriotism.

"Sure," said Peter. "Greatest race in the world! We're all Americuns! Have another."

They had another.

VI

At one o'clock a special orchestra, special even in a day of special orchestras, arrived at Delmonico's, and its members, seating themselves arrogantly around the piano, took up the burden of providing music for the Gamma Psi Fraternity. They were headed by a famous flute-player, distinguished throughout New York for his feat of standing on his head and shimmying with his shoulders while he played the latest jazz on his flute. During his performance the lights were extinguished except for the spotlight on the flute-player and another roving beam that threw flickering shadows and changing kaleidoscopic colors over the massed dancers.

Edith had danced herself into that tired, dreamy state habitual only with débutantes, a state equivalent to the glow of a noble soul after several long highballs. Her mind floated vaguely on the bosom of her music; her partners changed with the unreality of phantoms under the colorful shifting dusk, and to her present coma it seemed as if days had passed since the dance began. She had talked on many fragmentary subjects with many men. She had been kissed once and made love to six times. Earlier in the evening different undergraduates had danced with her, but now, like all the more popular girls there, she had her own entourage—that is, half a dozen gallants had singled her out or were alternating her charms with those of some other chosen beauty; they cut in on her in regular, inevitable succession.

Several times she had seen Gordon—he had been sitting a long time on the stairway with his palm to his head, his dull eyes fixed at an infinite speck on the floor before him, very depressed, he looked, and quite drunk—but Edith each time had averted her glance hurriedly. All that seemed long ago; her mind was passive now, her senses were lulled to trance-like sleep; only her feet danced and her voice talked on in hazy sentimental banter.

But Edith was not nearly so tired as to be incapable of moral indignation when Peter Himmel cut in on her, sublimely and happily drunk. She gasped and looked up at him.

"Why, *Peter!*"

"I'm a li'l' stewed, Edith."

"Why, Peter, you're a *peach,* you are! Don't you think it's a bum way of doing—when you're with me?"

Then she smiled unwillingly, for he was looking at her with owlish sentimentality varied with a silly spasmodic smile.

"Darlin' Edith," he began earnestly, "you know I love you, don't you?"

"You tell it well."

"I love you—and I merely wanted you to kiss me," he added sadly.

His embarrassment, his shame, were both gone. She was a mos' beautiful girl in whole worl'. Mos' beautiful eyes, like stars above. He wanted to 'pologize—firs', for presuming try to kiss her; second, for drinking—but he'd been so discouraged 'cause he had thought she was mad at him—

The red-fat man cut in, and looking up at Edith smiled radiantly.

"Did you bring any one?" she asked.

No. The red-fat man was a stag.

"Well, would you mind—would it be an awful bother for you to—to take me home to-night?" (this extreme diffidence was a charming affectation on Edith's part—she knew that the red-fat man would immediately dissolve into a paroxysm of delight).

"Bother? Why, good Lord, I'd be darn glad to! You know I'd be darn glad to."

"Thanks *loads!* You're awfully sweet."

She glanced at her wrist-watch. It was half-past one. And, as she said "half-past one" to herself, it floated vaguely into her mind that her brother had told her at luncheon that he worked in the office of his newspaper until after one-thirty every evening.

Edith turned suddenly to her current partner.

"What street is Delmonico's on, anyway?"

"Street? Oh, why Fifth Avenue, of course."

"I mean, what cross street?"

"Why—let's see—it's on Forty-fourth Street."

This verified what she had thought. Henry's office must be across the street and just around the corner, and it occurred to her immediately that she might slip over for a moment and surprise him, float in on him, a shimmering marvel in her new crimson opera cloak and "cheer him up." It was exactly the sort of thing Edith revelled in doing—an unconventional, jaunty thing. The idea reached out and gripped at her imagination—after an instant's hesitation she had decided.

"My hair is just about to tumble entirely down," she said pleasantly to her partner; "would you mind if I go and fix it?"

"Not at all."

"You're a peach."

A few minutes later, wrapped in her crimson opera cloak, she flitted down a side-stairs, her cheeks glowing with excitement at her little adventure. She ran by a couple who stood at the door—a weak-chinned waiter and an over-rouged young lady, in hot dispute—and opening the outer door stepped into the warm May night.

VII

The over-rouged young lady followed her with a brief, bitter glance—then turned again to the weak-chinned waiter and took up her argument.

"You better go up and tell him I'm here," she said defiantly, "or I'll go up myself."

"No, you don't!" said George sternly.

The girl smiled sardonically.

"Oh, I don't, don't I? Well, let me tell you I know more college fellas and more of 'em know me, and are glad to take me out on a party, than you ever saw in your whole life."

"Maybe so——"

"Maybe so," she interrupted. "Oh, it's all right for any of 'em like that one that just ran out—God knows where *she* went—it's all right for them that are asked here to come or go as they like—but when I want to see a friend they have some cheap, ham-slinging, bring-me-a-doughnut waiter to stand here and keep me out."

"See here," said the elder Key indignantly, "I can't lose my job. Maybe this fella you're talkin' about doesn't want to see you."

"Oh, he wants to see me all right."

"Anyways, how could I find him in all that crowd?"

"Oh, he'll be there," she asserted confidently. "You just ask anybody for Gordon Sterrett and they'll point him out to you. They all know each other, those fellas."

She produced a mesh bag, and taking out a dollar bill handed it to George.

"Here," she said, "here's a bribe. You find him and give him my message. You tell him if he isn't here in five minutes I'm coming up."

George shook his head pessimistically, considered the question for a moment, wavered violently, and then withdrew.

In less than the allotted time Gordon came down-stairs. He was drunker than he had been earlier in the evening and in a different way. The liquor seemed to have hardened on him like a crust. He was heavy and lurching—almost incoherent when he talked.

" 'Lo, Jewel," he said thickly. "Came right away. Jewel, I couldn't get that money. Tried my best."

"Money nothing!" she snapped. "You haven't been near me for ten days. What's the matter?"

He shook his head slowly.

"Been very low, Jewel. Been sick."

"Why didn't you tell me if you were sick. I don't care about the money that bad. I didn't start bothering you about it at all until you began neglecting me."

Again he shook his head.

"Haven't been neglecting you. Not at all."

"Haven't! You haven't been near me for three weeks, unless you been so drunk you didn't know what you were doing."

"Been sick, Jewel," he repeated, turning his eyes upon her wearily.

"You're well enough to come and play with your society friends here all right. You told me you'd meet me for dinner, and you said you'd have some money for me. You didn't even bother to ring me up."

"I couldn't get any money."

"Haven't I just been saying that doesn't matter? I wanted to see *you,* Gordon, but you seem to prefer your somebody else."

He denied this bitterly.

"Then get your hat and come along," she suggested.

Gordon hesitated—and she came suddenly close to him and slipped her arms around his neck.

"Come on with me, Gordon," she said in a half whisper. "We'll go over to Devineries' and have a drink, and then we can go up to my apartment."

"I can't, Jewel,——"

"You can," she said intensely.

"I'm sick as a dog!"

"Well, then, you oughtn't to stay here and dance."

With a glance around him in which relief and despair were

mingled, Gordon hesitated; then she suddenly pulled him to her and kissed him with soft, pulpy lips.

"All right," he said heavily. "I'll get my hat."

VIII

When Edith came out into the clear blue of the May night she found the Avenue deserted. The windows of the big shops were dark; over their doors were drawn great iron masks until they were only shadowy tombs of the late day's splendor. Glancing down toward Forty-second Street she saw a commingled blur of lights from the all-night restaurants. Over on Sixth Avenue the elevated, a flare of fire, roared across the street between the glimmering parallels of light at the station and streaked along into the crisp dark. But at Forty-fourth Street it was very quiet.

Pulling her cloak close about her Edith darted across the Avenue. She started nervously as a solitary man passed her and said in a hoarse whisper—"Where bound, kiddo?" She was reminded of a night in her childhood when she had walked around the block in her pajamas and a dog had howled at her from a mystery-big back yard.

In a minute she had reached her destination, a two-story, comparatively old building on Forty-fourth, in the upper window of which she thankfully detected a wisp of light. It was bright enough outside for her to make out the sign beside the window—the *New York Trumpet*. She stepped inside a dark hall and after a second saw the stairs in the corner.

Then she was in a long, low room furnished with many desks and hung on all sides with file copies of newspapers. There were only two occupants. They were sitting at different ends of the room, each wearing a green eye-shade and writing by a solitary desk light.

For a moment she stood uncertainly in the doorway, and then both men turned around simultaneously and she recognized her brother.

"Why, Edith!" He rose quickly and approached her in surprise, removing his eye-shade. He was tall, lean, and dark, with black, piercing eyes under very thick glasses. They were far-away eyes that seemed always fixed just over the head of the person to whom he was talking.

He put his hands on her arms and kissed her cheek.

"What is it?" he repeated in some alarm.

"I was at a dance across at Delmonico's, Henry," she said excitedly, "and I couldn't resist tearing over to see you."

"I'm glad you did." His alertness gave way quickly to a habitual vagueness. "You oughtn't to be out alone at night though, ought you?"

The man at the other end of the room had been looking at them curiously, but at Henry's beckoning gesture he approached. He was loosely fat with little twinkling eyes, and, having removed his collar and tie, he gave the impression of a Middle-Western farmer on a Sunday afternoon.

"This is my sister," said Henry. "She dropped in to see me."

"How do you do?" said the fat man, smiling. "My name's Bartholomew, Miss Bradin. I know your brother has forgotten it long ago."

Edith laughed politely.

"Well," he continued, "not exactly gorgeous quarters we have here, are they?"

Edith looked around the room.

"They seem very nice," she replied. "Where do you keep the bombs?"

"The bombs?" repeated Bartholomew, laughing. "That's pretty good—the bombs. Did you hear her, Henry? She wants to know where we keep the bombs. Say, that's pretty good."

Edith swung herself onto a vacant desk and sat dangling her feet over the edge. Her brother took a seat beside her.

"Well," he asked, absent-mindedly, "how do you like New York this trip?"

"Not bad. I'll be over at the Biltmore with the Hoyts until Sunday. Can't you come to luncheon to-morrow?"

He thought a moment.

"I'm especially busy," he objected, "and I hate women in groups."

"All right," she agreed, unruffled. "Let's you and me have luncheon together."

"Very well."

"I'll call for you at twelve."

Bartholomew was obviously anxious to return to his desk, but apparently considered that it would be rude to leave without some parting pleasantry.

"Well"—he began awkwardly.

They both turned to him.

"Well, we—we had an exciting time earlier in the evening."

The two men exchanged glances.

"You should have come earlier," continued Bartholomew, somewhat encouraged. "We had a regular vaudeville."

"Did you really?"

"A serenade," said Henry. "A lot of soldiers gathered down there in the street and began to yell at the sign."

"Why?" she demanded.

"Just a crowd," said Henry, abstractedly. "All crowds have to howl. They didn't have anybody with much initiative in the lead, or they'd probably have forced their way in here and smashed things up."

"Yes," said Bartholomew, turning again to Edith, "you should have been here."

He seemed to consider this a sufficient cue for withdrawal, for he turned abruptly and went back to his desk.

"Are the soldiers all set against the Socialists?" demanded Edith of her brother. "I mean do they attack you violently and all that?"

Henry replaced his eye-shade and yawned.

"The human race has come a long way," he said casually, "but most of us are throw-backs; the soldiers don't know what they want, or what they hate, or what they like. They're used to acting in large bodies, and they seem to have to make demonstrations. So it happens to be against us. There've been riots all over the city to-night. It's May Day, you see."

"Was the disturbance here pretty serious?"

"Not a bit," he said scornfully. "About twenty-five of them stopped in the street about nine o'clock, and began to bellow at the moon."

"Oh"— She changed the subject. "You're glad to see me, Henry?"

"Why, sure."

"You don't seem to be."

"I am."

"I suppose you think I'm a—a waster. Sort of the World's Worst Butterfly."

Henry laughed.

"Not at all. Have a good time while you're young. Why? Do I seem like the priggish and earnest youth?"

"No—" She paused, "—but somehow I began thinking how absolutely different the party I'm on is from—from all your purposes. It seems sort of—of incongruous, doesn't it?—me being at a party like that, and you over here working for a thing that'll make that sort of party impossible ever any more, if your ideas work."

"I don't think of it that way. You're young, and you're acting just as you were brought up to act. Go ahead—have a good time?"

Her feet, which had been idly swinging, stopped and her voice dropped a note.

"I wish you'd—you'd come back to Harrisburg and have a good time. Do you feel sure that you're on the right track——"

"You're wearing beautiful stockings," he interrupted. "What on earth are they?"

"They're embroidered," she replied, glancing down. "Aren't they cunning?" She raised her skirts and uncovered slim, silk-sheathed calves. "Or do you disapprove of silk stockings?"

He seemed slightly exasperated, bent his dark eyes on her piercingly.

"Are you trying to make me out as criticizing you in any way, Edith?"

"Not at all——"

She paused. Bartholomew had uttered a grunt. She turned and saw that he had left his desk and was standing at the window.

"What is it?" demanded Henry.

"People," said Bartholomew, and then after an instant: "Whole jam of them. They're coming from Sixth Avenue."

"People?"

The fat man pressed his nose to the pane.

"Soldiers, by God!" he said emphatically. "I had an idea they'd come back."

Edith jumped to her feet, and running over joined Bartholomew at the window.

"There's a lot of them!" she cried excitedly. "Come here, Henry!"

Henry readjusted his shade, but kept his seat.

"Hadn't we better turn out the lights?" suggested Bartholomew.

"No. They'll go away in a minute."

"They're not," said Edith, peering from the window. "They're not even thinking of going away. There's more of them coming. Look—there's a whole crowd turning the corner of Sixth Avenue."

By the yellow glow and blue shadows of the street lamp she could see that the sidewalk was crowded with men. They were mostly in uniform, some sober, some enthusiastically drunk, and over the whole swept an incoherent clamor and shouting.

Henry rose, and going to the window exposed himself as a long silhouette against the office lights. Immediately the shouting became a steady yell, and a rattling fusillade of small missiles, corners of tobacco plugs, cigarette-boxes, and even pennies beat against the window. The sounds of the racket now began floating up the stairs as the folding doors revolved.

"They're coming up!" cried Bartholomew.

Edith turned anxiously to Henry.

"They're coming up, Henry."

From down-stairs in the lower hall their cries were now quite audible.

"—God damn Socialists!"

"Pro-Germans! Boche-lovers!"

"Second floor, front! Come on!"

"We'll get the sons——"

The next five minutes passed in a dream. Edith was conscious that the clamor burst suddenly upon the three of them like a cloud of rain, that there was a thunder of many feet on the stairs, that Henry had seized her arm and drawn her back toward the rear of the office. Then the door opened and an overflow of men were forced into the room—not the leaders, but simply those who happened to be in front.

"Hello, Bo!"

"Up late, ain't you?"

"You an' your girl. Damn *you!*"

She noticed that two very drunken soldiers had been forced to the front, where they wobbled fatuously—one of them was short and dark, the other was tall and weak of chin.

Henry stepped forward and raised his hand.

"Friends!" he said.

The clamor faded into a momentary stillness, punctuated with mutterings.

"Friends!" he repeated, his far-away eyes fixed over the heads of the crowd, "you're injuring no one but yourselves by breaking in here to-night. Do we look like rich men? Do we look like Germans? I ask you in all fairness——"

"Pipe down!"

"I'll say you do!"

"Say, who's your lady friend, buddy?"

A man in civilian clothes, who had been pawing over a table, suddenly held up a newspaper.

"Here it is!" he shouted. "They wanted the Germans to win the war!"

A new overflow from the stairs was shouldered in and of a sudden the room was full of men all closing around the pale little group at the back. Edith saw that the tall soldier with the weak chin was still in front. The short dark one had disappeared.

She edged slightly backward, stood close to the open window, through which came a clear breath of cool night air.

Then the room was a riot. She realized that the soldiers were surging forward, glimpsed the fat man swinging a chair over his head—instantly the lights went out, and she felt the push of warm bodies under rough cloth, and her ears were full of shouting and trampling and hard breathing.

A figure flashed by her out of nowhere, tottered, was edged sideways, and of a sudden disappeared helplessly out through the open window with a frightened, fragmentary cry that died staccato on the bosom of the clamor. By the faint light streaming from the building backing on the area Edith had a quick impression that it had been the tall soldier with the weak chin.

Anger rose astonishingly in her. She swung her arms wildly, edged blindly toward the thickest of the scuffling. She heard grunts, curses, the muffled impact of fists.

"Henry!" she called frantically, "Henry!"

Then, it was minutes later, she felt suddenly that there were other figures in the room. She heard a voice, deep, bullying, authoritative; she saw yellow rays of light sweeping here and there in the fracas. The cries became more scattered. The scuffling increased and then stopped.

Suddenly the lights were on and the room was full of policemen, clubbing left and right. The deep voice boomed out:

"Here now! Here now! Here now!"

And then:

"Quiet down and get out! Here now!"

The room seemed to empty like a wash-bowl. A policeman fast-grappled in the corner released his hold on his soldier antagonist and started him with a shove toward the door. The deep voice continued. Edith perceived now that it came from a bull-necked police captain standing near the door.

"Here now! This is no way! One of your own sojers got shoved out of the back window an' killed hisself!"

"Henry!" called Edith, "Henry!"

She beat wildly with her fists on the back of the man in front of her; she brushed between two others; fought, shrieked, and beat her way to a very pale figure sitting on the floor close to a desk.

"Henry," she cried passionately, "what's the matter? What's the matter? Did they hurt you?"

His eyes were shut. He groaned and then looking up said disgustedly——

"They broke my leg. My God, the fools!"

"Here now!" called the police captain. "Here now! Here now!"

IX

"Childs', Fifty-ninth Street," at eight o'clock of any morning differs from its sisters by less than the width of their marble tables or the degree of polish on the frying-pans. You will see there a crowd of poor people with sleep in the corners of their eyes, trying to look straight before them at their food so as not to see the other poor people. But Childs', Fifty-ninth, four hours earlier is quite unlike any Childs' restaurant from Portland, Oregon, to Portland, Maine. Within its pale but sanitary walls one finds a noisy medley of chorus girls, college boys, débutantes, rakes, *filles de joie*—a not unrepresentative mixture of the gayest of Broadway, and even of Fifth Avenue.

In the early morning of May the second it was unusually full. Over the marble-topped tables were bent the excited faces of flappers whose fathers owned individual villages. They were eating buckwheat cakes and scrambled eggs with relish and gusto, an accomplishment that it would have been utterly impossible for them to repeat in the same place four hours later.

Almost the entire crowd were from the Gamma Psi dance at Delmonico's except for several chorus girls from a midnight revue who sat at a side table and wished they'd taken off a little more make-up after the show. Here and there a drab, mouse-like figure, desperately out of place, watched the butterflies with a weary, puzzled curiosity. But the drab figure was the exception. This was the morning after May Day, and celebration was still in the air.

Gus Rose, sober but a little dazed, must be classed as one of the drab figures. How he had got himself from Forty-fourth Street to Fifty-ninth Street after the riot was only a hazy half-memory. He had seen the body of Carrol Key put in an ambulance and driven off, and then he had started up town with two or three soldiers. Somewhere between Forty-fourth Street and Fifty-ninth Street the other soldiers had met some women and disappeared. Rose had wandered to Columbus Circle and chosen the gleaming lights of Childs' to minister to his craving for coffee and doughnuts. He walked in and sat down.

All around him floated airy, inconsequential chatter and high-pitched laughter. At first he failed to understand, but after a puzzled five minutes he realized that this was the aftermath of some gay party. Here and there a restless, hilarious young man wandered fraternally and familiarly between the tables, shaking hands indiscriminately and pausing occasionally for a facetious chat, while excited waiters, bearing cakes and eggs aloft, swore at him silently, and bumped him out of the way. To Rose, seated at the most inconspicuous and least crowded table, the whole scene was a colorful circus of beauty and riotous pleasure.

He became gradually aware, after a few moments, that the couple seated diagonally across from him, with their backs to the crowd, were not the least interesting pair in the room. The man was drunk. He wore a dinner coat with a dishevelled tie and shirt swollen by spillings of water and wine. His eyes, dim and bloodshot, roved unnaturally from side to side. His breath came short between his lips.

"He's been on a spree!" thought Rose.

The woman was almost if not quite sober. She was pretty, with dark eyes and feverish high color, and she kept her active eyes fixed on her companion with the alertness of a hawk. From time to time she would lean and whisper intently to him, and he would answer by inclining his head heavily or by a particularly ghoulish and repellent wink.

Rose scrutinized them dumbly for some minutes, until the woman gave him a quick, resentful look; then he shifted his gaze to two of the most conspicuously hilarious of the promenaders who were on a protracted circuit of the tables. To his surprise he recognized in one of them the young man by whom he had been so ludicrously entertained at Delmonico's. This started him thinking of Key with a vague sentimentality, not unmixed with awe. Key was dead. He had fallen thirty-five feet and split his skull like a cracked cocoanut.

"He was a darn good guy," thought Rose mournfully. "He was a darn good guy, o'right. That was awful hard luck about him."

The two promenaders approached and started down between Rose's table and the next, addressing friends and strangers alike with jovial familiarity. Suddenly Rose saw the fair-haired one with the prominent teeth stop, look unsteadily at the man and girl opposite, and then begin to move his head disapprovingly from side to side.

The man with the blood-shot eyes looked up.

"Gordy," said the promenader with the prominent teeth, "Gordy."

"Hello," said the man with the stained shirt thickly.

Prominent Teeth shook his finger pessimistically at the pair, giving the woman a glance of aloof condemnation.

"What'd I tell you, Gordy?"

Gordon stirred in his seat.

"Go to hell!" he said.

Dean continued to stand there shaking his finger. The woman began to get angry.

"You go way!" she cried fiercely. "You're drunk, that's what you are!"

"So's he," suggested Dean, staying the motion of his finger and pointing it at Gordon.

Peter Himmel ambled up, owlish now and oratorically inclined.

"Here now," he began as if called upon to deal with some petty dispute between children. "Wha's all trouble?"

"You take your friend away," said Jewel tartly. "He's bothering us."

"What's 'at?"

"You heard me!" she said shrilly. "I said to take your drunken friend away."

Her rising voice rang out above the clatter of the restaurant and a waiter came hurrying up.

"You gotta be more quiet!"

"That fella's drunk," she cried. "He's insulting us."

"Ah-ha, Gordy," persisted the accused. "What'd I tell you." He turned to the waiter. "Gordy an' I friends. Been tryin' help him, haven't I, Gordy?"

Gordy looked up.

"Help me? Hell, no!"

Jewel rose suddenly, and seizing Gordon's arm assisted him to his feet.

"Come on, Gordy!" she said, leaning toward him and speaking in a half whisper. "Let's us get out of here. This fella's got a mean drunk on."

Gordon allowed himself to be urged to his feet and started toward the door. Jewel turned for a second and addressed the provoker of their flight.

"I know all about *you!*" she said fiercely. "Nice friend, you are, I'll say. He told me about you."

Then she seized Gordon's arm, and together they made their way through the curious crowd, paid their check, and went out.

"You'll have to sit down," said the waiter to Pete after they had gone.

"What's 'at? Sit down?"

"Yes—or get out."

Peter turned to Dean.

"Come on," he suggested. "Let's beat up this waiter."

"All right."

They advanced toward him, their faces grown stern. The waiter retreated.

Peter suddenly reached over to a plate on the table beside him and picking up a handful of hash tossed it into the air. It descended as a languid parabola in snowflake effect on the heads of those near by.

"Hey! Ease up!"

"Put him out!"

"Sit down, Peter!"

"Cut out that stuff!"

Peter laughed and bowed.

"Thank you for your kind applause, ladies and gents. If some one will lend me some more hash and a tall hat we will go on with the act."

The bouncer bustled up.

"You've gotta get out!" he said to Peter.

"Hell, no!"

"He's my friend!" put in Dean indignantly.

A crowd of waiters were gathering. "Put him out!"

"Better go, Peter."

There was a short struggle and the two were edged and pushed toward the door.

"I got a hat and a coat here!" cried Peter.

"Well, go get 'em and be spry about it!"

The bouncer released his hold on Peter, who, adopting a ludicrous air of extreme cunning, rushed immediately around to the other table, where he burst into derisive laughter and thumbed his nose at the exasperated waiters.

"Think I just better wait a l'il' longer," he announced.

The chase began. Four waiters were sent around one way and four another. Dean caught hold of two of them by the coat, and another struggle took place before the pursuit of Peter could be resumed; he was finally pinioned after overturning a sugar-bowl and several cups of coffee. A fresh argument ensued at the cashier's desk, where Peter attempted to buy another dish of hash to take with him and throw at policemen.

But the commotion upon his exit proper was dwarfed by another phenomenon which drew admiring glances and a prolonged involuntary "Oh-h-h!" from every person in the restaurant.

The great plate-glass front had turned to a deep creamy blue, the color of a Maxfield Parrish moonlight—a blue that seemed to press close upon the pane as if to crowd its way into the restaurant.

Dawn had come up in Columbus Circle, magical, breathless dawn, silhouetting the great statue of the immortal Christopher, and mingling in a curious and uncanny manner with the fading yellow electric light inside.

X

Mr. In and Mr. Out are not listed by the census-taker. You will search for them in vain through the social register or the births, marriages, and deaths, or the grocer's credit list. Oblivion has swallowed them and the testimony that they ever existed at all is vague and shadowy, and inadmissible in a court of law. Yet I have it upon the best authority that for a brief space Mr. In and Mr. Out lived, breathed, answered to their names and radiated vivid personalities of their own.

During the brief span of their lives they walked in their native garments down the great highway of a great nation; were laughed at, sworn at, chased, and fled from. Then they passed and were heard of no more.

They were already taking form dimly, when a taxicab with the top open breezed down Broadway in the faintest glimmer of May dawn. In this car sat the souls of Mr. In and Mr. Out discussing with amazement the blue light that had so precipitately colored the sky behind the statue of Christopher Columbus, discussing with bewilderment the old, gray faces of the early risers which skimmed palely along the street like blown bits of paper on a gray lake. They were agreed on all things, from the absurdity of the bouncer in Childs' to the absurdity of the business of life. They were dizzy with the extreme maudlin happiness that the morning had awakened in their glowing souls. Indeed, so fresh and vigorous was their pleasure in living that they felt it should be expressed by loud cries.

"Ye-ow-ow!" hooted Peter, making a megaphone with his hands—and Dean joined in with a call that, though equally significant and symbolic, derived its resonance from its very inarticulateness.

"Yo-ho! Yea! Yoho! Yo-buba!"

Fifty-third Street was a bus with a dark, bobbed-hair beauty atop; Fifty-second was a street cleaner who dodged, escaped, and sent up a yell of, "Look where you're aimin'!" in a pained and grieved voice. At Fiftieth Street a group of men on a very white sidewalk in front of a very white building turned to stare after them, and shouted:

"Some party, boys!"

At Forty-ninth Street Peter turned to Dean. "Beautiful morning," he said gravely, squinting up his owlish eyes.

"Probably is."

"Go get some breakfast, hey?"

Dean agreed—with additions.

"Breakfast and liquor."

"Breakfast and liquor," repeated Peter, and they looked at each other, nodding. "That's logical."

Then they both burst into loud laughter.

"Breakfast and liquor! Oh, gosh!"

"No such thing," announced Peter.

"Don't serve it? Ne'mind. We force 'em serve it. Bring pressure bear."

"Bring logic bear."

The taxi cut suddenly off Broadway, sailed along a cross street, and stopped in front of a heavy tomb-like building in Fifth Avenue.

"What's idea?"

The taxi-driver informed them that this was Delmonico's.

This was somewhat puzzling. They were forced to devote several minutes to intense concentration, for if such an order had been given there must have been a reason for it.

"Somep'm 'bouta coat," suggested the taxi-man.

That was it. Peter's overcoat and hat. He had left them at Delmonico's. Having decided this, they disembarked from the taxi and strolled toward the entrance arm in arm.

"Hey!" said the taxi-driver.

"Huh?"

"You better pay me."

They shook their heads in shocked negation.

"Later, not now—we give orders, you wait."

The taxi-driver objected; he wanted his money now. With the scornful condescension of men exercising tremendous self-control they paid him.

Inside Peter groped in vain through a dim, deserted check-room in search of his coat and derby.

"Gone, I guess. Somebody stole it."

"Some Sheff student."

"All probability."

"Never mind," said Dean, nobly. "I'll leave mine here too—then we'll both be dressed the same."

He removed his overcoat and hat and was hanging them up when his roving glance was caught and held magnetically by two large squares of cardboard tacked to the two coat-room doors. The one on the left-hand door bore the word "In" in big black letters, and the one on the right-hand door flaunted the equally emphatic word "Out."

"Look!" he exclaimed happily——

Peter's eyes followed his pointing finger.

"What?"

"Look at the signs. Let's take 'em."

"Good idea."

"Probably pair very rare an' valuable signs. Probably come in handy."

Peter removed the left-hand sign from the door and endeavored to conceal it about his person. The sign being of considerable proportions, this was a matter of some difficulty. An idea flung itself at him, and with an air of dignified mystery he turned his back. After an instant he wheeled dramatically around, and stretching out his arms displayed himself to the admiring Dean. He had inserted the sign in his vest, completely covering his shirt front. In effect, the word "In" had been painted upon his shirt in large black letters.

"Yoho!" cheered Dean. "Mister In."

He inserted his own sign in like manner.

"Mister Out!" he announced triumphantly. "Mr. In meet Mr. Out."

They advanced and shook hands. Again laughter overcame them and they rocked in a shaken spasm of mirth.

"Yoho!"

"We probably get a flock of breakfast."

"We'll go—go to the Commodore."

Arm in arm they sallied out the door, and turning east in Forty-fourth Street set out for the Commodore.

As they came out a short dark soldier, very pale and tired, who had been wandering listlessly along the sidewalk, turned to look at them.

He started over as though to address them, but as they immediately bent on him glances of withering unrecognition, he waited until they had started unsteadily down the street, and then followed at about forty paces, chuckling to himself and saying "Oh, boy!" over and over under his breath, in delighted, anticipatory tones.

Mr. In and Mr. Out were meanwhile exchanging pleasantries concerning their future plans.

"We want liquor; we want breakfast. Neither without the other. One and indivisible."

"We want both 'em!"

"Both 'em!"

It was quite light now, and passers-by began to bend curious eyes on the pair. Obviously they were engaged in a discussion, which afforded each of them intense amusement, for occasionally a fit of laughter would seize upon them so violently that, still with their arms interlocked, they would bend nearly double.

Reaching the Commodore, they exchanged a few spicy epigrams with the sleepy-eyed doorman, navigated the revolving door with some difficulty, and then made their way through a thinly populated but startled lobby to the dining-room, where a puzzled waiter showed them an obscure table in a corner. They studied the bill of fare helplessly, telling over the items to each other in puzzled mumbles.

"Don't see any liquor here," said Peter reproachfully.

The waiter became audible but unintelligible.

"Repeat," continued Peter, with patient tolerance, "that there seems to be unexplained and quite distasteful lack of liquor upon bill of fare."

"Here!" said Dean confidently, "let me handle him." He turned to the waiter—"Bring us—bring us—" he scanned the bill of fare anxiously. "Bring us a quart of champagne and a—a—probably ham sandwich."

The waiter looked doubtful.

"Bring it!" roared Mr. In and Mr. Out in chorus.

The waiter coughed and disappeared. There was a short wait during which they were subjected without their knowledge to a careful scrutiny by the headwaiter. Then the champagne arrived, and at the sight of it Mr. In and Mr. Out became jubilant.

"Imagine their objecting to us having champagne for breakfast—jus' imagine."

They both concentrated upon the vision of such an awesome possibility, but the feat was too much for them. It was impossible for their joint imaginations to conjure up a world where any one might object to any one else having champagne for breakfast. The waiter drew the cork with an enormous *pop*—and their glasses immediately foamed with pale yellow froth.

"Here's health, Mr. In."

"Here's same to you, Mr. Out."

The waiter withdrew; the minutes passed; the champagne became low in the bottle.

"It's—it's mortifying," said Dean suddenly.

"Wha's mortifying?"

"The idea their objecting us having champagne breakfast."

"Mortifying?" Peter considered. "Yes, tha's word—mortifying."

Again they collapsed into laughter, howled, swayed, rocked back and forth in their chairs, repeating the word "mortifying" over and over to each other—each repetition seeming to make it only more brilliantly absurd.

After a few more gorgeous minutes they decided on another quart. Their anxious waiter consulted his immediate superior, and this discreet person gave implicit instructions that no more champagne should be served. Their check was brought.

Five minutes later, arm in arm, they left the Commodore and made their way through a curious, staring crowd along Forty-second Street, and up Vanderbilt Avenue to the Biltmore. There, with sudden cunning, they rose to the occasion and traversed the lobby, walking fast and standing unnaturally erect.

Once in the dining-room they repeated their performance. They were torn between intermittent convulsive laughter and sudden spasmodic discussions of politics, college, and the sunny state of their dispositions. Their watches told them that it was now nine o'clock, and a dim idea was born in them that they were on a memorable party, something that they would remember always. They lingered over the second bottle. Either of them had only to mention the word "mortifying" to send them both into riotous gasps. The dining-room was whirring and shifting now; a curious lightness permeated and rarefied the heavy air.

They paid their check and walked out into the lobby.

It was at this moment that the exterior doors revolved for the thousandth time that morning, and admitted into the lobby a very pale young beauty with dark circles under her eyes, attired in a much-rumpled evening dress. She was accompanied by a plain stout man, obviously not an appropriate escort.

At the top of the stairs this couple encountered Mr. In and Mr. Out.

"Edith," began Mr. In, stepping toward her hilariously and making a sweeping bow, "darling, good morning."

The stout man glanced questioningly at Edith, as if merely asking her permission to throw this man summarily out of the way.

" 'Scuse familiarity," added Peter, as an afterthought. "Edith, good-morning."

He seized Dean's elbow and impelled him into the foreground.

"Meet Mr. In, Edith, my bes' frien'. Inseparable. Mr. In and Mr. Out."

Mr. Out advanced and bowed; in fact, he advanced so far and bowed so low that he tipped slightly forward and only kept his balance by placing a hand lightly on Edith's shoulder.

"I'm Mr. Out, Edith," he mumbled pleasantly, "S'misterin Misterout."

" 'Smisterinanout," said Peter proudly.

But Edith stared straight by them, her eyes fixed on some infinite speck in the gallery above her. She nodded slightly to the stout man, who advanced bull-like and with a sturdy brisk gesture pushed Mr. In and Mr. Out to either side. Through this alley he and Edith walked.

But ten paces farther on Edith stopped again—stopped and pointed to a short, dark soldier who was eying the crowd in general, and the tableau of Mr. In and Mr. Out in particular, with a sort of puzzled, spell-bound awe.

"There," cried Edith. "See there!"

Her voice rose, became somewhat shrill. Her pointing finger shook slightly.

"There's the soldier who broke my brother's leg."

There were a dozen exclamations; a man in a cutaway coat left his place near the desk and advanced alertly; the stout person made a sort of lightning-like spring toward the short, dark soldier, and then the lobby closed around the little group and blotted them from the sight of Mr. In and Mr. Out.

But to Mr. In and Mr. Out this event was merely a particolored iridescent segment of a whirring, spinning world.

They heard loud voices; they saw the stout man spring; the picture suddenly blurred.

Then they were in an elevator bound skyward.

"What floor, please?" said the elevator man.

"Any floor," said Mr. In.

"Top floor," said Mr. Out.

"This is the top floor," said the elevator man.

"Have another floor put on," said Mr. Out.

"Higher," said Mr. In.

"Heaven," said Mr. Out.

XI

In a bedroom of a small hotel just off Sixth Avenue Gordon Sterrett awoke with a pain in the back of his head and a sick throbbing in all his veins. He looked at the dusky gray shadows in the corners of the room and at a raw place on a large leather chair in the corner where it had long been in use. He saw clothes, dishevelled, rumpled clothes on the floor and he smelt stale cigarette smoke and stale liquor. The windows were tight shut. Outside the bright sunlight had thrown a dust-filled beam across the sill—a beam broken by the head of the wide wooden bed in which he had slept. He lay very quiet—comatose, drugged, his eyes wide, his mind clicking wildly like an unoiled machine.

It must have been thirty seconds after he perceived the sunbeam with the dust on it and the rip on the large leather chair that he had the sense of life close beside him, and it was another thirty seconds after that before he realized that he was irrevocably married to Jewel Hudson.

He went out half an hour later and bought a revolver at a sporting goods store. Then he took a taxi to the room where he had been living on East Twenty-seventh Street, and leaning across the table that held his drawing materials, fired a cartridge into his head just behind the temple.

My Own People

Anzia Yezierska (1889–1970)

Anzia Yezierska was born to a poor family in Plinsk, Russian Poland. She moved to New York City's Lower East Side in the 1890s, and there, amidst night classes and work in sweatshops, she began to write novels and short stories. Yezierska describes a poverty-stricken America, a land of immigrants in search of the America of their dreams. Her writing contains a realistic intensity of feeling, with characters—especially women—who yearn for dignity, respect, and independence. Her novels include *Salome of the Tenements* (1922); *Bread Givers* (1925), and *All I Could Never Be* (1932), which are autobiographical; and *Arrogant Beggar* (1927). Her short story collections are *Hungry Hearts* (1920), which is her most well-known collection and where "My Own People" is included, and *Children of Loneliness* (1923).

With the suitcase containing all her worldly possessions under her arm, Sophie Sapinsky elbowed her way through the noisy ghetto crowds. Pushcart peddlers and pullers-in shouted and gesticulated. Women with market-baskets pushed and shoved one another, eyes straining with the one thought—how to get the food a penny cheaper. With the same strained intentness, Sophie scanned each tenement, searching for a room cheap enough for her dwindling means.

In a dingy basement window a crooked sign, in straggling, penciled letters, caught Sophie's eye: "Room to let, a bargain, cheap."

The exuberant phrasing was quite in keeping with the extravagant dilapidation of the surroundings. "This is the very now—a restless spirit pawing at the air. The intensity of experience, the surge of emotion that had been hers when she wrote—where were they? The words had failed to catch the lifebeat—had failed to register the passion she had poured into them.

Perhaps she was not a writer, after all. Had the years and years of night-study been in vain? Choked with discouragement, the cry broke from her, "O—God—God help me! I feel—I see, but it all dies in me—dumb!"

Tedious days passed into weeks. Again Sophie sat staring into her notebook. "There's nothing here that's alive. Not a word yet says what's in me . . .

"But it *is* in me!" With clenched fist she smote her bosom. "It must be in me! I believe in it! I got to get it out—even if it tears my flesh in pieces—even if it kills me! . . .

"But these words—these flat, dead words . . .

"Whether I can write or can't write—I can't stop writing. I can't rest. I can't breathe. There's no peace, no running away for me on earth except in the struggle to give out what's in me. The beat from my heart—the blood from my veins—must flow out into my words."

She returned to her unfinished essay, "Believe in Yourself." Her mind groping—clutching at the misty incoherence that clouded her thoughts—she wrote on.

"These sentences are yet only wood—lead; but I can't help it—I'll push on—on—I'll not eat—I'll not sleep—I'll not move from this spot till I get it to say on the paper what I got in my heart!"

Slowly the dead words seemed to begin to breathe. Her eyes brightened. Her cheeks flushed. Her very pencil trembled with the eager onrush of words.

Then a sharp rap sounded on her door. With a gesture of irritation Sophie put down her pencil and looked into the burning, sunken eyes of her neighbor, Hanneh Breineh.

"I got yourself a glass of tea, good friend. It ain't much I got to give away, but it's warm even if it's nothing."

Sophie scowled. "You must n't bother yourself with me. I'm so busy—thanks."

"Don't thank me yet so quick. I got no sugar." Hanneh

Story is all about peoples beliefs
Self centered perspective - to a more encompassing one

Breineh edged herself into the room confidingly. "At home, in Poland, I not only had sugar for tea—but even jelly—a jelly that would lift you up to heaven. I thought in America everything would be so plenty, I could drink the tea out from my sugarbowl. But ach! Not in Poland did my children starve like in America!"

Hanneh Breineh, in a friendly manner, settled herself on the sound end of the bed, and began her jeremiad.

"Yosef, my man, ain't no bread-giver. Already he got consumption the second year. One week he works and nine weeks he lays sick."

In despair Sophie gathered her papers, wondering how to get the woman out of her room. She glanced through the page she had written, but Hanneh Breineh, unconscious of her indifference, went right on.

"How many times it is tearing the heart out from my body—should I take Yosef's milk to give to the baby, or the baby's milk to give to Yosef? If he was dead the pensions they give to widows would help feed my children. Now I got only the charities to help me. A black year on them! They should only have to feed their own children on what they give me."

Resolved not to listen to the intruder, Sophie debated within herself: "Should I call my essay 'Believe in Yourself,' or would n't it be stronger to say, 'Trust Yourself? But if I say, 'Trust Yourself,' would n't they think that I got the words from Emerson?"

Hanneh Breineh's voice went on, but it sounded to Sophie like a faint buzzing from afar. "Gotteniu! How much did it cost me my life to go and swear myself that my little Fannie—only skin and bones—that she is already fourteen! How it chokes me the tears every morning when I got to wake her and push her out to the shop when her eyes are yet shutting themselves with sleep!"

Sophie glanced at her wrist-watch as it ticked away the precious minutes. She must get rid of the woman! Had she not left her own sister, sacrificed all comfort, all association, for solitude and its golden possibilities? For the first time in her life she had the chance to be by herself and think. And now, the thoughts which a moment ago had seemed like a flock of fluttering birds had come so close—and this woman with her sordid wailing had scattered them.

"I'm a savage, a beast, but I got to ask her to get out—this very minute," resolved Sophie. But before she could summon the courage to do what she wanted to do, there was a timid knock at the door, and the wizened little Fannie, her face streaked with tears, stumbled in.

"The inspector said it's a lie. I ain't yet fourteen," she whimpered.

Hanneh Breineh paled. "Woe is me! Sent back from the shop? God from the world—is there no end to my troubles? Why did n't you hide yourself when you saw the inspector come?"

"I was running to hide myself under the table, but she caught me and she said she'll take me to the Children's Society and arrest me and my mother for sending me to work too soon."

"Arrest me?" shrieked Hanneh Breineh, beating her breast. "Let them only come and arrest me! I'll show America who I am! Let them only begin themselves with me! . . . Black is for my eyes . . . the groceryman will not give us another bread till we pay him the bill!"

"The inspector said . . ." The child's brow puckered in an effort to recall the words.

"What did the inspector said? Gotteniu!" Hanneh Breineh wrung her hands in passionate entreaty. "Listen only once to my prayer! Send on the inspector only a quick death! I only wish her to have her own house with twenty-four rooms and each of the twenty-four rooms should be twenty-four beds and the chills and the fever should throw her from one bed to another!"

"Hanneh Breineh, still yourself a little," entreated Sophie.

"How can I still myself without Fannie's wages? Bitter is me! Why do I have to live so long?"

"The inspector said . . ."

"What did the inspector said? A thunder should strike the inspector! Ain't I as good a mother as other mothers? Would n't I better send my children to school? But who'll give us to eat? And who'll pay us the rent?"

Hanneh Breineh wiped her red-lidded eyes with the corner of her apron.

"The president from America should only come to my bitter heart. Let him go fighting himself with the pushcarts how to get the eating a penny cheaper. Let him try to feed his children on the money the charities give me and we'd see if he would n't better send his littlest ones to the shop better than to let them starve before his eyes. Woe is me! What for did I come to America? What's my life—nothing but one terrible, never-stopping fight with the grocer and the butcher and the landlord . . ."

Suddenly Sophie's resentment for her lost morning was forgotten. The crying waste of Hanneh Breineh's life lay open before her eyes like pictures in a book. She saw her own life in Hanneh Breineh's life. Her efforts to write were like Hanneh Breineh's efforts to feed her children. Behind her life and Hanneh Breineh's life she saw the massed ghosts of thousands upon thousands beating—beating out their hearts against rock barriers.

"The inspector said . . ." Fannie timidly attempted again to explain.

"The inspector!" shrieked Hanneh Breineh, as she seized hold of Fannie in a rage. "Hellfire should burn the inspector! Tell me again about the inspector and I'll choke the life out from you—"

Sophie sprang forward to protect the child from the mother. "She's only trying to tell you something."

"Why should she yet throw salt on my wounds? If there was enough bread in the house would I need an inspector to tell me to send her to school? If America is so interested in poor people's children, then why don't they give them to eat till they should go to work? What learning can come into a child's head when the stomach is empty?"

A clutter of feet down the creaking cellar steps, a scuffle of broken shoes and a chorus of shrill voices, as the younger children rushed in from school.

"Mamma—what's to eat?"

"It smells potatoes!"

"Pfui! The pot is empty! It smells over from Cohen's."

"Jake grabbed all the bread!"

"Mamma—he kicked the piece out from my hands!"

"Mamma—it's so empty in my stomach! Ain't there nothing?"

"Gluttons—wolves—thieves!" Hanneh Breineh shrieked. "I should only live to bury you all in one day!"

The children, regardless of Hanneh Breineh's invectives, swarmed around her like hungry bees, tearing at her apron, her skirt. Their voices rose in increased clamor, topped only by their mother's imprecations. "Gotteniu! Tear me away from these leeches on my neck! Send on them only a quick death! . . . Only a minute's peace before I die!"

"Hanneh Breineh—children! What's the matter?" Shmendrik stood at the door. The sweet quiet of the old man stilled the raucous voices as the coming of evening stills the noises of the day.

"There's no end to my troubles! Hear them hollering for bread, and the grocer stopped to give till the bill is paid. Woe is me! Fannie sent home by the inspector and not a crumb in the house!"

"I got something." The old man put his hands over the heads of the children in silent benediction. "All come in by me. I got sent me a box of cake."

"Cake!" The children cried, catching at the kind hands and snuggling about the shabby coat.

"Yes. Cake and nuts and raisins and even a bottle of wine."

The children leaped and danced around him in their wild burst of joy.

"Cake and wine—a box—to you? Have the charities gone crazy?" Hanneh Breineh's eyes sparkled with light and laughter.

"No—no," Shmendrik explained hastily. "Not from the charities—from a friend—for the holidays."

Shmendrik nodded invitingly to Sophie, who was standing in the door of her room. "The roomerkeh will also give a taste with us our party?"

"Sure will she!" Hanneh Breineh took Sophie by the arm. "Who'll say no in this black life to cake and wine?"

Young throats burst into shrill cries: "Cake and wine—wine and cake—raisins and nuts—nuts and raisins!" The words rose in a triumphant chorus. The children leaped and danced in time to their chant, almost carrying the old man bodily into his room in the wildness of their joy.

The contagion of this sudden hilarity erased from Sophie's mind the last thought of work and she found herself seated with the others on the cobbler's bench.

From under his cot the old man drew forth a wooden box. Lifting the cover he held up before wondering eyes a large frosted cake embedded in raisins and nuts.

Amid the shouts of glee Shmendrik now waved aloft a large bottle of grape-juice.

The children could contain themselves no longer and dashed forward.

"Shah—shah! Wait only!" He gently halted their onrush and waved them back to their seats.

"The glasses for the wine!" Hanneh Breineh rushed about hither and thither in happy confusion. From the sink, the shelf, the windowsill, she gathered cracked glasses, cups without handles—anything that would hold even a few drops of the yellow wine.

Sacrificial solemnity filled the basement as the children breathlessly watched Shmendrik cut the precious cake. Mouths—even eyes—watered with the intensity of their emotion.

With almost religious fervor Hanneh Breineh poured the grape-juice into the glasses held in the trembling hands of the children. So overwhelming was the occasion that none dared to taste till the ritual was completed. The suspense was agonizing as one and all waited for Shmendrik's signal.

"Hanneh Breineh—you drink from my Sabbath wine-glass!"

Hanneh Breineh clinked glasses with Schmendrik. "Long years on us all!" Then she turned to Sophie, clinked glasses once more. "May you yet marry yourself from our basement to a millionaire!" Then she lifted the glass to her lips.

The spell was broken. With a yell of triumph the children gobbled the cake in huge mouthfuls and sucked the golden liquid. All the traditions of wealth and joy that ever sparkled from the bubbles of champagne smiled at Hanneh Breineh from her glass of California grape-juice.

"Ach!" she sighed. "How good it is to forget your troubles, and only those that's got troubles have the chance to forget them."

She sipped the grape-juice leisurely, thrilled into ecstasy with each lingering drop. "How it laughs yet in me, the life, the minute I turn my head from my worries!"

With growing wonder in her eyes, Sophie watched Hanneh Breineh. This ragged wreck of a woman—how passionately she clung to every atom of life! Hungrily, she burned through the depths of every experience. How she flared against wrongs—and how every tiny spark of pleasure blazed into joy!

Within a half-hour this woman had touched the whole range of human emotions, from bitterest agony to dancing joy. The terrible despair at the onrush of her starving children when she cried out, "O that I should only bury you all in one day!" And now the leaping light of the words: "How it laughs yet in me, the life, the minute I turn my head from my worries."

"Ach, if I could only write like Hanneh Breineh talks!" thought Sophie. "Her words dance with a thousand colors. Like a rainbow it flows from her lips." Sentences from her own essays marched before her, stiff and wooden. How clumsy, how unreal, were her most labored phrases compared to Hanneh Breineh's spontaneity. Fascinated, she listened to Hanneh Breineh, drinking her words as a thirst-perishing man drinks water. Every bubbling phrase filled her with a drunken rapture to create.

"Up till now I was only trying to write from my head. It was n't real—it was n't life. Hanneh Breineh is real. Hanneh Breineh is life."

"Ach! What do the rich people got but dried-up dollars? Pfui on them and their money!" Hanneh Breineh held up her glass to be refilled. "Let me only win a fortune on the lotteree and move myself in my own bought house. Let me only have my first hundred dollars in the bank and I'll lift up my head like a person and tell the charities to eat their own cornmeal. I'll get myself an automobile like the kind rich ladies and ride up to their houses on

Fifth Avenue and feed them only once on the eating they like so good for me and my children."

With a smile of benediction Shmendrik refilled the glasses and cut for each of his guests another slice of cake. Then came the handful of nuts and raisins.

As the children were scurrying about for hammers and iron lasts with which to crack their nuts, the basement door creaked. Unannounced, a woman entered—the "friendly visitor" of the charities. Her look of awful amazement swept the group of merrymakers.

"Mr. Shmendrik!—Hanneh Breineh!" Indignation seethed in her voice. "What's this? A feast—a birthday?"

Gasps—bewildered glances—a struggle for utterance!

"I came to make my monthly visit—evidently I'm not needed."

Shmendrik faced the accusing eyes of the "friendly visitor." "Holiday eating . . ."

"Oh—I'm glad you're so prosperous."

Before any one had gained presence of mind enough to explain things; the door had clanked. The "friendly visitor" had vanished.

"Pfui!" Hanneh Breineh snatched up her glass and drained its contents. "What will she do now? Will we get no more dry bread from the charities because once we ate cake?"

"What for did she come?" asked Sophie.

"To see that we don't over-eat ourselves!" returned Hanneh Breineh. "She's a 'friendly visitor'! She learns us how to cook cornmeal. By pictures and lectures she shows us how the poor people should live without meat, without milk, without butter, and without eggs. Always it's on the end of my tongue to ask her, 'You learned us to do without so much, why can't you yet learn us how to eat without eating?' "

The children seized the last crumbs of cake that Shmendrik handed them and rushed for the street.

"What a killing look was on her face," said Sophie. "Could n't she be a little glad for your gladness?"

"Charity ladies—gladness?" The joy of the grape-wine still rip-

Hanneh knows the score

pled in Hanneh Breineh's laughter. "For poor people is only cornmeal. Ten cents a day—to feed my children!"

Still in her rollicking mood Hanneh Breineh picked up the baby and tossed it like a Bacchante. "Could you be happy a lot with ten cents in your stomach? Ten cents—half a can of condensed milk—then fill yourself the rest with water! . . . Maybe yet feed you with all water and save the ten-cent pieces to buy you a carriage like the Fifth Avenue babies! . . ."

The soft sound of a limousine purred through the area grating and two well-fed figures in sealskin coats, led by the "friendly visitor," appeared at the door.

"Mr. Bernstein, you can see for yourself." The "friendly visitor" pointed to the table.

The merry group shrank back. It was as if a gust of icy wind had swept all the joy and laughter from the basement.

"You are charged with intent to deceive and obtain assistance by dishonest means," said Mr. Bernstein.

"Dishonest?" Shmendrik paled.

Sophie's throat strained with passionate protest, but no words came to her release.

"A friend—a friend"—stammered Shmendrik—"sent me the holiday eating."

The superintendent of the Social Betterment Society faced him accusingly. "You told us that you had no friends when you applied to us for assistance."

"My friend—he knew me in my better time." Shmendrik flushed painfully. "I was once a scholar—respected. I wanted by this one friend to hold myself like I was."

Mr. Bernstein had taken from the bookshelf a number of letters, glanced through them rapidly and handed them one by one to the deferential superintendent.

Shmendrik clutched at his heart in an agony of humiliation. Suddenly his bent body straightened. His eyes dilated. "My letters—my life—you dare?"

"Of course we dare!" The superintendent returned Shmendrik's livid gaze, made bold by the confidence that what he was doing was the only scientific method of administering philanthropy. "These dollars, so generously given, must go to those most worthy. . . . I find in these letters references to gifts of fruit and other luxuries you did not report at our office."

"He never kept nothing for himself!" Hanneh Breineh broke in defensively. "He gave it all for the children."

Ignoring the interruption Mr. Bernstein turned to the "friendly visitor." "I'm glad you brought my attention to this case. It's but one of the many impositions on our charity . . . Come . . ."

"Kossacks! Pogromschiks!" Sophie's rage broke at last. "You call yourselves Americans? You dare call yourselves Jews? You bosses of the poor! This man Shmendrik, whose house you broke into, whom you made to shame like a beggar—he is the one Jew from whom the Jews can be proud! He gives all he is—all he has—as God gives. *He* is charity.

"But you—you are the greed—the shame of the Jews! *All-rightniks*—fat bellies in fur coats! What do you give from yourselves? You may eat and bust eating! Nothing you give till you've stuffed yourselves so full that your hearts are dead!"

The door closed in her face. Her wrath fell on indifferent backs as the visitors mounted the steps to the street.

Shmendrik groped blindly for the Bible. In a low, quavering voice, he began the chant of the oppressed—the wail of the downtrodden. "I am afraid, and a trembling taketh hold of my flesh. Wherefore do the wicked live, become old, yea, mighty in power?"

Hanneh Breineh and the children drew close around the old man. They were weeping—unconscious of their weeping—deep-buried memories roused by the music, the age-old music of the Hebrew race.

Through the grating Sophie saw the limousine pass. The chant flowed on: "Their houses are safe from fear; neither is the rod of God upon them."

Silently Sophie stole back to her room. She flung herself on the cot, pressed her fingers to her burning eyeballs. For a long time she lay rigid, clenched—listening to the drumming of her heart like the sea against rock barriers. Presently the barriers burst. Something in her began pouring itself out. She felt for her pencil—paper—and began to write. Whether she reached out to God or man she knew not, but she wrote on and on all through that night.

The gray light entering her grated window told her that beyond was dawn. Sophie looked up: "Ach! At last it writes itself in me!" she whispered triumphantly. "It's not me—it's their cries—my own people—crying in me! Hanneh Breineh, Shmendrik, they will not be stilled in me, till all America stops to listen."

The House in Turk Street

Dashiell Hammett (1894–1961)

Dashiell Hammett, a Maryland native, worked as an operative in a detective agency before becoming a well-known detective writer considered to be "the father of hard-boiled detective fiction." He is the creator of Sam Spade, a hard-edged sleuth devoted to finding answers and protecting people in the midst of tough, urban surroundings. His most well-known novels include *Red Harvest* (1929), *The Dain Curse* (1929), *The Maltese Falcon* (1930), *The Thin Man,* and *The Glass Key* (both 1931). He has written short stories as well, including *The Adventures of Sam Spade and Other Stories* (1944), *Hammett Homicides* (1946), and *Nightmare Town* (1948). "The House in Turk Street" is part of *The Continent Op* (1974).

I had been told that the man for whom I was hunting lived in a certain Turk Street block, but my informant hadn't been able to give me his house number. Thus it came about that late one rainy afternoon I was canvassing this certain block, ringing each bell, and reciting a myth that went like this:

"I'm from the law office of Wellington and Berkeley. One of our clients—an elderly lady—was thrown from the rear platform of a street car last week and severely injured. Among those who witnessed the accident was a young man whose name we don't know. But we have been told that he lives in this neighborhood." Then I would describe the man I wanted, and wind up: "Do you know of anyone who looks like that?"

All down one side of the block the answers were: "No," "No," "No."

I crossed the street and started on the other side. The first house: "No." The second: "No." The third. The fourth. The fifth—

No one came to the door in answer to my first ring. After a while, I rang again. I had just decided that no one was at home, when the knob turned slowly and a little old woman opened the door. She was a very fragile little old woman, with a piece of gray knitting in one hand, and faded eyes that twinkled pleasantly behind goldrimmed spectacles. She wore a stiffly starched apron over a black dress.

"Good evening," she said in a thin friendly voice. "I hope you didn't mind waiting. I always have to peep out to see who's there before I open the door—an old woman's timidity."

"Sorry to disturb you," I apologized. "But—"

"Won't you come in, please?"

"No; I just want a little information. I won't take much time."

"I wish you would come in," she said, and then added with mock severity, "I'm sure my tea is getting cold."

She took my damp hat and coat, and I followed her down a narrow hall to a dim room, where a man got up as we entered. He was old too, and stout, with a thin white beard that fell upon a white vest that was as stiffly starched as the woman's apron.

"Thomas," the little fragile woman told him; "this is Mr.—"

"Tracy," I said, because that was the name I had given the other residents of the block; but I came as near blushing when I said it as I have in fifteen years. These folks weren't made to be lied to.

Their name, I learned, was Quarre; and they were an affectionate old couple. She called him "Thomas" every time she spoke to him, rolling the name around in her mouth as if she liked the taste of it. He called her "my dear" just as frequently, and twice he got up to adjust a cushion more comfortably to her frail back.

I had to drink a cup of tea with them and eat some little spiced cookies before I could get them to listen to a question. Then Mrs. Quarre made little sympathetic clicking sounds with her tongue and teeth, while I told about the elderly lady who had fallen off a street car. The old man rumbled in his beard that it was "a damn shame," and gave me a fat cigar.

Finally I got away from the accident, and described the man I wanted.

"Thomas," Mrs. Quarre said, "isn't that the young man who lives in the house with the railing—the one who always looks so worried?"

The old man stroked his snowy beard and pondered for a moment.

"But, my dear," he rumbled at last, "hasn't he got dark hair?"

She beamed upon her husband. "Thomas is *so* observant," she said with pride. "I had forgotten; but the young man I spoke of does have dark hair, so he couldn't be the one."

The old man then suggested that one who lived in the block below might be my man. They discussed this one at some length before they decided that he was too tall and too old. Mrs. Quarre suggested another. They discussed that one, and voted against him. Thomas offered a candidate; he was weighed and discarded. They chattered on.

Darkness settled. The old man turned on a light in a tall lamp that threw a soft yellow circle upon us, and left the rest of the room dim. The room was a large one, and heavy with the thick hangings and bulky horsehair furniture of a generation ago. I didn't expect to get any information here; but I was comfortable, and the cigar was a good one. Time enough to go out into the drizzle when I had finished my smoke.

Something cold touched the nape of my neck.

"Stand up!"

I didn't stand up: I couldn't. I was paralyzed. I sat and blinked at the Quarres.

And looking at them, I knew that something cold *couldn't* be against the back of my neck; a harsh voice *couldn't* have ordered me to stand up. It wasn't possible!

Mrs. Quarre still sat primly upright against the cushions her husband had adjusted to her back; her eyes still twinkled with friendliness behind her glasses. The old man still stroked his white beard, and let cigar smoke drift unhurriedly from his nostrils.

They would go on talking about the young men in the neighborhood who might be the man I wanted. Nothing had happened. I had dozed.

"Get up!" The cold thing against my neck jabbed deep into the flesh.

I stood up. "Frisk him," the harsh voice came from behind.

The old man carefully laid his cigar down, came to me, and ran his hands over my body. Satisfied that I was unarmed, he emptied my pockets, dropping the contents upon the chair that I had just left.

"That's all," he told the man behind me, and returned to his chair.

"Turn around, you!" the harsh voice ordered.

I turned and faced a tall, gaunt, raw-boned man of about my own age, which is thirty-five. He had an ugly face—hollow-cheeked, bony, and spattered with big pale freckles. His eyes were of a watery blue, and his nose and chin stuck out abruptly. "Know me?" he asked.

"No."

"You're a liar!"

I didn't argue the point; he was holding a gun in one big freckled hand.

"You're going to know me pretty well before you're through with me," this big ugly man threatened. "You're going to—"

"Hook!" a voice came from a portièred doorway—the doorway through which the ugly man had no doubt crept up behind me. "Hook, come here!" The voice was feminine—young, clear, and musical.

"What do you want?" the ugly man called over his shoulder.

"*He's* here."

"All right!" He turned to Thomas Quarre. "Keep this joker safe."

From somewhere among his whiskers, his coat, and his stiff

white vest, the old man brought out a big black revolver, which he handled with no signs of unfamiliarity.

The ugly man swept up the things that had been taken from my pockets, and carried them through the portières with him.

Mrs. Quarre smiled up at me. "Do sit down, Mr. Tracy," she said.

I sat.

Through the portières a new voice came from the next room; a drawling baritone voice whose accent was unmistakably British; cultured British. "What's up, Hook?" this voice was asking.

The harsh voice of the ugly man:

"Plenty's up, I'm telling you! They're on to us! I started out a while ago; and as soon as I got to the street, I seen a man I knowed on the other side. He was pointed out to me in Philly five–six years ago. I don't know his name, but I remember his mug—he's a Continental Detective Agency man. I came back in right away, and me and Elvira watched him out of the window. He went to every house on the other side of the street, asking questions or something. Then he came over and started to give this side a whirl, and after a while he rings the bell. I tell the old woman and her husband to get him in, stall him along, and see what he says for himself. He's got a song and dance about looking for a guy what seen an old woman bumped by a street car—but that's the bunk! He's gunning for us. I went in and stuck him up just now. I meant to wait till you come, but I was scared he'd get nervous and beat it."

The British voice: "You shouldn't have shown yourself to him. The others could have taken care of him."

Hook: "What's the diff? Chances is he knows us all anyway. But supposing he didn't, what diff does it make?"

The drawling British voice: "It may make a deal of difference. It was stupid."

Hook, blustering: "Stupid, huh? You're always bellyaching about other people being stupid. To hell with you, I say! Who does all the work? Who's the guy that swings all the jobs? Huh? Where—"

The young feminine voice: "Now, Hook, for God's sake don't make that speech again. I've listened to it until I know it by heart!"

A rustle of papers, and the British voice: "I say, Hook, you're correct about his being a detective. Here is an identification card."

The feminine voice from the next room: "Well, what's to be done? What's our play?"

Hook: "That's easy to answer. We're going to knock this sleuth off!"

The feminine voice: "And put our necks in the noose?"

Hook, scornfully: "As if they ain't there if we don't! You don't think this guy ain't after us for the L.A. job, do you?"

The British voice: "You're an ass, Hook, and a quite hopeless one. Suppose this chap is interested in the Los Angeles affair, as is probable; what then? He is a Continental operative. Is it likely that his organization doesn't know where he is? Don't you think they know he was coming up here? And don't they know as much about us—chances are—as he does? There's no use killing him. That would only make matters worse. The thing to do is to tie him up and leave him here. His associates will hardly come looking for him until tomorrow."

My gratitude went out to the British voice! Somebody was in my favor, at least to the extent of letting me live. I hadn't been feeling very cheerful these last few minutes. Somehow, the fact that I couldn't see these people who were deciding whether I was to live or die, made my plight seem all the more desperate. I felt better now, though far from gay; I had confidence in the drawling British voice; it was the voice of a man who habitually carries his point.

Hook, bellowing: "Let me tell you something, brother: that guy's going to be knocked off! That's flat! I'm taking no chances. You can jaw all you want to about it, but I'm looking out for my own neck and it'll be a lot safer with that guy where he can't talk. That's flat."

The feminine voice, disgustedly: "Aw, Hook, be reasonable!"

The British voice, still drawling, but dead cold: "There's no use reasoning with you, Hook, you've the instincts and the intellect of a troglodyte. There is only one sort of language that you understand; and I'm going to talk that language to you, my son. If you are tempted to do anything silly between now and the time of our departure, just say this to yourself two or three times: 'If he dies, I die.' Say it as if it were out of the Bible—because it's that true."

There followed a long space of silence, with a tenseness that made my not particularly sensitive scalp tingle.

When, at last, a voice cut the silence, I jumped as if a gun had been fired; though the voice was low and smooth enough.

It was the British voice, confidently victorious, and I breathed again.

"We'll get the old people away first," the voice was saying. "You take charge of our guest, Hook. Tie him up while I get the bonds, and we'll be gone in less than half an hour."

The portières parted and Hook came into the room—a scowling Hook whose freckles had a greenish tinge against the sallowness of his face. He pointed a revolver at me, and spoke to the Quarres, short and harsh:

"He wants you." They got up and went into the next room.

Hook, meanwhile, had stepped back to the doorway, still menacing me with his revolver; and pulled loose the plush ropes that were around the heavy curtains. Then he came around behind me, and tied me securely to the highbacked chair; my arms to the chair's arms, my legs to the chair's legs, my body to the chair's back and seat; and he wound up by gagging me with the corner of a cushion that was too well-stuffed.

As he finished lashing me into place, and stepped back to scowl at me, I heard the street door close softly, and then light footsteps ran back and forth overhead.

Hook looked in the direction of those footsteps, and his little watery blue eyes grew cunning. "Elvira!" he called softly.

The portières bulged as if someone had touched them, and the musical feminine voice came through. "What?"

"Come here."

"I'd better not. He wouldn't—"

"Damn him!" Hook flared up. "Come here!"

She came into the room and into the circle of light from the tall lamp; a girl in her early twenties, slender and lithe, and dressed for the street, except that she carried her hat in one hand. A white face beneath a bobbed mass of flame-colored hair. Smoke-gray eyes that were set too far apart for trustworthiness—though not for beauty—laughed at me; and her red mouth laughed at me, exposing the edges of little sharp animal-teeth. She was as beautiful as the devil, and twice as dangerous.

She laughed at me—a fat man, all trussed up with red plush rope, and with the corner of a green cushion in my mouth—and she turned to the ugly man. "What do you want?"

He spoke in an undertone, with a furtive glance at the ceiling, above which soft steps still padded back and forth.

"What say we shake him?"

Her smoke-gray eyes lost their merriment and became calculating.

"There's a hundred thousand he's holding—a third of it's mine. You don't think I'm going to take a Mickey Finn on that, do you?"

"Course not! Supposing we get the hundred-grand?"

"How?"

"Leave it to me, kid; leave it to me! If I swing it, will you go with me? You know I'll be good to you."

She smiled contemptuously, I thought—but he seemed to like it.

"You're whooping right you'll be good to me," she said. "But listen, Hook: we couldn't get away with it—not unless you *get him*. I know him! I'm not running away with anything that belongs to him unless he is fixed so that he can't come after it."

Hook moistened his lips and looked around the room at nothing. Apparently he didn't like the thought of tangling with the owner of the British drawl. But his desire for the girl was too strong for his fear.

"I'll do it!" he blurted. "I'll get him! Do you mean it, kid? If I get him, you'll go with me?"

She held out her hand. "It's a bet," she said and he believed her.

His ugly face grew warm and red and utterly happy, and he took a deep breath and straightened his shoulders. In his place, I might have believed her myself—all of us have fallen for that sort of thing at one time or another—but sitting tied up on the sidelines, I knew that he'd have been better off playing with a gallon of nitro than with this baby. She was dangerous! There was a rough time ahead for Hook!

"This is the lay—" Hook began, and stopped, tongue-tied.

A step had sounded in the next room.

Immediately the British voice came through the portières, and there was exasperation to the drawl now:

"This is really too much! I can't"—he said *reahly* and *cawnt*—"leave for a moment without having things done all wrong. Now just what got into you, Elvira, that you must go in and exhibit yourself to our detective?"

Fear flashed into her smoke-gray eyes, and out again, and she spoke airily. "Don't be altogether yellow," she said. "Your precious neck can get along all right without so much guarding."

The portières parted, and I twisted my head around as far as I could get it for my first look at this man who was responsible for my still being alive. I saw a short fat man, hatted and coated for the street, and carrying a tan traveling bag in one hand.

Then his face came into the yellow circle of light, and I saw that it was a Chinese face. A short fat Chinese, immaculately clothed in garments that were as British as his accent.

"It isn't a matter of color," he told the girl—and I understood now the full sting of her jibe; "it's simply a matter of ordinary wisdom."

His face was a round yellow mask, and his voice was the same emotionless drawl that I had heard before; but I knew that he was as surely under the girl's sway as the ugly man—or he wouldn't have let her taunt bring him into the room. But I doubted that she'd find this Anglicized Oriental as easily handled as Hook.

"There was no particular need," the Chinese was still talking, "for this chap to have seen any of us." He looked at me now for the first time, with little opaque eyes that were like two black seeds. "It's quite possible that he didn't know any of us, even by description. This showing ourselves to him is the most arrant sort of nonsense."

"Aw, hell, Tai!" Hook blustered. "Quit your bellyaching, will you? What's the diff? I'll knock him off, and that takes care of that!"

The Chinese set down his tan bag and shook his head.

"There will be no killing," he drawled, "or there will be quite a bit of killing. You don't mistake my meaning, do you, Hook?"

Hook didn't. His Adam's apple ran up and down with the effort of his swallowing and behind the cushion that was choking me, I thanked the yellow man again.

Then this red-haired she-devil put her spoon in the dish.

"Hook's always offering to do things that he has no intention of doing," she told the Chinese.

Hook's ugly face blazed red at this reminder of his promise to get the Chinese, and he swallowed again, and his eyes looked as if nothing would have suited him better than an opportunity to crawl under something. But the girl had him; her influence was stronger than his cowardice.

He suddenly stepped close to the Chinese, and from his advantage of a full head in height scowled down into the round yellow face.

"Tai," the ugly man snarled; "you're done. I'm sick and tired of all this dog you put on—acting like you was a king or something. I'm going to—"

He faltered, and his words faded away into silence. Tai looked up at him with eyes that were as hard and black and inhuman as two pieces of coal. Hook's lips twitched and he flinched away a little.

I stopped sweating. The yellow man had won again. But I had forgotten the red-haired she-devil. She laughed now—a mocking laugh that must have been like a knife to the ugly man.

A bellow came from deep in his chest, and he hurled one big fist into the round blank face of the yellow man.

The force of the punch carried Tai all the way across the room, and threw him on his side in one corner.

But he had twisted his body around to face the ugly man even as he went hurtling across the room—a gun was in his hand before he went down—and he was speaking before his legs had settled upon the floor—and his voice was a cultured British drawl.

"Later," he was saying; "we will settle this thing that is between us. Just now you will drop your pistol and stand very still while I get up."

Hook's revolver—only half out of his pocket when the Oriental had covered him—thudded to the rug. He stood rigidly still while Tai got to his feet, and Hook's breath came out noisily, and each freckle stood ghastlily out against the dirty scared white of his face.

I looked at the girl. There was contempt in the eyes with which she looked at Hook, but no disappointment.

Then I made a discovery: *something had changed in the room near her!*

I shut my eyes and tried to picture that part of the room as it had been before the two men had clashed. Opening my eyes suddenly, I had the answer.

On the table beside the girl had been a book and some magazines. They were gone now. Not two feet from the girl was the tan bag that Tai had brought into the room. Suppose the bag had held the bonds from the Los Angeles job that they had mentioned. It probably had. What then? It probably now held the book and magazines that had been on the table. The girl had stirred up the trouble between the two men to distract their attention while she made a switch. Where would the loot be, then? I didn't know, but I suspected that it was too bulky to be on the girl's slender person.

Just beyond the table was a couch, with a wide red cover that went all the way down to the floor. I looked from the couch to the girl. She was watching me, and her eyes twinkled with a flash of mirth as they met mine coming from the couch. The couch it was!

By now the Chinese had pocketed Hook's revolver, and was talking to him: "If I hadn't a dislike for murder, and didn't think that you will perhaps be of some value to Elvira and me in effecting our departure, I should certainly relieve us of the handicap of your stupidity now. But I'll give you one more chance. I would suggest, however, that you think carefully before you give way to any more of your violent impulses." He turned to the girl. "Have you been putting foolish ideas in our Hook's head?"

She laughed. "Nobody could put any kind in it."

"Perhaps you're right," he said, and then came over to test the lashings about my arms and body.

Finding them satisfactory, he picked up the tan bag, and held out the gun he had taken from the ugly man a few minutes before.

"Here's your revolver, Hook, now try to be sensible. We may as well go now. The old man and his wife will do as they were told. They are on their way to a city that we needn't mention by name in front of our friend here, to wait for us and their share of the bonds. Needless to say, they will wait a long while—they are out of it now. But between ourselves there must be no more treachery. If we're to get clear, we must help each other."

According to the best dramatic rules, these folks should have made sarcastic speeches to me before they left, but they didn't. They passed me without even a farewell look, and went out of sight into the darkness of the hall.

Suddenly the Chinese was in the room again, running tiptoe—an open knife in one hand, a gun in the other. This was the man I had been thanking for saving my life! He bent over me.

The knife moved on my right side, and the rope that held that arm slackened its grip. I breathed again, and my heart went back to beating.

"Hook will be back," Tai whispered, and was gone.

On the carpet, three feet in front of me, lay a revolver.

The street door closed, and I was alone in the house for a while.

You may believe that I spent that while struggling with the red plush ropes that bound me. Tai had cut one length, loosening my right arm somewhat and giving my body more play, but I was far from free. And his whispered "Hook will be back" was all the spur I needed to throw my strength against my bonds.

I understood now why the Chinese had insisted so strongly upon my life being spared. *I was the weapon with which Hook was to be removed!* The Chinese figured that Hook would make some excuse as soon as they reached the street, slip back into the house, knock me off, and rejoin his confederates. If he didn't do it on his own initiative, I suppose the Chinese would suggest it.

So he had put a gun within reach and had loosened my ropes as much as he could, not to have me free before he himself got away.

This thinking was a side-issue. I didn't let it slow up my efforts to get loose. The *why* wasn't important to me just now—the important thing was to have that revolver in my hand when the ugly man came back.

Just as the front door opened, I got my right arm completely free, and plucked the strangling cushion from my mouth. The rest of my body was still held by the ropes—held loosely—but held.

I threw myself, chair and all, forward, breaking the fall with my free arm. The carpet was thick. I went down on my face, with the heavy chair atop me, all doubled up, but my right arm was free of the tangle, and my right hand grasped the gun. The dim light hit upon a man hurrying into the room—a glint of metal in his hand.

I fired.

He caught both hands to his belly, bent double, and slid out across the carpet.

That was over. But that was far from being all. I wrenched at the plush ropes that held me, while my mind tried to sketch what lay ahead.

The girl had switched the bonds, hiding them under the couch—there was no question of that. She had intended coming back for them before I had time to get free. But Hook had come back first, and she would have to change her plan. What more likely than that she would now tell the Chinese that Hook had made the switch? What then? There was only one answer: Tai would come back for the bonds—both of them would come. Tai knew that I was armed now, but they had said that the bonds represented a hundred thousand dollars. That would be enough to bring them back!

I kicked the last rope loose and scrambled to the couch. The bonds were beneath it: four thick bundles, done up with heavy rubber bands. I tucked them under one arm, and went over to the man who was dying near the door. His gun was under one of his legs. I pulled it out, stepped over him, and went into the dark hall. Then I stopped to consider.

The girl and the Chinese would split to tackle me. One would come in the front door and the other in the rear. That would be the safest way for them to handle me. My play, obviously, was to wait just inside one of those doors for them. It would be foolish for me to leave the house. That's exactly what they would be expecting at first—and they would be lying in ambush.

Decidedly, my play was to lie low within sight of this front door and wait until one of them came through it—as one of them surely would, when they had tired of waiting for me to come out.

Toward the street door, the hall was lighted with the glow that filtered through the glass from the street lights. The stairway leading to the second-story threw a triangular shadow across part of the hall—a shadow that was black enough for any purpose. I crouched low in this three-cornered slice of night, and waited.

I had two guns: the one the Chinese had given me, and the one I had taken from Hook. I had fired one shot; that would leave me eleven still to use—unless one of the weapons had been used since it was loaded. I broke the gun Tai had given me, and in the dark ran my fingers across the back of the cylinder. My fingers touched *one* shell—under the hammer. Tai had taken no chances; he had given me one bullet—the bullet with which I had dropped Hook.

I put that gun down on the floor, and examined the one I had taken from Hook. It was *empty*. The Chinese had taken no chances at all! He had emptied Hook's gun before returning it to him after their quarrel.

I was in a hole! Alone, unarmed, in a strange house that would presently hold two who were hunting me—and that one of them was a woman didn't soothe me any—she was none the less deadly on that account.

For a moment I was tempted to make a dash for it; the thought of being out in the street again was pleasant; but I put the idea away. That would be foolishness, and plenty of it. Then I remembered the bonds under my arm. They would have to be my weapon; and if they were to serve me, they would have to be concealed.

I slipped out of my triangular shadow and went up the stairs. Thanks to the street lights, the upstairs rooms were not too dark for me to move around. Around and around I went through the rooms, hunting for a place to hide the bonds. But when suddenly a window rattled, as if from the draught created by the opening of an outside door somewhere, I still had the loot in my hands.

There was nothing to do now but to chuck them out of a window and trust to luck. I grabbed a pillow from a bed, stripped off the white case, and dumped the bonds into it. Then I leaned out of an already open window and looked down into the night, searching for a desirable dumping place: I didn't want the bonds to land on anything that would make a racket.

And, looking out of the window, I found a better hiding place. The window opened into a narrow court, on the other side of which was a house of the same sort as the one I was in. That house was of the same height as this one, with a flat tin roof that sloped down the other way. The roof wasn't far from me—not too far to chuck the pillow case. I chucked it. It disappeared over the edge of the roof and crackled softly on the tin.

Then I turned on all the lights in the room, lighted a cigarette (we all like to pose a little now and then), and sat down on the bed to await my capture. I might have stalked my enemies through the dark house, and possibly have nabbed them; but most likely I would simply have succeeded in getting myself shot. And I don't like to be shot.

The girl found me.

She came creeping up the hall, an automatic in each hand, hesitated for an instant outside the door, and then came in on the jump. And when she saw me sitting peacefully on the side of the bed, her eyes snapped scornfully at me, as if I had done something mean. I suppose she thought I should have given her an opportunity to shoot.

"I got him, Tai," she called, and the Chinese joined us.

"What did Hook do with the bonds?" he asked point blank.

I grinned into his round yellow face and led my ace.

"Why don't you ask the girl?"

His face showed nothing, but I imagined that his fat body stiffened a little within its fashionable British clothing. That encouraged me, and I went on with my little lie that was meant to stir things up.

"Haven't you rapped to it," I asked, "that they were fixing up to ditch you?"

"You dirty liar!" the girl screamed, and took a step toward me.

Tai halted her with an imperative gesture. He stared through her with his opaque black eyes, and as he stared the blood slid out of his face. She had this fat yellow man on her string, right enough, but he wasn't exactly a harmless toy.

"So that's how it is?" he said slowly, to no one in particular. Then to me: "Where did they put the bonds?"

The girl went close to him and her words came out tumbling over each other:

"Here's the truth of it, Tai, so help me God! I switched the stuff myself. Hook wasn't in it. I was going to run out on both of you. I stuck them under the couch downstairs, but they're not there now. That's the God's truth!"

He was eager to believe her, and her words had the ring of truth to them. And I knew that—in love with her as he was—he'd more readily forgive her treachery with the bonds than he would forgive her for planning to run off with Hook; so I made haste to stir things up again.

"Part of that is right enough," I said. "She did stick the bonds under the couch—but Hook was in on it. They fixed it up between them while you were upstairs. He was to pick a fight with you, and during the argument she was to make the switch, and that is exactly what they did."

I had him! As she wheeled savagely toward me, he stuck the muzzle of an automatic in her side—a smart jab that checked the angry words she was hurling at me.

"I'll take your guns, Elvira," he said, and took them.

"Where are the bonds now?" he asked me.

I grinned. "I'm not with you, Tai. I'm against you."

"I don't like violence," he said slowly, "and I believe you are a sensible person. Let us traffic, my friend."

"You name it," I suggested.

"Gladly! As a basis for our bargaining, we will stipulate that you have hidden the bonds where they cannot be found by anyone else; and that I have you completely in my power, as the shilling shockers used to have it."

"Reasonable enough," I said; "go on."

"The situation, then, is what gamblers call a standoff. Neither of us has the advantage. As a detective, you want us; but we have you. As thieves, we want the bonds; but you have them. I offer you the girl in exchange for the bonds, and that seems to me an equitable offer. It will give me the bonds and a chance to get away. It will give you no small degree of success in your task as a detective. Hook is dead. You will have the girl. All that will remain is to find me and the bonds again—by no means a hopeless task. You will have turned a defeat into half a victory, with an excellent chance to make it a complete one."

"How do I know that you'll give me the girl?"

He shrugged. "Naturally, there can be no guarantee. But, knowing that she planned to desert me for the swine who lies dead below, you can't imagine that my feelings for her are the most friendly. Too, if I take her with me, she will want a share in the loot."

I turned the lay-out over in my mind.

"This is the way it looks to me," I told him at last. "You aren't a killer. I'll come through alive no matter what happens. All right, why should I swap? You and the girl will be easier to find again than the bonds, and they are the most important part of the job anyway. I'll hold on to them, and take my chances on finding you folks again. Yes, I'm playing it safe."

"No, I'm not a killer," he said, very softly; and he smiled the first smile I had seen on his face. It wasn't a pleasant smile: and there was something in it that made you want to shudder. "But I am other things, perhaps, of which you haven't thought. But this talking is to no purpose. Elvira!"

The girl came obediently forward.

"You will find sheets in one of the bureau drawers," he told her. "Tear one or two of them into strips strong enough to tie up our friend securely."

The girl went to the bureau. I wrinkled my head, trying to find a not too disagreeable answer to the question in my mind. The answer that came first wasn't nice: *torture.*

Then a faint sound brought us all into tense motionlessness.

The room we were in had two doors: one leading into the hall, the other into another bedroom. It was through the hall door that the faint sound had come—the sound of creeping feet.

Swiftly, silently, Tai moved backward to a position from which he could watch the hall door without losing sight of the girl and me—and the gun poised like a live thing in his fat hand was all the warning we needed to make no noise.

The faint sound again, just outside the door.

The gun in Tai's hand seemed to quiver with eagerness.

Through the other door—the door that gave to the next room—popped Mrs. Quarre, an enormous cocked revolver in her thin hand.

"Let it go, you nasty heathen," she screeched.

Tai dropped his pistol before he turned to face her, and he held his hands up high—all of which was very wise.

Thomas Quarre came through the hall door then; he also held a cocked revolver—the mate of his wife's—though, in front of his bulk, his didn't look so enormously large.

I looked at the old woman again, and found little of the

friendly fragile one who had poured tea and chatted about the neighbors. This was a witch if there ever was one—a witch of the blackest, most malignant sort. Her little faded eyes were sharp with ferocity, her withered lips were taut in a wolfish snarl, and her thin body fairly quivered with hate.

"I knew it," she was shrilling. "I told Tom as soon as we got far enough away to think things over. I knew it was a frame-up! I knew this supposed detective was a pal of yours! I knew it was just a scheme to beat Thomas and me out of our shares! Well, I'll show you, you yellow monkey! Where are them bonds? Where are they?"

The Chinese had recovered his poise, if he had ever lost it.

"Our stout friend can tell you perhaps," he said. "I was about to extract the information from him when you so—ah—dramatically arrived."

"Thomas, for goodness sakes don't stand there dreaming," she snapped at her husband, who to all appearances was still the same mild old man who had given me an excellent cigar. "Tie up this Chinaman! I don't trust him an inch, and I won't feel easy until he's tied up."

I got up from my seat on the side of the bed, and moved cautiously to a spot that I thought would be out of the line of fire if the thing I expected happened.

Tai had dropped the gun that had been in his hand, but he hadn't been searched. The Chinese are a thorough people; if one of them carries a gun at all, he usually carries two or three or more. One gun had been taken from Tai, and if they tried to truss him up without frisking him, there was likely to be fireworks. So I moved to one side.

Fat Thomas Quarre went phlegmatically up to the Chinese to carry out his wife's orders—and bungled the job perfectly.

He put his bulk between Tai and the old woman's gun.

Tai's hands moved. An automatic was in each.

Once more Tai ran true to racial form. When a Chinese shoots he keeps on until his gun is empty.

When I yanked Tai over backward by his fat throat, and

slammed him to the floor, his guns were still barking metal; and they clicked empty as I got a knee on one of his arms. I didn't take any chances. I worked on his throat until his eyes and tongue told me that he was out of things for a while. Then I looked around.

Thomas Quarre was against the bed, plainly dead, with three round holes in his starched white vest.

Across the room, Mrs. Quarre lay on her back. Her clothes had somehow settled in place around her fragile body, and death had given her once more the gentle friendly look she had worn when I first saw her.

The red-haired girl Elvira was gone.

Presently Tai stirred, and after taking another gun from his clothes, I helped him sit up. He stroked his bruised throat with one fat hand and looked coolly around the room.

"Where's Elvira?" he asked.

"Got away—for the time being."

He shrugged. "Well, you can call it a decidedly successful operation. The Quarres and Hook dead; the bonds and I in your hands."

"Not so bad," I admitted, "but will you do me a favor?"

"If I may."

"Tell me what the hell this is all about!"

"All about?" he asked.

"Exactly! From what you people have let me overhear, I gather that you pulled some sort of job in Los Angeles that netted you a hundred-thousand-dollars' worth of bonds; but I can't remember any recent job of that size down there."

"Why, that's preposterous!" he said with what, for him, was almost wild-eyed amazement. "Preposterous! Of course you know all about it!"

"I do not! I was trying to find a young fellow named Fisher who left his Tacoma home in anger a week or two ago. His father wants him found on the quiet, so that he can come down and try to talk him into going home again. I was told that I might find Fisher in this block of Turk Street, and that's what brought me here."

He didn't believe me. He never believed me. He went to the gallows thinking me a liar.

When I got out into the street again (and Turk Street was a lovely place when I came free into it after my evening in that house!) I bought a newspaper that told me most of what I wanted to know.

A boy of twenty—a messenger in the employ of a Los Angeles stock and bond house—had disappeared two days before, while on his way to a bank with a wad of bonds. That same night this boy and a slender girl with bobbed red hair had registered at a hotel in Fresno as *J. M. Riordan and wife.* The next morning the boy had been found in his room—murdered. The girl was gone. The bonds were gone.

That much the paper told me. During the next few days, digging up a little here and a little there, I succeeded in piecing together most of the story.

The Chinese—whose full name was Tai Choon Tau—had been the brains of the mob. Their game had been a variation of the always-reliable badger game. Tai would pick out some youth who was messenger or runner for a banker or broker—one who carried either cash or negotiable securities in large quantities.

The girl Elvira would then *make* this lad, get him all fussed up over her—which shouldn't have been very hard for her—and then lead him gently around to running away with her and whatever he could grab in the way of his employer's bonds or currency.

Wherever they spent the first night of their flight, there Hook would appear—foaming at the mouth and loaded for bear. The girl would plead and tear her hair and so forth, trying to keep Hook—in his rôle of irate husband—from butchering the youth. Finally she would succeed, and in the end the youth would find himself without either girl or the fruits of his thievery.

Sometimes he had surrendered to the police. Two we found had committed suicide. The Los Angeles lad had been built of tougher stuff than the others. He had put up a fight, and Hook had had to kill him. You can measure the girl's skill in her end of the game by the fact that not one of the half dozen youths who had been trimmed had said the least thing to implicate her; and some of them had gone to great trouble to keep her out of it.

The house in Turk Street had been the mob's retreat, and, that it might be always a safe one, they had not worked their game in San Francisco. Hook and the girl were supposed by the neighbors to be the Quarres' son and daughter—and Tai was the Chinese cook. The Quarres' benign and respectable appearances had also come in handy when the mob had securities to be disposed of.

The Chinese went to the gallows. We threw out the widest and finest-meshed of dragnets for the red-haired girl; and we turned up girls with bobbed red hair by the scores. But the girl Elvira was not among them.

I promised myself that some day . . .

The Jolly Corner

Henry James (1843–1916)

A novelist, short story writer, and critic, **Henry James** was born in New York City and, because of his wealthy father, had a unique schooling. His father believed that James and his brothers should learn the ways of European society and, using this knowledge, form well-rounded views of the world and of their place in it. Thus, James and his family traveled across the Atlantic numerous times, an experience that instilled in him a fascination for European-American relations. His collections of stories reflect this fascination: *A Passionate Pilgrim and Other Tales* (1875), *Transatlantic Sketches* (1875), *The Siege of London* (1883), *Embarrassments* (1896), and *The Two Magics* (1898). James is also known for his oftentimes cerebral novels, which are set in affluent and leisurely surroundings where central concerns are manners, conversation, and character values. His novels include *Roderick Hudson* (1875), *The American* (1877), *The Europeans* (1878), *Portrait of a Lady* (1881), *The Bostonians* (1886), and *The Golden Bowl* (1903). In these novels, he uses a complex and formal prose style, a style that has greatly influenced many later writers.

I

"Every one asks me what I 'think' of everything," said Spencer Brydon; "and I make answer as I can—begging or dodging the question, putting them off with any nonsense. It wouldn't matter to any of them really," he went on, "for, even were it possible to meet in that stand-and-deliver way so silly a demand on so big a subject, my 'thoughts' would still be almost altogether about something that concerns only myself." He was talking to Miss Staverton, with whom for a couple of months now he had availed himself of every possible occasion to talk; this disposition and this resource, this comfort and support, as the situation in fact presented itself, having promptly enough taken the first place in the considerable array of rather unattenuated surprises attending his so strangely belated return to America. Everything was somehow a surprise; and that might be natural when one had so long and so consistently neglected everything, taken pains to give surprises so much margin for play. He had given them more than thirty years—thirty-three, to be exact; and they now seemed to him to have organised their performance quite on the scale of that licence. He had been twenty-three on leaving New York—he was fifty-six today: unless indeed he were to reckon as he had sometimes, since his repatriation, found himself feeling; in which case he would have lived longer than is often allotted to man. It would have taken a century, he repeatedly said to himself, and said also to Alice Staverton, it would have taken a longer absence and a more averted mind than those even of which he had been guilty, to pile up the differences, the newnesses, the queernesses, above all the bignesses, for the better or the worse, that at present assaulted his vision wherever he looked.

The great fact all the while however had been the incalculability; since he *had* supposed himself, from decade to decade, to be allowing, and in the most liberal and intelligent manner, for brilliancy of change. He actually saw that he had allowed for nothing; he missed what he would have been sure of finding, he found what he would never have imagined. Proportions and values were upside-down; the ugly things he had expected, the ugly things of his far-away youth, when he had too promptly waked up to a sense of the ugly—these uncanny phenomena placed him rather, as it happened, under the charm; whereas the "swagger" things, the modern, the monstrous, the famous things, those he had more particularly, like thousands of ingenuous enquirers every year, come over to see, were exactly his sources of dismay. They were as so many set traps for displeasure, above all for reaction, of which his restless tread was constantly pressing the spring. It was interesting, doubtless, the whole show, but it would have been too disconcerting hadn't a certain finer truth saved the situation. He had distinctly not, in this steadier light, come over *all* for the monstrosities; he had come, not only in the last analysis but quite on the face of the act, under an impulse with which they had nothing to do. He had come—putting the thing pompously—to look at his "property," which he had thus for a third of a century not been within four thousand miles of; or, expressing it less sordidly, he had yielded to the humour of seeing again his house on the jolly corner, as he usually, and quite fondly, described it—the one in which he had first seen the light, in which various members of his family had lived and had died, in which the holidays of his overschooled boyhood had been passed and the few social flowers of his chilled adolescence gathered, and which, alienated then for so long a period, had, through the successive deaths of his two brothers and the termination of old arrangements, come wholly into his hands. He was the owner of another, not quite so "good"—the jolly corner having been, from far back, superlatively extended and consecrated; and the value of the pair represented his main capital, with an income consisting, in these later years, of their respective rents which (thanks precisely to their original excellent type) had never been depressingly low. He could live in "Europe," as he had been in the habit of living, on the product of these flourishing New York leases, and all the better since, that of the second structure, the mere number in its long row, having within a twelvemonth fallen in, renovation at a high advance had proved beautifully possible.

These were items of property indeed, but he had found himself since his arrival distinguishing more than ever between them. The house within the street, two bristling blocks westward, was already in course of reconstruction as a tall mass of flats; he had acceded, some time before, to overtures for this conversion—in which, now that it was going forward, it had been not the least of his astonishments to find himself able, on the spot, and though without a previous ounce of such experience, to participate with a certain intelligence, almost with a certain authority. He had lived his life with his back so turned to such concerns and his face addressed to those of so different an order that he scarce knew what to make of this lively stir, in a compartment of his mind never yet penetrated, of a capacity for business and a sense for construction. These virtues, so common all round him now, had been dormant in his own organism—where it might be said of them perhaps that they had slept the sleep of the just. At present, in the splendid autumn weather—the autumn at least was a pure boon in the terrible place—he loafed about his "work" undeterred, secretly agitated; not in the least "minding" that the whole proposition, as they said, was vulgar and sordid, and ready to climb ladders, to walk the plank, to handle materials and look wise about them, to ask questions, in fine, and challenge explanations and really "go into" figures.

It amused, it verily quite charmed him; and, by the same stroke, it amused, and even more, Alice Staverton, though perhaps charming her perceptibly less. She wasn't however going to be better off for it, as *he* was—and so astonishingly much: nothing was now likely, he knew, ever to make her better off than she found herself, in the afternoon of life, as the delicately frugal possessor and tenant of the small house in Irving Place to which she had subtly managed to cling through her almost unbroken New York career. If he knew the way to it now better than to any other address among the dreadful multiplied numberings which seemed to him to reduce the whole place to some vast ledger-page, overgrown, fantastic, of ruled and criss-crossed lines and figures—if he had formed, for his consolation, that habit, it was really not a little because of the charm of his having encountered and recognised, in the vast wilderness of the wholesale, breaking through the mere gross generalisation of wealth and force and success, a small still scene where items and shades, all delicate things, kept the sharpness of the notes of a high voice perfectly trained, and where economy hung about like the scent of a garden. His old friend lived with one maid and herself dusted her relics and trimmed her lamps and polished her silver; she stood off, in the awful modern crush, when she could, but she sallied forth and did battle when the challenge was really to "spirit," the spirit she after all confessed to, proudly and a little shyly, as to that of the better time, that of *their* common, their quite far-away and antediluvian social period and order. She made use of the street-cars when need be, the terrible things that people scrambled for as the panic-stricken at sea scramble for the boats; she affronted, inscrutably, under stress, all the public concussions and ordeals; and yet, with that slim mystifying grace of her appearance, which defied you to say if she were a fair young woman who looked older through trouble, or a fine smooth older one who looked young through successful indifference; with her precious reference, above all, to memories and histories into which he could enter, she was as exquisite for him as some pale pressed flower (a rarity to begin with), and, failing other sweetnesses, she was a sufficient reward of his effort. They had communities of knowledge, "their" knowledge (this discriminating possessive was always on her lips) of presences of the other age, presences all overlaid, in his case, by the experience of a man and the freedom of a wanderer, overlaid by pleasure, by infidelity, by passages of life that were strange and dim to her, just by "Europe" in short, but still unobscured, still exposed and cherished, under that pious visitation of the *spirit* from which she had never been diverted.

She had come with him one day to see how his "apartment-house" was rising; he had helped her over gaps and explained to her plans, and while they were there had happened to have, before her, a brief but lively discussion with the man in charge, the representative of the building-firm that had undertaken his work. He had found himself quite "standing-up" to this personage over a failure on the latter's part to observe some detail of one of their noted conditions, and had so lucidly urged his case that, besides ever so prettily flushing, at the time, for sympathy in his triumph, she had afterwards said to him (though to a slightly greater effect of irony) that he had clearly for too many years neglected a real gift. If he had but stayed at home he would have anticipated the inventor of the sky-scraper. If he had but stayed at home he would have discovered his genius in time really to start some new variety of awful architectural hare and run it till it burrowed in a gold-mine. He was to remember these words, while the weeks elapsed, for the small silver ring they had sounded over the queerest and deepest of his own lately most disguised and most muffled vibrations.

It had begun to be present to him after the first fortnight, it had broken out with the oddest abruptness, this particular wanton wonderment: it met him there—and this was the image under which he himself judged the matter, or at least, not a little, thrilled and flushed with it—very much as he might have been met by some strange figure, some unexpected occupant, at a turn of one of the dim passages of an empty house. The quaint analogy quite hauntingly remained with him, when he didn't indeed rather improve it by a still intenser form: that of his opening a door behind which he would have made sure of finding nothing, a door into a room shuttered and void, and yet so coming, with a great suppressed start, on some quite erect confronting presence, something planted in the middle of the place and facing him through the dusk. After that visit to the house in construction he walked with his companion to see the other and always so much the better one, which in the eastward direction formed one of the corners, the "jolly" one precisely, of the street now so generally dishonoured and disfigured in its westward reaches, and of the comparatively conservative Avenue. The Avenue still had pretensions, as Miss Staverton said, to decency; the old people had mostly gone, the old names were unknown, and here and there an old association seemed to stray, all vaguely, like some very aged person, out too late, whom you might meet and feel the impulse to watch or follow, in kindness, for safe restoration to shelter.

They went in together, our friends; he admitted himself with his key, as he kept no one there, he explained, preferring, for his reasons, to leave the place empty, under a simple arrangement with a good woman living in the neighbourhood and who came for a daily hour to open windows and dust and sweep. Spencer Brydon had his reasons and was growingly aware of them; they seemed to him better each time he was there, though he didn't name them all to his companion, any more than he told her as yet how often, how quite absurdly often, he himself came. He only let her see for the present, while they walked through the great blank rooms, that absolute vacancy reigned and that, from top to bottom, there was nothing but Mrs. Muldoon's broomstick, in a corner, to tempt the burglar. Mrs. Muldoon was then on the premises, and she loquaciously attended the visitors, preceding them from room to room and pushing back shutters and throwing up sashes—all to show them, as she remarked, how little there was to see. There was little indeed to see in the great gaunt shell where the main dispositions and the general apportionment of space the style of an age of ampler allowances, had nevertheless for its masters their honest pleading message, affecting him as some good old servant's, some lifelong retainer's appeal for a character, or even for a retiring-pension; yet it was also a remark of Mrs. Muldoon's that, glad as she was to oblige him by her noonday round, there was a request she greatly hoped he would never make of her. If he should wish her for any reason to come in after dark she would just tell him, if he "plased," that he must ask it of somebody else.

The fact that there was nothing to see didn't militate for the worthy woman against what one *might* see, and she put it frankly to Miss Staverton that no lady could be expected to like, could she? "craping up to thim top storeys in the ayvil hours." The gas and the electric light were off the house, and she fairly evoked a gruesome vision of her march through the great grey rooms—so many of them as there were too!—with her glimmering taper. Miss Staverton met her honest glare with a smile and the profession that she herself certainly would recoil from such an adventure. Spencer Brydon meanwhile held his peace—for the moment; the question of the "evil" hours in his old home had already become too grave for him. He had begun some time since to "crape," and he knew just why a packet of candles addressed to that pursuit had been stowed by his own hand, three weeks before, at the back of a drawer of the fine old sideboard that occupied, as a "fixture," the deep recess in the dining-room. Just now he laughed at his companions—quickly however changing the subject; for the reason that, in the first place, his laugh struck him even at that moment as starting the odd echo, the conscious human resonance (he scarce knew how to qualify it) that sounds made while he was there alone sent back to his ear or his fancy; and that, in the second, he imagined Alice Staverton for the instant on the point of asking him, with a divination, if he ever so prowled. There were divinations he was unprepared for, and he had at all events averted enquiry by the time Mrs. Muldoon had left them, passing on to other parts.

There was happily enough to say, on so consecrated a spot, that could be said freely and fairly; so that a whole train of declarations was precipitated by his friend's having herself broken out, after a yearning look round: "But I hope you don't mean they want you to pull *this* to pieces!" His answer came, promptly, with his reawakened wrath: it was of course exactly what they wanted, and what they were "at" him for, daily, with the iteration of people who couldn't for their life understand a man's liability to decent feelings. He had found the place, just as it stood and beyond what he could express, an interest and a joy. There were values other than the beastly rent-values, and in short, in short—! But it was thus Miss Staverton took him up. "In short you're to make so good a thing of your sky-scraper that, living in luxury on *those* ill-gotten gains, you can afford for a while to be sentimental here!" Her smile had for him, with the words, the particular mild irony with which he found half her talk suffused; an irony without bitterness and that came, exactly, from her having so much imagination—not, like the cheap sarcasms with which one heard most people, about the world of "society," bid for the reputation of cleverness, from nobody's really having any. It was agreeable to him at this very moment to be sure that when he had answered, after a brief demur, "Well yes: so, precisely, you may put it!" her imagination would still do him justice. He explained that even if never a dollar were to come to him from the other house he would nevertheless cherish this one; and he dwelt, further, while they lingered and wandered, on the fact of the stupefaction he was already exciting, the positive mystification he felt himself create.

He spoke of the value of all he read into it, into the mere sight of the walls, mere shapes of the rooms, mere sound of the floors, mere feel, in his hand, of the old silver-plated knobs of the several mahogany doors, which suggested the pressure of the palms of the dead; the seventy years of the past in fine that these things represented, the annals of nearly three generations, counting his grandfather's, the one that had ended there, and the impalpable ashes of his long-extinct youth, afloat in the very air like microscopic motes. She listened to everything; she was a woman who answered intimately but who utterly didn't chatter. She scattered abroad therefore no cloud of words; she could assent, she could agree, above all she could encourage, without doing that. Only at the last she went a little further than he had done himself. "And then how do you know? You may still, after all, want to live here." It rather indeed pulled him up, for it wasn't what he had been thinking, at least in her sense of the words. "You mean I may decide to stay on for the sake of it?"

"Well, *with* such a home—!" But, quite beautifully, she had too much tact to dot so monstrous an *i,* and it was precisely an illustration of the way she didn't rattle. How could any one—of any wit—insist on any one else's "wanting" to live in New York?

"Oh," he said, "I *might* have lived here (since I had my opportunity early in life); I might have put in here all these years. Then everything would have been different enough—and, I dare say, 'funny' enough. But that's another matter. And then the beauty of it—I mean of my perversity, of my refusal to agree to a 'deal'—is just in the total absence of a reason. Don't you see that if I had a reason about the matter at all it would *have* to be the other way, and would then be inevitably a reason of dollars? There are no reasons here *but* of dollars. Let us therefore have none whatever—not the ghost of one."

They were back in the hall then for departure, but from where they stood the vista was large, through an open door, into the great square main saloon, with its almost antique felicity of brave spaces between windows. Her eyes came back from that reach and met his own a moment. "Are you very sure the 'ghost' of one doesn't, much rather, serve—?"

He had a positive sense of turning pale. But it was as near as they were then to come. For he made answer, he believed, between a glare and a grin: "Oh ghosts—of course the place must swarm with them! I should be ashamed of it if it didn't. Poor Mrs. Muldoon's right, and it's why I haven't asked her to do more than look in."

Miss Staverton's gaze again lost itself, and things she didn't utter, it was clear, came and went in her mind. She might even for the minute, off there in the fine room, have imagined some element dimly gathering. Simplified like the death-mask of a handsome face, it perhaps produced for her just then an effect akin to the stir of an expression in the "set" commemorative plaster. Yet whatever her impression may have been she produced instead a vague platitude. "Well, if it were only furnished and lived in—!"

She appeared to imply that in case of its being still furnished he might have been a little less opposed to the idea of a return. But she passed straight into the vestibule, as if to leave her words behind her, and the next moment he had opened the house-door and was standing with her on the steps. He closed the door and, while he re-pocketed his key, looking up and down, they took in the comparatively harsh actuality of the Avenue, which reminded him of the assault of the outer light of the Desert on the traveller emerging from an Egyptian tomb. But he risked before they stepped into the street his gathered answer to her speech. "For me it is lived in. For me it *is* furnished." At which it was easy for her to sigh "Ah yes—!" all vaguely and discreetly; since his parents and his favourite sister, to say nothing of other kin, in numbers, had run their course and met their end there. That represented, within the walls, ineffaceable life.

It was a few days after this that, during an hour passed with her again, he had expressed his impatience of the too flattering curiosity—among the people he met—about his appreciation of New York. He had arrived at none at all that was socially producible, and as for that matter of his "thinking" (thinking the better or the worse of anything there) he was wholly taken up with one subject of thought. It was mere vain egoism, and it was moreover, if she liked, a morbid obsession. He found all things come back to the question of what he personally might have been, how he might have led his life and "turned out," if he had not so, at the outset, given it up. And confessing for the first time to the intensity within him of this absurd speculation—which but proved also, no doubt, the habit of too selfishly thinking—he affirmed the impotence there of any other source of interest, any other native appeal. "What would it have made of me, what would it have made of me? I keep for ever wondering, all idiotically; as if I could possibly know! I see what it has made of dozens of others, those I meet, and it positively aches within me, to the point of exasperation, that it would have made something of me as well. Only I can't make out *what,* and the worry of it, the small rage of curiosity never to be satisfied, brings back what I remember to have felt, once or twice, after judging best, for reasons, to burn some important letter unopened. I've been sorry, I've hated it—I've never known what was in the letter. You may of course say it's a trifle—!"

"I don't say it's a trifle," Miss Staverton gravely interrupted.

She was seated by her fire, and before her, on his feet and restless, he turned to and fro between this intensity of his idea and a fitful and unseeing inspection, through his single eye-glass, of the dear little old objects on her chimney-piece. Her interruption made him for an instant look at her harder. "I shouldn't care if you did!" he laughed, however; "and it's only a figure, at any rate, for the way I now feel. *Not* to have followed my perverse young course—and almost in the teeth of my father's curse, as I may say; not to have kept it up, so, 'over there,' from that day to this, without a doubt or a pang; not, above all, to have liked it, to have loved it, so much, loved it, no doubt, with such an abysmal conceit of my own preference: some variation from *that,* I say, must have produced some different effect for my life and for my 'form.' I should have stuck here—if it had been possible; and I was too young, at twenty-three, to judge, *pour deux sous,* whether it *were* possible. If I had waited I might have seen it was, and then I might have been, by staying here, something nearer to one of these types who have been hammered so hard and made so keen by their conditions. It isn't that I admire them so much—the question of any charm in them, or of any charm, beyond that of the rank money-passion, exerted by their conditions *for* them, has nothing to do with the matter: it's only a question of what fantastic, yet perfectly possible, development of my own nature I mayn't have missed. It comes over me that I had then a strange *alter ego* deep down somewhere within me, as the full-blown flower is in the small tight bud, and that I just took the course, I just transferred him to the climate, that blighted him for once and for ever."

"And you wonder about the flower," Miss Staverton said. "So do I, if you want to know; and so I've been wondering these several weeks. I believe in the flower," she continued, "I feel it would have been quite splendid, quite huge and monstrous."

"Monstrous above all!" her visitor echoed; "and I imagine, by the same stroke, quite hideous and offensive."

"You don't believe that," she returned; "if you did you wouldn't wonder. You'd know, and that would be enough for you. What you feel—and what I feel *for* you—is that you'd have had power."

"You'd have liked me that way?" he asked.

She barely hung fire. "How should I not have liked you?"

"I see. You'd have liked me, have preferred me, a billionaire!"

"How should I not have liked you?" she simply again asked.

He stood before her still—her question kept him motionless. He took it in, so much there was of it; and indeed his not otherwise meeting it testified to that. "I know at least what I am," he simply went on; "the other side of the medal's clear enough. I've not been edifying—I believe I'm thought in a hundred quarters to have been barely decent. I've followed strange paths and worshipped strange gods; it must have come to you again and again—in fact you've admitted to me as much—that I was leading, at any time these thirty years, a selfish frivolous scandalous life. And you see what it has made of me."

She just waited, smiling at him. "You see what it has made of *me*."

"Oh you're a person whom nothing can have altered. You were born to be what you are, anywhere, anyway: you've the perfection nothing else could have blighted. And don't you see how, without my exile, I shouldn't have been waiting till now—?" But he pulled up for the strange pang.

"The great thing to see," she presently said, "seems to me to be that it has spoiled nothing. It hasn't spoiled your being here at last. It hasn't spoiled this. It hasn't spoiled your speaking—" She also however faltered.

He wondered at everything her controlled emotion might mean. "Do you believe then—too dreadfully!—that I *am* as good as I might ever have been?"

"Oh no! Far from it!" With which she got up from her chair and was nearer to him. "But I don't care," she smiled.

"You mean I'm good enough?"

She considered a little. "Will you believe it if I say so? I mean will you let that settle your question for you?" And then as if making out in his face that he drew back from this, that he had some idea which, however absurd, he couldn't yet bargain away: "Oh you don't care either—but very differently: you don't care for anything but yourself."

Spencer Brydon recognised it—it was in fact what he had absolutely professed. Yet he importantly qualified. "*He* isn't myself. He's the just so totally other person. But I do want to see him," he added. "And I can. And I shall."

Their eyes met for a minute while he guessed from something in hers that she divined his strange sense. But neither of them otherwise expressed it, and her apparent understanding, with no protesting shock, no easy derision, touched him more deeply than anything yet, constituting for his stifled perversity, on the spot, an element that was like breatheable air. What she said however was unexpected. "Well, *I've* seen him."

"You—?"

"I've seen him in a dream."

"Oh a 'dream'—!" It let him down.

"But twice over," she continued. "I saw him as I see you now."

"You've dreamed the same dream—?"

"Twice over," she repeated. "The very same."

This did somehow a little speak to him, as it also gratified him. "You dream about me at that rate?"

"Ah about *him!*" she smiled.

His eyes again sounded her. "Then you know all about him." And as she said nothing more: "What's the wretch like?"

She hesitated, and it was as if he were pressing her so hard that, resisting for reasons of her own, she had to turn away. "I'll tell you some other time!"

II

It was after this that there was most of a virtue for him, most of a cultivated charm, most of a preposterous secret thrill, in the particular form of surrender to his obsession and of address to what he more and more believed to be his privilege. It was what in these weeks he was living for—since he really felt life to begin but after Mrs. Muldoon had retired from the scene and, visiting the ample house from attic to cellar, making sure he was alone, he knew himself in safe possession and, as he tacitly expressed it, let himself go. He sometimes came twice in the twenty-four hours; the moments he liked best were those of gathering dusk, of the short autumn twilight; this was the time of which, again and again, he found himself hoping most. Then he could, as seemed to him, most intimately wander and wait, linger and listen, feel his fine attention, never in his life before so fine, on the pulse of the great vague place: he preferred the lampless hour and only wished he might have prolonged each day the deep crepuscular spell. Later—rarely much before midnight, but then for a considerable vigil—he watched with his glimmering light; moving slowly, holding it high, playing it far, rejoicing above all, as much as he might, in open vistas, reaches of communication between rooms and by passages; the long straight chance or show, as he would have called it, for the revelation he pretended to invite. It was practice he found he could perfectly "work" without exciting remark; no one was in the least the wiser for it; even Alice

Staverton, who was moreover a well of discretion, didn't quite fully imagine.

He let himself in and let himself out with the assurance of calm proprietorship; and accident so far favoured him that, if a fat Avenue "officer" had happened on occasion to see him entering at eleven-thirty, he had never yet, to the best of his belief, been noticed as emerging at two. He walked there on the crisp November nights, arrived regularly at the evening's end; it was as easy to do this after dining out as to take his way to a club or to his hotel. When he left his club, if he hadn't been dining out, it was ostensibly to go to his hotel; and when he left his hotel, if he had spent a part of the evening there, it was ostensibly to go to his club. Everything was easy in fine; everything conspired and promoted: there was truly even in the strain of his experience something that glossed over, something that salved and simplified, all the rest of consciousness. He circulated, talked, renewed, loosely and pleasantly, old relations—met indeed, so far as he could, new expectations and seemed to make out on the whole that in spite of the career, of such different contacts, which he had spoken of to Miss Staverton as ministering so little, for those who might have watched it, to edification, he was positively rather liked than not. He was a dim secondary social success—and all with people who had truly not an idea of him. It was all mere surface sound, this murmur of their welcome, this popping of their corks—just as his gestures of response were the extravagant shadows, emphatic in proportion as they meant little, of some game of *ombres chinoises*. He projected himself all day, in thought, straight over the bristling line of hard unconscious heads and into the other, the real, the waiting life; the life that, as soon as he had heard behind him the click of his great house-door, began for him, on the jolly corner, as beguilingly as the slow opening bars of some rich music follows the tap of the conductor's wand.

He always caught the first effect of the steel point of his stick on the old marble of the hall pavement, large black-and-white squares that he remembered as the admiration of his childhood and that had then made in him, as he now saw, for the growth of an early conception of style. This effect was the dim reverberating tinkle as of some faroff bell hung who should say where?—in the depths of the house, of the past, of that mystical other world that might have flourished for him had he not, for weal or woe, abandoned it. On this impression he did ever the same thing; he put his stick noiselessly away in a corner—feeling the place once more in the likeness of some great glass bowl, all precious concave crystal, set delicately humming by the play of a moist finger round its edge. The concave crystal held, as it were, this mystical other world, and the indescribably fine murmur of its rim was the sigh there, the scarce audible pathetic wail to his strained ear, of all the old baffled forsworn possibilities. What he did therefore by this appeal of his hushed presence was to wake them into such measure of ghostly life as they might still enjoy. They were shy, all but unappeasably shy, but they weren't really sinister; at least they weren't as he had hitherto felt them—before they had taken the Form he so yearned to make them take, the Form he at moments saw himself in the light of fairly hunting on tiptoe, the points of his evening-shoes, from room to room and from storey to storey.

That was the essence of his vision—which was all rank folly, if one would, while he was out of the house and otherwise occupied, but which took on the last verisimilitude as soon as he was placed and posted. He knew what he meant and what he wanted; it was as clear as the figure on a cheque presented in demand for cash. His *alter ego* "walked"—that was the note of his image of him, while his image of his motive for his own odd pastime was the desire to waylay him and meet him. He roamed, slowly, warily, but all restlessly, he himself did—Mrs. Muldoon had been right, absolutely, with her figure of their "craping"; and the presence he watched for would roam restlessly too. But it would be as cautious and as shifty; the conviction of its probable, in fact its already quite sensible, quite audible evasion of pursuit grew for him from night to night, laying on him finally a rigour to which nothing in his life had been comparable. It had been the theory of many superficially-judging persons, he knew, that he was wasting that life in a surrender to sensations, but he had tasted of no pleasure so fine as his actual tension, had been introduced to no sport that demanded at once the patience and the nerve of this stalking of a creature more subtle, yet at bay perhaps more formidable, than any beast of the forest. The terms, the comparisons, the very practices of the chase positively came again into play; there were even moments when passages of his occasional experience as a sportsman, stirred memories, from his younger time, of moor and mountain and desert, revived for him—and to the increase of his keenness—by the tremendous force of analogy. He found himself at moments—once he had placed his single light on some mantel-shelf or in some recess—stepping back into shelter or shade, effacing himself behind a door or in an embrasure, as he had sought of old the vantage of rock and tree; he found himself holding his breath and living in the joy of the instant, the supreme suspense created by big game alone.

He wasn't afraid (though putting himself the question as he believed gentlemen on Bengal tiger-shoots or in close quarters with the great bear of the Rockies had been known to confess to having put it); and this indeed—since here at least he might be frank!—because of the impression, so intimate and so strange, that he himself produced as yet a dread, produced certainly a strain, beyond the liveliest he was likely to feel. They fell for him into categories, they fairly became familiar, the signs, for his own perception, of the alarm his presence and his vigilance created; though leaving him always to remark, portentously, on his probably having formed a relation, his probably enjoying a consciousness, unique in the experience of man. People enough, first and last, had been in terror of apparitions, but who had ever before so turned the tables and become himself, in the apparitional world, an incalculable terror? He might have found this sublime had he quite dared to think of it; but he didn't too much insist, truly, on that side of his privilege. With habit and repetition he gained to an extraordinary degree the power to penetrate the dusk of distances and the darkness of corners, to resolve back into their innocence the treacheries of uncertain light, the evil-looking forms taken in the gloom by mere shadows, by accidents of the air, by shifting effects of perspective; putting down his dim luminary he could still wander on without it, pass into other rooms and, only knowing it was there behind him in case of need, see his way about, visually project for his purpose a comparative clearness. It made him feel, this acquired faculty, like some monstrous stealthy cat; he wondered if he would have glared at these moments with large shining yellow eyes, and what it mightn't verily be, for the poor hard-pressed *alter ego,* to be confronted with such a type.

He liked however the open shutters; he opened everywhere those Mrs. Muldoon had closed, closing them as carefully afterwards, so that she shouldn't notice: he liked—oh this he did like, and above all in the upper rooms!—the sense of the hard silver of the autumn stars through the window-panes, and scarcely less the flare of the street-lamps below, the white electric lustre which it would have taken curtains to keep out. This was human actual social; this was of the world he had lived in, and he was more at his ease certainly for the countenance, coldly general and impersonal, that all the while and in spite of his detachment it seemed to give him. He had support of course mostly in the rooms at the wide front and the prolonged side; it failed him considerably in the central shades and the parts at the back. But if he sometimes, on his rounds, was glad of his optical reach, so none the less often the rear of the house affected him as the very jungle of his prey. The place was there more subdivided; a large "extension" in particular, where small rooms for servants had been multiplied, abounded in nooks and corners, in closets and passages, in the ramifications especially of an ample back staircase over which he leaned, many a time, to look far down—not deterred from his gravity even while aware that he might, for a spectator, have figured some solemn simpleton playing at hide-and-seek. Outside in fact he might himself make that ironic *rapprochement;* but within the walls, and in spite of the clear windows, his consistency was proof against the cynical light of New York.

It had belonged to that idea of the exasperated consciousness of his victim to become a real test for him; since he had quite put it to himself from the first that, oh distinctly! he could "cultivate" his whole perception. He had felt it as above all open to cultivation—which indeed was but another name for his manner of spending his time. He was bringing it on, bringing it to perfection, by practice; in consequence of which it had grown so fine that he was now aware of impressions, attestations of his general postulate, that couldn't have broken upon him at once. This was the case more specifically with a phenomenon at last quite frequent for him in the upper rooms, the recognition—absolutely unmistakeable, and by a turn dating from a particular hour, his resumption of his campaign after a diplomatic drop, a calculated absence of three nights—of his being definitely followed, tracked at a distance carefully taken and to the express end that he should the less confidently, less arrogantly, appear to himself merely to pursue. It worried, it finally quite broke him up, for it proved, of all the conceivable impressions, the one least suited to his book. He was kept in sight while remaining himself—as regards the essence of his position—sightless, and his only recourse then was in abrupt turns, rapid recoveries of ground. He wheeled about, retracing his steps, as if he might so catch in his face at least the stirred air of some other quick revolution. It was indeed true that his fully dislocalised thought of these manoeuvres recalled to him Pantaloon, at the Christmas farce, buffeted and tricked from behind by ubiquitous Harlequin; but it left intact the influence of the conditions themselves each time he was reexposed to them, so that in fact this association, had he suffered it to become constant, would on a certain side have but ministered to his intenser gravity. He had made, as I have said, to create on the premises the baseless sense of a reprieve, his three absences; and the result of the third was to confirm the after-effect of the second.

On his return, that night—the night succeeding his last intermission—he stood in the hall and looked up the staircase with a certainty more intimate than any he had yet known. "He's *there,* at the top, and waiting—not, as in general, falling back for disappearance. He's holding his ground, and it's the first time—which is a proof, isn't it? that something has happened for him." So Brydon argued with his hand on the banister and his foot on the lowest stair; in which position he felt as never before the air chilled by his logic. He himself turned cold in it, for he seemed of a sudden to know what now was involved. "Harder pressed?—yes, he takes it in, with its thus making clear to him that I've come, as they say, 'to stay.' He finally doesn't like and can't bear it, in the sense, I mean, that his wrath, his menaced interest, now balances with his dread. I've hunted him till he has 'turned': that, up there, is what has happened—he's the fanged or the antlered animal brought at last to bay." There came to him, as I say—but determined by an influence beyond my notation!—the acuteness of this certainty; under which however the next moment he had broken into a sweat that he would as little have consented to attribute to fear as he would have dared immediately to act upon it for enterprise. It marked none the less a prodigious thrill, a thrill that represented sudden dismay, no doubt, but also represented, and with the selfsame throb, the strangest, the most joyous, possibly the next minute almost the proudest, duplication of consciousness.

"He has been dodging, retreating, hiding, but now, worked up to anger, he'll fight!"—this intense impression made a single mouthful, as it were, of terror and applause. But what was wondrous was that the applause, for the felt fact, was so eager, since, if it was his other self he was running to earth, this ineffable identity was thus in the last resort not unworthy of him. It bristled there—somewhere near at hand, however unseen still—as the hunted thing, even as the trodden worm of the adage *must* at last bristle; and Brydon at this instant tasted probably of a sensation more complex than had ever before found itself consistent with sanity. It was as if it would have shamed him that a character so associated with his own should triumphantly succeed in just skulking, should to the end not risk the open, so that the drop of this danger was, on the spot, a great lift of the whole situation. Yet with another rare shift of the same subtlety he was already trying to measure by how much more he himself might now be in peril of fear; so rejoicing that he could, in another form, actively inspire that fear, and simultaneously quaking for the form in which he might passively know it.

The apprehension of knowing it must after a little have grown in him, and the strangest moment of his adventure perhaps, the most memorable or really most interesting, afterwares, of his crisis, was the lapse of certain instants of concentrated conscious *combat,* the sense of a need to hold on to something, even after the manner of a man slipping and slipping on some awful incline; the vivid impulse, above all, to move, to act, to charge, somehow and upon something—to show himself, in a word, that he wasn't afraid. The state of "holding-on" was thus the state to which he was momentarily reduced; if there had been anything, in the great vacancy, to seize, he would presently have been aware of having clutched it as he might under a shock at home have clutched the nearest chair-back. He had been surprised at any rate—of this he *was* aware—into something unprecedented since his original appropriation of the place; he had closed his eyes, held them tight, for a long minute, as with that instinct of dismay and that terror of vision. When he opened them the room, the other contiguous rooms, extraordinarily, seemed lighter—so light, almost, that at first he took the change for day. He stood firm, however that might be, just where he had paused; his resistance had helped him—it was as if there were something he had tided over. He knew after a little what this was—it had been in the imminent danger of flight. He had stiffened his will against going; without this he would have made for the stairs, and it seemed to him that, still with his eyes closed, he would have descended them, would have known how, straight and swiftly, to the bottom.

Well, as he had held out, here he was—still at the top, among the more intricate upper rooms and with the gauntlet of the others, of all the rest of the house, still to run when it should be his time to go. He would go at his time—only at his time: didn't he go every night very much at the same hour? He took out his watch—there was light for that: it was scarcely a quarter past one, and he had never withdrawn so soon. He reached his lodgings for the most part at two—with his walk of a quarter of an hour. He would wait for the last quarter—he wouldn't stir till then; and he kept his watch there with his eyes on it, reflecting while he held it that this deliberate wait, a wait with an effort, which he recognised, would serve perfectly for the attestation he desired to make. It would prove his courage—unless indeed the latter might most be proved by his budging at last from his place. What he mainly felt now was that, since he hadn't originally scuttled, he had his dignities—which had never in his life seemed so many—all to preserve and to carry aloft. This was before him in truth as a physical image, an image almost worthy of an age of greater romance. That remark indeed glimmered for him only to glow the next instant with a finer light; since what age of romance, after all, could have matched either the state of his mind or, "objectively," as they said, the wonder of his situation? The only difference would have been that, brandishing his dignities over his head as in a parchment scroll, he might then—that is in the heroic time—have proceeded downstairs with a drawn sword in his other grasp.

At present, really, the light he had set down on the mantel of the next room would have to figure his sword; which utensil, in the course of a minute, he had taken the requisite number of steps to possess himself of. The door between the rooms was open, and from the second another door opened to a third. These rooms, as he remembered, gave all three upon a common corridor as well, but there was a fourth, beyond them, without issue save through the preceding. To have moved, to have heard his step again, was appreciably a help; though even in recognising this he lingered once more a little by the chimney-piece on which his light had rested. When he next moved, just hesitating where to turn, he found himself considering a circumstance that, after his first and comparatively vague apprehension of it, produced in him the start that often attends some pang of recollection, the violent shock of having ceased happily to forget. He had come into sight of the door in which the brief chain of communication ended and which he now surveyed from the nearer threshold, the one not directly facing it. Placed at some distance to the left of this point, it would have admitted him to the last room of the four, the room without other approach or egress, had it not, to his intimate conviction, been closed *since* his former visitation, the matter probably of a quarter of an hour before. He stared with all his eyes at the wonder of the fact, arrested again where he stood and again holding his breath while he sounded its sense. Surely it had been *subsequently* closed—that is it had been on his previous passage indubitably open!

He took it full in the face that something had happened between—that he couldn't not have noticed before (by which he meant on his original tour of all the rooms that evening) that such a barrier had exceptionally presented itself. He had indeed since that moment undergone an agitation so extraordinary that it might have muddled for him any earlier view; and he tried to convince himself that he might perhaps then have gone into the room and, inadvertently, automatically, on coming out, have drawn the door after him. The difficulty was that this exactly was what he never did; it was against his whole policy, as he might have said, the essence of which was to keep vistas clear. He had them from the first, as he was well aware, quite on the brain: the strange apparition, at the far end of one of them, of his baffled "prey" (which had become by so sharp an irony so little the term now to apply!) was the form of success his imagination had most cherished, projecting into it always a refinement of beauty. He had known fifty times the start of perception that had afterwards dropped; had fifty times gasped to himself "There!" under some fond brief hallucination. The house, as the case stood, admirably lent itself; he might wonder at the taste, the native architecture of the particular time, which could rejoice so in the multiplication of doors—the opposite extreme to the modern, the actual almost complete proscription of them; but it had fairly contributed to provoke this obsession of the presence encountered telescopically, as he might say, focussed and studied in diminishing perspective and as by a rest for the elbow.

It was with these considerations that his present attention was charged—they perfectly availed to make what he saw portentous. He *couldn't,* by any lapse, have blocked that aperture; and if he hadn't, if it was unthinkable, why what else was clear but that there had been another agent? Another agent?—he had been catching, as he felt, a moment back, the very breath of him; but when had he been so close as in this simple, this logical, this completely personal act? It was so logical, that is, that one might have *taken* it for personal; yet for what did Brydon take it, he asked himself, while, softly panting, he felt his eyes almost leave their sockets. Ah this time at last they *were,* the two, the opposed projections of him, in presence; and this time, as much as one would, the question of danger loomed. With it rose, as not before, the question of courage—for what he knew the blank face of the door to say to him was "Show us how much you have!" It stared, it glared back at him with that challenge; it put to him the two alternatives: should he just push it open or not? Oh to have this consciousness was to *think*—and to think, Brydon knew, as he stood there, was, with the lapsing moments, not to have acted! Not to have acted—that was the misery and the pang—was even still not to act; was in fact *all* to feel the thing in another, in a new and terrible way. How long did he pause and how long did he debate? There was presently nothing to measure it; for his vibration had already changed—as just by the effect of its intensity. Shut up there, at bay, defiant, and with the prodigy of the thing palpably proveably *done,* thus giving notice like some stark signboard—under that accession of accent the situation itself had turned; and Brydon at last remarkably made up his mind on what it had turned to.

It had turned altogether to a different admonition; to a supreme hint, for him, of the value of Discretion! This slowly dawned, no doubt—for it could take its time; so perfectly, on his threshold, had he been stayed, so little as yet had he either advanced or retreated. It was the strangest of all things that now when, by his taking ten steps and applying his hand to a latch, or even his shoulder and his knee, if necessary, to a panel, all the hunger of his prime need might have been met, his high curiosity crowned, his unrest assuaged—it was amazing, but it was also exquisite and rare, that insistence should have, at a touch, quite dropped from him. Discretion—he jumped at that; and yet not, verily, at such a pitch, because it saved his nerves or his skin, but because, much more valuably, it saved the situation. When I say he "jumped" at it I feel the consonance of this term with the fact that—at the end indeed of I know not how long—he did move again, he crossed straight to the door. He wouldn't touch it—it seemed now that he might *if* he would: he would only just wait there a little, to show, to prove, that he wouldn't. He had thus another station, close to the thin partition by which revelation was denied him; but with his eyes bent and his hands held off in a mere intensity of stillness. He listened as if there had been something to hear, but this attitude, while it lasted, was his own communication. "If you won't then—good: I spare you and I give up. You affect me as by the appeal positively for pity: you convince me that for reasons rigid and sublime—what do I know?—we both of us should have suffered. I respect them then, and, though moved and privileged as, I believe, it has never been given to man, I retire, I renounce—never, on my honour, to try again. So rest for ever—and let *me!*"

That, for Brydon was the deep sense of this last demonstration—solemn, measured, directed, as he felt it to be. He brought it to a close, he turned away; and now verily he knew how deeply he had been stirred. He retraced his steps, taking up his candle, burnt, he observed, well-nigh to the socket, and marking again, lighten it as he would, the distinctness of his footfall; after which, in a moment, he knew himself at the other side of the house. He did here what he had not yet done at these hours—he opened half a casement, one of those in the front, and let in the air of the night; a thing he would have taken at any time previous for a sharp rupture of his spell. His spell was broken now, and it didn't matter—broken by his concession and his surrender, which made it idle henceforth that he should ever come back. The empty street—its other life so marked even by the great lamplit vacancy—was within call, within touch; he stayed there as to be in it again, high above it though he was still perched; he watched as for some comforting common fact, some vulgar human note, the passage of a scavenger or a thief, some night-bird however base. He would have blessed that sign of life; he would have welcomed positively the slow approach of his friend the policeman, whom he had hitherto only sought to avoid, and was not sure that if the patrol had come into sight he mightn't have felt the impulse to get into relation with it, to hail it, on some pretext, from his fourth floor.

The pretext that wouldn't have been too silly or too compromising, the explanation that would have saved his dignity and kept his name, in such a case, out of the papers, was not definite to him: he was so occupied with the thought of recording his Discretion—as an effect of the vow he had just uttered to his intimate adversary—that the importance of this loomed large and something had overtaken all ironically his sense of proportion. If there had been a ladder applied to the front of the house, even one of the vertiginous perpendiculars employed by painters and roofers and sometimes left standing overnight, he would have managed somehow, astride of the window-sill, to compass by outstretched leg and arm that mode of descent. If there had been some such uncanny thing as he had found in his room at hotels, a workable fire-escape in the form of notched cable or a canvas shoot, he would have availed himself of it as a proof—well, of his present delicacy. He nursed that sentiment, as the question stood, a little in vain, and even—at the end of he scarce knew, once more, how long—found it, as by the action on his mind of the failure of response of the outer world, sinking back to vague anguish. It seemed to him he had waited an age for some stir of the great grim hush; the life of the town was itself under a spell—so unnaturally, up and down the whole prospect of known and rather ugly objects, the blankness and the silence lasted. Had they ever, he asked himself, the hard-faced houses, which had begun to look livid in the dim dawn, had they ever spoken so little to any need of his spirit? Great builded voids, great crowded stillnesses put on, often, in the heart of cities, for the small hours, a sort of sinister mask, and it was of this large collective negation that Brydon presently became conscious—all the more that the break of day was, almost incredibly, now at hand, proving to him what a night he had made of it.

He looked again at his watch, saw what had become of his

time-values (he had taken hours for minutes—not, as in other tense situations, minutes for hours) and the strange air of the streets was but the weak, the sullen flush of a dawn in which everything was still locked up. His choked appeal from his own open window had been the sole note of life, and he could but break off at last as for a worse despair. Yet while so deeply demoralised he was capable again of an impulse denoting—at least by his present measure—extraordinary resolution; of retracing his steps to the spot where he had turned cold with the extinction of his last pulse of doubt as to there being in the place another presence than his own. This required an effort strong enough to sicken him; but he had his reason, which over-mastered for the moment everything else. There was the whole of the rest of the house to traverse, and how should he screw himself to that if the door he had seen closed were at present open? He could hold to the idea that the closing had practically been for him an act of mercy, a chance offered him to descend, depart, get off the ground and never again profane it. This conception held together, it worked; but what it meant for him depended now clearly on the amount of forbearance his recent action, or rather his recent inaction, had engendered. The image of the "presence," whatever it was, waiting there for him to go—this image had not yet been so concrete for his nerves as when he stopped short of the point at which certainty would have come to him. For, with all his resolution, or more exactly with all his dread, he did stop short—he hung back from really seeing. The risk was too great and his fear too definite: it took at this moment an awful specific form.

He knew—yes, as he had never known anything—that, *should* he see the door open, it would all too abjectly be the end of him. It would mean that the agent of his shame—for his shame was the deep abjection—was once more at large and in general possession; and what glared him thus in the face was the act that this would determine for him. It would send him straight about to the window he had left open, and by that window, be long ladder and dangling rope as absent as they would, he saw himself uncontrollably insanely fatally take his way to the street. The hideous chance of this he at least could avert; but he could only avert it by recoiling in time from assurance. He had the whole house to deal with, this fact was still there; only he now knew that uncertainty alone could start him. He stole back from where he had checked himself—merely to do so was suddenly like safety—and, making blindly for the greater staircase, left gaping rooms and sounding passages behind. Here was the top of the stairs, with a fine large dim descent and three spacious landings to mark off. His instinct was all for mildness, but his feet were harsh on the floors, and, strangely, when he had in a couple of minutes become aware of this, it counted somehow for help. He couldn't have spoken, the tone of his voice would have scared him, and the common conceit or resource of "whistling in the dark" (whether literally or figuratively) have appeared basely vulgar; yet he liked none the less to hear himself go, and when he had reached his first landing—taking it all with no rush, but quite steadily—that stage of success drew from him a gasp of relief.

The house, withal, seemed immense, the scale of space again inordinate; the open rooms to no one of which his eyes deflected, gloomed in their shuttered state like mouths of caverns; only the high skylight that formed the crown of the deep well created for him a medium in which he could advance, but which might have been, for queerness of colour, some watery under-world. He tried to think of something noble, as that his property was really grand, a splendid possession; but this nobleness took the form too of the clear delight with which he was finally to sacrifice it. They might come in now, the builders, the destroyers—they might come as soon as they would. At the end of two flights he had dropped to another zone, and from the middle of the third, with only one more left, he recognised the influence of the lower windows, of half-drawn blinds, of the occasional gleam of street-lamps, of the glazed spaces of the vestibule. This was the bottom of the sea, which showed an illumination of its own and which he even saw paved—when at a given moment he drew up to sink a long look over the banisters—with the marble squares of his childhood. By that time indubitably he felt, as he might have said in a commoner cause, better; it had allowed him to stop and draw breath, and the ease increased with the sight of the old black-and-white slabs. But what he most felt was that now surely, with the element of impunity pulling him as by hard firm hands, the case was settled for what he might have seen above had he dared that last look. The closed door, blessedly remote now, was still closed—and he had only in short to reach that of the house.

He came down further, he crossed the passage forming the access to the last flight; and if here again he stopped an instant it was almost for the sharpness of the thrill of assured escape. It made him shut his eyes—which opened again to the straight slope of the remainder of the stairs. Here was impunity still, but impunity almost excessive; inasmuch as the side-lights and the high fan-tracery of the entrance were glimmering straight into the hall; an appearance produced, he the next instant saw, by the fact that the vestibule gaped wide, that the hinged halves of the inner door had been thrown far back. Out of that again the *question* sprang at him, making his eyes, as he felt, half-start from his head, as they had done, at the top of the house, before the sign of the other door. If he had left that one open, hadn't he left this one closed, and wasn't he now in *most* immediate presence of some inconceivable occult activity? It was as sharp, the question, as a knife in his side, but the answer hung fire still and seemed to lose itself in the vague darkness to which the thin admitted dawn, glimmering archwise over the whole outer door, made a semicircular margin, a cold silvery nimbus that seemed to play a little as he looked—to shift and expand and contract.

It was as if there had been something within it, protected by indistinctness and corresponding in extent with the opaque surface behind, the painted panels of the last barrier to his escape, of which the key was in his pocket. The indistinctness mocked him even while he stared, affected him as somehow shrouding or challenging certitude, so that after faltering an instant on his step he let himself go with the sense that here *was* at last something to meet, to touch, to take, to know—something all unnatural and dreadful, but to advance upon which was the condition for him either of liberation or of supreme defeat. The penumbra, dense and dark, was the virtual screen of a figure which stood in it as still as some image erect in a niche or as some black-vizored sentinel guarding a treasure. Brydon was to know afterwards, was to recall and make out, the particular thing he had believed during the rest of his descent. He saw, in its great grey glimmering margin, the central vagueness diminish, and he felt it to be taking the very form toward which, for so many days, the passion of his curiosity had yearned. It gloomed, it loomed, it was something, it was somebody, the prodigy of a personal presence.

Rigid and conscious, spectral yet human, a man of his own substance and stature waited there to measure himself with his power to dismay. This only could it be—this only till he recognised, with his advance, that what made the face dim was the pair of raised hands that covered it and in which, so far from being offered in defiance, it was buried as for dark deprecation. So Brydon, before him, took him in; with every fact of him now, in the higher light, hard and acute—his planted stillness, his vivid truth, his grizzled bent head and white masking hands, his queer actuality of evening-dress, of dangling double eye-glass, of gleaming silk lappet and white linen, of pearl button and gold watch-guard and polished shoe. No portrait by a great modern master could have presented him with more intensity, thrust him out of his frame with more art, as if there had been "treatment," of the consummate sort, in his every shade and salience. The revulsion, for our friend, had become, before he knew it, immense—this drop, in the act of apprehension, to the sense of his adversary's inscrutable manoeuvre. That meaning at least, while he gaped, it offered him; for he could but gape at his other self in this other anguish, gape as a proof that *he,* standing there for the achieved, the enjoyed, the triumphant life, couldn't be faced in his triumph. Wasn't the proof in the splendid covering hands, strong and completely spread?—so spread and so intentional that, in spite of a special verity that surpassed every other, the fact that one of these hands had lost two fingers, which were reduced to stumps, as if accidentally shot away, the face was effectually guarded and saved.

"Saved," though, *would* it be?—Brydon breathed his wonder till the very impunity of his attitude and the very insistence of his eyes produced, as he felt, a sudden stir which showed the next instant as a deeper portent, while the head raised itself, the betrayal of a braver purpose. The hands, as he looked, began to move, to open; then, as if deciding in a flash, dropped from the face and left it uncovered and presented. Horror, with the sight, had leaped into Brydon's throat, gasping there in a sound he couldn't utter; for the bared identity was too hideous as *his,* and his glare was the passion of his protest. The face, *that* face, Spencer Brydon's?—he searched it still, but looking away from it in dismay and denial, falling straight from his height of sublimity. It was unknown, inconceivable, awful, disconnected from any possibility—! He had been "sold," he inwardly moaned, stalking such game as this: the presence before him was a presence, the horror within him a horror, but the waste of his nights had been only grotesque and the success of his adventure an irony. Such an identity fitted his at *no* point, made its alternative monstrous. A thousand times yes, as it came upon him nearer now—the face was the face of a stranger. It came upon him nearer now, quite as one of those expanding fantastic images projected by the magic lantern of childhood; for the stranger, whoever he might be, evil, odious, blatant, vulgar, had advanced as for aggression, and he knew himself give ground. Then harder pressed still, sick with the force of his shock, and falling back as under the hot breath and the roused passion of a life larger than his own, a rage of personality before which his own collapsed, he felt the whole vision turn to darkness and his very feet give way. His head went round; he was going; he had gone.

III

What had next brought him back, clearly—though after how long?—was Mrs. Muldoon's voice, coming to him from quite near, from so near that he seemed presently to see her as kneeling on the ground before him while he lay looking up at her; himself not wholly on the ground, but half-raised and upheld—conscious, yes, of tenderness of support and, more particularly, of a head pillowed in extraordinary softness and faintly refreshing fragrance. He considered, he wondered, his wit but half at his service; then another face intervened, bending more directly over him, and he finally knew that Alice Staverton had made her lap an ample and perfect cushion to him, and that she had to this end seated herself on the lowest degree of the staircase, the rest of his long person remaining stretched on his old black-and-white slabs. They were cold, these marble squares of his youth; but *he* somehow was not, in this rich return of consciousness—the most wonderful hour, little by little, that he had ever known, leaving him, as it did, so gratefully, so abysmally passive, and yet as with a treasure of intelligence waiting all round him for quiet appropriation; dissolved, he might call it, in the air of the place and producing the golden glow of a late autumn afternoon. He had come back, yes—come back from further away than any man but himself had ever travelled; but it was strange how with this sense what he had come back *to* seemed really the great thing, and as if his prodigious journey had been all for the sake of it. Slowly but surely his consciousness grew, his vision of his state thus completing itself: he had been miraculously *carried* back—lifted and carefully borne as from where he had been picked up, the uttermost end of an interminable grey passage. Even with this he was suffered to rest, and what had now brought him to knowledge was the break in the long mild motion.

It had brought him to knowledge, to knowledge—yes, this was the beauty of his state; which came to resemble more and more that of a man who has gone to sleep on some news of a great inheritance, and then, after dreaming it away, after profaning it with matters strange to it, has waked up again to serenity of certitude and has only to lie and watch it grow. This was the drift of his patience—that he had only to let it shine on him. He must moreover, with intermissions, still have been lifted and borne; since why and how else should he have known himself, later on, with the afternoon glow intenser, no longer at the foot of his stairs—situated as these now seemed at that dark other end of his tunnel—but on a deep window-bench of his high saloon, over which had been spread, couch-fashion, a mantle of soft stuff lined with grey fur that was familiar to his eyes and that one of his hands kept fondly feeling as for its pledge of truth. Mrs. Muldoon's face had gone, but the other, the second he had recognised, hung over him in a way that showed how he was still propped and pillowed. He took it all in, and the more he took it the more it seemed to suffice: he was as much at peace as if he had had food and drink. It was the two women who had found him, on Mrs. Muldoon's having plied, at her usual hour, her latch-key—and on her having above all arrived while Miss Staverton still lingered near the house. She had been turning away, all anxiety, from worrying the vain bell-handle—her calculation having been of the hour of the good woman's visit; but the latter, blessedly, had come up while she was still there, and they had entered together. He had then lain, beyond the vestibule, very much as he was lying now—quite, that is, as he appeared to have fallen, but all so wondrously without bruise or gash; only in a depth of stupor. What he most took in, however, at present, with the steadier clearance, was that Alice Staverton had for a long unspeakable moment not doubted he was dead.

"It must have been that I *was*." He made it out as she held him. "Yes—I can only have died. You brought me literally to life. Only," he wondered, his eyes rising to her, "only, in the name of all the benedictions, how?"

It took her but an instant to bend her face and kiss him, and something in the manner of it, and in the way her hands clasped and locked his head while he felt the cool charity and virtue of her lips, something in all this beatitude somehow answered everything. "And now I keep you," she said.

"Oh keep me, keep me!" he pleaded while her face still hung over him: in response to which it dropped again and stayed close, clingingly close. It was the seal of their situation—of which he tasted the impress for a long blissful moment in silence. But he came back. "Yet how did you know—?"

"I was uneasy. You were to have come, you remember—and you had sent no word."

"Yes, I remember—I was to have gone to you at one today." It caught on to their "old" life and relation—which were so near and so far. "I was still out there in my strange darkness—where was it, what was it? I must have stayed there so long." He could but wonder at the depth and the duration of his swoon.

"Since last night?" she asked with a shade of fear for her possible indiscretion.

"Since this morning—it must have been: the cold dim dawn of today. Where have I been," he vaguely wailed, "where have I been?" He felt her hold him close, and it was as if this helped him now to make in all security his mild moan. "What a long dark day!"

All in her tenderness she had waited a moment. "In the cold dim dawn?" she quavered.

But he had already gone on piecing together the parts of the whole prodigy. "As I didn't turn up you came straight—?"

She barely cast about. "I went first to your hotel—where they told me of your absence. You had dined out last evening and hadn't been back since. But they appeared to know you had been at your club."

"So you had the idea of *this*—?"

"Of what?" she asked in a moment.

"Well—of what has happened."

"I believed at least you'd have been here. I've known, all along," she said, "that you've been coming."

" 'Known' it—?"

"Well, I've believed it. I said nothing to you after that talk we had a month ago—but I felt sure. I knew you *would*," she declared.

"That I'd persist, you mean?"

"That you'd see him."

"Ah but I didn't!" cried Brydon with his long wail. "There's somebody—an awful beast; whom I brought, too horribly, to bay. But it's not me."

At this she bent over him again, and her eyes were in his eyes. "No—it's not you." And it was as if, while her face hovered, he might have made out in it, hadn't it been so near, some particular meaning blurred by a smile. "No, thank heaven," she repeated—"it's not you! Of course it wasn't to have been."

"Ah but it *was,*" he gently insisted. And he stared before him now as he had been staring for so many weeks. "I was to have known myself."

"You couldn't!" she returned consolingly. And then reverting, and as if to account further for what she had herself done, "But it wasn't only *that,* that you hadn't been at home," she went on. "I waited till the hour at which we had found Mrs. Muldoon that day of my going with you; and she arrived, as I've told you, while, failing to bring any one to the door, I lingered in my despair on the steps. After a little, if she hadn't come, by such a mercy, I should have found means to hunt her up. But it wasn't," said Alice Staverton, as if once more with her fine intention—"it wasn't only that."

His eyes, as he lay, turned back to her. "What more then?"

She met it, the wonder she had stirred. "In the cold dim dawn, you say? Well, in the cold dim dawn of this morning I too saw you."

"Saw me—?"

"Saw *him,*" said Alice Staverton. "It must have been at the same moment."

He lay an instant taking it in—as if he wished to be quite reasonable. "At the same moment?"

"Yes—in my dream again, the same one I've named to you. He came back to me. Then I knew it for a sign. He had come to you."

At this Brydon raised himself; he had to see her better. She helped him when she understood his movement, and he sat up, steadying himself beside her there on the window-bench and with his right hand grasping her left. "*He* didn't come to me."

"You came to yourself," she beautifully smiled.

"Ah I've come to myself now—thanks to you, dearest. But this brute, with his awful face—this brute's a black stranger. He's none of *me,* even as I *might* have been," Brydon sturdily declared.

But she kept the clearness that was like the breath of infallibility. "Isn't the whole point that you'd have been different?"

He almost scowled for it. "As different as *that*—?"

Her look again was more beautiful to him than the things of this world. "Haven't you exactly wanted to know *how* different? So this morning," she said, "you appeared to me."

"Like *him?*"

"A black stranger!"

"Then how did you know it was I?"

"Because, as I told you weeks ago, my mind, my imagination, had worked so over what you might, what you mightn't have been—to show you, you see, how I've thought of you. In the midst of that you came to me—that my wonder might be answered. So I knew," she went on; "and believed that, since the question held you too so fast, as you told me that day, you too would see for yourself. And when this morning I again saw I knew it would be because you had—and also then, from the first moment, because you somehow wanted me. *He* seemed to tell me of that. So why," she strangely smiled, "shouldn't I like him?"

It brought Spencer Brydon to his feet. "You 'like' that horror—?"

"I *could* have liked him. And to me," she said, "he was no horror. I had accepted him."

" 'Accepted'—?" Brydon oddly sounded.

"Before, for the interest of his difference—yes. And as *I* didn't disown him, as *I* knew him—which you at last, confronted with him in his difference, so cruelly didn't, my dear—well, he must have been, you see, less dreadful to me. And it may have pleased him that I pitied him."

She was beside him on her feet, but still holding his hand—still with her arm supporting him. But though it all brought for him thus a dim light, "You 'pitied' him?" he grudgingly, resentfully asked.

"He has been unhappy; he has been ravaged," she said.

"And haven't I been unhappy? Am not I—you've only to look at me!—ravaged?"

"Ah I don't say I like him *better,*" she granted after a thought. "But he's grim, he's worn—and things have happened to him. He doesn't make shift, for sight, with your charming monocle."

"No"—it struck Brydon: "I couldn't have sported mine 'downtown.' They'd have guyed me there."

"His great convex pince-nez—I saw it, I recognised the kind—is for his poor ruined sight. And his poor right hand—!"

"Ah!" Brydon winced—whether for his proved identity or for his lost fingers. Then, "He has a million a year," he lucidly added. "But he hasn't you."

"And he isn't—no, he isn't *you!*" she murmured as he drew her to his breast.

Looking for Mr. Green

Saul Bellow (1915–)

Saul Bellow is considered one of the greatest novelists of the twentieth century—and his Pulitzer Prize, three National Book Awards, and 1976 Nobel Prize attest to this. Born in Canada, he grew up in Montreal and Chicago, two urban settings that greatly influenced his writing. Bellow focuses on the marginal and alienated, on those attempting to make sense of the chaotic environment surrounding them. Dignity, not success, is the essential ingredient for clarity in chaos. He writes forcefully, using his vibrant prose to remind readers that words equal power. Notable works include *Dangling Man* (1944); *The Victim* (1947); *The Adventures of Augie March* (1953), which won the National Book Award; *Henderson the Rain King* (1959); *Herzog* (1964); *Mr. Sammler's Planet* (1969); *Humboldt's Gift* (1975), which won the Pulitzer Prize; *More Die of Heartbreak* (1987); and *The Bellarosa Connection* (1989). "Looking for Mr. Green," first published in 1951, is part of *Mosby's Memoirs and Other Stories* (1968).

Whatsoever thy hand findeth to do, do it with thy might. . . .
—Ecclesiastes 9:10

Hard work? No, it wasn't really so hard. He wasn't used to walking and stair-climbing, but the physical difficulty of his new job was not what George Grebe felt most. He was delivering relief checks in the Negro district, and although he was a native Chicagoan this was not a part of the city he knew much about—it needed a depression to introduce him to it. No, it wasn't literally hard work, not as reckoned in foot-pounds, but yet he was beginning to feel the strain of it, to grow aware of its peculiar difficulty. He could find the streets and numbers, but the clients were not where they were supposed to be, and he felt like a hunter inexperienced in the camouflage of his game. It was an unfavorable day, too—fall, and cold, dark weather, windy. But, anyway, instead of shells in his deep trenchcoat pocket he had the cardboard of checks, punctured for the spindles of the file, the holes reminding him of the holes in player-piano paper. And he didn't look much like a hunter, either; his was a city figure entirely, belted up in this Irish conspirator's coat. He was slender without being tall, stiff in the back, his legs looking shabby in a pair of old tweed pants gone through and fringy at the cuffs. With this stiffness, he kept his head forward, so that his face was red from the sharpness of the weather; and it was an indoors sort of face with gray eyes that persisted in some kind of thought and yet seemed to avoid definiteness of conclusion. He wore sideburns that surprised you somewhat by the tough curl of the blond hair and the effect of assertion in their length. He was not so mild as he looked, nor so youthful; and nevertheless there was no effort on his part to seem what he was not. He was an educated man; he was a bachelor; he was in some ways simple; without lushing, he liked a drink; his luck had not been good. Nothing was deliberately hidden.

He felt that his luck was better than usual today. When he had reported for work that morning he had expected to be shut up in the relief office at a clerk's job, for he had been hired downtown as a clerk, and he was glad to have, instead, the freedom of the streets and welcomed, at least at first, the vigor of the cold and even the blowing of the hard wind. But on the other hand he was not getting on with the distribution of the checks. It was true that it was a city job; nobody expected you to push too hard at a city job. His supervisor, that young Mr. Raynor, had practically told him that. Still, he wanted to do well at it. For one thing, when he knew how quickly he could deliver a batch of checks, he would know also how much time he could expect to clip for himself. And then, too, the clients would be waiting for their money. That was not the most important consideration, though it certainly mattered to him. No, but he wanted to do well, simply for doing-well's sake, to acquit himself decently of a job because he so rarely had a job to do that required just this sort of energy. Of this peculiar energy he now had a superabundance; once it had started to flow, it flowed all too heavily. And, for the time being anyway, he was balked. He could not find Mr. Green.

So he stood in his big-skirted trenchcoat with a large envelope in his hand and papers showing from his pocket, wondering why people should be so hard to locate who were too feeble or sick to come to the station to collect their own checks. But Raynor had told him that tracking them down was not easy at first and had offered him some advice on how to proceed. "If you can see the postman, he's your first man to ask, and your best bet. If you can't connect with him, try the stores and tradespeople around. Then the janitor and the neighbors. But you'll find the closer you come to your man the less people will tell you. They don't want to tell you anything."

"Because I'm a stranger."

"Because you're white. We ought to have a Negro doing this, but we don't at the moment, and of course you've got to eat, too, and this is public employment. Jobs have to be made. Oh, that holds for me too. Mind you, I'm not letting myself out. I've got three years of seniority on you, that's all. And a law degree. Otherwise, you might be back of the desk and I might be going out into the field this cold day. The same dough pays us both and for the same, exact, identical reason. What's my law degree got to do with it? But you have to pass out these checks, Mr. Grebe, and it'll help if you're stubborn, so I hope you are."

"Yes, I'm fairly stubborn."

Raynor sketched hard with an eraser in the old dirt of his desk, left-handed, and said, "Sure, what else can you answer to such a question. Anyhow, the trouble you're going to have is that they don't like to give information about anybody. They think you're a plain-clothes dick or an installment collector, or summons-server or something like that. Till you've been seen around the neighborhood for a few months and people know you're only from the relief."

It was dark, ground-freezing, pre-Thanksgiving weather; the wind played hob with the smoke, rushing it down, and Grebe missed his gloves, which he had left in Raynor's office. And no one would admit knowing Green. It was past three o'clock and the postman had made his last delivery. The nearest grocer, himself a Negro, had never heard the name Tulliver Green, or said he hadn't. Grebe was inclined to think that it was true, that he had in the end convinced the man that he wanted only to deliver a check. But he wasn't sure. He needed experience in interpreting looks and signs and, even more, the will not to be put off or denied and even the force to bully if need be. If the grocer did know, he had got rid of him easily. But since most of his trade was with reliefers, why should he prevent the delivery of a check? Maybe Green, or Mrs. Green, if there was a Mrs. Green, patronized another grocer. And was there a Mrs. Green? It was one of Grebe's great handicaps that he hadn't looked at any of the case records. Raynor should have let him read files for a few hours. But he apparently saw no need for that, probably considering the job unimportant. Why prepare systematically to deliver a few checks?

But now it was time to look for the janitor. Grebe took in the building in the wind and gloom of the late November day—trampled, frost-hardened lots on one side; on the other, an automobile junk yard and then the infinite work of Elevated frames, weak-looking, gaping with rubbish fires; two sets of leaning brick porches three stories high and a flight of cement stairs to the cellar. Descending, he entered the underground passage, where he tried the doors until one opened and he found himself in the furnace room. There someone rose toward him and approached, scraping on the coal grit and bending under the canvas-jacketed pipes.

"Are you the janitor?"

"What do you want?"

"I'm looking for a man who's supposed to be living here. Green."

"What Green?"

"Oh, you maybe have more than one Green?" said Grebe with new, pleasant hope. "This is Tulliver Green."

"I don't think I c'n help you, mister. I don't know any."

"A crippled man."

The janitor stood bent before him. Could it be that he was crippled? Oh, God! what if he was. Grebe's gray eyes sought with excited difficulty to see. But no, he was only very short and stooped. A head awakened from meditation, a strong-haired beard, low, wide shoulders. A staleness of sweat and coal rose from his black shirt and the burlap sack he wore as an apron.

"Crippled how?"

Grebe thought and then answered with the light voice of unmixed candor, "I don't know. I've never seen him." This was damaging, but his only other choice was to make a lying guess, and he was not up to it. "I'm delivering checks for the relief to shut-in cases. If he weren't crippled he'd come to collect himself. That's why I said crippled. Bedridden, chair-ridden—is there anybody like that?"

This sort of frankness was one of Grebe's oldest talents, going back to childhood. But it gained him nothing here.

"No suh. I've got four buildin's same as this that I take care of. I don' know all the tenants, leave alone the tenants' tenants. The rooms turn over so fast, people movin' in and out every day. I can't tell you."

The janitor opened his grimy lips but Grebe did not hear him in the piping of the valves and the consuming pull of air to flame in the body of the furnace. He knew, however, what he had said.

"Well, all the same, thanks. Sorry I bothered you. I'll prowl around upstairs again and see if I can turn up someone who knows him."

Once more in the cold air and early darkness he made the short circle from the cellarway to the entrance crowded between the brickwork pillars and began to climb to the third floor. Pieces of plaster ground under his feet; strips of brass tape from which the carpeting had been torn away marked old boundaries at the sides. In the passage, the cold reached him worse than in the street; it touched him to the bone. The hall toilets ran like springs. He thought grimly as he heard the wind burning around the building with a sound like that of the furnace, that this was a great piece of constructed shelter. Then he struck a match in the gloom and searched for names and numbers among the writings and scribbles on the walls. He saw WHOODY-DOODY GO TO JESUS, and zigzags, caricatures, sexual scrawls, and curses. So the sealed rooms of pyramids were also decorated, and the caves of human dawn.

The information on his card was, TULLIVER GREEN—APT 3D. There were no names, however, and no numbers. His shoulders drawn up, tears of cold in his eyes, breathing vapor, he went the length of the corridor and told himself that if he had been lucky enough to have the temperament for it he would bang on one of the doors and bawl out "Tulliver Green!" until he got results. But it wasn't in him to make an uproar and he continued to burn matches, passing the light over the walls. At the rear, in a corner off the hall, he discovered a door he had not seen before and he thought it best to investigate. It sounded empty when he knocked, but a young Negress answered, hardly more than a girl. She opened only a bit, to guard the warmth of the room.

"Yes suh?"

"I'm from the district relief station on Prairie Avenue. I'm looking for a man named Tulliver Green to give him his check. Do you know him?"

No, she didn't; but he thought she had not understood anything of what he had said. She had a dream-bound, dream-blind face, very soft and black, shut off. She wore a man's jacket and pulled the ends together at her throat. Her hair was parted in three directions, at the sides and transversely, standing up at the front in a dull puff.

"Is there somebody around here who might know?"

"I jus' taken this room las' week."

He observed that she shivered, but even her shiver was somnambulistic and there was no sharp consciousness of cold in the big smooth eyes of her handsome face.

"All right, miss, thank you. Thanks," he said, and went to try another place.

Here he was admitted. He was grateful, for the room was warm. It was full of people, and they were silent as he entered—ten people, or a dozen, perhaps more, sitting on benches like a parliament. There was no light, properly speaking, but a tempered darkness that the window gave, and everyone seemed to him enormous, the men padded out in heavy work clothes and winter coats, and the women huge, too, in their sweaters, hats, and old furs. And, besides, bed and bedding, a black cooking range, a piano piled towering to the ceiling with papers, a dining-room table of the old style of prosperous Chicago. Among these people Grebe, with his cold-heightened fresh color and his smaller stature, entered like a schoolboy. Even though he was met with smiles and good will, he knew, before a single word was spoken, that all the currents ran against him and that he would make no headway. Nevertheless he began. "Does anybody here know how I can deliver a check to Mr. Tulliver Green?"

"Green?" It was the man that had let him in who answered. He was in short sleeves, in a checkered shirt, and had a queer, high head, profusely overgrown and long as a shako; the veins entered it strongly from his forehead. "I never heard mention of him. Is this where he live?"

"This is the address they gave me at the station. He's a sick man, and he'll need his check. Can't anybody tell me where to find him?"

He stood his ground and waited for a reply, his crimson wool scarf wound about his neck and drooping outside his trenchcoat, pockets weighted with the block of checks and official forms. They must have realized that he was not a college boy employed afternoons by a bill collector, trying foxily to pass for a relief clerk, recognized that he was an older man who knew himself what need was, who had had more than an average seasoning in hardship. It was evident enough if you looked at the marks under his eyes and at the sides of his mouth.

"Anybody know this sick man?"

"No suh." On all sides he saw heads shaken and smiles of denial. No one knew. And maybe it was true, he considered, standing silent in the earthen, musky human gloom of the place as the rumble continued. But he could never really be sure.

"What's the matter with this man?" said shako-head.

"I've never seen him. All I can tell you is that he can't come in person for his money. It's my first day in this district."

"Maybe they given you the wrong number?"

"I don't believe so. But where else can I ask about him?" He felt that this persistence amused them deeply, and in a way he shared their amusement that he should stand up so tenaciously to them. Though smaller, though slight, he was his own man, he retracted nothing about himself, and he looked back at them, gray-eyed, with amusement and also with a sort of courage. On the bench some man spoke in his throat, the words impossible to catch, and a woman answered with a wild, shrieking laugh, which was quickly cut off.

"Well, so nobody will tell me?"

"Ain't nobody who knows."

"At least, if he lives here, he pays rent to someone. Who manages the building?"

"Greatham Company. That's on Thirty-ninth Street."

Grebe wrote it in his pad. But, in the street again, a sheet of wind-driven paper clinging to his leg while he deliberated what direction to take next, it seemed a feeble lead to follow. Probably this Green didn't rent a flat, but a room. Sometimes there were as many as twenty people in an apartment; the real-estate agent would know only the lessee. And not even the agent could tell you who the renters were. In some places the beds were even used in shifts, watchmen or jitney drivers or short-order cooks in night joints turning out after a day's sleep and surrendering their beds to a sister, a nephew, or perhaps a stranger, just off the bus. There were large numbers of newcomers in this terrific, blight-bitten portion of the city between Cottage Grove and Ashland, wandering from house to house and room to room. When you saw them, how could you know them? They didn't carry bundles on their backs or look picturesque. You only saw a man, a Negro, walking in the street or riding in the car, like everyone else, with his thumb closed on a transfer. And therefore how were you supposed to tell? Grebe thought the Greatham agent would only laugh at his question.

But how much it would have simplified the job to be able to say that Green was old, or blind, or consumptive. An hour in the files, taking a few notes, and he needn't have been at such a disadvantage. When Raynor gave him the block of checks he asked, "How much should I know about these people?" Then Raynor had looked as though he were preparing to accuse him of trying to make the job more important than it was. He smiled, because by then they were on fine terms, but nevertheless he had been getting ready to say something like that when the confusion began in the station over Staika and her children.

Grebe had waited a long time for this job. It came to him through the pull of an old schoolmate in the Corporation Counsel's office, never a close friend, but suddenly sympathetic and interested—pleased to show, moreover, how well he had done, how strongly he was coming on even in these miserable times. Well, he was coming through strongly, along with the Democratic administration itself. Grebe had gone to see him in City Hall, and they had had a counter lunch or beers at least once a month for a year, and finally it had been possible to swing the job. He didn't mind being assigned the lowest clerical grade, nor even being a messenger, though Raynor thought he did.

This Raynor was an original sort of guy and Grebe had taken to him immediately. As was proper on the first day, Grebe had come early, but he waited long, for Raynor was late. At last he darted into his cubicle of an office as though he had just jumped from one of those hurtling huge red Indiana Avenue cars. His thin, rough face was wind-stung and he was grinning and saying something breathlessly to himself. In his hat, a small fedora, and his coat, the velvet collar a neat fit about his neck, and his silk muffler that set off the nervous twist of his chin, he swayed and turned himself in his swivel chair, feet leaving the ground; so that he pranced a little as he sat. Meanwhile he took Grebe's measure out of his eyes, eyes of an unusual vertical length and slightly sardonic. So the two men sat for a while, saying nothing, while the supervisor raised his hat from his miscombed hair and put it in his lap. His cold-darkened hands were not clean. A steel beam passed through the little makeshift room, from which machine belts once had hung. The building was an old factory.

"I'm younger than you; I hope you won't find it hard taking orders from me," said Raynor. "But I don't make them up, either. You're how old, about?"

"Thirty-five."

"And you thought you'd be inside doing paper work. But it so happens I have to send you out."

"I don't mind."

"And it's mostly a Negro load we have in this district."

"So I thought it would be."

"Fine. You'll get along. *C'est un bon boulot.* Do you know French?"

"Some."

"I thought you'd be a university man."

"Have you been in France?" said Grebe.

"No, that's the French of the Berlitz School. I've been at it for more than a year, just as I'm sure people have been, all over the world, office boys in China and braves in Tanganyika. In fact, I damn well know it. Such is the attractive power of civilization. It's overrated, but what do you want? *Que voulez-vous?* I get *Le Rire* and all the spicy papers, just like in Tanganyika. It must be mystifying, out there. But my reason is that I'm aiming at the diplomatic service. I have a cousin who's a courier, and the way he describes it is awfully attractive. He rides in the *wagon-lits* and reads books. While we— What did you do before?"

"I sold."

"Where?"

"Canned meat at Stop and Shop. In the basement."

"And before that?"

"Window shades, at Goldblatt's."

"Steady work?"

"No, Thursdays and Saturdays. I also sold shoes."

"You've been a shoe-dog too. Well. And prior to that? Here it is in your folder." He opened the record. "Saint Olaf's College, instructor in classical languages. Fellow, University of Chicago,

1926–27. I've had Latin, too. Let's trade quotations—'*Dum spiro spero.*' "

" '*Da dextram misero.*' "

" '*Alea jacta est.*' "

" '*Excelsior.*' "

Raynor shouted with laughter, and other workers came to look at him over the partition. Grebe also laughed, feeling pleased and easy. The luxury of fun on a nervous morning.

When they were done and no one was watching or listening, Raynor said rather seriously, "What made you study Latin in the first place? Was it for the priesthood?"

"No."

"Just for the hell of it? For the culture? Oh, the things people think they can pull!" He made his cry hilarious and tragic. "I ran my pants off so I could study for the bar, and I've passed the bar, so I get twelve dollars a week more than you as a bonus for having seen life straight and whole. I'll tell you, as a man of culture, that even though nothing looks to be real, and everything stands for something else, and that thing for another thing, and that thing for a still further one—there ain't any comparison between twenty-five and thirty-seven dollars a week, regardless of the last reality. Don't you think that was clear to your Greeks? They were a thoughtful people, but they didn't part with their slaves."

This was a great deal more than Grebe had looked for in his first interview with his supervisor. He was too shy to show all the astonishment he felt. He laughed a little, aroused, and brushed at the sunbeam that covered his head with its dust. "Do you think my mistake was so terrible?"

"Damn right it was terrible, and you know it now that you've had the whip of hard times laid on your back. You should have been preparing yourself for trouble. Your people must have been well off to send you to the university. Stop me, if I'm stepping on your toes. Did your mother pamper you? Did your father give in to you? Were you brought up tenderly, with permission to go and find out what were the last things that everything else stands for while everybody else labored in the fallen world of appearances?"

"Well, no, it wasn't exactly like that." Grebe smiled. *The fallen world of appearances!* no less. But now it was his turn to deliver a surprise. "We weren't rich. My father was the last genuine English butler in Chicago—"

"Are you kidding?"

"Why should I be?"

"In a livery?"

"In livery. Up on the Gold Coast."

"And he wanted you to be educated like a gentleman?"

"He did not. He sent me to the Armour Institute to study chemical engineering. But when he died I changed schools."

He stopped himself, and considered how quickly Raynor had reached him. In no time he had your valise on the table and all your stuff unpacked. And afterward, in the streets, he was still reviewing how far he might have gone, and how much he might have been led to tell if they had not been interrupted by Mrs. Staika's great noise.

But just then a young woman, one of Raynor's workers, ran into the cubicle exclaiming, "Haven't you heard all the fuss?"

"We haven't heard anything."

"It's Staika, giving out with all her might. The reporters are coming. She said she phoned the papers, and you know she did."

"But what is she up to?" said Raynor.

"She brought her wash and she's ironing it here, with our current, because the relief won't pay her electric bill. She has her ironing board set up by the admitting desk, and her kids are with her, all six. They never are in school more than once a week. She's always dragging them around with her because of her reputation."

"I don't want to miss any of this," said Raynor, jumping up. Grebe, as he followed with the secretary, said, "Who is this Staika?"

"They call her the 'Blood Mother of Federal Street.' She's a professional donor at the hospitals. I think they pay ten dollars a pint. Of course it's no joke, but she makes a very big thing out of it and she and the kids are in the papers all the time."

A small crowd, staff and clients divided by a plywood barrier, stood in the narrow space of the entrance, and Staika was shouting in a gruff, mannish voice, plunging the iron on the board and slamming it on the metal rest.

"My father and mother came in a steerage, and I was born in our house, Robey by Huron. I'm no dirty immigrant. I'm a U.S. citizen. My husband is a gassed veteran from France with lungs weaker'n paper, that hardly can he go to the toilet by himself. These six children of mine, I have to buy the shoes for their feet with my own blood. Even a lousy little white Communion necktie, that's a couple of drops of blood; a little piece of mosquito veil for my Vadja so she won't be ashamed in church for the other girls, they take my blood for it by Goldblatt. That's how I keep goin'. A fine thing if I had to depend on the relief. And there's plenty of people on the rolls—fakes! There's nothin' *they* can't get, that can go and wrap bacon at Swift and Armour any time. They're lookin' for them by the Yards. They never have to be out of work. Only they rather lay in their lousy beds and eat the public's money." She was not afraid, in a predominantly Negro station, to shout this way about Negroes.

Grebe and Raynor worked themselves forward to get a closer view of the woman. She was flaming with anger and with pleasure at herself, broad and huge, a golden-headed woman who wore a cotton cap laced with pink ribbon. She was barelegged and had on black gym shoes, her Hoover apron was open and her great breasts, not much restrained by a man's undershirt, hampered her arms as she worked at the kid's dress on the ironing board. And the children, silent and white, with a kind of locked obstinacy, in sheepskins and lumberjackets, stood behind her. She had captured the station, and the pleasure this gave her was enormous. Yet her grievances were true grievances. She was telling the truth. But she behaved like a liar. The look of her small eyes was hidden, and while she raged she also seemed to be spinning and planning.

"They send me out college case workers in silk pants to talk me out of what I got comin'. Are they better'n me? Who told them? Fire them. Let 'em go and get married, and then you won't have to cut electric from people's budget."

The chief supervisor, Mr. Ewing, couldn't silence her and he stood with folded arms at the head of his staff, bald, bald-headed, saying to his subordinates like the ex-school principal he was, "Pretty soon she'll be tired and go."

"No she won't," said Raynor to Grebe. "She'll get what she wants. She knows more about the relief even than Ewing. She's been on the rolls for years, and she always gets what she wants because she puts on a noisy show. Ewing knows it. He'll give in soon. He's only saving face. If he gets bad publicity, the Commissioner'll have him on the carpet, downtown. She's got him submerged; she'll submerge everybody in time, and that includes nations and governments."

Grebe replied with his characteristic smile, disagreeing completely. Who would take Staika's orders, and what changes could her yelling ever bring about?

No, what Grebe saw in her, the power that made people listen, was that her cry expressed the war of flesh and blood, perhaps turned a little crazy and certainly ugly, on this place and this condition. And at first, when he went out, the spirit of Staika somehow presided over the whole district for him, and it took color from her; he saw her color, in the spotty curb fires, and the fires under the El, the straight alley of flamy gloom. Later, too, when he went into a tavern for a shot of rye, the sweat of beer, association with West Side Polish streets, made him think of her again.

He wiped the corners of his mouth with his muffler, his handkerchief being inconvenient to reach for, and went out again to get on with the delivery of his checks. The air bit cold and hard and a few flakes of snow formed near him. A train struck by and left a quiver in the frames and a bristling icy hiss over the rails.

Crossing the street, he descended a flight of board steps into a basement grocery, setting off a little bell. It was a dark, long store and it caught you with its stinks of smoked meat, soap, dried peaches, and fish. There was a fire wrinkling and flapping in the little stove, and the proprietor was waiting, an Italian with a long, hollow face and stubborn bristles. He kept his hands warm under his apron.

No, he didn't know Green. You knew people but not names. The same man might not have the same name twice. The police didn't know, either, and mostly didn't care. When somebody was shot or knifed they took the body away and didn't look for the murderer. In the first place, nobody would tell them anything. So they made up a name for the coroner and called it quits. And in the second place, they didn't give a goddamn anyhow. But they couldn't get to the bottom of a thing even if they wanted to. Nobody would get to know even a tenth of what went on among these people. They stabbed and stole, they did every crime and abomination you ever heard of, men and men, women and women, parents and children, worse than the animals. They carried on their own way, and the horrors passed off like a smoke. There was never anything like it in the history of the whole world.

It was a long speech, deepening with every word in its fantasy and passion and becoming increasingly senseless and terrible: a swarm amassed by suggestion and invention, a huge, hugging, despairing knot, a human wheel of heads, legs, bellies, arms, rolling through his shop.

Grebe felt that he must interrupt him. He said sharply, "What are you talking about! All I asked was whether you knew this man."

"That isn't even the half of it. I been here six years. You probably don't want to believe this. But suppose it's true?"

"All the same," said Grebe, "there must be a way to find a person."

The Italian's close-spaced eyes had been queerly concentrated, as were his muscles, while he leaned across the counter trying to convince Grebe. Now he gave up the effort and sat down on his stool. "Oh—I suppose. Once in a while. But I been telling you, even the cops don't get anywhere."

"They're always after somebody. It's not the same thing."

"Well, keep trying if you want. I can't help you."

But he didn't keep trying. He had no more time to spend on

Green. He slipped Green's check to the back of the block. The next name on the list was FIELD, WINSTON.

He found the back-yard bungalow without the least trouble; it shared a lot with another house, a few feet of yard between. Grebe knew these two-shack arrangements. They had been built in vast numbers in the days before the swamps were filled and the streets raised, and they were all the same—a boardwalk along the fence, well under street level, three or four ball-headed posts for clotheslines, greening wood, dead shingles, and a long, long flight of stairs to the rear door.

A twelve-year-old boy let him into the kitchen, and there the old man was, sitting by the table in a wheel chair.

"Oh, it's d' Government man," he said to the boy when Grebe drew out his checks. "Go bring me my box of papers." He cleared a space on the table.

"Oh, you don't have to go to all that trouble," said Grebe. But Field laid out his papers: Social Security card, relief certification, letters from the state hospital in Manteno, and a naval discharge dated San Diego, 1920.

"That's plenty," Grebe said. "Just sign."

"You got to know who I am," the old man said. "You're from the Government. It's not your check, it's a Government check and you got no business to hand it over till everything is proved."

He loved the ceremony of it, and Grebe made no more objections. Field emptied his box and finished out the circle of cards and letters.

"There's everything I done and been. Just the death certificate and they can close book on me." He said this with a certain happy pride and magnificence. Still he did not sign; he merely held the little pen upright on the golden-green corduroy of his thigh. Grebe did not hurry him. He felt the old man's hunger for conversation.

"I got to get better coal," he said. "I send my little gran'son to the yard with my order and they fill his wagon with screening. The stove ain't made for it. It fall through the grate. The order says Franklin County egg-size coal."

"I'll report it and see what can be done."

"Nothing can be done, I expect. You know and I know. There ain't no little ways to make things better, and the only big thing is money. That's the only sunbeams, money. Nothing is black where it shines, and the only place you see black is where it ain't shining. What we colored have to have is our own rich. There ain't no other way."

Grebe sat, his reddened forehead bridged levelly by his close-cut hair and his cheeks lowered in the wings of his collar—the caked fire shone hard within the isinglass-and-iron frames but the room was not comfortable—sat and listened while the old man unfolded his scheme. This was to create one Negro millionaire a month by subscription. One clever, good-hearted young fellow elected every month would sign a contract to use the money to start a business employing Negroes. This would be advertised by chain letters and word of mouth, and every Negro wage earner would contribute a dollar a month. Within five years there would be sixty millionaires.

"That'll fetch respect," he said with a throat-stopped sound that came out like a foreign syllable. "You got to take and organize all the money that gets thrown away on the policy wheel and horse race. As long as they can take it away from you, they got no respect for you. Money, that's d' sun of human kind!" Field was a Negro of mixed blood, perhaps Cherokee, or Natchez; his skin was reddish. And he sounded, speaking about a golden sun in this dark room, and looked, shaggy and slab-headed, with the mingled blood of his face and broad lips, the little pen still upright in his hand, like one of the underground kings of mythology, old judge Minos himself.

And now he accepted the check and signed. Not to soil the slip, he held it down with his knuckles. The table budged and creaked, the center of the gloomy, heathen midden of the kitchen covered with bread, meat, and cans, and the scramble of papers.

"Don't you think my scheme'd work?"

"It's worth thinking about. Something ought to be done, I agree."

"It'll work if people will do it. That's all. That's the only thing, any time. When they understand it in the same way, all of them."

"That's true," said Grebe, rising. His glance met the old man's.

"I know you got to go," he said. "Well, God bless you, boy, you ain't been sly with me. I can tell it in a minute."

He went back through the buried yard. Someone nursed a candle in a shed, where a man unloaded kindling wood from a sprawl-wheeled baby buggy and two voices carried on a high conversation. As he came up the sheltered passage he heard the hard boost of the wind in the branches and against the house fronts, and then, reaching the sidewalk, he saw the needle-eye red of cable towers in the open icy height hundreds of feet above the river and the factories—those keen points. From here, his view was obstructed all the way to the South Branch and its timber banks, and the cranes beside the water. Rebuilt after the Great Fire, this part of the city was, not fifty years later, in ruins again, factories boarded up, buildings deserted or fallen, gaps of prairie between. But it wasn't desolation that this made you feel, but rather a faltering of organization that set free a huge energy, an escaped, unattached, unregulated power from the giant raw place. Not only must people feel it but, it seemed to Grebe, they were compelled to match it. In their very bodies. He no less than others, he realized. Say that his parents had been servants in their time, whereas he was not supposed to be one. He thought that they had never done any service like this, which no one visible asked for, and probably flesh and blood could not even perform. Nor could anyone show why it should be performed; or see where the performance would lead. That did not mean that he wanted to be released from it, he realized with a grimly pensive face. On the contrary. He had something to do. To be compelled to feel this energy and yet have no task to do—that was horrible; that was suffering; he knew what that was. It was now quitting time. Six o'clock. He could go home if he liked, to his room, that is, to wash in hot water, to pour a drink, lie down on his quilt, read the paper, eat some liver paste on crackers before going out to dinner. But to think of this actually made him feel a little sick, as though he had swallowed hard air. He had six checks left, and he was determined to deliver at least one of these: Mr. Green's check.

So he started again. He had four or five dark blocks to go, past open lots, condemned houses, old foundations, closed schools, black churches, mounds, and he reflected that there must be many people alive who had once seen the neighborhood rebuilt and new. Now there was a second layer of ruins; centuries of history accomplished through human massing. Numbers had given the place forced growth; enormous numbers had also broken it down. Objects once so new, so concrete that it could have occurred to anyone they stood for other things, had crumbled. Therefore, reflected Grebe, the secret of them was out. It was that they stood for themselves by agreement, and were natural and not unnatural by agreement, and when the things themselves collapsed the agreement became visible. What was it, otherwise, that kept cities from looking peculiar? Rome, that was almost permanent, did not give rise to thoughts like these. And was it abidingly real? But in Chicago, where the cycles were so fast and the familiar died out, and again rose changed, and died again in thirty years, you saw the common agreement or covenant, and you were forced to think about appearances and realities. (He remembered Raynor and he smiled. Raynor was a clever boy.) Once you had grasped this, a great many things became intelligible. For instance, why Mr. Field should conceive such a scheme. Of course, if people were to agree to create a millionaire, a real millionaire would come into existence. And if you wanted to know how Mr. Field was inspired to think of this, why, he had within sight of his kitchen window the chart, the very bones of a successful scheme—the El with its blue and green confetti of signals. People consented to pay dimes and ride the crash-box cars, and so it was a success. Yet how absurd it looked; how little reality there was to start with. And yet Yerkes, the great financier who built it, had known that he could get people to agree to do it. Viewed as itself, what a scheme of a scheme it seemed, how close to an appearance. Then why wonder at Mr. Field's idea? He had grasped a principle. And then Grebe remembered, too, that Mr. Yerkes had established the Yerkes Observatory and endowed it with millions. Now how did the notion come to him in his New York museum of a palace or his Aegean-bound yacht to give money to astronomers? Was he awed by the success of his bizarre enterprise and therefore ready to spend money to find out where in the universe being and seeming were identical? Yes, he wanted to know what abides; and whether flesh is Bible grass; and he offered money to be burned in the fire of suns. Okay, then, Grebe thought further, these things exist because people consent to exist with them—we have got so far—and also there is a reality which doesn't depend on consent but within which consent is a game. But what about need, the need that keeps so many vast thousands in position? You tell me that, you *private* little gentleman and decent soul—he used these words against himself scornfully. Why is the consent given to misery? And why so painfully ugly? Because there is *something* that is dismal and permanently ugly? Here he sighed and gave it up, and thought it was enough for the present moment that he had a real check in his pocket for a Mr. Green who must be real beyond question. If only his neighbors didn't think they had to conceal him.

This time he stopped at the second floor. He struck a match and found a door. Presently a man answered his knock and Grebe had the check ready and showed it even before he began. "Does Tulliver Green live here? I'm from the relief."

The man narrowed the opening and spoke to someone at his back.

"Does he live here?"

"Uh-uh. No."

"Or anywhere in this building? He's a sick man and he can't come for his dough." He exhibited the check in the light, which was smoky—the air smelled of charred lard—and the man held off the brim of his cap to study it.

"Uh-uh. Never seen the name."

"There's nobody around here that uses crutches?"

He seemed to think, but it was Grebe's impression that he was simply waiting for a decent interval to pass.

"No, suh. Nobody I ever see."

"I've been looking for this man all afternoon"—Grebe spoke out with sudden force—"and I'm going to have to carry this check back to the station. It seems strange not to be able to find a person to *give* him something when you're looking for him for a good reason. I suppose if I had bad news for him I'd find him quick enough."

There was a responsive motion in the other man's face. "That's right, I reckon."

"It almost doesn't do any good to have a name if you can't be found by it. It doesn't stand for anything. He might as well not have any," he went on, smiling. It was as much of a concession as he could make to his desire to laugh.

"Well, now, there's a little old knot-back man I see once in a while. He might be the one you lookin' for. Downstairs."

"Where? Right side or left? Which door?"

"I don't know which. Thin-face little knot-back with a stick."

But no one answered at any of the doors on the first floor. He went to the end of the corridor, searching by matchlight, and found only a stairless exit to the yard, a drop of about six feet. But there was a bungalow near the alley, an old house like Mr. Field's. To jump was unsafe. He ran from the front door, through the underground passage and into the yard. The place was occupied. There was a light through the curtains, upstairs. The name on the ticket under the broken, scoop-shaped mailbox was Green! He exultantly rang the bell and pressed against the locked door. Then the lock clicked faintly and a long staircase opened before him. Someone was slowly coming down—a woman. He had the impression in the weak light that she was shaping her hair as she came, making herself presentable, for he saw her arms raised. But it was for support that they were raised; she was feeling her way downward, down the wall, stumbling. Next he wondered about the pressure of her feet on the treads; she did not seem to be wearing shoes. And it was a freezing stairway. His ring had got her out of bed, perhaps, and she had forgotten to put them on. And then he saw that she was not only shoeless but naked; she was

fragile existence

entirely naked, climbing down while she talked to herself, a heavy woman, naked and drunk. She blundered into him. The contact of her breasts, though they touched only his coat, made him go back against the door with a blind shock. See what he had tracked down, in his hunting game!

The woman was saying to herself, furious with insult, "So I cain't ——k, huh? I'll show that son-of-a-bitch kin I, cain't I."

What should he do now? Grebe asked himself. Why, he should go. He should turn away and go. He couldn't talk to this woman. He couldn't keep her standing naked in the cold. But when he tried he found himself unable to turn away.

He said, "Is this where Mr. Green lives?"

But she was still talking to herself and did not hear him.

"Is this Mr. Green's house?"

At last she turned her furious drunken glance on him. "What do you want?"

Again her eyes wandered from him; there was a dot of blood in their enraged brilliance. He wondered why she didn't feel the cold.

"I'm from the relief."

"Awright, what?"

"I've got a check for Tulliver Green."

This time she heard him and put out her hand.

"No, no, for *Mr.* Green. He's got to sign," he said. How was he going to get Green's signature tonight!

"I'll take it. He cain't."

He desperately shook his head, thinking of Mr. Field's precautions about identification. "I can't let you have it. It's for him. Are you Mrs. Green?"

"Maybe I is, and maybe I ain't. Who want to know?"

"Is he upstairs?"

"Awright. Take it up yourself, you goddamn fool."

Sure, he was a goddamn fool. Of course he could not go up because Green would probably be drunk and naked, too. And perhaps he would appear on the landing soon. He looked eagerly upward. Under the light was a high narrow brown wall. Empty! It remained empty!

"Hell with you, then!" he heard her cry. To deliver a check for coal and clothes, he was keeping her in the cold. She did not feel it, but his face was burning with frost and self-ridicule. He backed away from her.

"I'll come tomorrow, tell him."

"Ah, hell with you. Don' never come. What you doin' here in the nighttime? Don' come back." She yelled so that he saw the breadth of her tongue. She stood astride in the long cold box of the hall and held on to the banister and the wall. The bungalow itself was shaped something like a box, a clumsy, high box pointing into the freezing air with its sharp, wintry lights.

"If you are Mrs. Green, I'll give you the check," he said, changing his mind.

"Give here, then." She took it, took the pen offered with it in her left hand, and tried to sign the receipt on the wall. He looked around, almost as though to see whether his madness was being observed, and came near believing that someone was standing on a mountain of used tires in the auto-junking shop next door.

"But are you Mrs. Green?" he now thought to ask. But she was already climbing the stairs with the check, and it was too late, if he had made an error, if he was now in trouble, to undo the thing. But he wasn't going to worry about it. Though she might not be Mrs. Green, he was convinced that Mr. Green was upstairs. Whoever she was, the woman stood for Green, whom he was not to see this time. Well, you silly bastard, he said to himself, so you think you found him. So what? Maybe you really did find him—what of it? But it was important that there was a real Mr. Green whom they could not keep him from reaching because he seemed to come as an emissary from hostile appearances. And though the self-ridicule was slow to diminish, and his face still blazed with it, he had, nevertheless, a feeling of elation, too. "For after all," he said, "he *could* be found!"

From the Diary of a New York Lady

During Days of Horror, Despair, and World Change

Dorothy Parker (1893–1967)

Dorothy Parker was an urbane New York City native and a satirical critic, poet, and short story writer famous for her verbal bite and sharp wit. She led the famed "Algonquin Round Table" discussions, composed of writers who enjoyed acerbic commentary and malicious verbal exchanges at least as much as Parker did. Her works, written concisely and with an easy conversational tone, ironically describe alienation, loss of love, and the failure of idealism within American society. Her poetry collections include *Enough Rope* (1926), *Sunset Gun* (1928), and *Death and Taxes* (1931). These are collected in *Not So Deep as a Well* (1936). *Laments for the Living* (1930) and *After Such Pleasures* (1933) are two of her short story collections, all collected in *Here Lies* (1939). For years Parker wrote a book-review column entitled "Constant Reader" for *The New Yorker,* a magazine still influenced by her character and wit. "From the Diary of a New York Lady" is part of *The Collected Stories of Dorothy Parker* (1939).

Monday. Breakfast tray about eleven; didn't want it. The champagne at the Amorys' last night was *too* revolting, but what *can* you do? You can't stay until five o'clock on just *nothing.* They had those *divine* Hungarian musicians in the green coats, and Stewie Hunter took off one of his shoes and led them with it, and it *couldn't* have been funnier. He is *the* wittiest number in the *entire* world; he *couldn't* be more perfect. Ollie Martin brought me home and we both fell asleep in the car—*too* screaming. Miss Rose came about noon to do my nails, simply *covered* with *the* most divine gossip. The Morrises are going to separate *any minute,* and Freddie

Warren *definitely* has ulcers, and Gertie Leonard simply *won't* let Bill Crawford out of her sight even with Jack Leonard *right there in the room,* and it's all *true* about Sheila Phillips and Babs Deering. It *couldn't* have been more thrilling. Miss Rose is *too* marvelous; I really think that a lot of times people like that are a lot more intelligent than a lot of people. Didn't notice until after she had gone that the damn fool had put that *revolting* tangerine-colored polish on my nails; *couldn't* have been more furious. Started to read a book, but too nervous. Called up and found I could get two tickets for the opening of "Run like a Rabbit" tonight for forty-eight dollars. Told them they had *the* nerve of the world, but what *can* you do? Think Joe said he was dining out, so telephoned some *divine* numbers to get someone to go to the theater with me, but they were all tied up. Finally got Ollie Martin. He *couldn't* have more poise, and what do *I* care if he *is* one? *Can't* decide whether to wear the green crepe or the red wool. Every time I look at my finger nails, I could *spit. Damn* Miss Rose.

Tuesday. Joe came barging in my room this morning at *practically nine o'clock. Couldn't* have been more furious. Started to fight, but *too* dead. Know he said he wouldn't be home to dinner. Absolutely *cold* all day; couldn't *move.* Last night *couldn't* have been more perfect. Ollie and I dined at Thirty-Eight East, absolutely *poisonous* food, and not one *living* soul that you'd be seen *dead* with, and "Run like a Rabbit" was *the* world's worst. Took Ollie up to the Barlows' party and it *couldn't* have been more attractive—*couldn't* have been more people absolutely *stinking.* They had those Hungarians in the green coats, and Stewie Hunter was leading them with a fork—everybody simply *died.* He had *yards* of green toilet paper hung around his neck like a lei; he *couldn't* have been in better form. Met a *really new number,* very tall, *too* marvelous, and one of those people that you can *really* talk to them. I told him sometimes I get so *nauseated* I could *yip,* and I felt I absolutely *had* to do something like write or paint. He said why didn't I write or paint. Came home alone; Ollie passed out *stiff.* Called up the new number three times today to get him to come to dinner and go with me to the opening of "Never Say Good Morning," but first he was out and then he was all tied up with his mother. Finally got Ollie Martin. Tried to read a book, but couldn't sit still. *Can't* decide whether to wear the red lace or the pink with the feathers. Feel *too* exhausted, but what *can* you do?

Wednesday. The most terrible thing happened *just this minute.* Broke one of my finger nails *right off short.* Absolutely *the* most horrible thing I ever had happen to me in my life. Called up Miss Rose to come over and shape it for me, but she was out for the day. I do have *the* worst luck in the *entire* world. Now I'll have to go around like this all day and all night, but what *can* you do? *Damn* Miss Rose. Last night *too* hectic. "Never Say Good Morning" *too* foul, *never* saw more poisonous clothes on the stage. Took Ollie up to the Ballards' party; *couldn't* have been better. They had those Hungarians in the green coats and Stewie Hunter was leading them with a freesia—*too* perfect. He had on Peggy Cooper's ermine coat and Phyllis Minton's silver turban; *simply* unbelievable. Asked simply *sheaves* of *divine* people to come here Friday night; got the address of those Hungarians in the green coats from Betty Ballard. She says just engage them until four, and then whoever gives them another three hundred dollars, they'll stay till five. *Couldn't* be cheaper. Started home with Ollie, but had to drop him at his house; he *couldn't* have been sicker. Called up the new number today to get him to come to dinner and go to the opening of "Everybody Up" with me tonight, but he was tied up. Joe's going to be out; he didn't *condescend* to say *where, of course.* Started to read the papers, but nothing in them except that Mona Wheatley is in Reno charging *intolerable cruelty.* Called up Jim Wheatley to see if he had anything to do tonight, but he was tied up. Finally got Ollie Martin. *Can't* decide whether to wear the white satin or the black chiffon or the yellow pebble crepe. Simply *wrecked* to the *core* about my finger nail. Can't *bear* it. *Never* knew *anybody* to have such *unbelievable* things happen to them.

★ ★ ★

Thursday. Simply *collapsing* on my *feet.* Last night *too* marvelous. "Everybody Up" *too* divine, *couldn't* be filthier, and the new number was there, *too* celestial, only he didn't see me. He was with Florence Keeler in that *loathsome* gold Schiaparelli model of hers that every *shopgirl* has had since *God* knows. He must be out of his *mind;* she wouldn't *look* at a man. Took Ollie to the Watsons' party; *couldn't* have been more thrilling. Everybody simply *blind.* They had those Hungarians in the green coats and Stewie Hunter was leading them with a lamp, and, after the lamp got broken, he and Tommy Thomas did adagio dances—*too* wonderful. Somebody told me Tommy's doctor told him he had to absolutely get *right out of town,* he has *the* world's worst stomach, but you'd *never* know it. Came home alone, couldn't find Ollie *anywhere.* Miss Rose came at noon to shape my nail, *couldn't* have been more fascinating. Sylvia Eaton can't go *out the door* unless she's had a hypodermic, and Doris Mason *knows every single word* about Douggie Mason and that girl up in Harlem, and Evelyn North won't be *induced* to keep away from those three acrobats, and they don't *dare* tell Stuyvie Raymond *what* he's got the matter with him. *Never* knew anyone that had a more simply *fascinating* life than Miss Rose. Made her take that *vile* tangerine polish off my nails and put on dark red. Didn't notice until after she had gone that it's practically *black* in electric light; *couldn't* be in a worse state. *Damn* Miss Rose. Joe left a note saying he was going to dine out, so telephoned the new number to get him to come to dinner and go with me to that new movie tonight, but he didn't answer. Sent him three telegrams to *absolutely surely* come tomorrow night. Finally got Ollie Martin for tonight. Looked at the papers, but nothing in them except that the Harry Motts are throwing a tea with Hungarian music on Sunday. Think will ask the new number to go to it with me; they must have meant to invite me. Began to read a book, but too exhausted. *Can't* decide whether to wear the new blue with the white jacket or save it till tomorrow night and wear the ivory moire. Simply *heartsick* every time I think of my nails. *Couldn't* be wilder. Could *kill* Miss Rose, but what *can* you do?

★ ★ ★

Friday. Absolutely *sunk; couldn't* be worse. Last night *too* divine, movie *simply* deadly. Took Ollie to the Kingslands' party, *too* unbelievable, everybody absolutely *rolling*. They had those Hungarians in the green coats, but Stewie Hunter wasn't there. He's got a *complete* nervous breakdown. Worried *sick* for fear he won't be well by tonight; will absolutely *never* forgive him if he doesn't come. Started home with Ollie, but dropped him at his house because he *couldn't* stop crying. Joe left word with the butler he's going to the country this afternoon for the week-end; of *course* he wouldn't *stoop* to say *what* country. Called up *streams* of marvelous numbers to get someone to come dine and go with me to the opening of "White Man's Folly," and then go somewhere after to dance for a while; can't *bear* to be the first one there at your own party. Everybody was tied up. Finally got Ollie Martin. *Couldn't* feel more depressed; never should have gone *anywhere near* champagne and Scotch together. Started to read a book, but too restless. Called up Anne Lyman to ask about the new baby and *couldn't* remember if it was a boy or girl—*must* get a secretary *next week*. Anne *couldn't* have been more of a help; she said she didn't know whether to name it Patricia or Gloria, so then of course I knew it was a girl *right away*. Suggested calling it Barbara; forgot she already had one. Absolutely *walking the floor* like a *panther* all day. Could *spit* about Stewie Hunter. Can't *face* deciding whether to wear the blue with the white jacket or the purple with the beige roses. Every time I look at those *revolting* black nails, I want to absolutely *yip*. I really have *the* most horrible things happen to me of anybody in the *entire* world. *Damn* Miss Rose.

Little Dog

Langston Hughes (1902–1967)

Although **Langston Hughes** is celebrated mainly as a poet, he was a novelist, playwright, journalist, and lyricist as well. Hughes was born in Joplin, Missouri, and spent most of his childhood in the Midwest. He then traveled to Europe and Africa, which, along with urban life experiences, inspired his first volume of verse, *The Weary Blues* (1926). This volume is filled with Hughes' blues and jazz poetry; poetry which evokes the rhythm and feeling of black urban life. Other volumes of verse include *Fine Clothes to the Jew* (1927), *Fields of Wonder* (1947), and *Montage of a Dream Deferred* (1951). Hughes was a key figure in the Harlem Renaissance; he looked especially to the people of Harlem for inspiration and thrived on their praise. His works portray various aspects of African-American life, including art, music, and history. Examples of Hughes' novels are *Not Without Laughter* (1930), *Simple Speaks His Mind* (1950), *The Sweet Flypaper of Life* (1955), and *I Wonder as I Wander: An Autobiographical Journey* (1956). His short story collections include *Laughing to Keep from Crying* (1952) and *Something in Common* (1963), where "Little Dog" is included.

Miss Briggs had a little apartment all alone in a four-story block just where Oakwood Drive curved past the park and the lake. Across the street, beneath her window, kids skated in winter, and in the spring the grass grew green. In summer, lovers walked and necked by the lake in the moonlight. In fall brown and red-gold leaves went skithering into the water when the wind blew.

Miss Briggs came home from work every night at eight, unless she went to the movies or the Women's Civics Club. On Sunday evenings she sometimes went to a lecture on Theosophy. But she was never one to gad about, Miss Briggs. Besides, she worked too hard. She was the head bookkeeper for the firm of Wilkins and Bryant, Wood, Coal and Coke. And since 1930, when they had cut down the staff, she had only one assistant. Just two of them now to take care of the books, bills, and everything. But Miss Briggs was very efficient. She had been head bookkeeper for twenty-one years. Wilkins and Bryant didn't know what they would do without her.

Miss Briggs was proud of her record as a bookkeeper. Once the City Hall had tried to get her, but Wilkins and Bryant said, "No, indeed. We can pay as much as the city, if not more. You stay right here with us." Miss Briggs stayed. She was never a person to move about much or change jobs.

As a young girl she had studied very hard in business school. She never had much time to go out. A widowed mother, more or less dependent on her then, later became completely dependent—paralyzed. Her mother had been dead for six years now.

Perhaps it was the old woman's long illness that had got Miss Briggs in the habit of staying home every night in her youth, instead of going out to the theatre or to parties. They had never been able to afford a maid even after Miss Briggs became so well paid—for doctors' bills were such a drain, and in those last months a trained nurse was needed for her mother—God rest her soul.

Now, alone, Miss Briggs usually ate her dinner in the Rose Bud Tea Shoppe. A number of genteel businesswomen ate there, and the colored waiters were so nice. She had been served by Joe or Perry, flat-footed old Negro gentlemen, for three or four years now. They knew her tastes, and would get the cook to make little special dishes for her if she wasn't feeling very well.

After dinner, with a walk of five or six blocks from the Rose Bud, the park would come into view with its trees and lights. The Lyle Apartments loomed up. A pretty place to live, facing the park. Miss Briggs had moved there after her mother died. Trying to keep house alone was just a little too much. And there was no man in view to marry. Most of them would want her only for her money now, at her age, anyway. To move with another woman, Miss Briggs thought, would be a sort of sacrilege so soon after her mother's death. Besides, she really didn't know any other woman who, like herself, was without connections. Almost everybody had somebody, Miss Briggs reflected. Every woman she knew had either a husband, or sisters, or a friend of long standing with whom she resided. But Miss Briggs had nobody at all. Nobody.

Not that she thought about it very much. Miss Briggs was too used to facing the world alone, minding her own business, and going her own way. But one summer, while returning from Michigan, where she had taken her two weeks' rest, as she came through Cleveland, on her way from the boat to the station there, she happened to pass a dog shop with a window full of fuzzy little white dogs. Miss Briggs called to the taxi man to stop. She got out and went in. When she came back to the taxi, she carried a little white dog named Flips. At least, the dealer said he had been calling it Flips because its ears were so floppy.

"They just flip and flop," the man said, smiling at the tall middle-aged woman.

"How much is he?" Miss Briggs asked, holding the puppy up.

"I'll let you have him for twenty-five dollars," the man said.

Miss Briggs put the puppy down. She thought that was a pretty steep price. But there was something about Flips that she liked, so she picked him up again and took him with her. After all, she allowed herself very few indulgences. And somehow, this summer, Miss Briggs sort of hated going back to an empty flat—even if it did overlook the park.

Or maybe it was because it overlooked the park that had made it so terrible a place to live lately. Miss Briggs had never felt lonely, not *very* lonely, in the old house after her mother died. Only when she moved to the flat did her loneliness really come down on her. There were some nights there, especially summer nights, when she thought she couldn't stand it, to sit in her window and see so many people going by, couple by couple, arms locked; or else in groups, laughing and talking. Miss Briggs wondered why she knew no one, male or female, to walk out with, laughing and talking. She knew only the employees where she worked, and with whom she associated but little (for she hated to have people know her business). She knew, of course, the members of the Women's Civics Club, but in a cultural sort of way. The warmth of friendship seldom mellowed her contacts there. Only one or two of the clubwomen had ever called on her. Miss Briggs always believed in keeping her distance, too. Her mother used to say she'd been born poor but proud, and would stay that way.

"Folks have to amount to something before Clara takes up with them," old Mrs. Briggs always said. "Men'll have a hard time getting Clara."

Men did. Now, with no especial attractions to make them keep trying, Miss Briggs, tall and rail-like, found herself left husbandless at an age when youth had gone.

So, in her forty-fifth year, coming back from a summer boardinghouse in Michigan, Miss Briggs bought herself a little white dog. When she got home, she called on the janitor and asked him to bring her up a small box for Flips. The janitor, a tow-headed young Swede, brought her a grapefruit crate from the A & P. Miss Briggs put it in the kitchen for Flips.

She told the janitor to bring her, too, three times a week, a dime's worth of dog meat or bones, and leave it on the back porch where she could find it when she came home. On other nights Flips ate dog biscuits.

Flips and Miss Briggs soon settled on a routine. Each evening when she got home she would feed him. Then she would take him for a walk. This gave Miss Briggs an excuse for getting out, too. In warm weather she would walk around the little lake fronting her apartment with Flips on a string. Sometimes she would even smile at other people walking around the lake with dogs at night. It was nice the way dogs made things friendly. It was nice the way people with dogs smiled at her occasionally because she had a dog, too. But whenever (as seldom happened) someone in the park, dog or no dog, tried to draw her into conversation, Miss Briggs would move on as quickly as she could without being rude. You could never tell just who people were, Miss Briggs thought, or what they might have in their minds. No, you shouldn't think of taking up with strange people in parks. Besides, she was head bookkeeper for Wilkins and Bryant, and in these days of robberies and kidnapings maybe they just wanted to find out when she went for the payroll, and how much cash the firm kept on hand. Miss Briggs didn't trust people.

Always, by ten o'clock, she was back with Flips in her flat. A cup of hot milk then maybe, with a little in a saucer for Flips, and to bed. In the morning she would let Flips run down the back steps for a few minutes, then she gave him more milk, left a pan of water, and went to work. A regular routine, for Miss Briggs took care of Flips with great seriousness. At night when she got back from the Rose Bud Tea Shoppe, she fed him biscuits; or if it were dog meat night, she looked out on the back porch for the package the janitor was paid to leave. (That is, Miss Briggs allowed the Swede fifty cents a week to buy bones. He could keep the change.)

But one night, the meat was not there. Miss Briggs thought perhaps he had forgotten. Still, he had been bringing it regularly for nearly two years. Maybe the warm spring this year made the young janitor listless, Miss Briggs mused. She fed Flips biscuits.

But two days later, another dog meat night, the package was not there either. "This is too much!" thought Miss Briggs. "Come on, Flipsy, let's go downstairs and see. I'm sure I gave him fifty cents this week to buy your bones."

Miss Briggs and the little white beast went downstairs to ask why there was no meat for her dog to eat. When they got to the janitor's quarters in the basement, they heard a mighty lot of happy laughter and kids squalling, and people moving. They didn't sound like Swedes, either. Miss Briggs was a bit timid about knocking, but she finally mustered up courage with Flips there beside her. A sudden silence fell inside.

"You Leroy," a voice said. "Go to de door."

A child's feet came running. The door opened like a flash and a small colored boy stood there grinning.

"Where—where is the janitor?" Miss Briggs said, taken aback.

"You mean my papa?" asked the child, looking at the gaunt white lady. "He's here." And off he went to call his father.

Surrounded by children, a tall broad-shouldered Negro of perhaps forty, gentle of face and a little stooped, came to the door.

"Good evenin'," he said pleasantly.

"Why, are you the janitor?" stammered Miss Briggs. Flips had already begun to jump up on him with friendly mien.

"Yes'm, I'm the new janitor," said the Negro in a softly beautiful voice, kids all around him. "Is there something I can help you to do?"

"Well," said Miss Briggs, "I'd like some bones for my little dog. He's missed his meat two times now. Can you get him some?"

"Yes'm, sure can," said the new janitor, "if all the stores ain't closed." He was so much taller than Miss Briggs that she had to look up at him.

"I'd appreciate it," said Miss Briggs, "please."

As she went back upstairs she heard the new janitor calling in his rich voice, "Lora, you reckon that meat store's still open?" And a woman's voice and a lot of children answered him.

It turned out that the store was closed. So Miss Briggs gave the Negro janitor ten cents and told him to have the meat there the next night when she came home.

"Flips, you shan't starve," she said to the little white dog, "new janitor or no new janitor."

"Wruff!" said Flips.

But the next day when she came home there was no meat on the back porch either. Miss Briggs was puzzled, and a little hurt. Had the Negro forgotten?

Scarcely had she left the kitchen, however, when someone knocked on the back door and there stood the colored man with the meat. He was almost as old as Miss Briggs, she was certain of it, looking at him. Not a young man at all, but he was awfully big and brown and kind looking. So sort of sure about life as he handed her the package.

"I thought some other dog might get it if I left it on the

porch," said the colored man. "So I kept it downstairs till you come."

Miss Briggs was touched. "Well, thank you very much," she said.

When the man had gone, she remembered that she had not told him how often to get meat for the dog.

The next night he came again with bones, and every night from then on. Miss Briggs did not stop him, or limit him to three nights a week. Just after eight, whenever she got home, up the back porch steps the Negro would come with the dog meat. Sometimes there would be two or three kids with him. Pretty little brown-black rather dirty kids, Miss Briggs thought, who were shy in front of her, but nice.

Once or twice during the spring the janitor's wife, instead, brought the dog meat up on Saturday nights. Flips barked rudely at her. Miss Briggs didn't take to the creature, either. She was fat and yellow, and certainly too old to just keep on having children as she evidently did. The janitor himself was so solid and big and strong! Miss Briggs felt better when he brought her the bones for her dog. She didn't like his wife.

That June, on warm nights, as soon as she got home, Miss Briggs would open the back door and let the draft blow through. She could hear the janitor better coming up the rear stairs when he brought the bones. And, of course, she never said more than good evening to him and thank you. Or here's a dollar for the week. Keep the change.

Flips ate an awful lot of meat that spring. "Your little dog's a regular meat-hound," the janitor said one night as he handed her the bones; and Miss Briggs blushed, for no good reason.

"He does eat a lot," she said. "Good night."

As she spread the bones out on paper for the dog, she felt that her hands were trembling. She left Flips eating and went into the parlor, but found that she could not keep her mind on the book she was reading. She kept looking at the big kind face of the janitor in her mind, perturbed that it was a Negro face, and that it stayed with her so.

The next night she found herself waiting for the dog meat to arrive with more anxiety than Flips himself. When the colored man handed it to her, she quickly closed the door, before her face got red again.

"Funny old white lady," thought the janitor as he went back downstairs to his basement full of kids. "Just crazy about that dog," he added to his wife. "I ought to tell her it ain't good to feed a dog so much meat."

"What do you care, long as she wants to?" asked his wife.

The next day in the office Miss Briggs found herself making errors over the books. That night she hurried home to be sure and be there on time when he brought the dog meat up, in case he came early.

"What's the matter with me," she said sharply to herself, "rushing this way just to feed Flips? Whatever is the matter with me?" But all the way through the warm dusky streets, she seemed to hear the janitor's deep voice saying, "Good evenin'," to her.

Then, when the Negro really knocked on the door with the meat, she was trembling so that she could not go to the kitchen to get it. "Leave it right there by the sink," she managed to call out. "Thank you, Joe."

She heard the man going back downstairs sort of humming to himself, a kid or so following him. Miss Briggs felt as if she were going to faint, but Flips kept jumping up on her, barking for his meat.

"Oh, Flips," she said, "I'm so hungry." She meant to say, "*You're* so hungry." So she repeated it. "You're so hungry! Heh, Flipsy, dog?"

And from the way the little dog barked, he must have been hungry. He loved meat.

The next evening, Miss Briggs was standing in the kitchen when the colored man came with the bones.

"Lay them down," she said, "thank you," trying not to look at him. But as he went downstairs, she watched through the window his beautifully heavy body finding the rhythm of the steps, his big brown neck moving just a little.

"Get down!" she said sharply to Flips barking for his dinner.

To herself she said earnestly, "I've got to move. I can't be worried being so far from a meat shop, or from where I eat my dinner. I think I'll move downtown where the shops are open at night. I can't stand this. Most of my friends live downtown anyway."

But even as she said it, she wondered what friends she meant. She had a little white dog named Flips, that was all. And she was acquainted with other people who worked at Wilkins and Bryant, but she had nothing to do with them. She was the head bookkeeper. She knew a few women in the Civics Club fairly well. And the Negro waiters at the Rose Bud Shoppe.

And this janitor!

Miss Briggs decided that she could not bear to have this janitor come upstairs with a package of bones for Flips again. She was sure he was happy down there with his portly yellow wife and his house full of children. Let him stay in the basement, then, where he belonged. She never wanted to see him again, never.

The next night Miss Briggs made herself go to a movie before coming home. And when she got home, she fed Flips dog biscuits. That week she began looking for a new apartment, a small one for two, her and the dog. Fortunately, there were plenty to be had, what with people turned out for not being able to pay their rent—which would never happen to her, thank God! She had saved her money. When she found an apartment, she deposited the first month's rent at once. On her coming Saturday afternoon off, she planned to move.

Friday night, when the janitor came up with the bones, she decided to be just a little pleasant to him. Probably she would never see him again. Perhaps she would give him a dollar for a tip, then. Something to remember her by.

When he came upstairs, she was aware a long time of his feet approaching. Coming up, up, up, bringing bones for her dog. Flips began to bark. Miss Briggs went to the door. She took the package in one hand. With the other she offered the bill.

"Thank you so much for buying bones for my little dog," she said. "Here, here is a dollar for your trouble. You keep it all."

"Much obliged, m'am," said the astonished janitor. He had never seen Miss Briggs so generous before. "Thank you, m'am! He sure do eat a heap o'bones, your little dog."

"He almost keeps me broke buying bones," Miss Briggs said, holding the door.

"True," said the janitor. "But I reckon you don't have much other expenses on hand, do you? No family and all like me?"

"You're right," answered Miss Briggs. "But a little dog is so much company, too."

"Guess they are, m'am," said the janitor, turning to go. "Well, good night, Miss Briggs. I'm much obliged."

"Good night, Joe."

As his broad shoulders and tall brown body disappeared down the stairs, Miss Briggs slowly turned her back, shut the door, and put the bones on the floor for Flipsy. Then suddenly she began to cry.

The next day she moved away as she had planned to do. The janitor never saw her any more. For a few days the walkers in the park beside the lake wondered where a rather gaunt middle-aged woman who used to come out at night with a little white dog had gone. But in a very short while the neighborhood had completely forgotten her.

My Kinsman, Major Molineux

Nathaniel Hawthorne (1804–1864)

Nathaniel Hawthorne's works, often infused with a strong sense of morality, have been fundamental to the development of the American short story genre. Born in Salem, Massachusetts, to a prominent Puritan family, Hawthorne grew up to be a solitary man, deeply aware of and interested in the role of Puritanism in colonial New England. His puritanical background is clearly evident in his works. Allegory and symbolism also are key; thus, his characters tend to be representational—of morality or spirituality, for instance. Hawthorne's novels include *The Scarlet Letter* (1850), his most well-known work; *The House of the Seven Gables* (1851); *The Blithedale Romance* (1852); and *The Marble Faun* (1860). Two of his short story collections are *Twice-Told Tales* (1837) and *Mosses from an Old Manse* (1846), both of which explore the Puritan psyche in a New England setting.

After the kings of Great Britain had assumed the right of appointing the colonial governors, the measures of the latter seldom met with the ready and general approbation, which had been paid to those of their predecessors, under the original charters. The people looked with most jealous scrutiny to the exercise of power, which did not emanate from themselves, and they usually rewarded the rulers with slender gratitude, for the compliances, by which, in softening their instructions from beyond the sea, they had incurred the reprehension of those who gave them. The annals of Massachusetts Bay will inform us, that of six governors, in the space of about forty years from the surrender of the old charter, under James II., two were imprisoned by a popular insurrection; a third, as Hutchinson inclines to believe, was driven from the province by the whizzing of a musket ball; a fourth, in the opinion of the same historian, was hastened to his grave by continual bickerings with the House of Representatives; and the remaining two, as well as their successors, till the Revolution, were favored with few and brief intervals of peaceful sway. The inferior members of the court party, in times of high political excitement, led scarcely a more desirable life. These remarks may serve as preface to the following adventures, which chanced upon a summer night, not far from a hundred years ago. The reader, in order to avoid a long and dry detail of colonial affairs, is requested to dispense with an account of the train of circumstances, that had caused much temporary inflammation of the popular mind.

It was near nine o'clock of a moonlight evening, when a boat crossed the ferry with a single passenger, who had obtained his conveyance, at that unusual hour, by the promise of an extra fare. While he stood on the landing-place, searching in either pocket for the means of fulfilling his agreement, the ferryman lifted a lantern, by the aid of which, and the newly risen moon, he took a very accurate survey of the stranger's figure. He was a youth of barely eighteen years, evidently country-bred, and now, as it should seem, upon his first visit to town. He was clad in a coarse grey coat, well worn, but in excellent repair; his under garments were durably constructed of leather, and sat tight to a pair of serviceable and well-shaped limbs; his stockings of blue yarn, were the incontrovertible handiwork of a mother or a sister; and on his head was a three-cornered hat, which in its better days had perhaps sheltered the graver brow of the lad's father. Under his left arm was a heavy cudgel, formed of an oak sapling, and retaining a part of the hardened root; and his equipment was completed by a wallet, not so abundantly stocked as to incommode the vigorous shoulders on which it hung. Brown, curly hair, well-shaped features, and bright, cheerful eyes, were nature's gifts, and worth all that art could have done for his adornment.

The youth, one of whose names was Robin, finally drew from his pocket the half of a little province-bill of five shillings, which, in the depreciation of that sort of currency, did but satisfy the ferryman's demand, with the surplus of a sexangular piece of parchment valued at three pence. He then walked forward into the town, with as light a step, as if his day's journey had not already exceeded thirty miles, and with as eager an eye, as if he were entering London city, instead of the little metropolis of a New England colony. Before Robin had proceeded far, however, it occurred to him, that he knew not whither to direct his steps; so he paused, and looked up and down the narrow street, scrutinizing the small and mean wooden buildings, that were scattered on either side.

"This low hovel cannot be my kinsman's dwelling," thought he, "nor yonder old house, where the moonlight enters at the broken casement; and truly I see none hereabouts that might be worthy of him. It would have been wise to inquire my way of the ferryman, and doubtless he would have gone with me, and earned a shilling from the Major for his pains. But the next man I meet will do as well."

He resumed his walk, and was glad to perceive that the street now became wider, and the houses more respectable in their appearance. He soon discerned a figure moving on moderately in advance, and hastened his steps to overtake it. As Robin drew nigh, he saw that the passenger was a man in years, with a full periwig of grey hair, a wide-skirted coat of dark cloth, and silk stockings rolled about his knees. He carried a long and polished cane, which he struck down perpendicularly before him, at every step; and at regular intervals he uttered two successive hems, of a peculiarly solemn and sepulchral intonation. Having made these observations, Robin laid hold of the skirt of the old man's coat, just when the light from the open door and windows of a barber's shop, fell upon both their figures.

"Good evening to you, honored Sir," said he, making a low bow, and still retaining his hold of the skirt. "I pray you to tell me whereabouts is the dwelling of my kinsman, Major Molineux?"

The youth's question was uttered very loudly; and one of the barbers, whose razor was descending on a well-soaped chin, and another who was dressing a Ramillies wig, left their occupations, and came to the door. The citizen, in the meantime, turned a long favored countenance upon Robin, and answered him in a tone of excessive anger and annoyance. His two sepulchral hems, however, broke into the very centre of his rebuke, with most singular effect, like a thought of the cold grave obtruding among wrathful passions.

"Let go my garment, fellow! I tell you, I know not the man you speak of. What! I have authority, I have—hem, hem—authority; and if this be the respect you show your betters, your feet shall be brought acquainted with the stocks, by daylight, tomorrow morning!"

Robin released the old man's skirt, and hastened away, pursued by an ill-mannered roar of laughter from the barber's shop. He was at first considerably surprised by the result of his question, but, being a shrewd youth, soon thought himself able to account for the mystery.

"This is some country representative," was his conclusion, "who has never seen the inside of my kinsman's door, and lacks the breeding to answer a stranger civilly. The man is old, or verily—I might be tempted to turn back and smite him on the nose. Ah, Robin, Robin! even the barber's boys laugh at you, for choosing such a guide! You will be wiser in time, friend Robin."

He now became entangled in a succession of crooked and narrow streets, which crossed each other, and meandered at no great distance from the water-side. The smell of tar was obvious to his nostrils, the masts of vessels pierced the moon-light above the tops of the buildings, and the numerous signs, which Robin paused to read, informed him that he was near the centre of business. But the streets were empty, the shops were closed, and lights were visible only in the second stories of a few dwelling-houses. At length, on the corner of a narrow lane, through which he was passing, he beheld the broad countenance of a British hero swinging before the door of an inn, whence proceeded the voices of many guests. The casement of one of the lower windows was thrown back, and a very thin curtain permitted Robin to distinguish a party at supper, round a well-furnished table. The fragrance of the good cheer steamed forth into the outer air, and the youth could not fail to recollect, that the last remnant of his travelling stock of provision had yielded to his morning appetite, and that noon had found, and left him, dinnerless.

"Oh, that a parchment three-penny might give me a right to sit down at yonder table," said Robin, with a sigh. "But the Major will make me welcome to the best of his victuals; so I will even step boldly in, and inquire my way to his dwelling."

He entered the tavern, and was guided by the murmur of voices, and fumes of tobacco, to the public room. It was a long and low apartment, with oaken walls, grown dark in the continual smoke, and a floor, which was thickly sanded, but of no immaculate purity. A number of persons, the larger part of whom appeared to be mariners, or in some way connected with the sea, occupied the wooden benches, or leather-bottomed chairs, conversing on various matters, and occasionally lending their attention to some topic of general interest. Three or four little groups were draining as many bowls of punch, which the great West India trade had long since made a familiar drink in the colony. Others, who had the aspect of men who lived by regular and laborious handicraft, preferred the insulated bliss of an unshared potation, and became more taciturn under its influence. Nearly all, in short, evinced a predilection for the Good Creature in some of its various shapes, for this is a vice, to which, as the Fast-day sermons of a hundred years ago will testify, we have a long hereditary claim. The only guests to whom Robin's sympathies inclined him, were two or three sheepish countrymen, who were using the inn somewhat after the fashion of a Turkish Caravansary; they had gotten themselves into the darkest corner of the room, and, heedless of the Nicotian atmosphere, were supping on the bread of their own ovens, and the bacon cured in their own chimney-smoke. But though Robin felt a sort of brotherhood with these strangers, his eyes were attracted from them, to a person who stood near the door, holding whispered conversation with a group of ill-dressed associates. His features were separately striking almost to grotesqueness, and the whole face left a deep impression in the memory. The forehead bulged out into a double prominence, with a vale between; the nose came boldly forth in an irregular curve, and its bridge was of more than a finger's breadth; the eyebrows were deep and shaggy, and the eyes glowed beneath them like fire in a cave.

While Robin deliberated of whom to inquire respecting his kinsman's dwelling, he was accosted by the innkeeper, a little man in a stained white apron, who had come to pay his professional welcome to the stranger. Being in the second generation from a French Protestant, he seemed to have inherited the courtesy of his parent nation; but no variety of circumstance was ever known to change his voice from the one shrill note in which he now addressed Robin.

"From the country, I presume, Sir?" said he, with a profound bow. "Beg to congratulate you on your arrival, and trust you intend a long stay with us. Fine town here, Sir, beautiful buildings, and much that may interest a stranger. May I hope for the honor of your commands in respect to supper?"

"The man sees a family likeness! the rogue has guessed that I am related to the Major!" thought Robin, who had hitherto experienced little superfluous civility.

All eyes were now turned on the country lad, standing at the door, in his worn three-cornered hat, grey coat, leather breeches, and blue yarn stockings, leaning on an oaken cudgel, and bearing a wallet on his back.

Robin replied to the courteous innkeeper, with such an assumption of consequence, as befitted the Major's relative.

"My honest friend," he said, "I shall make it a point to patronize your house on some occasion, when—" here he could not help lowering his voice—"I may have more than a parchment three-pence in my pocket. My present business," continued he, speaking with lofty confidence, "is merely to inquire the way to the dwelling of my kinsman, Major Molineux."

There was a sudden and general movement in the room, which Robin interpreted as expressing the eagerness of each individual to become his guide. But the innkeeper turned his eyes to a written paper on the wall, which he read, or seemed to read, with occasional recurrences to the young man's figure.

"What have we here?" said he, breaking his speech into little dry fragments. " 'Left the house of the subscriber, bounden servant, Hezekiah Mudge—had on, when he went away, grey coat, leather breeches, master's third best hat. One pound currency reward to whoever shall lodge him in any jail in the province.' Better trudge, boy, better trudge!"

Robin had begun to draw his hand towards the lighter end of the oak cudgel, but a strange hostility in every countenance, induced him to relinquish his purpose of breaking the courteous innkeeper's head. As he turned to leave the room, he encountered a sneering glance from the bold-featured personage whom he had before noticed; and no sooner was he beyond the door, than he heard a general laugh, in which the innkeeper's voice might be distinguished, like the dropping of small stones into a kettle.

"Now is it not strange," thought Robin, with his usual shrewdness, "is it not strange, that the confession of an empty pocket, should outweigh the name of my kinsman, Major Molineux? Oh, if I had one of these grinning rascals in the woods, where I and my oak sapling grew up together, I would teach him that my arm is heavy, though my purse be light!"

On turning the corner of the narrow lane, Robin found himself in a spacious street, with an unbroken line of lofty houses on each side, and a steepled building at the upper end, whence the ringing of a bell announced the hour of nine. The light of the moon, and the lamps from numerous shop windows, discovered people promenading on the pavement, and amongst them, Robin hoped to recognize his hitherto inscrutable relative. The result of his former inquiries made him unwilling to hazard another, in a scene of such publicity, and he determined to walk slowly and silently up the street, thrusting his face close to that of every elderly gentleman, in search of the Major's lineaments. In his progress, Robin encountered many gay and gallant figures. Embroidered garments, of showy colors, enormous periwigs, gold-laced hats, and silver hilted swords, glided past him and dazzled his optics. Travelled youths, imitators of the European fine gentlemen of the period, trod jauntily along, half-dancing to the fashionable tunes which they hummed, and making poor Robin ashamed of his quiet and natural gait. At length, after many pauses to examine the gorgeous display of goods in the shop windows, and after suffering some rebukes for the impertinence of his scrutiny into people's faces, the Major's kinsman found himself near the steepled building, still unsuccessful in his search. As yet, however, he had seen only one side of the thronged street; so Robin crossed, and continued the same sort of inquisition down the opposite pavement, with stronger hopes than the philosopher seeking an honest man, but with no better fortune. He had arrived about midway towards the lower end, from which his course began, when he overheard the approach of some one, who struck down a cane on the flag-stones at every step, uttering, at regular intervals, two sepulchral hems.

"Mercy on us!" quoth Robin, recognizing the sound.

Turning a corner, which chanced to be close at his right hand, he hastened to pursue his researches, in some other part of the town. His patience was now wearing low, and he seemed to feel more fatigue from his rambles since he crossed the ferry, than from his journey of several days on the other side. Hunger also pleaded loudly within him, and Robin began to balance the propriety of demanding, violently and with lifted cudgel, the necessary guidance from the first solitary passenger, whom he should meet. While a resolution to this effect was gaining strength, he entered a street of mean appearance, on either side of which, a row of ill-built houses was straggling towards the harbor. The moonlight fell upon no passenger along the whole extent, but in the third domicile which Robin passed, there was a half-opened door, and his keen glance detected a woman's garment within.

"My luck may be better here," said he to himself.

Accordingly, he approached the door, and beheld it shut closer as he did so; yet an open space remained, sufficing for the fair occupant to observe the stranger, without a corresponding display on her part. All that Robin could discern was a strip of scarlet petticoat, and the occasional sparkle of an eye, as if the moonbeams were trembling on some bright thing.

"Pretty mistress,"—for I may call her so with a good conscience, thought the shrewd youth, since I know nothing to the contrary—"my sweet pretty mistress, will you be kind enough to tell me whereabouts I must seek the dwelling of my kinsman, Major Molineux?"

Robin's voice was plaintive and winning, and the female, seeing nothing to be shunned in the handsome country youth, thrust open the door, and came forth into the moonlight. She was a dainty little figure, with a white neck, round arms, and a slender waist, at the extremity of which her scarlet petticoat jutted out over a hoop, as if she were standing in a balloon. Moreover, her face was oval and pretty, her hair dark beneath the little cap, and her bright eyes possessed a sly freedom, which triumphed over those of Robin.

"Major Molineux dwells here," said this fair woman.

Now her voice was the sweetest Robin had heard that night, the airy counterpart of a stream of melted silver; yet he could not help doubting whether that sweet voice spoke Gospel truth. He looked up and down the mean street, and then surveyed the house before which they stood. It was a small, dark edifice of two stories, the second of which projected over the lower floor; and the front apartment had the aspect of a shop for petty commodities.

"Now truly I am in luck," replied Robin, cunningly, "and so indeed is my kinsman, the Major, in having so pretty a housekeeper. But I prithee trouble him to step to the door; I will deliver him a message from his friends in the country, and then go back to my lodgings at the inn."

"Nay, the Major has been a-bed this hour or more," said the lady of the scarlet petticoat; "and it would be to little purpose to disturb him to-night, seeing his evening draught was of the strongest. But he is a kind-hearted man, and it would be as much as my life's worth, to let a kinsman of his turn away from the door. You are the good old gentleman's very picture, and I could swear that was his rainy-weather hat. Also, he has garments very much resembling those leather—But come in, I pray, for I bid you hearty welcome in his name."

So saying, the fair and hospitable dame took our hero by the hand; and though the touch was light, and the force was gentleness, and though Robin read in her eyes what he did not hear in her words, yet the slender waisted woman, in the scarlet petticoat, proved stronger than the athletic country youth. She had drawn his half-willing footsteps nearly to the threshold, when the opening of a door in the neighborhood, startled the Major's housekeeper, and, leaving the Major's kinsman, she vanished speedily into her own domicile. A heavy yawn preceded the appearance of a man, who, like the Moonshine of Pyramus and Thisbe, carried a lantern, needlessly aiding his sister luminary in the heavens. As he walked sleepily up the street, he turned his broad, dull face on Robin, and displayed a long staff, spiked at the end.

"Home, vagabond, home!" said the watchman, in accents that seemed to fall asleep as soon as they were uttered. "Home, or we'll set you in the stocks by peep of day!"

"This is the second hint of the kind," thought Robin. "I wish they would end my difficulties, by setting me there tonight."

Nevertheless, the youth felt an instinctive antipathy towards the guardian of midnight order, which at first prevented him from asking his usual question. But just when the man was about to vanish behind the corner, Robin resolved not to lose the opportunity, and shouted lustily after him—

"I say, friend! will you guide me to the house of my kinsman, Major Molineux?"

The watchman made no reply, but turned the corner and was gone; yet Robin seemed to hear the sound of drowsy laughter stealing along the solitary street. At that moment, also, a pleasant titter saluted him from the open window above his head; he looked up, and caught the sparkle of a saucy eye; a round arm beckoned to him, and next he heard light footsteps descending the staircase within. But Robin, being of the household of a New England clergyman, was a good youth, as well as a shrewd one; so he resisted temptation, and fled away.

He now roamed desperately, and at random, through the town, almost ready to believe that a spell was on him, like that, by which a wizard of his country, had once kept three pursuers wandering, a whole winter night, within twenty paces of the cottage which they sought. The streets lay before him, strange and desolate, and the lights were extinguished in almost every house. Twice, however, little parties of men, among whom Robin distinguished individuals in outlandish attire, came hurrying along, but though on both occasions they paused to address him, such intercourse did not at all enlighten his perplexity. They did but utter a few words in some language of which Robin knew nothing, and perceiving his inability to answer, bestowed a curse upon him in plain English, and hastened away. Finally, the lad determined to knock at the door of every mansion that might appear worthy to be occupied by his kinsman, trusting that perseverance would overcome the fatality which had hitherto thwarted him. Firm in this resolve, he was passing beneath the walls of a church, which formed the corner of two streets, when, as he turned into the shade of its steeple, he encountered a bulky stranger, muffled in a cloak. The man was proceeding with the speed of earnest business, but Robin planted himself full before him, holding the oak cudgel with both hands across his body, as a bar to further passage.

"Halt, honest man, and answer me a question," said he, very resolutely. "Tell me, this instant, whereabouts is the dwelling of my kinsman, Major Molineux?"

"Keep your tongue between your teeth, fool, and let me pass," said a deep, gruff voice, which Robin partly remembered. "Let me pass, I say, or I'll strike you to the earth!"

"No, no, neighbor!" cried Robin, flourishing his cudgel, and then thrusting its larger end close to the man's muffled face. "No, no, I'm not the fool you take me for, nor do you pass, till I have an answer to my question. Whereabouts is the dwelling of my kinsman, Major Molineux?"

The stranger, instead of attempting to force his passage, stept back into the moonlight, unmuffled his own face and stared full into that of Robin.

"Watch here an hour, and Major Molineux will pass by," said he.

Robin gazed with dismay and astonishment, on the unprecedented physiognomy of the speaker. The forehead with its double prominence, the broad-hooked nose, the shaggy eyebrows, and fiery eyes, were those which he had noticed at the inn, but the man's complexion had undergone a singular, or, more properly, a two-fold change. One side of the face blazed of an intense red, while the other was black as midnight, the division line being in the broad bridge of the nose; and a mouth, which seemed to extend from ear to ear, was black or red, in contrast to the color of the cheek. The effect was as if two individual devils, a fiend of fire and a fiend of darkness, had united themselves to form this infernal visage. The stranger grinned in Robin's face, muffled his parti-colored features, and was out of sight in a moment.

"Strange things we travellers see!" ejaculated Robin.

He seated himself, however, upon the steps of the church-door, resolving to wait the appointed time for his kinsman's appearance. A few moments were consumed in philosophical speculations, upon the species of the *genus homo,* who had just left him, but having settled this point shrewdly, rationally, and satisfactorily, he was compelled to look elsewhere for amusement. And first he threw his eyes along the street; it was of more respectable appearance than most of those into which he had wandered, and the moon, "creating, like the imaginative power, a beautiful strangeness in familiar objects," gave something of romance to a scene, that might not have possessed it in the light of day. The irregular, and often quaint architecture of the houses, some of whose roofs were broken into numerous little peaks; while others ascended, steep and narrow, into a single point; and others again were square; the pure milk-white of some of their complexions, the aged darkness of others, and the thousand sparklings, reflected from bright substances in the plastered walls of many; these matters engaged Robin's attention for awhile, and then began to grow wearisome. Next he endeavored to define the forms of distant objects, starting away with almost ghostly indistinctness, just as his eye appeared to grasp them; and finally he took a minute survey of an edifice, which stood on the opposite side of the street, directly in front of the church-door, where he was stationed. It was a large square mansion, distinguished from its neighbors by a balcony, which rested on tall pillars, and by an elaborate Gothic window, communicating therewith.

"Perhaps this is the very house I have been seeking," thought Robin.

Then he strove to speed away the time, by listening to a murmur, which swept continually along the street, yet was scarcely audible, except to an unaccustomed ear like his; it was a low, dull, dreamy sound, compounded of many noises, each of which was at too great a distance to be separately heard. Robin marvelled at this snore of a sleeping town, and marvelled more, whenever its continuity was broken, by now and then a distant shout, apparently loud where it originated. But altogether it was a sleep-inspiring sound, and to shake off its drowsy influence, Robin arose, and climbed a window-frame, that he might view the interior of the church. There the moonbeams came trembling in, and fell down upon the deserted pews, and extended along the quiet aisles. A fainter, yet more awful radiance, was hovering round the pulpit, and one solitary ray had dared to rest upon the opened page of the great Bible. Had Nature, in that deep hour, become a worshipper in the house, which man had builded? Or was that heavenly light the visible sanctity of the place, visible because no earthly and impure feet were within the walls? The scene made Robin's heart shiver with a sensation of loneliness, stronger than he had ever felt in the remotest depths of his native woods; so he turned away, and sat down again before the door. There were graves around the church, and now an uneasy thought obtruded into Robin's breast. What if the object of his search, which had been so often and so strangely thwarted, were all the time mouldering in his shroud? What if his kinsman should glide through yonder gate, and nod and smile to him in passing dimly by?

"Oh, that any breathing thing were here with me!" said Robin.

Recalling his thoughts from this uncomfortable track, he sent them over forest, hill, and stream, and attempted to imagine how that evening of ambiguity and weariness, had been spent by his father's household. He pictured them assembled at the door, beneath the tree, the great old tree, which had been spared for its huge twisted trunk, and venerable shade, when a thousand leafy brethren fell. There, at the going down of the summer sun, it was his father's custom to perform domestic worship, that the neighbors might come and join with him like brothers of the family, and that the wayfaring man might pause to drink at that fountain, and keep his heart pure by freshening the memory of home. Robin distinguished the seat of every individual of the little audience; he saw the good man in the midst, holding the Scriptures in the golden light that shone from the western clouds; he beheld him close the book, and all rise up to pray. He heard the old thanksgivings for daily mercies, the old supplications for their continuance, to which he had so often listened in weariness, but which were now among his dear remembrances. He perceived the slight inequality of his father's voice when he came to speak of the Absent One; he noted how his mother turned her face to the broad and knotted trunk; how his elder brother scorned, because the beard was rough upon his upper lip, to permit his features to be moved; how his younger sister drew down a low hanging branch before her eyes; and how the little one of all, whose sports had hitherto broken the decorum of the scene, understood the prayer for her playmate, and burst into clamorous grief. Then he saw them go in at the door; and when Robin would have entered also, the latch tinkled into its place, and he was excluded from his home.

"Am I here, or there?" cried Robin, starting; for all at once, when his thoughts had become visible and audible in a dream, the long, wide, solitary street shone out before him.

He aroused himself, and endeavored to fix his attention steadily upon the large edifice which he had surveyed before. But still his mind kept vibrating between fancy and reality; by turns, the pillars of the balcony lengthened into the tall, bare stems of pines, dwindled down to human figures, settled again in their true shape and size, and then commenced a new succession of changes. For a single moment, when he deemed himself awake, he could have sworn that a visage, one which he seemed to remember, yet could not absolutely name as his kinsman's, was looking towards him from the Gothic window. A deeper sleep wrestled with, and nearly overcame him, but fled at the sound of footsteps along the opposite pavement. Robin rubbed his eyes, discerned a man passing at the foot of the balcony, and addressed him in a loud, peevish, and lamentable cry.

"Halloo, friend! must I wait here all night for my kinsman, Major Molineux?"

The sleeping echoes awoke, and answered the voice; and the passenger, barely able to discern a figure sitting in the oblique shade of the steeple, traversed the street to obtain a nearer view. He was himself a gentleman in his prime, of open, intelligent, cheerful, and altogether prepossessing countenance. Perceiving a country youth, apparently homeless and without friends, he accosted him in a tone of real kindness, which had become strange to Robin's ears.

"Well, my good lad, why are you sitting here?" inquired he. "Can I be of service to you in any way?"

"I am afraid not, Sir," replied Robin, despondingly; "yet I shall take it kindly, if you'll answer me a single question. I've been searching half the night for one Major Molineux; now, Sir, is there really such a person in these parts, or am I dreaming?"

"Major Molineux! The name is not altogether strange to me," said the gentleman, smiling. "Have you any objection to telling me the nature of your business with him?"

Then Robin briefly related that his father was a clergyman, settled on a small salary, at a long distance back in the country, and that he and Major Molineux were brothers' children. The Major, having inherited riches, and acquired civil and military rank, had visited his cousin in great pomp a year or two before; had manifested much interest in Robin and an elder brother, and, being childless himself, had thrown out hints respecting the future establishment of one of them in life. The elder brother was destined to succeed to the farm, which his father cultivated, in the interval of sacred duties; it was therefore determined that Robin should profit by his kinsman's generous intentions, especially as he had seemed to be rather the favorite, and was thought to possess other necessary endowments.

"For I have the name of being a shrewd youth," observed Robin, in this part of his story.

"I doubt not you deserve it," replied his new friend, good naturedly; "but pray proceed."

"Well, Sir, being nearly eighteen years old, and well-grown, as you see," continued Robin, raising himself to his full height, "I thought it high time to begin the world. So my mother and sister put me in handsome trim, and my father gave me half the remnant of his last year's salary, and five days ago I started for this place, to pay the Major a visit. But would you believe it, Sir? I crossed the ferry a little after dusk, and have yet found nobody that would show me the way to his dwelling; only an hour or two since, I was told to wait here, and Major Molineux would pass by."

"Can you describe the man who told you this?" inquired the gentleman.

"Oh, he was a very ill-favored fellow, Sir," replied Robin, "with two great bumps on his forehead, a hook nose, fiery eyes, and, what struck me as the strangest, his face was of two different colors. Do you happen to know such a man, Sir?"

"Not intimately," answered the stranger, "but I chanced to meet him a little time previous to your stopping me. I believe you may trust his word, and that the Major will very shortly pass through this street. In the mean time, as I have a singular curiosity to witness your meeting, I will sit down here upon the steps, and bear you company."

He seated himself accordingly, and soon engaged his companion in animated discourse. It was but of brief continuance, however, for a noise of shouting, which had long been remotely audible, drew so much nearer, that Robin inquired its cause.

"What may be the meaning of this uproar?" asked he. "Truly,

if your town be always as noisy, I shall find little sleep, while I am an inhabitant."

"Why, indeed, friend Robin, there do appear to be three or four riotous fellows abroad to-night," replied the gentleman. "You must not expect all the stillness of your native woods, here in our streets. But the watch will shortly be at the heels of these lads, and—"

"Aye, and set them in the stocks by peep of day," interrupted Robin, recollecting his own encounter with the drowsy lantern-bearer. "But, dear Sir, if I may trust my ears, an army of watchmen would never make head against such a multitude of rioters. There were at least a thousand voices went to make up that one shout."

"May not one man have several voices, Robin, as well as two complexions?" said his friend.

"Perhaps a man may; but Heaven forbid that a woman should!" responded the shrewd youth, thinking of the seductive tones of the Major's housekeeper.

The sounds of a trumpet in some neighboring street now became so evident and continual, that Robin's curiosity was strongly excited. In addition to the shouts, he heard frequent bursts from many instruments of discord, and a wild and confused laughter filled up the intervals. Robin rose from the steps, and looked wistfully towards a point, whither several people seemed to be hastening.

"Surely some prodigious merrymaking is going on," exclaimed he. "I have laughed very little since I left home, Sir, and should be sorry to lose an opportunity. Shall we just step round the corner by that darkish house, and take our share of the fun?"

"Sit down again, sit down, good Robin," replied the gentleman, laying his hand on the skirt of the grey coat. "You forget that we must wait here for your kinsman; and there is reason to believe that he will pass by, in the course of a very few moments."

The near approach of the uproar had now disturbed the neighborhood; windows flew open on all sides; and many heads, in the attire of the pillow, and confused by sleep suddenly broken, were protruded to the gaze of whoever had leisure to observe them. Eager voices hailed each other from house to house, all demanding the explanation, which not a soul could give. Half-dressed men hurried towards the unknown commotion, stumbling as they went over the stone steps, that thrust themselves into the narrow foot-walk. The shouts, the laughter, and the tuneless bray, the antipodes of music, came onward with increasing din, till scattered individuals, and then denser bodies, began to appear round a corner, at the distance of a hundred yards.

"Will you recognize your kinsman, Robin, if he passes in this crowd?" inquired the gentleman.

"Indeed, I can't warrant it, Sir; but I'll take my stand here, and keep a bright look out," answered Robin, descending to the outer edge of the pavement.

A mighty stream of people now emptied into the street, and came rolling slowly towards the church. A single horseman wheeled the corner in the midst of them, and close behind him came a band of fearful wind-instruments, sending forth a fresher discord, now that no intervening buildings kept it from the ear. Then a redder light disturbed the moonbeams, and a dense multitude of torches shone along the street, concealing by their glare whatever object they illuminated. The single horseman, clad in a military dress, and bearing a drawn sword, rode onward as the leader, and, by his fierce and variegated countenance, appeared like war personified; the red of one cheek was an emblem of fire and sword; the blackness of the other betokened the mourning which attends them. In his train, were wild figures in the Indian dress, and many fantastic shapes without a model, giving the whole march a visionary air, as if a dream had broken forth from some feverish brain, and were sweeping visibly through the midnight streets. A mass of people, inactive, except as applauding spectators, hemmed the procession in, and several women ran along the sidewalks, piercing the confusion of heavier sounds, with their shrill voices of mirth or terror.

"The double-faced fellow has his eye upon me," muttered

Robin, with an indefinite but uncomfortable idea, that he was himself to bear a part in the pageantry.

The leader turned himself in the saddle, and fixed his glance full upon the country youth, as the steed went slowly by. When Robin had freed his eyes from those fiery ones, the musicians were passing before him, and the torches were close at hand; but the unsteady brightness of the latter formed a veil which he could not penetrate. The rattling of wheels over the stones sometimes found its way to his ear, and confused traces of a human form appeared at intervals, and then melted into the vivid light. A moment more, and the leader thundered a command to halt; the trumpets vomited a horrid breath, and held their peace; the shouts and laughter of the people died away, and there remained only a universal hum, nearly allied to silence. Right before Robin's eyes was an uncovered cart. There the torches blazed the brightest, there the moon shone out like day, and there, in tar-and-feathery dignity, sate his kinsman, Major Molineux!

He was an elderly man, of large and majestic person, and strong, square features, betokening a steady soul; but steady as it was, his enemies had found the means to shake it. His face was pale as death, and far more ghastly; the broad forehead was contracted in his agony, so that his eyebrows formed one grizzled line; his eyes were red and wild, and the foam hung white upon his quivering lip. His whole frame was agitated by a quick, and continual tremor, which his pride strove to quell, even in those circumstances of overwhelming humiliation. But perhaps the bitterest pang of all was when his eyes met those of Robin; for he evidently knew him on the instant, as the youth stood witnessing the foul disgrace of a head that had grown grey in honor. They stared at each other in silence, and Robin's knees shook, and his hair bristled, with a mixture of pity and terror. Soon, however, a bewildering excitement began to seize upon his mind; the preceding adventures of the night, the unexpected appearance of the crowd, the torches, the confused din, and the hush that followed, the spectre of his kinsman reviled by that great multitude, all this, and more than all, a perception of tremendous ridicule in the whole scene, affected him with a sort of mental inebriety. At that moment a voice of sluggish merriment saluted Robin's ears; he turned instinctively, and just behind the corner of the church stood the lantern-bearer, rubbing his eyes, and drowsily enjoying the lad's amazement. Then he heard a peal of laughter like the ringing of silvery bells; a woman twitched his arm, a saucy eye met his, and he saw the lady of the scarlet petticoat. A sharp, dry cachinnation appealed to his memory, and, standing on tiptoe in the crowd, with his white apron over his head, he beheld the courteous little innkeeper. And lastly, there sailed over the heads of the multitude a great, broad laugh, broken in the midst by two sepulchral hems; thus—

"Haw, haw, haw—hem, hem—haw, haw, haw, haw!"

The sound proceeded from the balcony of the opposite edifice, and thither Robin turned his eyes. In front of the Gothic window stood the old citizen, wrapped in a wide gown, his grey periwig exchanged for a nightcap, which was thrust back from his forehead, and his silk stockings hanging down about his legs. He supported himself on his polished cane in a fit of convulsive merriment, which manifested itself on his solemn old features, like a funny inscription on a tomb-stone. Then Robin seemed to hear the voices of the barbers; of the guests of the inn; and of all who had made sport of him that night. The contagion was spreading among the multitude, when, all at once, it seized upon Robin, and he sent forth a shout of laughter that echoed through the street; every man shook his sides, every man emptied his lungs, but Robin's shout was the loudest there. The cloud-spirits peeped from their silvery islands, as the congregated mirth went roaring up the sky! The Man in the Moon heard the far bellow; "Oho," quoth he, "the old Earth is frolicsome to-night!"

When there was a momentary calm in that tempestuous sea of sound, the leader gave the sign, the procession resumed its march. On they went, like fiends that throng in mockery round some dead potentate, mighty no more, but majestic still in his agony. On they went, in counterfeited pomp, in senseless uproar, in frenzied merriment, trampling all on an old man's heart. On swept the tumult, and left a silent street behind.

"Well, Robin, are you dreaming?" inquired the gentleman, laying his hand on the youth's shoulder.

Robin started, and withdrew his arm from the stone post, to which he had instinctively clung, while the living stream rolled by him. His cheek was somewhat pale, and his eye not quite so lively as in the earlier part of the evening.

"Will you be kind enough to show me the way to the ferry?" said he, after a moment's pause.

"You have then adopted a new subject of inquiry?" observed his companion, with a smile.

"Why, yes, Sir," replied Robin, rather dryly. "Thanks to you, and to my other friends, I have at last met my kinsman, and he will scarce desire to see my face again. I begin to grow weary of a town life, Sir. Will you show me the way to the ferry?"

"No, my good friend Robin, not to-night, at least," said the gentleman. "Some few days hence, if you continue to wish it, I will speed you on your journey. Or, if you prefer to remain with us, perhaps, as you are a shrewd youth, you may rise in the world, without the help of your kinsman, Major Molineux."

In Dreams Begin Responsibilities

Delmore Schwartz (1913–1966)

Delmore Schwartz was born in Brooklyn, New York, and grew up to be a poet, critic, story writer, teacher, and editor. Schwartz was known for his irony and for his concentration on the relations between the private individual and the outside world, and his works are full of intellectual energy. This energy was also reflected in his teaching career—he taught at Harvard, New York, Syracuse, and Princeton universities—and in his role as member of the editorial board of *The Partisan Review* (from 1943 to 1955) and of *The New Republic* (1955 to 1957). His poetry collections include *Vaudeville for a Princess* (1950) and *Summer Knowledge* (1959), which won the Bollingen Prize. *Shenandoah* (1941) is a verse play, *Genesis* (1943) collects both prose and poetry, and *The World Is a Wedding* (1948) is a compilation of short fiction. The story included in this anthology is from *In Dreams Begin Responsibilities* (1938).

I

I think it is the year 1909. I feel as if I were in a motion picture theatre, the long arm of light crossing the darkness and spinning, my eyes fixed on the screen. This is a silent picture as if an old Biograph one, in which the actors are dressed in ridiculously old-fashioned clothes, and one flash succeeds another with sudden jumps. The actors too seem to jump about and walk too fast. The shots themselves are full of dots and rays, as if it were raining when the picture was photographed. The light is bad.

It is Sunday afternoon, June 12th, 1909, and my father is walking down the quiet streets of Brooklyn on his way to visit my mother. His clothes are newly pressed and his tie is too tight in his high collar. He jingles the coins in his pockets, thinking of the witty things he will say. I feel as if I had by now relaxed entirely in the soft darkness of the theatre; the organist peals out the obvious and approximate emotions on which the audience rocks unknowingly. I am anonymous, and I have forgotten myself. It is always so when one goes to the movies, it is, as they say, a drug.

My father walks from street to street of trees, lawns and houses, once in a while coming to an avenue on which a street-car skates and gnaws, slowly progressing. The conductor, who has a handlebar mustache, helps a young lady wearing a hat like a bowl with feathers on to the car. She lifts her long skirts slightly as she mounts the steps. He leisurely makes change and rings his bell. It is obviously Sunday, for everyone is wearing Sunday clothes, and the street-car's noises emphasize the quiet of the holiday. Is not Brooklyn the City of Churches? The shops are closed and their shades drawn, but for an occasional stationery store or drug-store with great green balls in the window.

My father has chosen to take this long walk because he likes to walk and think. He thinks about himself in the future and so arrives at the place he is to visit in a state of mild exaltation. He pays no attention to the houses he is passing, in which the Sunday dinner is being eaten, nor to the many trees which patrol each street, now coming to their full leafage and the time when they will room the whole street in cool shadow. An occasional carriage passes, the horse's hooves falling like stones in the quiet afternoon, and once in a while an automobile, looking like an enormous upholstered sofa, puffs and passes.

My father thinks of my mother, of how nice it will be to introduce her to his family. But he is not yet sure that he wants to marry her, and once in a while he becomes panicky about the bond already established. He reassures himself by thinking of the big men he admires who are married: William Randolph Hearst, and William Howard Taft, who has just become President of the United States.

My father arrives at my mother's house. He has come too early and so is suddenly embarrassed. My aunt, my mother's sister, answers the loud bell with her napkin in her hand, for the family is still at dinner. As my father enters, my grandfather rises from the table and shakes hands with him. My mother has run upstairs to tidy herself. My grandmother asks my father if he has had dinner, and tells him that Rose will be downstairs soon. My grandfather opens the conversation by remarking on the mild June weather. My father sits uncomfortably near the table, holding his hat in his hand. My grandmother tells my aunt to take my father's hat. My uncle, twelve years old, runs into the house, his hair tousled. He shouts a greeting to my father, who has often given him a nickel, and then runs upstairs. It is evident that the respect in which my father is held in this household is tempered by a good deal of mirth. He is impressive, yet he is very awkward.

II

Finally my mother comes downstairs, all dressed up, and my father being engaged in conversation with my grandfather becomes uneasy, not knowing whether to greet my mother or continue the conversation. He get up from the chair clumsily and says "hello" gruffly. My grandfather watches, examining their congruence, such as it is, with a critical eye, and meanwhile rubbing his bearded cheek roughly, as he always does when he reflects. He is worried; he is afraid that my father will not make a good husband for his oldest daughter. At this point something happens to the film, just as my father is saying something funny to my mother; I am awakened to myself and my unhappiness just as my interest was rising. The audience begins to clap impatiently. Then the trouble is cared for but the film has been returned to a portion just shown, and once more I see my grandfather rubbing his bearded cheek and pondering my father's character. It is difficult to get back into the picture once more and forget myself, but as my mother giggles at my father's words, the darkness drowns me.

My father and mother depart from the house, my father shaking hands with my mother once more, out of some unknown uneasiness. I stir uneasily also, slouched in the hard chair of the theatre. Where is the older uncle, my mother's older brother? He is studying in his bedroom upstairs, studying for his final examination at the College of the City of New York, having been dead of rapid pneumonia for the last twenty-one years. My mother and father walk down the same quiet streets once more. My mother is holding my father's arm and telling him of the novel which she has been reading; and my father utters judgments of the characters as the plot is made clear to him. This is a habit which he very much enjoys, for he feels the utmost superiority and confidence when he approves and condemns the behavior of other people. At times he feels moved to utter a brief "Ugh"—whenever the story becomes what he would call sugary. This tribute is paid to his manliness. My mother feels satisfied by the interest which she has awakened; she is showing my father how intelligent she is, and how interesting.

They reach the avenue, and the street-car leisurely arrives. They are going to Coney Island this afternoon, although my mother considers that such pleasures are inferior. She has made up her mind to indulge only in a walk on the boardwalk and a pleasant dinner, avoiding the riotous amusements as being beneath the dignity of so dignified a couple.

My father tells my mother how much money he has made in the past week, exaggerating an amount which need not have been exaggerated. But my father has always felt that actualities somehow fall short. Suddenly I begin to weep. The determined old lady who sits next to me in the theatre is annoyed and looks at me with an angry face, and being intimidated, I stop. I drag out my handkerchief and dry my face, licking the drop which has fallen near my lips. Meanwhile I have missed something, for here are my mother and father alighting at the last stop, Coney Island.

III

They walk toward the boardwalk, and my father commands my mother to inhale the pungent air from the sea. They both breathe in deeply, both of them laughing as they do so. They have in common a great interest in health, although my father is strong and husky, my mother frail. Their minds are full of theories of what is good to eat and not good to eat, and sometimes they engage in heated discussions of the subject, the whole matter ending in my father's announcement, made with a scornful bluster, that you have to die sooner or later anyway. On the boardwalk's flagpole, the American flag is pulsing in an intermittent wind from the sea.

My father and mother go to the rail of the boardwalk and look down on the beach where a good many bathers are casually walking about. A few are in the surf. A peanut whistle pierces the air with its pleasant and active whine, and my father goes to buy peanuts. My mother remains at the rail and stares at the ocean. The ocean seems merry to her; it pointedly sparkles and again and again the pony waves are released. She notices the children digging in the wet sand, and the bathing costumes of the girls who are her own age. My father returns with the peanuts. Overhead the sun's lightning strikes and strikes, but neither of them are at all aware of it. The boardwalk is full of people dressed in their Sunday clothes and idly strolling. The tide does not reach as far as the boardwalk, and the strollers would feel no danger if it did. My mother and father lean on the rail of the boardwalk and absently stare at the ocean. The ocean is becoming rough; the waves come in slowly, tugging strength from far back. The moment before they somersault, the moment when they arch their backs so beautifully, showing green and white veins amid the black, that moment is intolerable. They finally crack, dashing fiercely upon the sand, actually driving, full force downward, against the sand, bouncing upward and forward, and at last petering out into a small stream which races up the beach and then is recalled. My parents gaze absentmindedly at the ocean, scarcely interested in its harshness. The sun overhead does not disturb them. But I stare at the terrible sun which breaks up sight, and the fatal, merciless, passionate ocean, I forget my parents. I stare fascinated and finally, shocked by the indifference of my father and mother, I burst out weeping once more. The old lady next to me pats me on the shoulder and says "There, there, all of this is only a movie, young man, only a movie," but I look up once more at the terrifying sun and the terrifying ocean, and being unable to control my tears, I get up and go to the men's room, stumbling over the feet of the other people seated in my row.

IV

When I return, feeling as if I had awakened in the morning sick for lack of sleep, several hours have apparently passed and my parents are riding on the merry-go-round. My father is on a black horse, my mother on a white one, and they seem to be making an eternal circuit for the single purpose of snatching the nickel rings which are attached to the arm of one of the posts. A hand-organ is playing; it is one with the ceaseless circling of the merry-go-round.

For a moment it seems that they will never get off the merry-go-round because it will never stop. I feel like one who looks down on the avenue from the fiftieth story of a building. But at length they do get off; even the music of the hand-organ has ceased for a moment. My father has acquired ten rings, my mother only two, although it was my mother who really wanted them.

They walk on along the boardwalk as the afternoon descends by imperceptible degrees into the incredible violet of dusk. Everything fades into a relaxed glow, even the ceaseless murmuring from the beach, and the revolutions of the merry-go-round. They look for a place to have dinner. My father suggests the best one on the boardwalk and my mother demurs, in accordance with her principles.

However they do go to the best place, asking for a table near the window, so that they can look out on the boardwalk and the mobile ocean. My father feels omnipotent as he places a quarter in the waiter's hand as he asks for a table. The place is crowded and here too there is music, this time from a kind of string trio. My father orders dinner with a fine confidence.

As the dinner is eaten, my father tells of his plans for the future, and my mother shows with expressive face how interested she is, and how impressed. My father becomes exultant. He is lifted up by the waltz that is being played, and his own future begins to intoxicate him. My father tells my mother that he is going to expand his business, for there is a great deal of money to be made. He wants to settle down. After all, he is twenty-nine, he has lived by himself since he was thirteen, he is making more and more money, and he is envious of his married friends when he visits them in the cozy security of their homes, surrounded, it seems, by the calm domestic pleasures, and by delightful children, and then, as the waltz reaches the moment when all the dancers swing madly, then, then with awful daring, then he asks my mother to marry him, although awkwardly enough and puzzled, even in his excitement, at how he had arrived at the proposal, and she, to make the whole business worse, begins to cry, and my father looks nervously about, not knowing at all what to do now, and my mother says: "It's all I've wanted from the moment I saw you," sobbing, and he finds all of this very difficult, scarcely to his taste, scarcely as he had thought it would be, on his long walks over Brooklyn Bridge in the revery of a fine cigar, and it was then that I stood up in the theatre and shouted: "Don't do it. It's not too late to change your minds, both of you. Nothing good will come of it, only remorse, hatred, scandal, and two children whose characters are monstrous." The whole audience turned to look at me, annoyed, the usher came hurrying down the aisle flashing his searchlight, and the old lady next to me tugged me down into my seat, saying: "Be quiet. You'll be put out, and you paid thirty-five cents to come in." And so I shut my eyes because I could not bear to see what was happening. I sat there quietly.

V

But after awhile I begin to take brief glimpses, and at length I watch again with thirsty interest, like a child who wants to maintain his sulk although offered the bribe of candy. My parents are now having their picture taken in a photographer's booth along the boardwalk. The place is shadowed in the mauve light which is apparently necessary. The camera is set to the side on its tripod and looks like a Martian man. The photographer is instructing my parents in how to pose. My father has his arm over my mother's shoulder, and both of them smile emphatically. The photographer brings my mother a bouquet of flowers to hold in her hand but she holds it at the wrong angle. Then the photographer covers himself with the black cloth which drapes the camera and all that one sees of him is one protruding arm and his hand which clutches the rubber ball which he will squeeze when the picture is finally taken. But he is not satisfied with their appearance. He feels with certainty that somehow there is something wrong in their pose. Again and again he issues from his hidden place with new directions. Each suggestion merely makes matters worse. My father is becoming impatient. They try a seated pose. The photographer explains that he has pride, he is not interested in all of this for the money, he wants to make beautiful pictures. My father says: "Hurry up, will you? We haven't got all night." But the photographer only scurries about apologetically, and issues new directions. The photographer charms me. I approve of him with all my heart, for I know just how he feels, and as he criticizes each revised pose according to some unknown idea of rightness, I become quite hopeful. But then my father says angrily: "Come on, you've had enough time, we're not going to wait any longer." And the photographer, sighing unhappily, goes back under his black covering, holds out his hand, says: "One, two, three, Now!", and the picture is taken, with my father's smile turned to a grimace and my mother's bright and false. It takes a few minutes for the picture to be developed and as my parents sit in the curious light they become quite depressed.

VI

They have passed a fortune-teller's booth, and my mother wishes to go in, but my father does not. They begin to argue about it. My mother becomes stubborn, my father once more impatient, and then they begin to quarrel, and what my father would like to do is walk off and leave my mother there, but he knows that that would never do. My mother refuses to budge. She is near to tears, but she feels an uncontrollable desire to hear what the palm-reader will say. My father consents angrily, and they both go into a booth which is in a way like the photographer's, since it is draped in black cloth and its light is shadowed. The place is too warm, and my father keeps saying this is all nonsense, pointing to the crystal ball on the table. The fortune-teller, a fat, short woman, garbed in what is supposed to be Oriental robes, comes into the room from the back and greets them, speaking with an accent. But suddenly my father feels that the whole thing is intolerable; he tugs at my mother's arm, but my mother refuses to budge. And then, in terrible anger, my father lets go of my mother's arm and strides out, leaving my mother stunned. She moves to go after my father, but the fortune-teller holds her arm tightly and begs her not to do so, and I in my seat am shocked more than can ever be said, for I feel as if I were walking a tight-rope a hundred feet over a circus-audience and suddenly the rope is showing signs of breaking, and I get up from my seat and begin to shout once more the first words I can think of to communicate my terrible fear and once more the usher comes hurrying down the aisle flashing his searchlight, and the old lady pleads with me, and the shocked audience has turned to stare at me, and I keep shouting: "What are they doing? Don't they know what they are doing? Why doesn't my mother go after my father? If she does not do that, what will she do? Doesn't my father know what he is doing?"—But the usher has seized my arm and is dragging me away, and as he does so, he says: "What are *you* doing? Don't you know that you can't do whatever you want to do? Why should a young man like you, with your whole life before you, get hysterical like this? Why don't you *think* of what you're doing? You can't act like this even if other people aren't around! You will be sorry if you do not do what you should do, you can't carry on like this, it is not right, you will find that out soon enough, everything you do matters too much," and he said that dragging me through the lobby of the theatre into the cold light, and I woke up into the bleak winter morning of my twenty-first birthday, the windowsill shining with its lip of snow, and the morning already begun.

The Pagan Rabbi

Cynthia Ozick (1928–)

A literary critic and fiction writer born in the Bronx, **Cynthia Ozick** was influenced greatly by Henry James—especially in her strongly Jamesian novel *Trust* (1966). Like James, Ozick writes of money, class, and status as a central societal force, using luscious imagery in her descriptions. Ozick also writes of Jewish-American culture and the dilemmas within it with a forceful, often fantastical style of expression. A fascination with pagan earth-gods begins in *The Pagan Rabbi and Other Stories* (1971), which includes the story in this anthology, continues in *The Shawl* (1989), and is most evident throughout her later works. Other short story collections include *Levitation: Five Fictions* (1982) and *The Cannibal Galaxy* (1983). Her essays are compiled in *Art and Ardor* (1983), *Metaphor and Memory* (1987), and *Fame and Folly* (1996).

Rabbi Jacob said: "He who is walking along and studying, but then breaks off to remark, 'How lovely is that tree!' or 'How beautiful is that fallow field!'—Scripture regards such a one as having hurt his own being."

—from THE ETHICS OF THE FATHERS

When I heard that Isaac Kornfeld, a man of piety and brains, had hanged himself in the public park, I put a token in the subway stile and journeyed out to see the tree.

We had been classmates in the rabbinical seminary. Our fathers were both rabbis. They were also friends, but only in a loose way of speaking: in actuality our fathers were enemies. They vied with one another in demonstrations of charitableness, in the captious glitter of their scholia, in the number of their adherents. Of the two, Isaac's father was the milder. I was afraid of my father; he had a certain disease of the larynx, and if he even uttered something so trivial as "Bring the tea" to my mother, it came out splintered, clamorous, and vindictive.

Neither man was philosophical in the slightest. It was the one thing they agreed on. "Philosophy is an abomination," Isaac's father used to say. "The Greeks were philosophers, but they remained children playing with their dolls. Even Socrates, a monotheist, nevertheless sent money down to the temple to pay for incense to their doll."

"Idolatry is the abomination," Isaac argued, "not philosophy."

"The latter is the corridor to the former," his father said.

My own father claimed that if not for philosophy I would never have been brought to the atheism which finally led me to withdraw, in my second year, from the seminary. The trouble was not philosophy—I had none of Isaac's talent: his teachers later said of him that his imagination was so remarkable he could concoct holiness out of the fine line of a serif. On the day of his funeral the president of his college was criticized for having commented that although a suicide could not be buried in consecrated earth, whatever earth enclosed Isaac Kornfeld was ipso facto consecrated. It should be noted that Isaac hanged himself several weeks short of his thirty-sixth birthday; he was then at the peak of his renown; and the president, of course, did not know the whole story. He judged by Isaac's reputation, which was at no time more impressive than just before his death.

I judged by the same, and marveled that all that holy genius and intellectual surprise should in the end be raised no higher than the next-to-lowest limb of a delicate young oak, with burly roots like the toes of a gryphon exposed in the wet ground.

The tree was almost alone in a long rough meadow, which sloped down to a bay filled with sickly clams and a bad smell. The place was called Trilham's Inlet, and I knew what the smell meant: that cold brown water covered half the city's turds.

On the day I came to see the tree the air was bleary with fog. The weather was well into autumn and, though it was Sunday, the walks were empty. There was something historical about the park just then, with its rusting grasses and deserted monuments. In front of a soldiers' cenotaph a plastic wreath left behind months before by some civic parade stood propped against a stone frieze of identical marchers in the costume of an old war. A banner across the wreath's belly explained that the purpose of war is peace. At the margins of the park they were building a gigantic highway. I felt I was making my way across a battlefield silenced by the victory of the peace machines. The bulldozers had bitten far into the park, and the rolled carcasses of the sacrificed trees were already cut up into logs. There were dozens of felled maples, elms, and oaks. Their moist inner wheels breathed out a fragrance of barns, countryside, decay.

In the bottommost meadow fringing the water I recognized the tree which had caused Isaac to sin against his own life. It looked curiously like a photograph—not only like that newspaper photograph I carried warmly in my pocket, which showed the field and its markers—the drinking-fountain a few yards off, the ruined brick wall of an old estate behind. The caption-writer had particularly remarked on the "rope." But the rope was no longer there; the widow had claimed it. It was his own prayer shawl that Isaac, a short man, had thrown over the comely neck of the next-to-lowest limb. A Jew is buried in his prayer shawl; the police had handed it over to Sheindel. I observed that the bark was rubbed at that spot. The tree lay back against the sky like a licked postage stamp. Rain began to beat it flatter yet. A stench of sewage came up like a veil in the nostril. It seemed to me I was a man in a photograph standing next to a gray blur of tree. I would stand through eternity beside Isaac's guilt if I did not run, so I ran that night to Sheindel herself.

I loved her at once. I am speaking now of the first time I saw her, though I don't exclude the last. The last—the last together with Isaac—was soon after my divorce; at one stroke I left my wife and my cousin's fur business to the small upstate city in which both had repined. Suddenly Isaac and Sheindel and two babies appeared in the lobby of my hotel—they were passing through:

Isaac had a lecture engagement in Canada. We sat under scarlet neon and Isaac told how my father could now not speak at all.

"He keeps his vow," I said.

"No, no, he's a sick man," Isaac said. "An obstruction in the throat."

"I'm the obstruction. You know what he said when I left the seminary. He meant it, never mind how many years it is. He's never addressed a word to me since."

"We were reading together. He blamed the reading, who can blame *him?* Fathers like ours don't know how to love. They live too much indoors."

It was an odd remark, though I was too much preoccupied with my own resentments to notice. "It wasn't what we read," I objected. "Torah tells that an illustrious man doesn't have an illustrious son. Otherwise he wouldn't be humble like other people. This much scholarly stuffing I retain. Well, so my father always believed he was more illustrious than anybody, especially more than your father. *There*fore," I delivered in Talmudic cadence, "what chance did I have? A nincompoop and no *sitzfleish.* Now you, you could answer questions that weren't even invented yet. Then you invented them."

"Torah isn't a spade," Isaac said. "A man should have a livelihood. You had yours."

"The pelt of a dead animal isn't a living either, it's an indecency."

All the while Sheindel was sitting perfectly still; the babies, female infants in long stockings, were asleep in her arms. She wore a dark thick woolen hat—it was July—that covered every part of her hair. But I had once seen it in all its streaming black shine.

"And Jane?" Isaac asked finally.

"Speaking of dead animals. Tell my father—he won't answer a letter, he won't come to the telephone—that in the matter of the marriage he was right, but for the wrong reason. If you share a bed with a Puritan you'll come into it cold and you'll go out of it cold. Listen, Isaac, my father calls me an atheist, but between the conjugal sheets every Jew is a believer in miracles, even the lapsed."

He said nothing then. He knew I envied him his Sheindel and his luck. Unlike our fathers, Isaac had never condemned me for my marriage, which his father regarded as his private triumph over my father, and which my father, in his public defeat, took as an occasion for declaring me as one dead. He rent his clothing and sat on a stool for eight days, while Isaac's father came to watch him mourn, secretly satisfied, though aloud he grieved for all apostates. Isaac did not like my wife. He called her a tall yellow straw. After we were married he never said a word against her, but he kept away.

I went with my wife to his wedding. We took the early train down especially, but when we arrived the feast was well under way, and the guests far into the dancing.

"Look, look, they don't dance together," Jane said.

"Who?"

"The men and the women. The bride and the groom."

"Count the babies," I advised. "The Jews are also Puritans, but only in public."

The bride was enclosed all by herself on a straight chair in the center of a spinning ring of young men. The floor heaved under their whirl. They stamped, the chandeliers shuddered, the guests cried out, the young men with linked arms spiraled and their skullcaps came flying off like centrifugal balloons. Isaac, a mist of black suit, a stamping foot, was lost in the planet's wake of black suits and emphatic feet. The dancing young men shouted bridal songs, the floor leaned like a plate, the whole room teetered.

Isaac had told me something of Sheindel. Before now I had never seen her. Her birth was in a concentration camp, and they were about to throw her against the electrified fence when an army mobbed the gate; the current vanished from the terrible wires, and she had nothing to show for it afterward but a mark on her cheek like an asterisk, cut by a barb. The asterisk pointed to certain dry footnotes: she had no mother to show, she had no father to show, but she had, extraordinarily, God to show—she was known to be, for her age and sex, astonishingly learned. She was only seventeen.

"What pretty hair she has," Jane said.

Now Sheindel was dancing with Isaac's mother. All the ladies made a fence, and the bride, twirling with her mother-in-law, lost a shoe and fell against the long laughing row. The ladies lifted their glistering breasts in their lacy dresses and laughed; the young men, stamping two by two, went on shouting their wedding songs. Sheindel danced without her shoe, and the black river of her hair followed her.

"After today she'll have to hide it all," I explained.

Jane asked why.

"So as not to be a temptation to men," I told her, and covertly looked for my father. There he was, in a shadow, apart. My eyes discovered his eyes. He turned his back and gripped his throat.

"It's a very anthropological experience," Jane said.

"A wedding is a wedding," I answered her, "among us even more so."

"Is that your father over there, that little scowly man?"

To Jane all Jews were little. "My father the man of the cloth. Yes."

"A wedding is not a wedding," said Jane: we had had only a license and a judge with bad breath.

"Everybody marries for the same reason."

"No," said my wife. "Some for love and some for spite."

"And everybody for bed."

"Some for spite," she insisted.

"I was never cut out for a man of the cloth," I said. "My poor father doesn't see that."

"He doesn't speak to you."

"A technicality. He's losing his voice."

"Well, he's not like you. He doesn't do it for spite," Jane said.

"You don't know him," I said.

He lost it altogether the very week Isaac published his first remarkable collection of responsa. Isaac's father crowed like a passionate rooster, and packed his wife and himself off to the Holy Land to boast on the holy soil. Isaac was a little relieved; he had just been made Professor of Mishnaic History, and his father's whims and pretenses and foolish rivalries were an embarrassment. It is easy to honor a father from afar, but bitter to honor one who is dead. A surgeon cut out my father's voice, and he died without a word.

Isaac and I no longer met. Our ways were too disparate. Isaac was famous, if not in the world, certainly in the kingdom of jurists and scholars. By this time I had acquired a partnership in a small book store in a basement. My partner sold me his share, and I put up a new sign: "The Book Cellar"; for reasons more obscure than filial (all the same I wished my father could have seen it) I established a department devoted especially to not-quite-rare theological works, chiefly in Hebrew and Aramaic, though I carried some Latin and Greek. When Isaac's second volume reached my shelves (I had now expanded to street level), I wrote him to congratulate him, and after that we corresponded, not with any regularity. He took to ordering all his books from me, and we exchanged awkward little jokes. "I'm still in the jacket business," I told him, "but now I feel I'm where I belong. Last time I went too fur." "Sheindel is well, and Naomi and Esther have a sister," he wrote. And later: "Naomi, Esther, and Miriam have a sister." And still later: "Naomi, Esther, Miriam, and Ophra have a sister." It went on until there were seven girls. "There's nothing in Torah that prevents an illustrious man from having illustrious daughters," I wrote him when he said he had given up hope of another rabbi in the family. "But where do you find seven illustrious husbands?" he asked. Every order brought another quip, and we bantered back and forth in this way for some years.

I noticed that he read everything. Long ago he had inflamed my taste, but I could never keep up. No sooner did I catch his joy in Saadia Gaon than he had already sprung ahead to Yehudah Halevi. One day he was weeping with Dostoyevski and the next leaping in the air over Thomas Mann. He introduced me to Hegel and Nietzsche while our fathers wailed. His mature reading was no more peaceable than those frenzies of his youth, when I would come upon him in an abandoned classroom at dusk, his stocking feet on the windowsill, the light already washed from the lowest city clouds, wearing the look of a man half-sotted with print.

But when the widow asked me—covering a certain excess of alertness or irritation—whether to my knowledge Isaac had lately been ordering any books on horticulture, I was astonished.

"He bought so much," I demurred.

"Yes, yes, yes," she said. "How could you remember?"

She poured the tea and then, with a discreetness of gesture, lifted my dripping raincoat from the chair where I had thrown it and took it out of the room. It was a crowded apartment, not very neat, far from slovenly, cluttered with dolls and tiny dishes and an array of tricycles. The dining table was as large as a desert. An old-fashioned crocheted lace runner divided it into two nations, and on the end of this, in the neutral zone, so to speak, Sheindel had placed my cup. There was no physical relic of Isaac: not even a book.

She returned. "My girls are all asleep, we can talk. What an ordeal for you, weather like this and going out so far to that place."

It was impossible to tell whether she was angry or not. I had rushed in on her like the rainfall itself, scattering drops, my shoes stuck all over with leaves.

"I comprehend exactly why you went out there. The impulse of a detective," she said. Her voice contained an irony that surprised me. It was brilliantly and unmistakably accented, and because of this jaggedly precise. It was as if every word emitted a quick white thread of great purity, like hard silk, which she was then obliged to bite cleanly off. "You went to find something? An atmosphere? The sadness itself?"

"There was nothing to see," I said, and thought I was lunatic to have put myself in her way.

"Did you dig in the ground? He might have buried a note for goodbye."

"Was there a note?" I asked, startled.

"He left nothing behind for ordinary humanity like yourself."

I saw she was playing with me. "Rebbetzin Kornfeld," I said, standing up, "forgive me. My coat, please, and I'll go."

"Sit," she commanded. "Isaac read less lately, did you notice that?"

I gave her a civil smile. "All the same he was buying more and more."

"Think," she said. "I depend on you. You're just the one who might know. I had forgotten this. God sent you perhaps."

"Rebbetzin Kornfeld, I'm only a bookseller."

"God in his judgment sent me a bookseller. For such a long time Isaac never read at home. Think! Agronomy?"

"I don't remember anything like that. What would a Professor of Mishnaic History want with agronomy?"

"If he had a new book under his arm he would take it straight to the seminary and hide it in his office."

"I mailed to his office. If you like I can look up some of the titles—"

"You were in the park and you saw nothing?"

"Nothing." Then I was ashamed. "I saw the tree."

"And what is that? A tree is nothing."

"Rebbetzin Kornfeld," I pleaded, "it's a stupidity that I came here. I don't know myself why I came, I beg your pardon, I had no idea—"

"You came to learn why Isaac took his life. Botany? Or even, please listen, even mycology? He never asked you to send something on mushrooms? Or having to do with herbs? Manure? Flowers? A certain kind of agricultural poetry? A book about gardening? Forestry? Vegetables? Cereal growing?"

"Nothing, nothing like that," I said excitedly. "Rebbetzin Kornfeld, your husband was a rabbi!"

"I know what my husband was. Something to do with vines? Arbors? Rice? Think, think, think! Anything to do with land—meadows—goats—a farm, hay—anything at all, anything rustic or lunar—"

"Lunar! My God! Was he a teacher or a nurseryman? Goats!

Was he a furrier? Sheindel, are you crazy? *I* was the furrier! What do you want from the dead?"

Without a word she replenished my cup, though it was more than half full, and sat down opposite me, on the other side of the lace boundary line. She leaned her face into her palms, but I saw her eyes. She kept them wide.

"Rebbetzin Kornfeld," I said, collecting myself, "with a tragedy like this—"

"You imagine I blame the books. I don't blame the books, whatever they were. If he had been faithful to his books he would have lived."

"He lived," I cried, "in books, what else?"

"No," said the widow.

"A scholar. A rabbi. A remarkable Jew!"

At this she spilled a furious laugh. "Tell me, I have always been very interested and shy to inquire. Tell me about your wife."

I intervened: "I haven't had a wife in years."

"What are they like, those people?"

"They're exactly like us, if you can think what we would be if we were like them."

"We are not like them. Their bodies are more to them than ours are to us. Our books are holy, to them their bodies are holy."

"Jane's was so holy she hardly ever let me get near it," I muttered to myself.

"Isaac used to run in the park, but he lost his breath too quickly. Instead he read in a book about runners with hats made of leaves."

"Sheindel, Sheindel, what did you expect of him? He was a student, he sat and he thought, he was a Jew."

She thrust her hands flat. "He was not."

I could not reply. I looked at her merely. She was thinner now than in her early young-womanhood, and her face had an in-between cast, poignant still at the mouth and jaw, beginning to grow coarse on either side of the nose.

"I think he was never a Jew," she said.

I wondered whether Isaac's suicide had unbalanced her.

"I'll tell you a story," she resumed. "A story about stories. These were the bedtime stories Isaac told Naomi and Esther: about mice that danced and children who laughed. When Miriam came he invented a speaking cloud. With Ophra it was a turtle that married a blade of withered grass. By Leah's time the stones had tears for their leglessness. Rebecca cried because of a tree that turned into a girl and could never grow colors again in autumn. Shiphrah, the littlest, believes that a pig has a soul."

"My own father used to drill me every night in sacred recitation. It was a terrible childhood."

"He insisted on picnics. Each time we went farther and farther into the country. It was a madness. Isaac never troubled to learn to drive a car, and there was always a clumsiness of baskets to carry and a clutter of buses and trains and seven exhausted wild girls. And he would look for special places—we couldn't settle just here or there, there had to be a brook or such-and-such a slope or else a little grove. And then, though he said it was all for the children's pleasure, he would leave them and go off alone and never come back until sunset, when everything was spilled and the air freezing and the babies crying."

"I was a grown man before I had the chance to go on a picnic," I admitted.

"I'm speaking of the beginning," said the widow. "Like you, wasn't I fooled? I was fooled, I was charmed. Going home with our baskets of berries and flowers we were a romantic huddle. Isaac's stories on those nights were full of dark invention. May God preserve me, I even begged him to write them down. Then suddenly he joined a club, and Sunday mornings he was up and away before dawn."

"A club? So early? What library opens at that hour?" I said, stunned that a man like Isaac should ally himself with anything so doubtful.

"Ah, you don't follow, you don't follow. It was a hiking club, they met under the moon. I thought it was a pity, the whole week Isaac was so inward, he needed air for the mind. He used to come home too fatigued to stand. He said he went for the landscape. I was like you, I took what I heard, I heard it all and never followed. He resigned from the hikers finally, and I believed all that strangeness was finished. He told me it was absurd to walk at such a pace, he was a teacher and not an athlete. Then he began to write."

"But he always wrote," I objected.

"Not this way. What he wrote was only fairy tales. He kept at it and for a while he neglected everything else. It was the strangeness in another form. The stories surprised me, they were so poor and dull. They were a little like the ideas he used to scare the girls with, but choked all over with notes, appendices, prefaces. It struck me then he didn't seem to understand he was only doing fairy tales. Yet they were really very ordinary—full of sprites, nymphs, gods, everything ordinary and old."

"Will you let me see them?"

"Burned, all burned."

"Isaac burned them?"

"You don't think I did! I see what you think."

It was true that I was marveling at her hatred. I supposed she was one of those born to dread imagination. I was overtaken by a coldness for her, though the sight of her small hands with their tremulous staves of fingers turning and turning in front of her face like a gate on a hinge reminded me of where she was born and who she was. She was an orphan and had been saved by magic and had a terror of it. The coldness fled. "Why should you be bothered by little stories?" I inquired. "It wasn't the stories that killed him."

"No, no, not the stories," she said. "Stupid corrupt things. I was glad when he gave them up. He piled them in the bathtub and lit them with a match. Then he put a notebook in his coat pocket and said he would walk in the park. Week after week he tried all the parks in the city. I didn't dream what he could be after. One day he took the subway and rode to the end of the line, and this was the right park at last. He went every day after class. An hour going, an hour back. Two, three in the morning he came home. 'Is it exercise?' I said. I thought he might be running again. He used to shiver with the chill of night and the dew. 'No, I sit quite still,' he said. 'Is it more stories you do out there?' 'No, I only jot down what I think.' 'A man should meditate in his own house, not by night near bad water,' I said. Six, seven in the morning he came home. I asked him if he meant to find his grave in that place."

She broke off with a cough, half artifice and half resignation, so loud that it made her crane toward the bedrooms to see if she had awakened a child. "I don't sleep any more," she told me. "Look around you. Look, look everywhere, look on the windowsills. Do you see any plants, any common house plants? I went down one evening and gave them to the garbage collector. I couldn't sleep in the same space with plants. They are like little trees. Am I deranged? Take Isaac's notebook and bring it back when you can."

I obeyed. In my own room, a sparse place, with no ornaments but a few pretty stalks in pots, I did not delay and seized the notebook. It was a tiny affair, three inches by five, with ruled pages that opened on a coiled wire. I read searchingly, hoping for something not easily evident. Sheindel by her melancholy innuendo had made me believe that in these few sheets Isaac had revealed the reason for his suicide. But it was all a disappointment. There was not a word of any importance. After a while I concluded that, whatever her motives, Sheindel was playing with me again. She meant to punish me for asking the unaskable. My inquisitiveness offended her; she had given me Isaac's notebook not to enlighten but to rebuke. The handwriting was recognizable yet oddly formed, shaky and even senile, like that of a man outdoors and deskless who scribbles in his palm or on his lifted knee or leaning on a bit of bark; and there was no doubt that the wrinkled leaves, with their ragged corners, had been in and out of someone's pocket. So I did not mistrust Sheindel's mad anecdote; this much was true: a park, Isaac, a notebook, all at once, but signifying no more than that a professor with a literary turn of mind had gone for a walk. There was even a green stain straight across one of the quotations, as if the pad had slipped grassward and been trod on.

I have forgotten to mention that the notebook, though scantily filled, was in three languages. The Greek I could not read at all, but it had the shape of verse. The Hebrew was simply a miscellany, drawn mostly from Leviticus and Deuteronomy. Among these I found the following extracts, transcribed not quite verbatim:

> Ye shall utterly destroy all the places of the gods, upon the high mountains, and upon the hills, and under every green tree.

> And the soul that turneth after familiar spirits to go a-whoring after them, I will cut him off from among his people.

These, of course, were ordinary unadorned notes, such as any classroom lecturer might commonly make to remind himself of the text, with a phrase cut out here and there for the sake of speeding his hand. Or I thought it possible that Isaac might at that time have been preparing a paper on the Talmudic commentaries for these passages. Whatever the case, the remaining quotations, chiefly from English poetry, interested me only slightly more. They were the elegiac favorites of a closeted Romantic. I was repelled by Isaac's Nature: it wore a capital letter, and smelled like my own Book Cellar. It was plain to me that he had lately grown painfully academic: he could not see a weed's tassel without finding a classical reference for it. He had put down a snatch of Byron, a smudge of Keats (like his Scriptural copyings, these too were quick and fragmented), a pair of truncated lines from Tennyson, and this unmarked and clumsy quatrain:

> *And yet all is not taken. Still one Dryad*
> *Flits through the wood, one Oread skims the hill;*
> *White in the whispering stream still gleams a Naiad;*
> *The beauty of the earth is haunted still.*

All of this was so cloying and mooning and ridiculous, and so pedantic besides, that I felt ashamed for him. And yet there was almost nothing else, nothing to redeem him and nothing personal, only a sentence or two in his rigid self-controlled scholar's style, not unlike the starched little jokes of our correspondence. "I am writing at dusk sitting on a stone in Trilham's Inlet Park, within sight of Trilham's Inlet, a bay to the north of the city, and within two yards of a slender tree, *Quercus velutina,* the age of which, should one desire to measure it, can be ascertained by (God forbid) cutting the bole and counting the rings. The man writing is thirty-five years old and aging too rapidly, which may be ascertained by counting the rings under his poor myopic eyes." Below this, deliberate and readily more legible than the rest, appeared three curious words:

Great Pan lives.

That was all. In a day or so I returned the notebook to Sheindel. I told myself that she had seven orphans to worry over, and repressed my anger at having been cheated.

She was waiting for me. "I am so sorry, there was a letter in the notebook, it had fallen out. I found it on the carpet after you left."

"Thank you, no," I said. "I've read enough out of Isaac's pockets."

"Then why did you come to see me to begin with?"

"I came," I said, "just to see you."

"You came for Isaac." But she was more mocking than distraught. "I gave you everything you needed to see what happened and still you don't follow. Here." She held out a large law-sized paper. "Read the letter."

"I've read his notebook. If everything I need to fathom Isaac is in the notebook I don't need the letter."

"It's a letter he wrote to explain himself," she persisted.

"You told me Isaac left you no notes."

"It was not written to me."

I sat down on one of the dining room chairs and Sheindel put the page before me on the table. It lay face up on the lace divider. I did not look at it.

"It's a love letter," Sheindel whispered. "When they cut him down they found the notebook in one pocket and the letter in the other."

I did not know what to say.

"The police gave me everything," Sheindel said. "Everything to keep."

"A love letter?" I repeated.

"That is what such letters are commonly called."

"And the police—they gave it to you, and that was the first you realized what"—I floundered after the inconceivable—"what could be occupying him?"

"What could be occupying him," she mimicked. "Yes. Not until they took the letter and the notebook out of his pocket."

"My God. His habit of life, his mind . . . I can't imagine it. You never guessed?"

"No."

"These trips to the park—"

"He had become aberrant in many ways. I have described them to you."

"But the park! Going off like that, alone—you didn't think he might be meeting a woman?"

"It was not a woman."

Disgust like a powder clotted my nose. "Sheindel, you're crazy."

"I'm crazy, is that it? Read his confession! Read it! How long can I be the only one to know this thing? Do you want my brain to melt? Be my confidant," she entreated so unexpectedly that I held my breath.

"You've said nothing to anyone?"

"Would they have recited such eulogies if I had? Read the letter!"

"I have no interest in the abnormal," I said coldly.

She raised her eyes and watched me for the smallest space. Without any change in the posture of her suppliant head her laughter began; I have never since heard sounds like those—almost mouselike in density for fear of waking her sleeping daughters, but so rational in intent that it was like listening to astonished sanity rendered into a cackling fugue. She kept it up for a minute and then calmed herself. "Please sit where you are. Please pay attention. I will read the letter to you myself."

She plucked the page from the table with an orderly gesture. I saw that this letter had been scrupulously prepared; it was closely written. Her tone was cleansed by scorn.

" 'My ancestors were led out of Egypt by the hand of God,' " she read.

"Is this how a love letter starts out?"

She moved on resolutely. "We were guilty of so-called abominations well-described elsewhere. Other peoples have been nourished on their mythologies. For aeons we have been weaned from all traces of the same."

I felt myself becoming impatient. The fact was I had returned with a single idea: I meant to marry Isaac's widow when enough time had passed to make it seemly. It was my intention to court her with great subtlety at first, so that I would not appear to be presuming on her sorrow. But she was possessed. "Sheindel, why do you want to inflict this treatise on me? Give it to the seminary, contribute it to a symposium of professors."

"I would sooner die."

At this I began to attend in earnest.

" 'I will leave aside the wholly plausible position of so-called animism within the concept of the One God. I will omit a historical illumination of its continuous but covert expression even within the Fence of the Law. Creature, I leave these aside—' "

"What?" I yelped.

" 'Creature,' " she repeated, spreading her nostrils. " 'What is human history? What is our philosophy? What is our religion? None of these teaches us poor human ones that we are alone in the universe, and even without them we would know that we are not. At a very young age I understood that a foolish man would not believe in a fish had he not had one enter his experience. Innumerable forms exist and have come to our eyes, and to the still deeper eye of the lens of our instruments; from this minute perception of what already is, it is easy to conclude that further forms are possible, that all forms are probable. God created the world not for Himself alone, or I would not now possess this consciousness with which I am enabled to address thee, Loveliness.' "

"Thee," I echoed, and swallowed a sad bewilderment.

"You must let me go on," Sheindel said, and grimly went on. " 'It is false history, false philosophy, and false religion which declare to us human ones that we live among Things. The arts of physics and chemistry begin to teach us differently, but their way of compassion is new, and finds few to carry fidelity to its logical and beautiful end. The molecules dance inside all forms, and within the molecules dance the atoms, and within the atoms dance still profounder sources of divine vitality. There is nothing that is Dead. There is no Non-life. Holy life subsists even in the stone, even in the bones of dead dogs and dead men. Hence in God's fecundating Creation there is no possibility of Idolatry, and therefore no possibility of committing this so-called abomination.' "

"My God, my God," I wailed. "Enough, Sheindel, it's more than enough, no more—"

"There is more," she said.

"I don't want to hear it."

"He stains his character for you? A spot, do you think? You will hear." She took up in a voice which all at once reminded me of my father's: it was unforgiving. " 'Creature, I rehearse these matters though all our language is as breath to thee; as baubles for the juggler. Where we struggle to understand from day to day, and contemplate the grave for its riddle, the other breeds are born fulfilled in wisdom. Animal races conduct themselves without self-investigations; instinct is a higher and not a lower thing. Alas that we human ones—but for certain pitifully primitive approximations in those few reflexes and involuntary actions left to our bodies—are born bare of instinct! All that we unfortunates must resort to through science, art, philosophy, religion, all our imaginings and tormented strivings, all our meditations and vain questionings, all!—are expressed naturally and rightly in the beasts, the plants, the rivers, the stones. The reason is simple, it is our tragedy: our soul is included in us, it inhabits us, we contain it, when we seek our soul we must seek in ourselves. To *see* the soul, to confront it—that is divine wisdom. Yet how can we see into our dark selves? With the other races of being it is differently ordered. The soul of the plant does not reside in the chlorophyll, it may roam if it wishes, it may choose whatever form or shape it pleases. Hence the other breeds, being largely free of their soul and able to witness it, can live in peace. To see one's soul is to know all, to know all is to own the peace our philosophies futilely envisage. Earth displays two categories of soul: the free and the indwelling. We human ones are cursed with the indwelling—' "

"Stop!" I cried.

"I will not," said the widow.

"Please, you told me he burned his fairy tales."

"Did I lie to you? Will you say I lied?"

"Then for Isaac's sake why didn't you? If this isn't a fairy tale what do you want me to think it could be?"

"Think what you like."

"Sheindel," I said, "I beg you, don't destroy a dead man's honor. Don't look at this thing again, tear it to pieces, don't continue with it."

"I don't destroy his honor. He had none."

"Please! Listen to yourself! My God, who was the man? Rabbi Isaac Kornfeld! Talk of honor! Wasn't he a teacher? Wasn't he a scholar?"

"He was a pagan."

Her eyes returned without hesitation to their task. She commenced: " 'All these truths I learned only gradually, against my will and desire. Our teacher Moses did not speak of them; much may be said under this head. It was not out of ignorance that Moses failed to teach about those souls that are free. If I have learned what Moses knew, is this not because we are both men? He was a man, but God addressed him; it was God's will that our ancestors should no longer be slaves. Yet our ancestors, being stiff-necked, would not have abandoned their slavery in Egypt had they been taught of the free souls. They would have said: "Let us stay, our bodies will remain enslaved in Egypt, but our souls will wander at their pleasure in Zion. If the cactus-plant stays rooted while its soul roams, why not also a man?" And if Moses had replied that only the world of Nature has the gift of the free soul, while man is chained to his, and that a man, to free his soul, must also free the body that is its vessel, they would have scoffed. "How is it that men, and men alone, are different from the world of Nature? If this is so, then the condition of men is evil and unjust, and if this condition of ours is evil and unjust in general, what does it matter whether we are slaves in Egypt or citizens in Zion?" And they would not have done God's will and abandoned their slavery. Therefore Moses never spoke to them of the free souls, lest the people not do God's will and go out from Egypt.' "

In an instant a sensation broke in me—it was entirely obscure, there was nothing I could compare it with, and yet I was certain I recognized it. And then I did. It hurtled me into childhood—it was the crisis of insight one experiences when one has just read out, for the first time, that conglomeration of figurines which makes a word. In that moment I penetrated beyond Isaac's alphabet into his language. I saw that he was on the side of possibility: he was both sane and inspired. His intention was not to accumulate mystery but to dispel it.

"All that part is brilliant," I burst out.

Sheindel meanwhile had gone to the sideboard to take a sip of cold tea that was standing there. "In a minute," she said, and pursued her thirst. "I have heard of drawings surpassing Rembrandt daubed by madmen who when released from the fit couldn't hold the chalk. What follows is beautiful, I warn you."

"The man was a genius."

"Yes."

"Go on," I urged.

She produced for me her clownish jeering smile. She read: " 'Sometimes in the desert journey on the way they would come to a watering place, and some quick spry boy would happen to glimpse the soul of the spring (which the wild Greeks afterward called naiad), but not knowing of the existence of the free souls he would suppose only that the moon had cast a momentary beam across the water. Loveliness, with the same innocence of accident I discovered thee. Loveliness, Loveliness.' "

She stopped.

"Is that all?"

"There is more."

"Read it."

"The rest is the love letter."

"Is it hard for you?" But I asked with more eagerness than pity.

"I was that man's wife, he scaled the Fence of the Law. For this God preserved me from the electric fence. Read it for yourself."

Incontinently I snatched the crowded page.

" 'Loveliness, in thee the joy, substantiation, and supernal succor of my theorem. How many hours through how many years I walked over the cilia-forests of our enormous aspirating vegetable-star, this light rootless seed that crawls in its single furrow, this shaggy mazy unimplanted cabbage-head of our earth!—never, all that time, all those days of unfulfillment, a white space like a desert thirst, never, never to grasp. I thought myself abandoned to the intrigue of my folly. At dawn, on a hillock, what seemed the very shape and seizing of the mound's nature—what was it? Only the haze of the sunball growing great through hoarfrost. The oread slipped from me, leaving her illusion; or was never there at all; or was there but for an instant, and ran away. What sly ones the free souls are! They have a comedy we human ones cannot dream: the laughing drunkard feels in himself the shadow of the shadow of the shadow of their wit, and only because he has made himself a vessel, as the two banks and the bed of a rivulet are the naiad's vessel. A naiad I may indeed have viewed whole: all seven of my daughters were once wading in a stream in a compact but beautiful park, of which I had much hope. The youngest being not yet two, and fretful, the older ones were told to keep her always by the hand, but they did not obey. I, having passed some way into the woods behind, all at once heard a scream and noise of splashes, and caught sight of a tiny body flying down into the water. Running back through the trees I could see the others bunched together, afraid, as the baby dived helplessly, all these little girls frozen in a garland—when suddenly one of them (it was too quick a movement for me to recognize which) darted to the struggler, who was now underwater, and pulled her up, and put an arm around her to soothe her. The arm was blue—blue. As blue as a lake. And fiercely, from my spot on the bank, panting, I began to count the little girls. I counted eight, thought myself not mad but delivered, again counted, counted seven, knew I had counted well before, knew I counted well even now. A blue-armed girl had come to wade among them. Which is to say the shape of a girl. I questioned my daughters: each in her fright believed one of the others had gone to pluck up the tiresome baby. None wore a dress with blue sleeves.' "

"Proofs," said the widow. "Isaac was meticulous, he used to account for all his proofs always."

"How?" My hand in tremor rustled Isaac's letter; the paper bleated as though whipped.

"By eventually finding a principle to cover them," she finished maliciously. "Well, don't rest even for me, you don't oblige me. You have a long story to go, long enough to make a fever."

"Tea," I said hoarsely.

She brought me her own cup from the sideboard, and I believed as I drank that I swallowed some of her mockery and gall.

"Sheindel, for a woman so pious you're a great skeptic." And now the tremor had command of my throat.

"An atheist's statement," she rejoined. "The more piety, the more skepticism. A religious man comprehends this. Superfluity, excess of custom, and superstition would climb like a choking vine on the Fence of the Law if skepticism did not continually hack them away to make freedom for purity."

I then thought her fully worthy of Isaac. Whether I was worthy of her I evaded putting to myself; instead I gargled some tea and returned to the letter.

" 'It pains me to confess,' " I read, " 'how after that I moved from clarity to doubt and back again. I had no trust in my conclusions because all my experiences were evanescent. Everything certain I attributed to some other cause less certain. Every voice out of the moss I blamed on rabbits and squirrels. Every motion among leaves I called a bird, though there positively was no bird. My first sight of the Little People struck me as no more than a shudder of literary delusion, and I determined they could only be an instantaneous crop of mushrooms. But one night, a little after ten o'clock at the crux of summer—the sky still showed strings of light—I was wandering in this place, this place where they will find my corpse—' "

"Not for my sake," said Sheindel when I hesitated.

"It's terrible," I croaked, "terrible."

"Withered like a shell," she said, as though speaking of the cosmos; and I understood from her manner that she had a fanatic's acquaintance with this letter, and knew it nearly by heart. She appeared to be thinking the words faster than I could bring them out, and for some reason I was constrained to hurry the pace of my reading.

" '—where they will find my corpse withered like the shell of an insect,' " I rushed on. " 'The smell of putrefaction lifted clearly from the bay. I began to speculate about my own body after I was dead—whether the soul would be set free immediately after the departure of life; or whether only gradually, as decomposition proceeded and more and more of the indwelling soul was released to freedom. But when I considered how a man's body is no better than a clay pot, a fact which none of our sages has ever contradicted, it seemed to me then that an indwelling soul by its own nature would be obliged to cling to its bit of pottery until the last crumb and grain had vanished into earth. I walked through the ditches of that black meadow grieving and swollen with self-pity. It came to me that while my poor bones went on decaying at their ease, my soul would have to linger inside them, waiting, despairing, longing to join the free ones. I cursed it for its gravity-despoiled, slow, interminably languishing purse of flesh; better to be encased in vapor, in wind, in a hair of a coconut! Who knows how long it takes the body of a man to shrink into gravel, and the gravel into sand, and the sand into vitamin? A hundred years? Two hundred, three hundred? A thousand perhaps! Is it not true that bones nearly intact are constantly being dug up by the paleontologists two million years after burial?'—Sheindel," I interrupted, "this is death, not love. Where's the love letter to be afraid of here? I don't find it."

"Continue," she ordered. And then: "You see I'm not afraid."

"Not of love?"

"No. But you recite much too slowly. Your mouth is shaking. Are you afraid of death?"

I did not reply.

"Continue," she said again. "Go rapidly. The next sentence begins with an extraordinary thought."

" 'An extraordinary thought emerged in me. It was luminous, profound, and practical. More than that, it had innumerable precedents; the mythologies had documented it a dozen dozen times over. I recalled all those mortals reputed to have coupled with gods (a collective word, showing much common sense, signifying what our philosophies more abstrusely call Shekhina), and all that poignant miscegenation represented by centaurs, satyrs, mermaids, fauns, and so forth, not to speak of that even more famous mingling in Genesis, whereby the sons of God took the daughters of men for brides, producing giants and possibly also those abortions, leviathan and behemoth, of which we read in Job, along with unicorns and other chimeras and monsters abundant in Scripture, hence far from fanciful. There existed also the example of the succubus Lilith, who was often known to couple in the mediaeval ghetto even with pre-pubescent boys. By all these evidences I was emboldened in my confidence that I was surely not the first man to conceive such a desire in the history of our earth. Creature, the thought that took hold of me was this: if only I could couple with one of the free souls, the strength of the connection would likely wrest my own soul from my body—seize it, as if by a tongs, draw it out, so to say, to its own freedom. The intensity and force of my desire to capture one of these beings now became prodigious. I avoided my wife—' "

Here the widow heard me falter.

"Please," she commanded, and I saw creeping in her face the completed turn of a sneer.

" '—lest I be depleted of potency at that moment (which might occur in any interval, even, I assumed, in my own bedroom) when I should encounter one of the free souls. I was borne back again and again to the fetid viscosities of the Inlet, borne there as if on the rising stink of my own enduring and tedious putrefaction, the idea of which I could no longer shake off—I envisaged my soul as trapped in my last granule, and that last granule itself perhaps petrified, never to dissolve, and my soul condemned to minister to it throughout eternity! It seemed to me my soul must be released at once or be lost to sweet air forever. In a gleamless dark, struggling with this singular panic, I stumbled from ditch to ditch, strained like a blind dog for the support of solid verticality; and smacked my palm against bark. I looked up and in the black could not fathom the size of the tree—my head lolled forward, my brow met the trunk with all its gravings. I busied my fingers in the interstices of the bark's cuneiform. Then with forehead flat on the tree, I embraced it with both arms to measure it. My hands united on the other side. It was a young narrow weed, I did not know of what family. I reached to the lowest branch and plucked a leaf and made my tongue travel meditatively along its periphery to assess its shape: oak. The taste was sticky and exaltingly bitter. A jubilation lightly carpeted my groin. I then placed one hand (the other I kept around the tree's waist, as it were) in the bifurcation (disgustingly termed crotch) of that lowest limb and the elegant and devoutly firm torso, and caressed that miraculous juncture with a certain languor, which gradually changed to vigor. I was all at once savagely alert and deeply daring: I chose that single tree together with the ground near it for an enemy which in two senses would not yield: it would neither give nor give in. "Come, come," I called aloud to Nature. A wind blew out a braid of excremental malodor into the heated air. "Come," I called, "couple with me, as thou didst with Cadmus, Rhoecus, Tithonus, Endymion, and that king Numa Pompilius to whom thou didst give secrets. As Lilith comes without a sign, so come thou. As the sons of God came to copulate with women, so now let a daughter of Shekhina the Emanation reveal herself to me. Nymph, come now, come now."

" 'Without warning I was flung to the ground. My face smashed into earth, and a flaky clump of dirt lodged in my open mouth. For the rest, I was on my knees, pressing down on my hands, with the fingernails clutching dirt. A superb ache lined my haunch. I began to weep because I was certain I had been ravished by some sinewy animal. I vomited the earth I had swallowed and believed I was defiled, as it is written: "Neither shalt thou lie with any beast." I lay sunk in the grass, afraid to lift my head to see if the animal still lurked. Through some curious means I had been fully positioned and aroused and exquisitely sated, all in half a second, in a fashion impossible to explain, in which, though I performed as with my own wife, I felt as if a preternatural rapine had been committed upon me. I continued prone, listening for the animal's breathing. Meanwhile, though every tissue of my flesh was gratified in its inmost awareness, a marvelous voluptuousness did not leave my body; sensual exultations of a wholly supreme and paradisal order, unlike anything our poets have ever defined, both flared and were intensely satisfied in the same moment. This salubrious and delightful perceptiveness excited my being for some time: a conjoining not dissimilar (in metaphor only; in actuality it cannot be described) from the magical contradiction of the tree and its issuance-of-branch at the point of bifurcation. In me were linked, *in the same instant,* appetite and fulfillment, delicacy and power, mastery and submissiveness, and other paradoxes of entirely remarkable emotional import.

" 'Then I heard what I took to be the animal treading through the grass quite near my head, all cunningly; it withheld its breathing, then snored it out in a cautious and wisplike whirr that resembled a light wind through rushes. With a huge energy (my muscular force seemed to have increased) I leaped up in fear of my life; I had nothing to use for a weapon but—oh, laughable!—the pen I had been writing with in a little notebook I always carried about with me in those days (and still keep on my person as a self-shaming souvenir of my insipidness, my bookishness, my pitiable conjecture and wishfulness in a time when, not yet knowing thee, I knew nothing). What I saw was not an animal but a girl no older than my oldest daughter, who was then fourteen. Her skin was as perfect as an eggplant's and nearly of that color. In height she was half as tall as I was. The second and third fingers of her hands—this I noticed at once—were peculiarly fused, one slotted into the other, like the ligula of a leaf. She was entirely bald and had no ears but rather a type of gill or envelope, one only, on the left side. Her toes displayed the same oddity I had observed in her fingers. She was neither naked nor clothed—that is to say, even though a part of her body, from hip to just below the breasts (each of which appeared to be a kind of velvety colorless pear, suspended from a very short, almost invisible stem), was luxuriantly covered with a flossy or spore-like material, this was a natural efflorescence in the manner of, with us, hair. All her sexual portion was wholly visible, as in any field flower. Aside from these express deviations, she was commandingly human in aspect, if unmistakably flowerlike. She was, in fact, the reverse of our hackneyed euphuism, as when we say a young girl blooms like a flower—she, on the contrary, seemed a flower transfigured into the shape of the most stupendously lovely child I had ever seen. Under the smallest push of wind she bent at her superlative waist; this, I recognized, and not the exhalations of some lecherous beast, was the breathlike sound that had alarmed me at her approach: these motions of hers made the blades of grass collide. (She herself, having no lungs, did not "breathe.") She stood bobbing joyfully before me, with a face as tender as a morning-glory, strangely phosphorescent: she shed her own light, in effect, and I had no difficulty in confronting her beauty.

" 'Moreover, by experiment I soon learned that she was not only capable of language, but that she delighted in playing with it. This she literally could do—if I had distinguished her hands before anything else, it was because she had held them out to catch my first cry of awe. She either caught my words like balls or let them roll, or caught them and then darted off to throw them into the

Inlet. I discovered that whenever I spoke I more or less pelted her; but she liked this, and told me ordinary human speech only tickled and amused, whereas laughter, being highly plosive, was something of an assault. I then took care to pretend much solemnity, though I was lightheaded with rapture. Her own "voice" I apprehended rather than heard—which she, unable to imagine how we human ones are prisoned in sensory perception, found hard to conceive. Her sentences came to me not as a series of differentiated frequencies but (impossible to develop this idea in language) as a diffused cloud of field fragrances; yet to say that I assimilated her thought through the olfactory nerve would be a pedestrian distortion. All the same it was clear that whatever she said reached me in a shimmer of pellucid perfumes, and I understood her meaning with an immediacy of glee and with none of the ambiguities and suspiciousness of motive that surround our human communication.

" 'Through this medium she explained that she was a dryad and that her name was Iripomoňoéià (as nearly as I can render it in our narrowly limited orthography, and in this dunce's alphabet of ours which is notoriously impervious to odoriferous categories). She told me what I had already seized: that she had given me her love in response to my call.

" ' "Wilt thou come to any man who calls?" I asked.

" ' "All men call, whether realizing it or not. I and my sisters sometimes come to those who do not realize. Almost never, unless for sport, do we come to that man who calls knowingly—he wishes only to inhabit us out of perversity or boastfulness or to indulge a dreamed-of disgust."

" ' "Scripture does not forbid sodomy with the plants," I exclaimed, but she did not comprehend any of this and lowered her hands so that my words would fly past her uncaught. "I too called thee knowingly, not for perversity but for love of Nature."

" ' "I have caught men's words before as they talked of Nature, you are not the first. It is not Nature they love so much as Death they fear. So Corylylyb my cousin received it in a season not long ago coupling in a harbor with one of your kind, one called Spinoza, one that had catarrh of the lung. I am of Nature and immortal and so I cannot pity your deaths. But return tomorrow and say Iripomoňoéià." Then she chased my last word to where she had kicked it, behind the tree. She did not come back. I ran to the tree and circled it diligently but she was lost for that night.

" 'Loveliness, all the foregoing, telling of my life and meditations until now, I have never before recounted to thee or any other. The rest is beyond mean telling: those rejoicings from midnight to dawn, when the greater phosphorescence of the whole shouting sky frightened thee home! How in a trance of happiness we coupled in the ditches, in the long grasses, behind a fountain, under a broken wall, once recklessly on the very pavement, with a bench for roof and trellis! How I was taught by natural arts to influence certain chemistries engendering explicit marvels, blisses, and transports no man has slaked himself with since Father Adam pressed out the forbidden chlorophyll of Eden! Loveliness, Loveliness, none like thee. No brow so sleek, no elbow-crook so fine, no eye so green, no waist so pliant, no limbs so pleasant and acute. None like immortal Iripomoňoéià.

" 'Creature, the moon filled and starved twice, and there was still no end to the glorious archaic newness of Iripomoňoéià.

" 'Then last night. Last night! I will record all with simplicity.

" 'We entered a shallow ditch. In a sweet-smelling voice of extraordinary redolence—so intense in its sweetness that even the barbaric stinks and wind-lifted farts of the Inlet were overpowered by it—Iripomoňoéià inquired of me how I felt without my soul. I replied that I did not know this was my condition. "Oh yes, your body is now an empty packet, that is why it is so light. Spring." I sprang in air and rose effortlessly. "You have spoiled yourself, spoiled yourself with confusions," she complained, "now by morning your body will be crumpled and withered and ugly, like a leaf in its sere hour, and never again after tonight will this place see you." "Nymph!" I roared, amazed by levitation. "Oh, oh, that damaged," she cried, "you hit my eye with that noise," and she wafted a deeper aroma, a leeklike mist, one that stung the mucous membranes. A white bruise disfigured her petally lid. I was repentant and sighed terribly for her injury. "Beauty marred is for our kind what physical hurt is for yours," she reproved me. "Where you have pain, we have ugliness. Where you profane yourselves by immorality, we are profaned by ugliness. Your soul has taken leave of you and spoils our pretty game." "Nymph!" I whispered, "heart, treasure, if my soul is separated how is it I am unaware?"

" ' "Poor man," she answered, "you have only to look and you will see the thing." Her speech had now turned as acrid as an herb, and all that place reeked bitterly. "You know I am a spirit. You know I must flash and dart. All my sisters flash and dart. Of all races we are the quickest. Our very religion is all-of-a-sudden. No one can hinder us, no one may delay us. But yesterday you undertook to detain me in your embrace, you stretched your kisses into years, you called me your treasure and your heart endlessly, your soul in its slow greed kept me close and captive, all the while knowing well how a spirit cannot stay and will not be fixed. I made to leap from you, but your obstinate soul held on until it was snatched straight from your frame and escaped with me. I saw it hurled out onto the pavement, the blue beginning of day was already seeping down, so I ran away and could say nothing until this moment."

" ' "My soul is free? Free entirely? And can be seen?"

" ' "Free. If I could pity any living thing under the sky I would pity you for the sight of your soul. I do not like it, it conjures against me."

" ' "My soul loves thee," I urged in all my triumph, "it is freed from the thousand-year grave!" I jumped out of the ditch like a frog, my legs had no weight; but the dryad sulked in the ground, stroking her ugly violated eye. "Iripomoňoéià, my soul will follow thee with thankfulness into eternity."

" ' "I would sooner be followed by the dirty fog. I do not like that soul of yours. It conjures against me. It denies me, it denies every spirit and all my sisters and every nereid of the harbor, it denies all our multiplicity, and all gods diversiform, it spites even Lord Pan, it is an enemy, and you, poor man, do not know your own soul. Go, look at it, there it is on the road."

" 'I scudded back and forth under the moon.

" ' "Nothing, only a dusty old man trudging up there."

" ' "A quite ugly old man?"

" ' "Yes, that is all. My soul is not there."

" ' "With a matted beard and great fierce eyebrows?"

" ' "Yes, yes, one like that is walking on the road. He is half bent over under the burden of a dusty old bag. The bag is stuffed with books—I can see their raveled bindings sticking out."

" ' "And he reads as he goes?"

" ' "Yes, he reads as he goes."

" ' "What is it he reads?"

" ' "Some huge and terrifying volume, heavy as a stone." I peered forward in the moonlight. "A Tractate. A Tractate of the Mishnah. Its leaves are so worn they break as he turns them, but he does not turn them often because there is much matter on a single page. He is so sad! Such antique weariness broods in his face! His throat is striped from the whip. His cheeks are folded like ancient flags, he reads the Law and breathes the dust."

" ' "And are there flowers on either side of the road?"

" ' "Incredible flowers! Of every color! And noble shrubs like mounds of green moss! And the cricket crackling in the field. He passes indifferent through the beauty of the field. His nostrils sniff his book as if flowers lay on the clotted page, but the flowers lick his feet. His feet are bandaged, his notched toenails gore the path. His prayer shawl droops on his studious back. He reads the Law and breathes the dust and doesn't see the flowers and won't heed the cricket spitting in the field."

" ' "That," said the dryad, "is your soul." And was gone with all her odors.

" 'My body sailed up to the road in a single hop. I alighted near the shape of the old man and demanded whether he were indeed the soul of Rabbi Isaac Kornfeld. He trembled but confessed. I asked if he intended to go with his books through the whole future without change, always with his Tractate in his hand, and he answered that he could do nothing else.

" ' "Nothing else! You, who I thought yearned for the earth! You, an immortal, free, and caring only to be bound to the Law!"

" 'He held a dry arm fearfully before his face, and with the other arm hitched up his merciless bag on his shoulder. "Sir," he said, still quavering, "didn't you wish to see me with your own eyes?"

" ' "I know your figure!" I shrieked. "Haven't I seen that figure a hundred times before? On a hundred roads? It is not mine! I will not have it be mine!"

" ' "If you had not contrived to be rid of me, I would have stayed with you till the end. The dryad, who does not exist, lies. It was not I who clung to her but you, my body. Sir, all that has no real existence lies. In your grave beside you I would have sung you David's songs, I would have moaned Solomon's voice to your last grain of bone. But you expelled me, your ribs exile me from their fate, and I will walk here alone always, in my garden"—he scratched on his page—"with my precious birds"—he scratched at the letters—"and my darling trees"—he scratched at the tall side-column of commentary.

" 'He was so impudent in his bravery—for I was all fleshliness and he all floppy wraith—that I seized him by the collar and shook him up and down, while the books on his back made a vast rubbing one on the other, and bits of shredding leather flew out like a rain.

" ' "The sound of the Law," he said, "is more beautiful than the crickets. The smell of the Law is more radiant than the moss. The taste of the Law exceeds clear water."

" 'At this nervy provocation—he more than any other knew my despair—I grabbed his prayer shawl by its tassels and whirled around him once or twice until I had unwrapped it from him altogether, and wound it on my own neck and in one bound came to the tree.

" ' "Nymph!" I called to it. "Spirit and saint! Iripomoňoéià, come! None like thee, no brow so sleek, no elbow-crook so fine, no eye so green, no waist so pliant, no limbs so pleasant and acute. For pity of me, come, come."

" 'But she does not come.

" ' "Loveliness, come."

" 'She does not come.

" 'Creature, see how I am coiled in the snail of this shawl as if in a leaf. I crouch to write my words. Let soul call thee lie, but body . . .

" '. . . body . . .

" '. . . fingers twist, knuckles dark as wood, tongue dries like grass, deeper now into silk . . .

" '. . . silk of pod of shawl, knees wilt, knuckles wither, neck . . .' "

Here the letter suddenly ended.

"You see? A pagan!" said Sheindel, and kept her spiteful smile. It was thick with audacity.

"You don't pity him," I said, watching the contempt that glittered in her teeth.

"Even now you don't see? You can't follow?"

"Pity him," I said.

"He who takes his own life does an abomination."

For a long moment I considered her. "You don't pity him? You don't pity him at all?"

"Let the world pity me."

"Goodbye," I said to the widow.

"You won't come back?"

I gave what amounted to a little bow of regret.

"I told you you came just for Isaac! But Isaac"—I was in terror of her cough, which was unmistakably laughter—"Isaac disappoints. 'A scholar. A rabbi. A remarkable Jew!' Ha! He disappoints you?"

"He was always an astonishing man."

"But not what you thought," she insisted. "An illusion."

"Only the pitiless are illusory. Go back to that park, Rebbetzin," I advised her.

"And what would you like me to do there? Dance around a tree and call Greek names to the weeds?"

"Your husband's soul is in that park. Consult it." But her low derisive cough accompanied me home: whereupon I remembered her earlier words and dropped three green house plants down the toilet; after a journey of some miles through conduits they straightway entered Trilham's Inlet, where they decayed amid the civic excrement.